IT BEGAN IN A NEBRASKA WHEAT FIELD.
IT COULD END IN NUCLEAR HOLOCAUST.

In an underground chamber, a vacillating President, an inexperienced President-elect, and the feuding elites of military and civilian power huddle in a last-ditch attempt to avert total annihilation.

For ten years, wheat exports to the Soviet Union have been secretly contaminated with silent killers—slow-acting, cancer-inducing chemicals. Now, an unscrupulous media mogul has leaked the news to a horror-stricken world.

In the wake of the revelations, a hawkish regime has seized control in Moscow and is hell-bent on nuclear revenge. Naked panic rages across the U.S.

As global terror mounts, as doomsday dawns, who can escape . . . who can stop the deadly consequences of . . .

THE CONTAMINANT

THE CONTAMINANT

Leonard Reiffel

A DELL BOOK

Published by
Dell Publishing Co., Inc.
1 Dag Hammarskjold Plaza
New York, New York 10017

Dell ® TM 681510, Dell Publishing Co., Inc.

ISBN: 0-440-11473-X

Reprinted by arrangement with Harper & Row,
Publishers, Inc.

Printed in the United States of America

First Dell printing—April 1980

To my mother, Sophie.
And to my wife, Nancy.

Acknowledgment

The author acknowledges with gratitude the tireless and long-suffering efforts (albeit not silent suffering) of his friend and secretary, Ronnie Goranson. Several conversations with Dr. Franklin C. Bing were most valuable in dealing with certain biochemical questions.

THE
CONTAMINANT

1

Wednesday, April 11

a412 AP
BULLETIN WASHINGTON D.C.
PRESIDENT DONLEY HAS APPOINTED ADMIRAL RANDOLPH
G. CLAYTON AS CHAIRMAN OF THE JOINT CHIEFS OF
STAFF. CLAYTON REPLACES PREVIOUS CHAIRMAN, ARMY
GENERAL WILLIAM R. JAMES. JAMES DIED SUDDENLY
LAST MONTH OF HEART ATTACK. AT 48 CLAYTON IS
YOUNGEST CHAIRMAN JOINT CHIEFS EVER. HE IS TOP
NAVAL AVIATOR AND STILL ACTIVE FLIER. FULL CLAY-
TON BIOG WILL FOLLOW IN APPROXIMATELY 30 MIN-
UTES.
1031 A ED 4-11

To anyone but an expert, the room appeared quite ordinary. It measured only seven feet by nine feet. Two
double fluorescent lights were mounted on the ceiling
behind three layers of copper screening, which provided
a hint of the room's special character. Behind the shad-
owless beige of the walls, under the medium brown of the
standard General Services Administration carpeting and
in the ceiling itself was more telltale evidence, but none
of it was visible. The structure of the little room was, in
fact, the culmination of five decades of the art of coun-
terintelligence. Like the oriental curiosity carvings of
sphere within sphere within sphere, the room was not one
chamber but three, each surrounding the next and each as
complete and as perfect as Pentagon engineers could make
it. Not the slightest sound nor the weakest electrical
signal could filter in or out. Only a single electronic cable
penetrated the tamperproof armor of the room; it terminated in a computer console mounted on a small gray
metal table with no drawers.

A man was seated in front of the console and he was
annoyed. For a long moment, he glared at the television-
like screen of the device, which was blank except for one

bright-green symbol in the upper-left-hand corner. The symbol winked at him coyly: M10.

Admiral Randolph Clayton swore to himself. What the hell could that one be? Still another to add to the list. With impatient quickness, he wrote the letter "M" and the number "10" in bold strokes of black marker ink on the seventh line of a long yellow tablet, tossed the marker down and sighed. The list was growing.

Clayton's eyes skimmed over the other entries he had made: six alphanumeric designators, each followed by a classification level—two Secrets, four Top Secrets—the enigmatic harvest of nearly twenty hours of work over two full weeks of stealing precious time from other, urgent demands. Each entry represented an unidentified Department of Defense project and was a puzzle Clayton knew he would have to solve.

A dryness in his mouth reminded Clayton that it was time for a midmorning break. He pushed a small red button and spoke toward the circular intercom grille on the right side of the computer console. "Katrinka, take a minute off and get me a cup of coffee, will you?" Her real name was Katherine, but he usually called her Katrinka when he had things under control. When he was not feeling playful, or when other people were around, he called her Kathy; on very formal occasions, Katherine. Today, all things considered and in spite of the vexing list in front of him, he was relatively relaxed.

Moments later, the heavy door to the small high-security area opened and a little-girl face framed in soft jet-black hair peeked in. Kathy Myrdal tiptoed into the room and placed a steaming mug on the table next to the yellow paper.

"How ya doing?" she asked cheerfully, as she brushed her hand lightly across his shoulder.

He glanced up at her. "Everything's okay. Except for these, that is." He gestured toward his list. "I got another one out of the program that I can't seem to attach to anything. Every one of them has a big budget or it wouldn't have shown up, but I'm damned if I can track them, even with the ACA."

"Why don't you put somebody else on them? I know you, and they'll drive you up the wall until you find out what they mean." Kathy laughed. "I would just as soon have a couple of captains or commanders worrying about them for you, so you don't get into one of your beastly 'I have got to find out about it' moods."

"Nope," Clayton replied. "Now that I've got so far into it, I'm damned if I'll turn it over to anyone else. Anyway, I have to do this part myself and you know it. I'll figure them out in another few hours, I'm sure."

"Yeah, that's what you always say." She patted his shoulder with her small hand. "Let me just remind you that you have to go to the CIA/DOD briefing on China-Burma in ten minutes, so don't get too involved." She shot him another smile and walked out, closing the perfectly balanced multilayered door behind her.

Katherine Myrdal was in love. Six months after she had gone to work for the then young red-headed rear admiral she had realized she was in love with him. That was fourteen whirlwind years ago, and she loved him now as she did then. A magic chemistry had somehow preserved her feelings over the years in spite of his belonging to another woman and in spite of his damnably old-fashioned attitudes about affairs and who should or shouldn't have them.

Once, on a beautiful evening in Brussels during a NATO conference in the mid 1970s, she had worked up the courage to tell him exactly how she felt about him. As she had almost expected but had desperately hoped against, he waved her words casually aside. All secretaries fall in love with their bosses, he had said, and that seemed to end the matter as far as he was concerned. He knew he could count on her anytime, anyplace, and that was that. She was like the mug of coffee she had just brought him: warm, comforting, and there when requested.

Perhaps because the world around Katherine was always swirling with large or small emergencies played out against the giant backdrop of global politics, she found it easier than most women might have to accept a limited role in Clayton's life. Knowing, as she did, that the admiral was far more devoted to his job and to his country than to a less than satisfactory marriage helped, too. It gave her another way to rationalize her willingness to let the years slip by. The Navy, of course, was always able to find ways to occupy an admiral's secretary, especially if trouble seemed to be brewing. Perversely, the crises were frequently the happiest times for her. She liked the way they distorted habits and schedules and pressed her boss close to her. In the quiet respites between flurries of action, she simply waited and contented herself with thinking about him and doing things for him, even though he hardly noticed. As she had told her worried mother in countless discussions over the years, when you love somebody, that's just the way you are.

Alone in the soundless room hidden behind his office, Clayton stretched his long arms toward the screened ceiling lights and then sipped his coffee. The glowing symbol was still on the screen. M10. What about a classification history? That, at least, ought to be in the data base. He brushed a wisp of graying rusty hair away from his forehead and, in surprisingly fast hunt-and-peck style, tapped out a query on the computer keyboard. In less than a second the answer came: TOP SECRET, SIGMA SIX, NO REVISIONS. Pretty tightly held, but not the tightest, by any means. Peculiarly, there had apparently been no automatic downgrading of the security level of M10. Even the five-year reviews had been skipped.

Admiral Clayton's gray-green eyes clouded for an instant, then brightened with aroused curosity. He leaned forward like a hunter sensing something nearby, then relaxed again. With only ten minutes to go before his next meeting, there was no time to really exercise the codes and the DOD computers in search of the details of M10. That would have to wait for another day. Instead, at least for now, the subject would have to be China-Burma. Clayton's index fingers danced over the keyboard again and instantly he submerged in a welter of maps and figures laying out the best knowledge the United States possessed on a series of dangerous but unpublicized border incidents which clearly were cause for more concern to a new Chairman of the Joint Chiefs than a mystery project called M10. The Burmese situation, as Clayton already knew, could easily mushroom into his first major fire drill.

It had been only a few weeks since the President had named Clayton to his new post. Donley had caught him by surprise with the appointment. Clayton had been certain the job would go to Mike Kallen of the Air Force because Kallen and the President were long-time friends. But the telephone call had come in the midst of his usual evening argument with his wife and was followed by one of those pleasant foregone-conclusion chats at the White House. Two weeks later, he was confirmed by a friendly Senate. Suddenly, he was there—in the highest position a U.S. military man could hold.

The mechanics of the promotion were easy enough. Kathy and his aides took care of moving his papers into the new suite—E Ring, Second Floor, Room 873—and he was even beginning to get used to finding his staff car in the new parking slot at the Pentagon's River Entrance. Futhermore, there were really few surprises in the job itself. Clayton had been too carefully molded and prepared: captain of the huge nuclear-powered carrier U.S.S. *Enterprise*, developer of the Navy's Advanced Helicopter Strike Force, and, finally, "chief sailor" of the U.S. Navy—the Chief of Naval Operations. Each step along the way the system had further shaped and readied him. The end product of the process was a hard-driving but immensely likable man with exceptional technical knowledge and an unquestioning, almost compulsive, will to use his mind and power to the fullest for the good, as he saw it, of his service and his country.

Clayton's last two years as CNO had been the perfect finishing school. Along with Kallen, and to a lesser degree Dandridge of the Army, he had worked side by side with General James, the previous JCS Chairman, helping the older man deal with one crisis after another. The system had done its job well. When James was stricken, both Kallen and Clayton were at least passingly acquainted with all the major problems the Joint Chiefs faced, and Clayton got the job.

There was, however, one seemingly minor exception to Clayton's sense of immediate mastery of his new assignment. If pressed, the admiral just might have flashed a boyish Iowa grin and admitted it: Before he'd had a chance to use them himself, he hadn't really appreciated the enormous power of ACA—the Associative Control and Analysis codes of the Department of Defense.

Each of the three services—Army, Navy, Air Force— provided separate portions of the codes and none knew those portions provided by the others. Only the President, the Vice President, the Secretary of Defense, the Secretary of State, and now Clayton as Chairman of the Joint Chiefs of Staff, had complete sets, and only these five men could open the miraculous Pandora's box of the ACA system.

The concepts underlying the system had begun as a series of learned papers by Professor Eugene P. Wigren of Harvard. Couched in the arcane language of pure mathematics, Wigren's ideas were published in six consecutive 1962 issues of the journal *Archives of Mathematics*.

Wigren and a few colleagues at Harvard had been exploring the deepest frontiers of mathematical models of human thought processes and they gradually realized that a procedure could be developed out of logic alone that would emulate the intuitive leaps of the mind. But the mere writing down of formulae and algorithms, the prescriptions for such a feat, wondrously logical though the procedures were, was a very long way from actually carrying them out. The vast high-speed computers required were not available in Wigren's day and the professor died in 1963 without ever seeing his work yield practical results. Indeed, it was nearly two decades before the hardware needed finally did come into being.

Nevertheless, the Harvard work was in no danger of being forgotten. To the contrary, from 1962 on, the U.S. Department of Defense poured ever-increasing millions into the development of "artificial intelligence" in general and the Wigren procedure in particular. At first a few dozen bright young minds from Harvard, MIT, and Cal Tech wrestled with the task. By 1968 there were hundreds of mathematicians, scientists, and engineers involved. At the peak of the effort, which occurred in the late 1970s, literally thousands of the free world's best brains were concentrated in a single mighty effort to build a computer that was more than a computer—that was, in fact, a *mind*.

In a sense the effort failed. A totally artificial intelligence proved to be beyond the reach of science, for reasons not fully understood. The brain still guarded its secrets. But even as the artificial-intelligence project faltered, it became apparent that a lesser goal, although one of monumental importance, could be attained. An *associative* computer memory could be created. Out of inert metal and plastic, man could create a device capable of sorting through trillions of bits of information and automatically searching out associations, connections, and relationships among seemingly unrelated data. It was possible to make a machine that, externally at least, could do what man does when he says to himself: "Aha! I have a strange feeling that A might be related to B."

Of course, it did not take long before such a system was actually built by the only institution that could afford to undertake its construction. The institution was the U.S. Department of Defense and the system came to be called ACA. Its ultrasecret sequences of words and numbers could give a user access not only to all the data stored in the entire U.S. military computer network but also to the associative memory process that could automatically scan the data for obscure or hidden meanings. Over a billion bits of information could be sifted each second.

Five small rooms—two in the White House, two in the Pentagon, and one in the State Department—were installed and equipped with the technical means for contacting the ACA system. Completed less than two years before, ACA was indisputably the ultimate achievement and the crowning glory of the computer art. It would have easily awed Professor Wigren had he been alive and cleared by security to see it. Without doubt, when he first confronted it in the sealed room behind his desk, it did awe Admiral Randolph G. Clayton.

But Clayton was not a man who stayed impressed for long, and by the end of his third week as Chairman of the Joint Chiefs, he no longer thought much about the ACA system as such. Instead he was voraciously devouring the welter of facts and ideas the system could provide him. He also began accumulating his special list of puzzle projects, now seven entries long, which neither the ACA system nor the rest of the DOD's superb computer facility could tell him much about.

"Admiral, it's time to join the group in the conference room." Katherine's voice from the intercom speaker snapped Clayton away from a map on the ACA display showing towns on the Burmese border where new clashes might be expected.

"Okay, Katrinka." Frowning, he punched a sign-off sequence into the black-and-chrome computer console. He was about to swing the door of the little room open when, on impulse, he reached back for the yellow note pad next to the terminal. As if to say seven puzzles were quite enough, he tore off the top sheet with its cryptic scrawls, folded it into a three-inch square, and shoved it into the left side pocket of his uniform tunic. One last slug of cold coffee signaled the end of the day's session with ACA. For a time at least, Admiral Clayton would come no closer to solving the riddle of M10.

With his usual unhurried, almost lazy gait—a walk that developed during his high school years, when he was playing basketball and trying to imitate the shuffle of the big pro stars—Clayton headed for his China-Burma briefing. He waved hello to the young MP manning the outer reception desk of his office suite and, in a dozen more steps, confronted the shiny black of the JCS conference room door. A long, bony finger punched in his identification number on the touch-tone pad mounted next to the door. Instantly, the "Activated" light on a video scanner blinked on and stared out at Clayton through a small lens in the center of the steel door. Somewhere in a distant part of the Pentagon, a small computer busily extracted the essential features of Clayton's face and compared them to data on file in its electronic memory. An automatic voice-response unit issued directions in flat metallic tones: "Physiognomy match accepted. Please enter handprint data."

Clayton, obedient to the system, placed his right hand flat against a dark plastic square mounted on the wall next to the door. The emotionless voice of the computer, apparently satisfied, responded. "Access controls activated. Four-second limit. Thank you."

The steel door opened onto a large room lined with spotlighted wall charts and clusters of men and women quietly talking and obviously waiting for Clayton to join them. His nostrils caught the faint scent of recently applied furniture polish. He smiled, nodded his hellos, and settled himself in a maroon swivel chair with slightly worn arms. The others in the room filed around the long table and into their preassigned places. With the too perfect precision of all well-rehearsed military briefings for top brass, the lights dimmed and the first visual flashed up on a large color television screen covering one wall of the room, just as a nervous one-star general reached the walnut podium to Clayton's left. "The purpose of today's briefing, sir, is to update you on our interpretations of Chinese activity in Burma. We assume you have already reviewed the formal data base. . . ."

To drive from the Pentagon—where the Chairman of the Joint Chiefs was listening patiently as his subordinates struggled to pronounce the names of Burmese officials and towns—to the elegant eight-room white colonial house at 4618 Mariston Road in Rockville, Maryland, required just over thirty minutes if rush-hour traffic had not jammed the Outer Beltway—Interstate 495—or I 270 beyond the turnoff. The owner of the house had not often made that specific trip, because even before he had retired, his final assignment as Deputy Commandant of the Army's Fort Deterling Research Center had usually taken him twenty miles in the opposite direction. And that, of course, had been fine with him: the farther he was from the soft-headed bureaucrats who infested the Pentagon, the better he liked it.

On this near perfect afternoon in May, Lieutenant General Robert Travis Mallon (U.S. Army, Retired) was at least momentarily much more concerned with the small black specks on the undersides of the glossy green leaves of his peonies than with anything going on in the capital. Bent close to the plants, he squinted behind his sunglasses as he tried to decide what the trouble might be and made a mental note to use a Malathion spray first thing in the morning. General Mallon straightened up and looked at his watch. Ten minutes before the usual weekly status report was due. He kneaded the stiffening muscles in the small of his bony back—damn the aches of growing old— then turned his attention to his white irises, now in full bloom and shining luminously in the midafternoon sun. Minutes later and exactly on schedule, the aging officer's garden puttering was interrupted by a distant ringing, which was followed quickly by the sound of a woman's voice coming from the screened windows of the den.

"Trav—it's your call. Can you come in now?"

"I'll be right there, dear. Tell him to hang on."

General Mallon eased himself into the worn brown leather wing chair next to his cluttered desk and waited for his wife to close the door behind her, then pressed the receiver to his ear. "This is Mallon. Go ahead. . . ."

The excitement that unfailingly came with each weekly call and that had maintained itself for nearly a decade gave his words an extra crispness. He listened without comment, merely nodding to himself as the voice on the line recited a seemingly meaningless series of numbers interspersed with a few foreign-sounding place names. At the end of the caller's two-minute monologue, the old general smiled, thanked his informant, and hung up.

The rest of the afternoon and evening was an unalloyed pleasure for Robert Mallon. A little more gardening, two very dry vodka martinis on the rocks, and an excellent meat loaf for dinner. At exactly 10:30 P.M., in accordance with his long-established schedule, General Mallon slipped into bed after giving his wife a courtly kiss on the cheek. He was a happy man. Despite his age and his retired status, he was suffused as always with a satisfying feeling of participation and action that transcended the best days of his active Army career. Almost immediately he dropped off to sleep, while his wife drowsily watched the late news on Channel 7 from her own bed nearby. Half the program was devoted to politics, politics, politics. The forthcoming national presidential elections were already beginning to sweep almost everything else aside in a Niagara of empty words and promises. Alice Mallon yawned, glanced across at her sleeping husband, and tripped the remote control to silence the TV. She reached up and switched off her bed-lamp. In a few minutes, she, too, was peacefully asleep.

It is entirely certain that neither of the Mallons would have fallen into sleep so easily if they had known that in another bedroom, not more than twenty miles away, in a neat three-story Georgetown town house, a man had just removed the tunic of his Navy admiral's uniform and, by the warm light of a single small table lamp, was fingering a folded sheet of yellow paper. On the paper was a hand-written list of seven Department of Defense projects.

2

By the time the awful heat and humidity of August descended like a hot, wet towel on Washington, Admiral Randolph Clayton felt as if he'd been running the JCS for years. Everything had settled into a steady routine of meetings, briefings, and budget arguments, spiced by just enough small but crackling crises around the world to remind him that he was not merely an administrator in some ordinary business corporation.

Implicit but never mentioned in the slides and viewgraphs that paraded endlessly before him were always those special elements that at once fascinated and frightened most military men: war and death. To Clayton, both were old and familiar. Although he had chosen to spend a lifetime dealing with them, he hated them. True and incandescent hate had joined familiarity only after Clayton's son, Marine Lieutenant Todd Randolph Clayton, was returned home to a waiting father and mother in a GI coffin containing a waterproof body bag closed with a sealed zipper.

Todd Clayton had not died in a war. Pure stupidity, as only an organization the size of the Department of Defense can practice it, had sliced the young man to pieces one moonless night when a communications garble during maneuvers sent helicopters directly into a lagoon area off Johnston Island where parachuting Marine frogmen and underwater demolition teams were also landing.

Randolph Clayton responded to that tragedy of five years earlier by retreating into his work. Where he had previously been thorough and precise in anything he undertook, he became obsessive. Behind his facile skill at assimilating mountains of data, which he shared with almost every other successful four-star officer, behind his deceptively easy smile and boyish face, was now a grim and absolute necessity to leave nothing whatsoever to chance or to accident.

Clayton looked up from his morning paper, whose bold headlines announced that the day was expected to be the

hottest August 14 in twenty-five years. The woman across
from him was staring into empty space. In spite of the
air conditioner, which filled the green-and-white kitchen
with a low hum, Clayton could see the beginnings of dark
stains of perspiration across the shoulders and under the
arms of her shiny blue housecoat. With a twinge of disgust, he returned to his newspaper.

"Don't you have anything at all to say to me?" the
woman finally asked.

"There's nothing more to say, Millie," Clayton answered. "As far as I'm concerned, we said it all last night
—for the ten thousandth time. I'm doing my job the best
way I can. It takes the hours it does and that's all there
is to it. I'm not going to start compromising and do it
halfway, and you know it.

"Furthermore, you also know damned well that the
fact that I'm not around enough to suit you is not the
root of the problem. Other women don't—" Clayton
stopped abruptly. He could feel himself getting angry
again and he didn't want to let it happen. Reducing his
wife to tears was easily done, but led absolutely nowhere.
Quickly he folded his paper, finished the dregs of his lukewarm coffee, and stood up. Looking down at his wife's
anguished face, he saw her chin begin to quiver as her
reddening eyes blinked nervously.

"Millie, look," he continued in a resigned half whisper.
"We both know you need help and you simply won't accept it. Until you make up your own mind to get well,
everything is going to stay like it is—or maybe get worse.
It's all up to you, can't you see that?"

Mildred Clayton did not answer. Instead she sat creas-
ing and recreasing a breakfast napkin as she waited for
the special signal she always sought when Clayton's words
turned in this direction. It was not long before she heard
it. The sound of the front door shutting with a slam behind her husband. Immediately she moved from the bright
sunlit kitchen to the softer gray light of the living room.
She paused on the way to open a glass-doored cabinet
and then settled gratefully into the overstuffed sofa with
its happy pattern of blue and green flowers.

In the early days of their marriage, most people would
have described Randolph Clayton's wife as pretty, if not
beautiful. Her skin was delicately translucent and her hair

a satisfying deep auburn. Now, at age forty-six and after twenty-five years of marriage, her skin had become merely a sallow wrapping over puffy, watery flesh and her hair was heavily threaded with streaks of gray which she no longer tried to conceal by dyeing. Rather than attempting to keep herself beautiful for herself or for her husband, Mildred Clayton had developed other skills, which were much more important to her survival. She had become adept at skipping backward through the years to when Todd was a little boy and Randy was just another promising young officer to whom the future was both beckoning and ambiguous. Hours or even days could pass without her returning from the protection of those long-vanished times and the simple joys they held—the picnics, the late dinners when Clayton's lanky but tired frame appeared at the door, the quick little vacations in the Caribbean, thanks to free, but unofficial, Navy transportation. She had found a wondrous time machine and it stood before her on the white marble coffee table within easy reach of the sofa. With a long sigh, she leaned forward and picked it up. The warm amber liquid gurgled into the water glass until it was almost full. Less than thirty minutes later, she was laughing aloud while she watched Todd's legs pumping furiously as he charged across the lawn on his bright new red tricycle. The water glass was empty and Mrs. Randolph Clayton was drunk.

In the isolated world of the small chamber behind the JCS Chairman's desk, immune to the August heat and protected from every possible intrusion, a black marker moved rapidly back and forth across the yellow paper, finally burying a brief notation in an opaque mass of intersecting lines. Admiral Clayton was satisfied with his morning's work. Two more of the puzzle projects on his list had finally yielded in a single session with the ACA codes.

The first, Program R607, turned out to be rather dull. The IRS had been experimenting with associative electronic memory technology, trying to nail high rollers at Las Vegas: it frustrated them to see so many anonymous people cashing in as big winners all year long, only to disappear into poverty around April 15. After hearing about the progress IRS was making, the previous Secretary of Defense had apparently established R607 to monitor their techniques for anything that the office of the SecDef might find useful. R607 had produced nothing special, but the Secretary must have been leery about being accused of picking brains at Internal Revenue or he wouldn't have been so careful about covering his project.

The second puzzle Clayton had cracked was a little more interesting. Early in the year, the President had run a major exercise analyzing probable effects of alternate strategies in southern Africa. No problem there, but after spending fifty million through State, Commerce, DOD, and Energy on the analyses, the wily old fox must have realized that the results, once they'd been completely pulled together, could be used to raise some very touchy racial questions at election time. Almost certainly that was the reason he had sprinkled the final, fully collated data around so subtly in the Federal Data Base that only the ACA system could reassemble the important results. If that was his notion, and it seemed reasonable, Donley had spent the last six months comfortably certain that he would have no leaks about his African strategy. Only one of the four men other than the President who were privileged to use the ACA codes could be a source, and quite aside from questions of loyalty, a leak from such an easily isolated originator would be unthinkable.

Clayton smiled, recognizing the ancient and answerless question faced daily by thousands of public servants in Washington: Where does national interest stop and self-interest begin? Generally, Clayton admitted to himself, Donley had done a good job in his first term of measuring off the pros and cons, the goods and bads, the "mes" and "theys." Nevertheless, given the country's economic troubles, the coming election could be stormy if the opposition found an issue around which to rally. Thus far, in mid-August, they'd only come up with the standard list, led, as usual, by the DOD budget. But they still had ten weeks to go and were turning over every rock they could. Using the ACA system as an ultimate means of classification and safe storage, Donley had obviously greatly reduced the visibility of his perhaps too neatly leveraged and balanced tactics in southern Africa. Or at least so it seemed to Clayton. What Donley's real motivations might have been mattered little to the admiral. The important facts were that Donley himself had initiated the program, and that Clayton now knew what it was and had provided himself with an explanation of why it existed. He could cross it off the tattered piece of yellow paper he had been carrying around since April. Eliminating it left only one entry on his list: Project M10, Top Secret, Sigma Six.

Clayton emerged from the ACA console room and filled his lungs with air as he dropped into the leather desk chair in his main office. He was always vaguely uneasy in the closed little room—the "tank," as he'd come to call it. It was too quiet, too perfectly controlled, and too damned small. Happy to be out of his self-inflicted confinement after the long morning session, Clayton flipped through his calendar to see when he could fit in another turn at the console. The paradox between his feelings and his action did not concern him.

The schedule did not look good. For most of the rest of the week, he'd be in the middle of the congressional dogfight over DOD funding and a major contract "jawboning" effort to cut costs. Next week was burdened with a fast trip to the Middle East and Pakistan and Australia. Then came site-inspection visits at the newly augmented BMEWS radars in northern Canada.

Clayton swore softly to himself. At this rate, it would be September before he could squeeze in another ACA session. For a brief moment, his hand hovered over the yellow paper which he had smoothed out on the cool glass covering his desk. Why not end it here? he thought. You've gotten all of them except one and none have been all that earth-shaking. On top of everything else, the biennial European war games were coming right after the election and not enough had been done on them. Quit now.

The entry on the seventh line of the paper stared back at him. Out of pure impulse, Clayton grunted and brought a hand down on the annoying sheet of paper, his strong fingers gathering it together and crushing it into a tight little wad. A sense of satisfaction flooded through him but was replaced immediately by a quietly insistent inner voice: Project M10. What is it? What is it?

Inexplicably, Clayton had been totally frustrated in his

attempts to penetrate its mystery. All he knew thus far, in spite of hours of effort with the world's most powerful computer system, was that M10 had been drawing funds from several services and that the first M10 funds were allocated sometime in the mid 1970s. Exact up-to-date expenditures did not appear in the DOD data file, but based on what the ACA codes had been able to uncover, the funds used on M10 must have exceeded twenty million dollars. Surprisingly, no data were available on the purpose of M10 nor on the elements of the DOD who were responsible for its successful prosecution.

Logic demanded that M10 be allowed to slip into the background of Clayton's mind. The multibillion-dollar issues of the entire DOD with which he was now contending made a matter of twenty million dollars a low-priority problem. But what guided Clayton, alone and toying with the tiny yellow ball of paper in his office, was not logic. Instead it was an almost primal need that had been born five years before in a sad funeral cortege and could not be satisfied with a quick flip into the gray metal wastebasket waiting under his desk. The admiral paused as if held by an invisible force. He rolled the wadded yellow ball around in his hand for a dozen heartbeats. Then, his decision made, he reopened it with great care and smoothed it flat against the desk. Folding it again, he slipped the paper into the pocket of his uniform where he had always carried it.

"Kathy, I'm going to lunch at the Corridor C commissary," he announced into his intercom. He had just fifteen minutes before his next meeting was scheduled.

3

Washington was feeling the edge of a huge Canadian cold front which had pushed its way across and down the continent long before it should have. Surprised morning commuters, dressed in clothing correct for the mid-September season but too light for the weather, stepped briskly along walkways whipped by a snapping wind.

For the first time in more than a month, Admiral Clayton felt a slight lessening of pressure. The budget hearings were behind him and, at least for the moment, the whirlwind tour schedule had abated. At last he had a chance to breathe. Through the gauzy curtains of his bedroom he could see that the day was going to be downright wintery. Well, that was okay. Cold weather always invigorated him. Fall and winter were his favorite times.

Clayton looked back toward the rumpled bed and the tightly curled form of his wife. "Millie, are you awake?"

"Yes, I guess so," came the sleepy answer.

"How do you feel?"

Mildred Clayton straightened her body and pushed a pillow under her head. "What did you say?" she asked with mock surprise.

"I merely asked you how you felt," he replied warily, beginning to sense the start of another argument. Their conversations always used the same scripts, he thought, as he watched her drag herself to a sitting position on the edge of the bed.

"If you really care, Randy, I feel ugly, as usual, and old, as usual, and I need a drink. . . ."

Clayton fought down the urge to add "as usual" to his wife's last phrase. He busied himself with fishing around in his closet for a warmer uniform. By the time he had pulled one away from the grasp of a plastic cleaner's bag, he had himself under full control. Like a physician with a very sick patient, he settled down on the bed beside his wife and put an arm around her shoulder. He felt her shiver. She wore only thin white nylon pajamas.

"Thank you," she murmured listlessly. "I was getting cold."

As she spoke, Clayton caught the dark odor of old alcohol on her breath and, in spite of himself, turned his face away. "Millie, things have eased off a bit at the office. It won't last long. Maybe a week or two, then the final election push will start and I'm sure to catch some of it. But in the meantime, we could plan a few things, perhaps even a weekend in the mountains if you like. . . ."

"You really mean that?" she said, cocking her head toward him in genuine disbelief.

Clayton nodded and forced a smile. "Yes, I really mean it. It'll do us both some good. Set up a few dates for us and

I'll make sure I don't cancel out on you. I promise. Now I've got to finish dressing. The car's downstairs."

Taking the narrow stairs two at a time, Clayton elbowed the jacket of a winter-weight uniform onto his slightly bony shoulders and headed for the door of his house. Just as the cold breeze of the morning washed over his face, he remembered something and quickly retraced his steps to the second-floor bedroom. He dug a hand into the left side pocket of his lightweight uniform tunic, still hanging across the back of a chair.

"Randy, is that you?" His wife's voice was barely audible over the distant sound of running water in the bathtub.

"Yes, of course it's me. I just forgot something."

"Listen, Randy," the voice behind the closed door of the bathroom continued. "There's a party at the Pulmans'. I think it's two weeks from Saturday. Could we go? I was planning to tell them you were too busy. My brother John will be there. I haven't seen him in ages."

Having found what he was looking for, Clayton was hardly aware of what his wife was saying. "Sure, that sounds good," he mumbled as he toyed with the tattered piece of yellow paper and headed back down the stairs.

By the time he reached the end of the red-brick walk in front of his house, Clayton was no longer concerned with playing the solicitous husband of an alcoholic wife. He had decided how he would spend the luxury of the free time that had crept into his daily schedule.

"Damn! Today's the day we finally get back to that one!" he said aloud as he shot a determined look at the puzzled driver, who was merely waiting to close the car door.

Clayton ducked low and the door of the "minimum transportation" sedan shut with a snap. He settled down in the rear seat and the car rolled slowly into Washington's morning traffic. As he watched the blurred faces of pedestrians flash by in the flat morning light, Clayton picked up the radiotelephone cradled in a niche to his left. He punched up his private office number and waited as the crackling noise on the line settled into a steady ringing tone, which was immediately followed by a girl's voice and an enthusiastic greeting.

"Listen, Katrinka," Clayton said, "did we ever get anything on M10 from the JCS staff after we put it on the follow-up list last month?"

"Can't you even say good morning?" Kathy answered. "But I must say, welcome back to the living! Now that you're onto subjects like that, I know things are getting back to normal. No, sir, we haven't got anything new about M10. As you well know, there has not been all that much time for chasing little puzzles."

"Well, listen," Clayton responded. "We're going to settle that one once and for all. I'll take an hour or two with the ACA codes to see whether anything new has come in and then, if it hasn't, I am going to bring it up again at the JCS meeting this afternoon. I'm going to get an answer if I have to take the Pentagon apart to do it."

"Jawohl, Herr General! Is there anything else?" Kathy giggled lightly.

Clayton laughed. "Let's not have any disrespect. This is an open link and we don't have a scrambler on it, so treat me gently, or you'll find yourself in a goddamned concentration camp!" With that, Clayton replaced the telephone in its cradle and smiled. He was pleased with himself.

Three and one half hours later, in the little windowless room behind his desk, Clayton was no longer pleased. The ACA codes had produced nothing new about M10 and Clayton's sense of frustration—a familiar feeling from his past encounters with the elusive project—had grown with each minute of fruitless effort. "It's the same goddamned blank wall I hit last winter," he mumbled at the blank screen of his console. "Sonofabitch! We spend a billion dollars creating this silly system and it can't even give me one simple answer on what this project is all about." As a diversion from the problems of his marriage and as an anesthetic for the still gnawing if subconscious pain of his son's death, M10 was doing its work well. It kept the admiral playing at what appeared to be merely an exercise in management-information retrieval until it was time for lunch.

Clayton decided to have a simple sandwich prior to joining his colleagues in the conference room of the Joint Chiefs. His heels clicked crisply through the wide greenish-yellow corridor of the Pentagon's innermost A Ring as he waved casual greetings at the parade of gold, blue, khaki, and olive drab that streamed past him. The smell of hamburgers and onions grilling on hot metal greeted his arrival at the tiny Y-shaped sandwich shop off A Ring at Corridors 5 and 6. He moved a cracked plastic tray, in an absurdly out-of-place tartan plaid pattern, through the sandwich line and ordered a sliced turkey on rye with lettuce and tomato, heavy on the mayo. The young black girl behind the counter smiled at him and the sandwich came back thick and heavy. They always give general officers good sandwiches here, mused Clayton, wondering how the lieutenants did. Carrying his sandwich on its paper plate to one of the long stand-up eating counters, Clayton was unaware of the impressed stares of the other people—the common folk of the Pentagon—lunching around him. Things were going pretty well at that, he thought. Hell, they *must* be, if I've got time to buy my own lunch and stand here watching the secretaries swinging by! He brushed a wisp of reddish hair away from his eye with the side of his hand. I really ought to be doing more about Millie. She reacted like a happy puppy today. Maybe she could start to pull out of it with enough help. I should talk to her again about AA. Maybe tonight . . .

His sandwich finished, Clayton dropped the paper plate and the other debris of his lunch into the almost filled plastic liner of a trash basket. It was nearly time for the JCS to convene as he walked back into the busy Pentagon corridor. Without knowing why, he suddenly felt compelled to pull the yellow paper from his pocket. "I'm going to get you, my friend," he muttered.

In one of the most carefully guarded and physically isolated areas of the Pentagon, behind thick ferroconcrete walls in which anti-eavesdropping sensors were buried every sixteen inches, the Joint Chiefs of Staff gathered for their weekly meeting. As usual, clusters of support personnel from each of the services milled around, gossiping about politics and promotions. When the tall figure of Admiral Clayton appeared, the conversations stopped instantly.

Clayton's rigid control of the time took the meeting through the formal agenda a full ten minutes ahead of schedule. At its close, as he looked from one side of the room to the other, Clayton icily reminded his colleagues that he had asked them previously for information about a project called M10. "I haven't gotten a thing from any of you," he said, purposely letting his annoyance show through his words. "I realize it's not a huge program, but it's still twenty million dollars that somebody thought was worth spending, and I want you to know I intend to find out what it is all about."

The men and women in the room explored each other's faces in silence. Most of them did not even remember Clayton's asking about M10. Too much had happened since he had brought up the subject. But the Chairman of the Joint Chiefs was the Chairman of the Joint Chiefs and on a dozen note pads as well as in the formal minutes of the meeting, the phrase "M10" was jotted down.

Clayton shoved his chair back abruptly and stood. "I expect detailed reports on M10 at next week's meeting," he said with emphasis. "I mean what I am saying. I want a full-scale check of every major element of DOD if that is necessary. I want to know which agency has cognizance of this project and what its objectives are. I presume now that my intentions are clear. The meeting is adjourned."

While the others stood at respectful attention behind him, Clayton wheeled from the room, certain that the last puzzle on his list would be resolved at the next JCS session. He was, as it turned out, completely wrong.

The meeting of the week of 19 September started with Clayton giving in to his curiosity by putting M10 first on the agenda. But one general or admiral after another answered Clayton's inquiring gaze or quick question with a helpless shrug. No one, literally no one, seemed to know what the project was about. Twenty million dollars' worth of nothing.

Clayton turned away from the conference table and polled the several dozen supporting staff people in the room. With obviously growing anger, his eyes flashed from one to the next. "Does the representative of the Defense Intelligence Agency have anything to report?"

"No, sir."

"The Defense Communications Agency?"

"No, sir."

"The Defense Nuclear Agency? Defense Civil Preparedness? NORAD? SAC?"

Every element of the DOD represented in the room,

each in its turn, gave the JCS Chairman the same blank look or slow side-to-side nod of the head.

The room flooded with tension as Clayton grimly completed his roll call and slumped deep into his chair. Finally, the CIA liaison representative, a blond, bushy-haired man in Harvard tweeds and a droopy mustache that had grown on a long trip through Eastern Europe and had never come off, suggested that M10 might be some kind of joint CIA-DOD catchall item in the budget that "fell between the cracks" for everybody.

"Well, I don't know what this damned project is," responded Clayton in a voice under too much control, "but I am certainly going to find out. I promise you that." He turned to Kathy, who was seated in her usual place at his left. Her responsibility in these meetings was to supplement the electronic record-keeping system with personal notes and observations for Clayton.

"Katherine, set up dates for me with Secretary Howetz and with Secretary Silverton. Since none of us seems to know what M10 is, maybe the Secretary of Defense or the Secretary of State will."

Again Clayton found that he was wrong. Conversations later in the week with Silverton and Howetz revealed that they had never heard of M10, or at least so they claimed, nor, for that matter, had other members of the President's cabinet, to whom Clayton addressed inquiries of steadily increasing urgency. It was as if no one in the entire federal government had ever had anything whatsoever to do with a project that appeared, albeit cryptically, in official classified records spanning nearly a decade.

While the Chairman of the Joint Chiefs pondered his next move on M10, the one man best equipped to answer all his questions was on the telephone conducting the business of the project. General Mallon had been through all the moralistic arguments many times before. He had no trouble deciding what to do.

"She must be neutralized," he said, and paused momentarily while the voice on the phone tried to argue with him. "Yes, yes, I understand all that," he continued impatiently, "but the fact is that her husband understood the risks. He knew the materials might affect him too, regardless of how careful he was. He was a loyal member of the project and

went into it with his eyes open because he believed in it. I
regret he has had to suffer so much and I certainly regret
his wife has made the threats she has. The point is, however,
that when Contrerras dies, and I gather it is a matter of
only hours or days now, there will be no one to control
her or monitor her actions. She must be removed for the
good of us all and to preserve the integrity of the entire
operation. . . .

"What? Yes, I understand that, too." Another pause.
"All right, we'll make those arrangements for the children.
But are we then agreed? Good. You'll send me the customary information afterward, of course. Have a good
weekend."

General Mallon hung up the telephone in his den and
stared thoughtfully out the window at his lawn. It was time
to use the power mower and he couldn't remember whether
or not there was any gas left in it.

Two days later, the obituary section of *La Prensa* noted
that Carlos Contrerras, age thirty-eight, transportation
manager for the giant Argentinian firm Pan-Sud Food and
Grain S.A., had died at the Buenos Aires Oncological
Hospital after a long illness. That evening his distraught
wife committed suicide with potassium cyanide, leaving
behind nine-year-old Julio and seven-year-old Martina
Contrerras.

4

Far below him, the blue-white diamonds of the ice wheeled
and undulated in a slow, majestic dance. Gliding through
the dark sky like a great hawk, his heart pounding exul-
tantly, he swooped closer and the diamonds became an
endless sea of gleaming crystal ridges, each locked against
the next by some enormous and incomprehensible force.
He threw back his arms and zoomed upward into the
infinite silence. Intoxicated by his freedom, he arched his
naked body and descended again, sweeping closer and
closer to the cold gleaming edges of the knives of ice. And
then there was no longer any will within him. He was
captured. He streaked downward, his skin taut and shiver-

ing against the sudden cold, every muscle and nerve ready
for the ecstatic touch of the reaching pillars. His long glide
leveled and the shining blades of ice were against him—
caressing, caressing. Thin red lines drew themselves down
across his chest and abdomen, and the tips of the blades
were tinged with running rosy blood.

Soaring into the sky again, whirling and bursting with
joy beyond imagining, he streaked upward in a towering
loop and plummeted back toward the beckoning blades.
Their steely edges met his flesh and painless crimson
furrows raced across his breast and dug their way down his
belly and his genitals, until they etched both quivering
thighs with dark-red bands. But still it was not enough. The
iridescent moonlit clouds pulled him skyward for another
plunging marriage with the waiting knives. Mindless, en-
raptured no longer, his mouth opened wide and then
exploded in a final voiceless shriek while the blades sliced
their way through throbbing muscle and hot splintering
bone. Thick, congealed ribbons of blood sloughed along
the edges of the cold, sharp metal and a gigantic crystal ax
whistled toward his face, which was now not his face at all,
but his son's face, Todd's face, crying out to him for help.

Admiral Clayton's eyes snapped open wide in the gloom
of his bedroom. His pulse raced. Whenever it came, the
dream was exactly the same and it always left him weak
with fear and self-disgust. He pulled the corner of the
pillowcase across his forehead to wipe away the cold film
of sweat. He lay still, listening for a time to the bubbly
snoring of his wife. After a long while, in the lonely morning just as dawn was breaking, he made a decision. He
would ask the President himself about Project M10.

A few hours later, as his staff car rolled out of Georgetown, joining the heavy stream of traffic crossing the
Potomac via the Key Bridge, Randolph Clayton dialed a
special White House number on his radiotelephone. By
the time the olive-drab automobile, sporting its JCS
Chairman's black emblem plate with four stars, had
rounded Rosslyn Circle below the Marriott Hotel and had
eased past Arlington Cemetery, leaving the Kennedy
Memorial Flame just visible in the cold mists of the fall
morning, Clayton had reached the office he was seeking.

"Mrs. Wilcox, this is Admiral Clayton."

"Oh, hello, Admiral, how are you?" responded the soft,

Texas-accented voice of the President's personal secretary.

"I'm fine, but look, I need a few minutes with the President. When could you fit me in for, say, fifteen minutes?"

"Admiral, he is really up to his ears. He is doing about four speeches a day, it seems. Let's see . . . about the soonest I can find anything clear is the week of October eighth. How 'bout Wednesday, October tenth . . . say at 6:00 P.M.? I'm assuming, of course, this isn't an emergency. It isn't, is it?"

"No, no, nothing like that," said Clayton casually. "It's just a little project I've uncovered that I can't seem to find out about. I thought perhaps the President might be running it himself, and I don't want to get into something I shouldn't be. The tenth will be fine."

"Well, why don't I put you down for, say, twenty minutes. Do you want to send over any paper work in advance?"

"I'm afraid I don't really have anything much. That's part of my problem. All I can tell you is the project designation—M10—and the classification—Top Secret, Sigma Six. That's all I can get out of the ACA system."

"M10 TS-S6. Okay. I'll give that to him in his daily calendar notes for that week. It may give him a chance to think about it."

"Thanks, Mrs. Wilcox. I'll see you then on the tenth."

"Good-bye, Admiral, and give my regards to Mildred."

Clayton slammed the phone back into its niche in the rear-seat armrest. He did not like the idea of waiting two weeks to get at M10, but there was nothing to be done about it. At least for a time, he mused to himself, he would just have to arrange to keep the project out of his mind. It was hurting other things he ought to be thinking about. Like a man counting sheep in an attempt to fall asleep, he began to list aloud the major problems to which he would turn his attention while waiting for October 10. He mouthed them slowly and deliberately one after another, oblivious of his driver's presence and noting their self-evident significance as compared to M10. But he did not believe in what he was doing. The puzzle had become an obsession.

* * *

On Saturday night, October 6, Randolph Clayton found himself struggling hard to keep a promise. Weeks earlier, he had encouraged his wife to make a few dates and social plans and had assured her of his cooperation. Now the chickens were coming home to roost. Tense with the nagging torment of his preoccupation with M10—during the endless days of waiting for his appointment with President Donley, he had found it increasingly difficult to concentrate on the business of his office—he was now enduring a Washington party. How he hated parties! What abominable wastes of time they were. A sport for idiots. On the other hand, he admitted to himself, watching the graceful white-haired hostess introducing the latest arrivals, the Pulmans were actually very decent people and Mildred seemed to be having a good time. So far, at least, she hadn't had too much to drink.

Suddenly in need of getting away from the babble of the crowd, Clayton moved from his corner position in the dining room and out the glass doors which opened onto the flagstone patio. Passing a cluster of men who were laughingly supervising George Pulman's adjustment of his huge charcoal grill, Clayton continued across the clipped lawn, following the long split-rail fence that guarded the four acres of the congressman's house outside Rockville. Against the glowing orange red of the sunset sky, the weathered cedar shingles of the rambling house looked like metallic silver and Clayton, conscious of the beauty of the evening, pulled a deep draught of cool air into his lungs. He continued his stroll until his nostrils caught the sharp scent of barbecuing meat drifting toward him on the light wind. The realization that he was getting hungry sent him back toward the house, just as a man's voice called to him in the fading twilight.

"Hey, Randy, wait a minute!" A short, heavy-set man with gray hair and the movements of an athlete sprinted over a low rise toward Clayton. It was John Schotty, his wife's older brother and the author of the Washington *Globe*'s top political column, "Schotty Says . . ." The admiral smiled. Schotty was a man's man and Clayton liked him immensely, though they seldom saw each other socially. The prospect of chatting with the perceptive Pulitzer Prize–winner at this party had been its most redeeming aspect and Clayton had been disappointed not to find him in the crowd.

The older man pumped Clayton's hand vigorously and fell into step beside him. By the time the two of them had reached the smoothly set flag walk leading back toward the crowded patio, which was decorated with gently swaying strings of bright red, green, and orange Japanese lanterns, the usual amenities were over and Schotty got down to what really mattered to him.

"How's Millie been doing lately?" he asked gravely.

"Not much different than usual," Clayton replied with resignation. "In fact, maybe a little worse. It's almost an everyday thing, and I can't get her to seek help. The moment I try, she just shuts me out."

"But what about Alcoholics Anonymous, Randy? You said you were going to try them the last time we talked. What happened?"

"Hell, nothing happened. She simply refuses to go to them, and I can't pick her up and carry her there," Clayton said quietly.

Schotty was about to say more when Mrs. Pulman tiptoed up to Clayton with exaggerated solicitousness and a pained expression on her face. She excused herself to Schotty and tugged on the admiral's sport coat, urging him off to one side of the crowded patio.

"I'm sorry, Randy, but I think you'd better go into the living room. Millie's . . . well, she's had too much and she's . . . getting awfully loud. She needs you. I'm sorry."

Clayton faced his hostess squarely. Under the warm glow of the paper lanterns, he could see the honest pity in her eyes. It infuriated and embarrassed him. "I'll take care of it . . . and thank you, Mrs. Pulman. It's been a lovely party."

"Let's have lunch, John. I'll give you a call," Clayton said as he shook Mildred's brother's hand in a hurried good-bye. Schotty nodded knowingly, but said nothing.

Randolph Clayton threaded his way through the laughing, milling crowd jammed into the Pulmans' living room. He had no trouble knowing where he was going. His wife, though not immediately visible, could be heard easily above the din of the mob. She was damning Washington, damning the Navy, and damning President Donley at the top of her voice.

"Millie, it's time we go," he whispered, hoping the others in the room were too busy to notice his hand moving under her armpit.

She looked at him with glazed and reddened eyes and licked her lips loudly. For an instant she struggled against him, but then, seeing the expression on his face, she heaved herself up from the deep cushions of the sofa to a standing position. "Sure, honey, anything you say . . . anything at all, Randy, honey."

Moving unsteadily along the Pulmans' curving driveway and through the briskly beautiful night toward their car, Admiral Clayton could not bring himself to look directly at his wife. "Millie," he said, staring straight ahead, "I want you to do something for me. I want you to call Alcoholics Anonymous tomorrow."

"Whafor? Whafor?"

"You know damned well what for. You're drinking like a fish."

"Aw, Randy, why do you say things . . . things like that? I don't drink so much . . . I don't . . . I'm over that. You're just trying to spoil everything . . . It's so pretty tonight, Randy. Come on . . . don't talk like that."

Clayton held his wife's arm as she stumbled along the crushed marble stone of the driveway. In the clear, dark air, his voice was tight with anger. "Mildred, I really mean it . . . Millie, you're going to call AA and you're going to call them tomorrow."

"Randy, I'm not drunk. I'm not. Honestly, I'm not. . . ."

They were at their car. With one hand Clayton reached for his keys, while the other still grasped Mildred's upper arm. "You're calling tomorrow, damn you," he repeated, half under his breath. As he opened the door to help her in, his fingers dug through the wool of her coat and into her flesh—imperceptibly at first, and then tighter and tighter and tighter. Finally, she began to sob softly with the pain.

5

The next three days were not pleasant ones for Admiral Clayton. Sunday was spent in futile assaults on his wife's stony silence. Monday and Tuesday he was like a man divided, outwardly conducting the routine business of his office but inwardly consumed with impatience at having to wait for his meeting with the President. Then Wednesday came and Clayton's appointment with the President was less than an hour away. His staff car and driver were outside.

"Good luck, Admiral," Kathy's voice followed him as he walked quickly past her desk. "Hope the boss can tell you what you want to find out."

"Well, if he can't," he called back to her, "I don't know what the next step is. We'll just have to see."

Clayton could feel a tightness begin to build in his stomach as he followed the now familiar route from his own inner office suite, through the reception area, past the ever-present MPs, and into the main corridor of E Ring. Taking the low, wide stairs of the Pentagon River Entrance three at a time, he set the gold-braided visor of his hat firmly against the October wind and motioned a quick "Let's go" to his driver. Ten minutes later the sedan was moving slowly down Fourteenth Street, caught in the stop-and-go traffic of the final stages of the Washington rush hour. After what seemed to be an endless journey, it came to a gentle stop at the thick greenish-glass windows of the guard gate which controlled access to the White House appointments gate off Pennsylvania Avenue. Clayton felt for the wallet in his right rear trousers pocket. He pushed an ID card toward the blue-uniformed federal policeman standing at the window of the car. The policeman had seen Clayton dozens of times in the past, but the rules were to be followed. Mechanically the guard checked the identification photo against the man holding it.

"Yes sir, Admiral. Go right ahead." The black iron gate swung open.

* * *

Clayton settled himself into the red-and-gold striped sofa outside the President's Oval Office. Mrs. Wilcox's assistant, who spoke with the same soft Texas accent, offered him a magazine. He looked up at her and laughed. Now that he was here, the tension was beginning to abate. "No, thanks, I think I'll just sit here and watch the world go by."

She smiled at him, showing smoothly polished even white teeth. Clayton allowed himself a closer look—blond, blue-eyed, thirtyish, and inviting. Reminding himself how little time he had had for such things and how little effort he had put into them, Clayton sucked in a deep breath and let it out slowly. If I had it all to do over again, he thought idly, I wonder if I would still keep the same set of priorities. With secret pleasure, he watched the girl's smooth body slide back into her desk chair.

At that moment, a muted buzzer on Mrs. Wilcox's own desk sounded. "Dorie, I got through a bit early with the ambassador, so when Randy Clayton shows up, why don't you shoot him on in here." It was the voice of President Frederick R. Donley.

Mrs. Wilcox pushed the first button on the small walnut box of the intercom. "Sir, he is here now. Shall I send him in?"

"Yes, yes, send him on in, by all means."

Clayton was already on his feet and walking toward the cream-colored door of the Oval Office. It opened abruptly and he found himself face to face with a tall man in his sixties. The President of the United States, obviously every inch a patrician, was a little heavier than he had been when he was governor of Texas and a bit less fit than he had been when he rowed against Harvard while attending Yale, but he was still a handsome, indeed striking, man. Randolph Clayton was slightly over six feet tall. He found that he had to look up at least two or three inches to meet the President's smiling eyes.

"Randy, Randy, good to see you. Come in. Sit down, sit down. Want some coffee?"

"No, thanks. It's good to see you, too, sir," responded Clayton respectfully.

"How are things going over there, Randy? You fellows in the DOD are giving me fits, as I'm sure you know. Everywhere I go these days, I hear nothing but hell-raising about all the money we're spending."

"Sir, we have a big effort under way to try to put some facts in place of all the speculation on the budget. I think we're getting someplace, too. The media are beginning to understand that there's plenty of good, valid information around. It's just a matter of getting it out to the people. We can't do that by ourselves."

"Yes, yes, I know," sighed the President, settling in behind his desk. "We had all those goddamned congressional investigations and nobody really came up with anything solid, but people just don't pay attention, and I haven't figured out a way to get them to. . . . Well, look, I gather that's not why you asked to see me. What can I do for you?"

"Sir, I know this may seem strange, but there is a little project I have run onto with the ACA codes—"

"Yeah," the President interrupted. "They *are* something, aren't they?"

"Yes, sir, they certainly are. Well, I ran onto this little project that I can't seem to get any information on, and so I thought maybe it was something you were using as a cover designator. I didn't want to pry into it any further until I checked with you. I don't want to be sticking my nose in where it doesn't belong."

The President frowned slightly. "Yes, Mrs. Wilcox gave me the information. Project M10, isn't it?"

"That's right, sir." Clayton nodded.

"Well, I tell you I have had Jim Willoughby check around and he can't find anything. I even played with the ACA system myself this morning and I didn't find anything, either. Nothing that jogged my memory. As far as I can tell, I've never heard of it. Look, whatever makes you curious about this thing, it's probably past history now. If it weren't, my OMB people would certainly have spotted it in this budget hassle we've been having. I didn't get a chance to check . . . how much money do you think we've spent on it?"

Clayton hesitated. He knew the relatively small amount of money involved would kill the President's interest. "Only about twenty million, but," he added hastily, "for all I know, that is just the tip of the iceberg. That's what worries me. I've got an uneasy feeling about this one. It's the only one that seems to be so hard to pin down of all the designators I tried to track."

"Well, hell," the President said airily, "if you've got time to play with it, you go right ahead. It's not any cover for something we are doing up here. But I really wonder whether it's worth your while. It makes me think you might not have enough to do, my friend." The President laughed and winked broadly at Clayton. Clayton could sense that the interview was over. Twenty-million-dollar projects were not presidential-level concerns, especially with just a month to go before the election.

Donley rose from his chair and walked around his ornately carved desk, a gift of Queen Victoria. Its polished surface was fastidiously clear, except for a corner covered with a collection of crystal paperweights. The President took Clayton's extended hand in both his own. "Randy," he said, giving Clayton the steady, intense eyeball-to-eyeball gaze of a practiced politician, "one thing I want you to do for me. Let's not have any surprises out of your shop between now and the election, okay? Things are relatively calm now and that's good. If it weren't for these damn strikes and cost of living problems, we would be a shoo-in next month. As it is, it's going to be close, so we are going to need all the help we can get. As far as you guys over there are concerned, that means a quiet world. You get me, Randy?"

"I understand, sir," Clayton affirmed.

"Good, good." The President nodded enthusiastically as he grasped Clayton's elbow and escorted him toward the door.

Clayton was passing Mrs. Wilcox and her bright Texas smile when the President called to him again. "And by the way, Admiral, if you ever do find out about M10, let me know. I would be curious. As a matter of fact, I'll bet you a steak dinner after the election that it's some damn fool nonsense involving the Boy Scouts or some congressional junkets you fellas have been running."

"We'll see, sir. I may look into it further . . . if I get time," Clayton answered as he waved a salute.

Neither man could have known it at the time, but they would never see each other again.

It was dusk when Admiral Clayton's car coasted to a stop in front of his house. Finding himself at home came as a surprise. He had spent the ride deep in thought. The

interview scheduled for twenty minutes by Mrs. Wilcox
had lasted only five. Was it cut short because M10 was too
small for Donley to worry about these days? Should Clayton not have mentioned the dollar figures? Would it have
piqued the President's interest if he knew the project was
ongoing for so long? Was the President trying to give him a
message without actually saying anything about M10?
What did he mean about not having enough to do? Was
that a hint to drop the matter? No, that didn't make sense.
At the end of the conversation, he had said he wanted to
know about M10 if Clayton found out anything. Well,
that's just marvelous, Clayton thought. We spend twenty
million dollars or more and nobody in the whole bloody
government knows what for, not even the President himself. M10 . . . M10 . . . M10 . . . The tires on the
road had whispered the phrase all the way to Georgetown
and home.

Clayton's key clicked sharply in the heavy brass colonial lock and his front door opened into deep shadows.
Not a single light was burning. Rubbing his taut neck
muscle, Clayton snapped on a hall switch and moved into
the living room. There, sprawled across the sofa, was
Mildred. The steady but labored clicks and gurgles of her
breathing told him she was asleep. On the coffee table in
front of her was a bottle of Scotch with only three fingers
left in it. Clayton's lips curled with disgust as he debated
shaking her into wakefulness. Instead he turned and
stalked back out of the house, slamming the door behind
him. This was another night for a long, long walk along the
back streets of Georgetown.

6
───────────

Throughout most of the week following that of his conversation with President Donley, Randolph Clayton was
unable to find time to devote to M10. If he had scraped
together the time, it is likely that he could not have used
it very effectively. He was too tense and too angry. He assumed the object of his anger was Mildred. Repeatedly
over the past few days, he had tried to talk to her about

psychiatric help or at least Alcoholics Anonymous, but each time she responded with sphinxlike silence or wild hysteria. Something made of iron seemed to lie beneath her behavior. Clayton could not fathom what it was, but he knew he was trapped by it. There was nothing, absolutely nothing, he could do for her, nor could he make her do anything for herself. It cannot go on like this, he told himself again and again. There was, however, no next step, no clear plan, in his mind.

Late in the week, and without being conscious of the fact that he had finally forgiven himself for letting his meeting with the President come to nothing, Clayton began to feel better. He found himself thinking seriously about M10 again. He thought it was still just an abstract, unemotional exercise for him and he never asked himself exactly why it had become so absolutely necessary to know about it. He did not see his renewed preoccupation with M10 as part of the special mixture of patterns in his life.

By Friday afternoon, Clayton had freed his mind and his calendar sufficiently to renew his full-scale sessions with the ACA codes. With instructions to Kathy to fend off all calls and visitors from 1800 hours onward, he slipped through the small door behind his desk and into the tiny computer console room. Settling into the chair in front of the console, he tapped in his ACA access identifiers and connected the console into the incredibly complex DOD supercomputer system. Access to the system instantly amplified Clayton's powers of analysis a millionfold. He himself was bright. He had a superb memory. He was inventive and creative. But he was human. The computer system with which he was now teamed was not bright; it was merely perfect. It was not human; it was merely tireless. It was not creative; it simply had infinite capacity to remember. It was not intuitive; it could only process broad, deep rivers of data that came and went with the speed of light.

But this system had one thing that none of its counterparts elsewhere had. Thanks to the genius of Professor Eugene Wigren and the monumental effort of the thousands of mathematicians and engineers who had followed his lead, this system had the ability to suggest *associations*. While the computer's power of suggestive association might result only in a few extra flickering hints and snips of data displayed in glowing green alphanumeric form on the console screen, this outwardly simple addition to its capabilities had changed it from servant to teacher, from dumb thing to true colleague. Man and machine could now become profoundly unified, bound together by an invisible flow of thoughts and ideas that could move with ease from one partner to the other and back again.

The computer, with its flawless efficiency and dazzling speed, could cross-check any fact with all other data in its enormous memory. It could look for correlations, for groupings, for those unusual coincidences that, if recognized by a human mind, might be called inspired insights. The computer could not judge the *value* of its insights. That, at least, was still a human function. Judgment remained the domain of man's intuitive genius alone. But the computer could provide the catalog, the table of contents, as it were. All that a man was asked to do was choose the best, the most intriguing, the most appealing possibility. Given that choice, the computer could execute a torrent of new correlation commands and open new directions in which to look for ever more penetrating answers.

It was this almost living, nearly omnipotent system that Clayton had been using in his unavailing attempts to understand Project M10. Ignoring the repeated failures of the past, Clayton now poked at the keyboard with renewed excitement. He had another new approach—perhaps the hundredth he had tried. He could feel himself becoming tense as he sent his message to the waiting machine: Do a statistical analysis on the timing of the use of travel funds on all projects at the Sigma Six level. What were the correlations among travel charges to the M10 accounts. Some of that twenty million dollars must certainly have been used by somebody to travel someplace. What could be made out of the patterns of that travel?

In obedience to Clayton's commands, the worldwide system began to pulsate with life. Electronic signals traveling 186,000 miles per second, the quicksilver lifeblood of the huge megamachine, flashed through cables, sprang from satellite antennas, and streaked along microwave and optical communications channels. Intricate code sequences faultlessly guided trillions of bits of information to destinations in dozens of processing centers. Like the brontosaur of prehistoric times, this greatest of all computer systems did not have a single brain. It had outgrown such an easy concept. A single brain would have been too slow, too limited. Instead, just as the brontosaur had one brain in its head and another halfway down its long back, this DOD supercomputer system relied upon a cooperative community of computers to solve the prodigious problems it undertook. Electronic data libraries—the memory of the megamachine—were dispersed across the entire globe and yet were drawn tightly together by the fabric of the system. In Kansas City, in Berlin, outside London, and in the basements of a dozen Washington buildings, in the IRS centers of the Midwest and the West Coast, the data were channeled, analyzed, shaped, and cross-checked. One large-scale computer, squatting silently in the subbasement of the Pentagon itself, had no other duty but to oversee the functioning of the other computers of the system. Nearby, a giant sister computer, in a guarded thick-walled concrete vault, ran the associative programs themselves and provided results accessible only to those few men entitled to use the ACA codes.

The act of creation of the ACA programs had, in some ways, come close to turning men into gods. Man had not yet created life, but he had created programs that almost duplicated the process of living thought. When and if it became possible to include such abstracts as "taste" and "judgment" and "beauty" in these codes and programs, then man would have, in effect, produced a thinking mind . . . a mechanical personality . . . a personality whose richness and complexity not only would rival those of man himself but could, in many very human ways, excel him.

Now, under Clayton's instructions to explore the nature of travel-fund expenditures at the Sigma Six classification level, the ACA codes slashed quickly through the records of a hundred thousand trips by tens of thousands of travelers. The system cross-checked, queried, cross-checked again—each time exploring a bewildering maze of possible relationships to other events. Finally, the results of its mighty effort flickered into view on the console before which Admiral Clayton waited impatiently.

NO SIGNIFICANT PATTERNS RECOGNIZABLE
IN TRAVEL BUDGETS OTHER THAN THOSE

ACCOUNTED FOR BY KNOWN PROJECTS. END
OF DIRECT RESPONSE. PLEASE ENTER NEXT REQUEST.

Clayton slammed his fist down against the metal table. The console screen facing him felt none of his frustration. The primary associative procedures had yielded nothing. There were, however, four less likely correlation procedures or subroutines in the program. Half-heartedly Clayton typed in another command: "Perform Correlation Subroutines 1, 2, 3, and 4."

The screen flickered once, then two words appeared: IN PROCESS. Clayton leaned back in the chair and clasped his hands behind his head. His gray-green eyes narrowed to slits. There was nothing to do now but wait. Moments later, the console screen went blank and a longer message scrolled into view:

SUBROUTINE 1: NO YIELD.
SUBROUTINE 2: NO YIELD.
SUBROUTINE 3: SUGGESTS POSSIBLE UNACCOUNTED-FOR RESIDUALS RELATING TO SCHEDULES OF NATIONAL AND INTERNATIONAL MEETINGS ON FOLLOWING SUBJECTS: POPULATION DYNAMICS; ECOLOGY; BIOCHEMISTRY; ORGANIC CHEMISTRY; ONCOLOGY; EPIDEMIOLOGY; PUBLIC HEALTH PLANNING; SOVIET CANCER RESEARCH; STATISTICAL TECHNIQUES AND MATHEMATICS.
SUBROUTINE 4: NO YIELD.

Clayton jolted forward in his chair. What did *that* all mean? Correlation Subroutine 3 had produced a laundry list of miscellaneous subjects. What could be the possible connection between international professional meetings on such a broad spectrum of subjects, on the one hand, and the puzzle of M10 on the other? Could it be that M10 was some kind of international ecology study? Why would Soviet health statistics be involved? And why would such a study have a classification level of Top Secret, Sigma Six?

None of the data seemed to make any sense. But at least now Clayton had a lead, however flimsy, that might take him somewhere. Okay, he thought, suppose it is an ecology project or perhaps a medical research project. Suppose we are collaborating with the USSR. Maybe someone in DOD didn't feel we were ready for joint research when M10 was started and so they covered it. Things have changed since and perhaps the bureaucracy never caught up. Let's pursue that possibility and see where it leads.

Admiral Clayton typed in a new series of commands. As his index fingers skipped awkwardly over the keyboard, he was aware of his heart beating a little faster and harder than usual. He sensed that he could be coming closer. He was right.

By 3:00 A.M., Saturday morning, October 20, Clayton had concluded that M10 was indeed some kind of international project in medical research being run in collaboration with the Soviets. He still did not know why it was Top Secret nor precisely what kind of research was involved. The project seemed to have something to do with population dynamics. The one really stupefying fact that he had unearthed was that M10 was no puny little twenty-million-dollar hobby for some anonymous project director, perhaps long gone into retirement. Clayton had located expenditures for M10 hidden in scores of different budget items for at least half a dozen Department of Defense and civilian federal labs. Like a team of bloodhounds on the scent, the computer system and its human partner had traced through trillions of facts with blinding speed to find costs exceeding 195 million dollars!

Except for dozing briefly as he waited for the machine to process particularly complex sequences, Clayton had not slept in twenty-one hours nor eaten in fifteen. But he was neither hungry nor tired. He knew that he was winning against M10, and furthermore, he knew that it was no simple little puzzle which, for some inexplicable reason, had grown into an irrational challenge. How could the U.S. have possibly spent nearly two hundred million dollars about which no one knew anything? Now a man helplessly addicted, Clayton could not control his need to end his struggle to *know*. He resolved that he would not stop, he would not leave the console, until he had torn M10 to shreds.

Oblivious of the time, he grabbed for the telephone and excitedly dialed Kathy at her home. Finally, a sleepy "Hello" greeted him after a long and persistent series of rings.

"Katrinka," Clayton shouted, in spite of the strange hour, "I think I've got it!"

"Admiral Clayton, for heaven's sake. What is the matter? What's wrong? What time is it?" Holding the telephone six inches from her ear for fear he would shout again, Katherine Myrdal felt around in the darkness for the switch on her bedlamp.

"It's three o'clock, Katrinka, and I am onto M10!"

"Oh," she replied huskily, as the knowledge that he was not ill or in trouble flooded through her. "That's nice, Admiral. . . . Ah, what did it turn out to be?"

"Listen, girl," he said, ignoring her question. "This is going to go on all weekend and I need you. If you're game, get out of bed and come down here. I can't let you have access to the ACA console, but I've got a feeling I am going to need your help getting supplementary stuff that you are cleared to use."

"I can be down there in an hour. Is that okay?" came the sleepy but willing response. "Just give me time to take a shower and put on some lipstick."

"Do whatever you have to do, but get the hell down here. And look, while you're at it, I'm starved. Find some kind of an all-night greasy spoon and bring me a ham n' cheese and a bottle of beer."

"Ugh! Okay, but please don't talk about beer at this hour."

Clayton laughed for the first time in days. "Incidentally," he said, "I'm sorry I woke you up, but you're used to that by now. You can make up the sleep after this is over."

"I'll never get used to you, sir, but I guess that's what I like about the job. See you shortly."

The line went dead with a soft click. Clayton was alone again with his computer console.

7

The final Saturday-afternoon shoppers were bustling their way through the aisles of Woodward and Lothrop, Washington's best-known department store, while anxious clerks wished them out onto the street, when Admiral Clayton finally permitted himself a momentary respite from his incessant pounding of the ACA console. He emerged from the high-security area to find Kathy sound asleep at her desk, her head down on her arms and her tousled black hair spilling across an open telephone directory. With a sudden start, she sat up, her eyes big and round with surprise.

"Oh! I guess I fell asleep," she said, flushing with embarrassment.

"No problem. Did you finish that list of contigency telephone numbers I asked for?" Clayton snapped out his words as if he were addressing a military strategy session.

"Yes, they're right here, *sir*." She hit the "sir" hard to let him know she was piqued by his tone, but he didn't seem to notice. Picking up the bottle of Dexedrine pills he had sent her for earlier, he headed back toward his office as if she were not there.

"Randy Clayton!" she shouted. "Are you going to stay in that goddamned tank all day?" All she received for an answer was the heavy thud of a door closing.

Kathy did not see Clayton again until the early hours of Sunday, when he stuck his head into her office after another of his brief prowls out of the console room. By then deep circles had settled in under her eyes and her legs and shoulders ached with fatigue. She had decided she hated him and would never speak to him again.

"Kathy, I need a copy of the *Encyclopedia Pharmacopeia*. Get Abelton at the Library of Congress to run it over here, will you?"

"But it's two o'clock Sunday morning!"

"I don't give a damn what time it is!"

With sudden awareness, Kathy realized she was watching a man whipping himself into a frenzy. His eyes were bright and burning, his face was dark and flushed. "I want that reference material, and I want it now," Clayton growled. "It's not anywhere in the DOD computerized files. Now, goddammit, get it over here. Incidentally, Katrinka, you look like hell. Get me another sandwich and cup of coffee, and go and get some sleep, but get me that encyclopedia first."

"Admiral, listen a moment," Kathy said. "You've lived with this Project M10 puzzle for a long time. Why don't you knock off and get some sleep and come at it fresh tomorrow? Why are you killing yourself like this?"

"Never mind me. I feel fine. Just get me that reference

material and that sandwich and go *home!*" The last few words just made it through the slamming door of the security area.

As she had countless times in the past twenty-four hours, Kathy wearily dialed a telephone number and jolted another of Clayton's friends into unquestioning but perplexed obedience to the admiral's demand for instant information. With a helpless shrug, she then picked up her purse, ran a hand through her disheveled hair, and walked slowly out of the office of the Chairman of the Joint Chiefs of Staff, wishing that she had either the strength to stay or the ability to get him to leave, but knowing she had neither. Her heels sounded hollowly through empty Pentagon hallways peopled only by occasional night janitors waxing the asphalt-tiled floors under cold blue-white fluorescent bulbs. The calves of her legs tingled with exhaustion as she half-walked, half-staggered down the ramp to the arcade area and negotiated the long flight of concrete steps to the Pentagon taxi stand. Three forlorn cabbies were sitting on a bench arguing the prospects of the Washington Redskins. Seconds later, in a cloud of exhaust fumes, she was on her way to Virginia and to sleep.

Churchgoers were emerging from Sunday-morning services when Kathy Myrdal woke with a start. What was going on with Admiral Clayton? She quickly dialed his Pentagon office number, but got no answer. Hesitating only briefly, she dialed Clayton's home. On the sixth ring, Mildred Clayton's sleepy and slightly slurred voice answered. "Just a moment," Mrs. Clayton replied. The background sounds on the line diminished sharply as she cupped a hand over the mouthpiece, but Kathy could hear her muffled shouting of the admiral's name. "Kathy, I guess he's not here. He called me sometime yesterday and told me he was working on something and he would be home when he got here. I haven't seen him yet."

Kathy hung up and paused to think. For security reasons and to control interruptions, the direct line into the little computer console room where Clayton was working could not be dialed from the outside. But she could call the duty officer in the Joint Chiefs area and get him to go by and see whether Admiral Clayton was still there.

Barely three minutes later Kathy had her answer. "Yes, ma'am, he's in there. He says to just leave him be; he does not want to be disturbed by anybody."

"But has he had anything to eat?" Kathy asked with a worried tremor in her voice.

"I'm sorry, ma'am, I don't know. I just came on duty at 0800 hours."

"Okay, Major. Thank you very much."

Too many years of Katherine Myrdal's life had been spent thinking and worrying about Randolph Clayton for her now simply to sit back and let whatever was happening in that little console room happen. She dressed, rapidly slipping on old jeans and pulling a warm turtleneck sweater of thick white wool over her head. A Red Top cab deadheading back to the District screeched to a stop for her in the crisp October sunshine and by 10:50 A.M. she was knocking on the locked door behind Admiral Clayton's desk. There was no answer. The knuckles of her small hand reddened with the impact as she knocked again and louder.

The door of the little room flew open and Clayton's big frame towered over his tiny secretary. "What the hell is it? What do you want?"

"Admiral, what's the matter? You look awful!"

"Goddammit, woman, nothing is the matter. Just get the hell out of here and leave me alone."

"But you're going to make yourself sick. It's already Sunday morning. You've got to get some sleep or you'll end up in the hospital."

A three-day beard shadowed the drawn, ashen skin of Randolph Clayton's face. A dull, milky membrane seemed to cover his eyes, which flicked away from her face to dart around his office as if seeking a path of escape. "Look, Katherine," he said in a peculiarly hoarse voice. "I know you mean well, coming down here like this, but I don't want you here. I simply want to be left alone. Completely left alone. Do you understand me?"

"Randy, please tell me what's wrong. What are you doing in there? Is it M10? What have you found out? Whatever it is, it's not worth tearing yourself apart over. Come out of there for a while and get something decent to eat."

"Sonofabitch! Can't you hear anymore, woman? Just

get the hell out of here and let me get back to work. When I need your advice, I'll ask for it!"

The small door slammed shut in Kathy's face as tears began to well up in her eyes. She turned to leave, but the door opened again and Clayton leaned out. "And don't, for chrissake, worry about me eating," he said with comparative calm. "I can always get the duty officer to take care of that. Just, goddammit, please go away and stop worrying about me."

Clayton returned to the ACA console. Oblivious to time and to the pain of fingers raw from ceaseless pounding of the computer keyboard, he entered another command, and another and another. The throbbing at his temples, the quivering ache in the muscles of his neck and back, did not exist. His whole world had funneled down into the ten-inch-wide sheet of dark glass which formed the face plate of the ACA electronic console. It was as if the megamachine and the man had become a single living creature whose sole purpose for existence was the pursuit of M10.

The incredible ordeal of man and system continued through all of Sunday. Hour after hour, relentless streams of information flickered onto the display screen and through Clayton's brain. Nitrosamines . . . current estimated death rates . . . ten million for shipboard systems . . . coverage in Moscow and Leningrad . . . possible countermeasures . . . Hour after hour, the global system responded and reacted to Clayton's urgent commands and filled his mind with a storm of facts which gradually converged into a single overwhelming idea.

And then suddenly, at 2:06 A.M., Monday morning, October 22, it all stopped. Clayton slumped back into the padded chair before the console. His arms and legs flopped crazily, as if he could no longer feel them.

Admiral Randolph Clayton had learned the secret of M10.

8

It was a long time until Clayton could pull himself erect again before the impassive glass face of the console. Like a lobotomized madman, he gaped vacantly into space while his shattered mind fought to reject, to somehow escape, the very knowledge he had struggled so hard to obtain. Feelings of disbelief and then finally of white-hot rage washed over him. It was all there and there was no escaping it. M10 was not a collaborative medical project with the USSR, nor was it a project in global ecology. M10 was not a project at all. It was a war—*a systematic biomedical war*. The most advanced ecological and biomedical knowledge that humanity possessed had been perverted and twisted into an obscene weapon aimed at deliberately *inducing cancer* in an unsuspecting Soviet population.

A chilling cold crept into his bones and Clayton's shoulders began to shiver uncontrollably. Even as he sat there, M10 was actively murdering tens of thousands of Russians. They were dying in hospital rooms or in their own beds, but they were being slaughtered as surely as if they were falling on a battlefield. While the world concentrated on controlling the threat of nuclear war, M10 had been coolly attacking Russia with devastating doses of "natural" death.

In the early 1970s, the U.S. had moved to wind down its biological and chemical warfare projects. But in contrast to M10, these projects were all aimed at finding weapons that could bring death with lightning quickness. Had not the very word "war" come to mean killing promptly and winning *now?* The usual active materials of biological and chemical warfare were aimed at annihilating specific opposing forces in a few hours with rampaging rabbit fever or with instantly fatal nerve gases. When the U.S. abandoned chemical and biological warfare, no one ever suggested the possibility of a fiendishly slow, hellishly general, and completely invisible attack on people who would never even realize they were victims of weapons that could reach over thousands of miles and decades of time. No one dreamed of waging such a war. No one except the men behind Project M10.

M10 depended upon one simple idea: Wage war by radically increasing the general susceptibility of an enemy population to fatal diseases. As a result, a nation could be weakened in countless ways, rendered less competitive, and finally laid open to more overt forms of attack. Cancer was the primary weapon of M10, but according to the ACA reports, its designers had considered and developed others—circulatory diseases, debilitating muscular disorders, a long list of misery, agony, and death.

Ecological and biomedical knowledge was what had made M10 possible. Such knowledge had expanded rapidly since the early days of the environmental crusade that forced more and more research dollars into studies of the connections between human disease and pollution, food additives, industrial wastes, and similar contaminants. The resulting quantum leaps in understanding springing from the well-intentioned efforts of thousands of dedicated minds had, Clayton now understood, been tainted by a fateful irony: Between the discovery of a causative agent for a fatal disease such as cancer, and the development of a successful treatment or cure, could lie a critical interval. In such an interval, mankind was vulnerable to the use of the disease-causing agent as a weapon of war. Less than a decade ago, researchers had found that minute amounts of certain chemicals, the nitrosamines, the metabolic products of certain molds, and the complex derivatives of particular coal-tar or petroleum products, could all reduce the body's resistance to various strains of viruses capable, in turn, of triggering wild cancerous growth in human cells. No one knew why or how. A cause was known, but not a cure. Mankind was in the critical interval and Project M10 was born.

In the small, bare room behind his office, Admiral Clayton struggled to comprehend what M10 had already done to the Soviet Union. The passionless statistics and graphs that marched across the ACA display screen showed clearly how key Russian leaders had been exterminated. Scientists, engineers, teachers, administrators, musicians, workers, farmers, and housewives all had been cut down, victims of seemingly natural diseases. Huge chunks of vital energy had been sapped from the Soviet Union without the slightest repercussion.

While to the public it appeared that real progress was being made in controlling cancer, peculiar rises in certain forms of the disease had, in fact, been widely discussed in the scientific community, which concluded that the "excess" deaths observed were just the inescapable consequences of modern life. They were "environmentally caused" cancers.

The major nations of the world, in the midst of heroic efforts to improve health and the environment, confidently assured themselves that they would one day eliminate both natural and inadvertent, manmade, causes of cancer. They did not consider looking for effects of chronic doses of cancer-causing agents *purposely employed*.

Nor would they have succeeded if they had tried. The weaponry of M10 was directed at no one target in particular. It was aimed at an entire society and there was no deadline for victory, hence the attack was easily hidden under "natural causes." Researchers who might have uncovered it were innocently baffled by the brute fact that there were far too many other variables that screened the onslaught. In spite of, or perhaps *because* of, the mountains of statistical and medical data that had become available over the past decade, this diabolical form of war simply could not be detected. There were no warnings; no thundering rockets; no great flashes of light; no giant mushroom clouds. There was only a slow draining away of national strength as people—leaders or simple hacks—died, one by one, each in his own bed or a quiet hospital room, each unknowing and each before his time.

Could America really be conducting this unthinkably obscene project? Admiral Clayton leaned forward, hovering over the keyboard of his computer console like a great shadowy bird, one hand again and again sweeping compulsively through his wispy reddish hair. The confirming data splashed across the glowing screen. The incredibly powerful programs of the megamachine had torn the problem apart. Formulas, production rates, effective agents, year-by-year calculations of the impact on various segments of the Russian population, preferred modes of delivery, estimates of annual reductions in Russian military effectiveness, gross national product, political leadership—

all the awesome effects of a cancer-induction project that had apparently run for more than seven years stood mutely before him. It was all there. There was no mistake.

Clayton's trembling fingers reached for an object lying on the table. It was the yellow paper he had carried with him for so long. Slowly he began to tear it into pieces. He tore at it and tore at it until the strength that remained in his shaking fingers drained away and he could not grasp the shreds. He let the bits fall like yellow snowflakes into the plastic plate containing a stale forgotten sandwich. He stared dumbly at the crusts of bread and then a new horror leaped out at him. The thought was like a physical blow. What about feedback effects? How much of the M10 material was finding its way back into the United States? Clayton lunged forward to interrogate the ACA system and moments later he had his answer.

The designers of M10, insanely committed to the decimation of Soviet power at whatever cost, had been willing to pay an awful price. The cancer-causing substances of M10 had not been successfully confined to Soviet territory and the impact of M10 had not fallen on the Soviets alone. The consequences were there on the dark glass screen of the console, illuminated by only a few simple words and numbers from the ACA codes:

M10 Data Summary

Soviet Union
    Lifespan reduction   8.5 years
    Total casualties to date   11,800,000

United States
    Lifespan reduction   0.5 years
    Total casualties to date   78,250
Estimated accuracy ± 7 percent

Nearly 80,000 Americans had already perished from the effects of M10 agents returning to the United States and contained not only in the obvious items, such as gourmet foods, vodka, and other imported beverages, but also in contaminated fabrics, furs, and leathers. From Baku and Krasnovodsk on the Caspian Sea to the truck farms encircling Leningrad, Russia had been poisoned, and small but lethal traces of the toxins were oozing out through every route of international commerce.

Like a long-captive jungle cat in a cage, insensible to the fatigue dragging at his every muscle and joint, Admiral Clayton paced to and fro in the tiny, utterly silent room. His burning eyes moved between the glowing green words on the screen and the curling dry bread of his sandwich under its dusting of yellow confetti. With sudden and furious energy, he hurled the plastic plate and its debris against the locked door, then bent low over the curved back of the ACA console. Slowly he rubbed his cheek against its comforting electronic warmth. He was a small boy again, hurt and seeking solace in the smooth silkiness of his pillow. And he was sobbing.

A long minute later, Clayton forced himself to stand erect and face the one aspect of M10 that he had not penetrated.

He now understood the project and its terrible intent. But somehow those who had created this monstrosity, those who had activated it, those who were now keeping it going, had eluded him. They could not have known, when they began their efforts, that the entire DOD computer system and the ACA codes would someday be arrayed against them, but nevertheless, whoever they were—these brilliant, inspired, satanic men—had taken sufficient precautions that their names still remained unknown. Nowhere in the data Clayton possessed were there any clear leads to their identities. They must be found out and they must be stopped. And above all, word of what they had been doing could never reach the outside world. The consequences would be cataclysmic. With a start, Clayton reminded himself of a second crucial task: The President of the United States must be told!

Could Frederick Donley be involved in M10? Clayton's heart pounded. Is that what the President meant by his light-hearted hint to leave the subject of M10 alone? No, that was impossible. The man was far too decent. Besides, M10 had started years before he became President. But might not the President have learned about it after his election and agreed to continue it?

Sagging deeply into his padded chair, Clayton considered his options. What should he do? It was now 5:00 A.M., Monday, October 22, and he could not go on much longer without rest. He could spend his strength pursuing the perpetrators or he could prepare to brief Frederick Donley. The choice seemed obvious. The President could not possibly be involved and so he must be warned promptly. If the Soviets were to learn of M10, the result would be instant nuclear war. The enormous complexity of M10, the great variety of results Clayton had uncovered in his nonstop three-day ordeal, would have to be laid out carefully and convincingly for the President. Tracking down the men behind the project would have to wait.

Sure now of what he must do, Clayton emerged from the small room behind his desk and walked through the deserted main office. The DOD duty officer routinely posted in the reception area looked up, startled. He had not known the admiral was even in the building. As he opened his mouth to greet his unexpected company, Clayton's eyes froze him instantly. The duty officer scanned the wrinkled uniform and heavy beard and knew he should mind his own business. He began an intensive study of the top of his desk.

Clayton faced the young captain, but looked past him into empty space as he spoke. His voice was hoarse and seemed to be coming from a faraway place in his body. "Captain, I need your help."

"Yes, sir," snapped the captain, as he rose to attention.

"I want this area isolated. I want four guards. I want one of them placed here. I want two men in the computer peripherals room, to which I am now going, and I want one man to stand by with you in case I need him."

As Clayton finished his commands, his head dropped forward for a moment like that of a man who had just been found guilty of a crime. He was no longer aware of where he was. He should have found out about M10 sooner. Why had it taken him so long? He should have pressed the Joint Chiefs for answers weeks ago. Why had he not . . . His tired mind was beginning to play tricks on itself. M10 was becoming his fault.

"Immediately, sir. I'll call the Support Center."

"Yes, do that." Clayton nodded as the duty officer's voice returned him from his brooding. "And see that they get here right away. Above all, I want those fellows at the peripherals room to make sure no one, absolutely no one, goes in there. I'm going to be outputting a report and it will be very sensitive, do you understand me? Very sensitive."

"Yes, sir, I understand," the blond young man replied as he reached for his phone to call the guards.

Clayton moved on, trancelike, to a large room just to the west of and adjacent to the JCS Conference Center. The Peripheral Equipments Room housed the apparatus through which the DOD computer system could quickly produce any written documentation needed by the Joint Chiefs. High-speed machines capable of printing ten thousand lines per minute of preformated and edited text waited next to graphic plotters, which could print instant full-color illustrations from almost any form of computerized information. Lightning-quick reproduction units and self-contained photographic systems stood along one wall, ready to disgorge detailed reports on any subject. Documents that might normally take days to create could be cascading out of such a facility in hours or even minutes.

While the ACA computer console where Clayton had been working was almost spartan in its appearance—an appearance which belied its enormous power—the control panels of the report preparation room were impressive in their complexity. Row after row of push-button switches and tiny indicator lights were arrayed on both sides of a set of large cathode ray tube screens used to display the texts, diagrams, and photographs with which the system worked. Years earlier, when he first became Chief of Naval Operations, Clayton had made himself thoroughly expert in their operation. It was his nature to do so.

The admiral, moving more by rote than by conscious thought, set up the machinery to produce two copies and only two copies of a report in paper-and-print "hard copy" form. Pressing a series of buttons, which began flashing in response to his touch, he picked up a "light pen" stylus and pressed it against one of the screens. A soft hum broke the silence as the printer typed out a trial line of text: "A Synopsis of Project M10, by Admiral Randolph G. Clayton." It was the title page of the automatically formated report that would summarize for the President of the United States all that Clayton had learned about the grisly secrets of M10.

Satisfied that the peripherals were now properly configured, Clayton waved the stylus of his light pen at the

screen like a conductor leading an orchestra. The electronic
eye of the pen sensed the glowing markings at which he was
pointing and instructed the computer to transfer overall
system control to the small ACA console in Clayton's
office suite. The system was ready.

Clayton trudged back toward his own office past the
two MPs now stationed at the entrance of the computer
peripherals room. "No one is to get into this room except
me. Do you men understand that?" he growled.

"Yes, sir!" the guards replied simultaneously as they
stiffened in crisp salutes. They did not know what was
going on, but they knew it was something important.

At the duty officer's desk, Clayton paused again. "Son,
get me some coffee, please, and keep a hot pot of it on my
desk. I'll be in the secure area for the next few hours and I
don't want to be disturbed. I expect you to check those
MPs regularly, you understand, regularly. No one gets into
this facility."

The officer nodded and Clayton closed the door of the
solitary cell of the ACA console just as the long, slanting
rays of sunrise were crisscrossing his outer office.

It was about 0830 Monday morning when Clayton heard
a barely audible tapping on the locked door behind him. It
was the duty officer. Clayton flipped on his intercom.
"Whoever you are, talk to me through the intercom on my
desk. I've opened the line."

"Admiral, this is Captain Gilton. Your secretary is in the
outer office. What do you want us to do? Do you want us
to let her into her desk area?"

"No," Clayton replied, speaking close to the microphone
grillwork. "Tell her to take the day off. Tell her I'll be
leaving town shortly for a day or so and I'll be in touch."
The admiral paused. "And tell her I feel fine and there's
nothing to worry about."

"Yes, sir . . . but, sir, she really wants to see you."

"Goddammit, soldier! Tell her what I said and get the
hell out of here."

"Yes, sir!" the duty officer said as he retreated rapidly
from the intercom.

An angry bellow followed him as he scurried toward the
JCS reception area. "And keep this area closed!"

By 3:30 Monday afternoon, a little over ten hours after

starting, Clayton had two copies of the report, "A Synopsis
of Project M10," in his hands. Shaking with fatigue, he
picked up the red scrambler phone on his desk and dialed
the White House on the NMCCS, America's top-level
communications network—the National Military Command and Control System. The President was not in
Washington and Clayton wanted instant access to him. He
could get it through the NMCCS.

The President of the United States is always accompanied by an aide who carries an attaché case handcuffed
to his wrist. Inside the case is Top Secret "red phone"
communications equipment, which permits a President to
be reached at any time and at any place in the world. On
this particular occasion, President Frederick Donley was
giving a luncheon speech at a political rally in Denver and
transfer of Admiral Clayton's call to the military aide with
the President's portable scrambler phone took a little longer
than usual—fifty seconds. The aide holding the equipment
was standing in the dark wing of the stage from which the
President was speaking and his arm jumped as though he
had been shot in the hand when the leather case began
buzzing. He had not received an actual message transfer for
the President in all the four months that he had been
carrying it.

"This is Admiral Clayton. I must arrange to see the
President immediately. Can I speak to him now? This is
not a military emergency."

"Why, yes, sir, I can get you to him, sir." A pause. "Sir,
he is actually in the middle of a speech, sir. You said it is
not an emergency. Shall I—"

"I said it is not a *military* emergency at the moment,"
came the slightly annoyed reply. "All right," Clayton continued. "If he is giving a speech, just pass him a note. I want
his okay to come out and see him right away. Tell him I
want to see him in the next couple of hours, and tell him it's
about Project M10."

"Yes, sir. I'll pass a note to him immediately, sir."

The aide put the phone down and, in the dim spillover of
the stage lights, carefully printed Clayton's message in large
letters on a three-by-five index card. With the air of someone embarrassed to be there, he then tiptoed onto the stage
before three thousand people and placed the note on the
podium where the President could see it.

Without skipping a beat in his speech, Frederick Donley glanced up at his blushing aide after reading the note and nodded his head. The aide walked quickly off the stage and picked up the red phone again. "All right, sir. He said okay. I guess you can come out right away."

"Tell the President I will be there in a couple of hours. Make the necessary arrangements to keep my pilot informed of his whereabouts. Is that clear?"

"Yes, sir. Is that all, sir?"

The line to the President's portable phone was dead.

Contact with the outside world, and indirectly with the President himself, had sent a surge of adrenaline through his body and Clayton felt better. He moved rapidly to a thick-walled storage room for JCS classified documents and was about to put one of the two copies of his report in a hulking steel safe when he stopped short. He could not trust even this highly secure area. He did not know who was behind M10. Whoever it was might have easy access to these facilities. Thoughtfully, he placed the two documents in his own worn black attaché case. He then headed out of the JCS area, after releasing the special guards he had posted earlier with an admonishment to say nothing about anything they might have heard or seen. Ignoring the puzzled stares of people in the bustling Pentagon corridors, he dashed for the Mall Entrance of the Pentagon, where his staff car was waiting.

The short drive to his home gave Clayton his first chance to relax. Over and over again he recited instructions to himself: Don't think about M10. Keep your mind on the details. Arrange for transportation to Denver. What do you want to take along?

His car crossed Key Bridge on its familiar route to Georgetown as Clayton dialed Andrews Air Force Base and ordered his Boeing 787 command jet rolled out immediately. "Have Danny Soltani and the crew ready to fly me to Denver in one hour," he said as he calculated his arrival time. The big plane ought to be able to make Denver in about two and one half hours, so he should be face to face with Donley by 5:30 P.M. Mountain Time. Clayton pressed his hands to painfully throbbing temples. The whole affair seemed so unreal. Had he really seen what he had seen? Were the two documents in his briefcase really there? Was he sleeping through some ghoulish nightmare? No, it was no illusion. M10 was real. The need to share the crushing weight of what he had learned with another human being suddenly became overwelming. Clayton looked up and blinked his burning eyes at the neatly barbered neck of the man in the front seat. "Sergeant . . ." he said in a half whisper.

"Sir? Did you say something?" The driver's gaze flicked up to the rear-view mirror.

Clayton caught himself. "No, nothing. Never mind. Just press on, Sergeant." Clayton warned himself with gritted teeth to guard against any further muddleheaded urges. Minutes later, clutching his attaché case tightly under his arm, he was running on wobbly legs up the brick walk to his house.

"Randy!" Mildred Clayton exclaimed as he finally got the front door open after fumbling wearily with his keys. "I've been so worried! Where in heaven's name have you been? What is going on?"

"I don't have time to talk," he said, mounting the stairs to the second floor. "Everything is okay. Something has come up and I've got to get out to Denver. I just came home to grab a shower and some fresh clothes."

"But you look awful. Sit down and rest a minute," she persisted as she gathered her terry-cloth robe tightly around her and padded after him in her bare feet. "I haven't seen you in three days and there are some things I've got to tell you—important things."

Clayton whirled to face her. "Mildred, goddammit, I told you I don't have time to talk now." His teeth were clenched and he was struggling to keep from screaming the horror of M10 full into her face.

"I only have time to get showered and shaved and get to Andrews. I've got to see someone on an urgent basis."

"Is it some kind of an emergency? Has somebody started shooting?"

"No, there's no problem. It's just that I've got to do something and there's no one else that can do it, and that's all I can tell you."

"Listen to me, honey," she was pleading now. "I've been thinking about things the last few days. Your being away has given me a lot of time to think."

"Yes, and I'll bet that's not all!" Clayton said bitterly. "I haven't had a drop in three days! Honestly I haven't."

On the edge of tears, she pressed herself against his chest. "Randy, I'm willing to do something about it now if you really think I could. I'm willing to talk about it. Please stay with me a few minutes and let's talk. I've felt so lonely the last few days. Randy, you mean so much to me. I can't ever seem to get through to you. Maybe that's why I drink so much. I don't know. I'll even go to AA if you want me to, but let's talk about it, okay? Come on, come back downstairs and sit with me a few minutes."

"Woman, you've picked the worst possible time to start talking this way." He looked a thousand years old. "I just haven't got the time now. I want to stay, but I can't. I have got to get out of here. Can't you understand that?" His voice was rising toward hysteria. "I have *got* to get out of here. Now just leave me alone. We'll talk about it later." The door to the yellow-tiled bathroom slammed shut.

Mildred Clayton stood before the door until its image began to wave and shimmer in her tears. The rushing sound of the shower followed her down the stairs and into the living room. She could still hear its rainlike hiss as she opened the door of the old white-and-gold cabinet against which Todd had fallen and broken his arm on his fifth birthday. A bottle and a glass were on the bottom shelf.

Twenty minutes later and blazing with a final surge of energy, Randolph Clayton bounded down the stairs two at a time. The black attaché case was under one arm as he walked past the living room doorway without looking toward his wife. In his den, he unlocked the top left-hand drawer of his well-traveled desk. He removed one copy of the M10 report from his case and slipped it into the drawer under his will and other important papers. Locking the drawer again, he dropped the key into the attaché case and snapped it shut with metallic finality.

In the Base Operations Center at Andrews, Clayton's crew was ready and waiting to go. The flight plan was filed for Denver, but a problem was developing. A strong early-winter storm had been moving across the western United States and heavy snows with extremely strong winds were now predicted for the Denver area about an hour before the seven-hundred-mile-per-hour Boeing 787 could get there. Clayton drummed his fingers on the scratched clear-plastic top of the operations counter as he studied the faded U.S. map that lay beneath it. There was little question about it

—the operations analysis computer showed that the flight plan was marginal at best. Traffic delays could be lengthy, and even worse, the jet might have to be diverted to another quite distant airport. Clayton slammed his fist down on the counter as his head started to throb again. His last reserves were almost gone. "Goddammit!" he mumbled. "I have got to get there. I have just got to get there." He looked up at the weather briefing officer, standing across from him. "Let me see the synoptic chart." The wavy lines of the chart told the same story as the computer print-out. The storm was a massive one and moving in at nearly forty knots. There was actually no chance for Clayton's big jet to get to Denver before the heavy weather settled in.

"What about the All-Weather Landing System at Denver?" Clayton asked of no one in particular. "What one is it?"

"It's an AWLS-20 sir," someone replied. "They're planning to replace it this year with a 55, but—"

"Okay, okay, we don't get any help there," Clayton said as he turned to face his pilot. "Danny, I'm scrubbing your trip. I'm going to go out alone in the A22."

Against the strongly expressed wishes of the Pentagon, which worried about high-ranking officers buzzing around the sky by themselves, Admiral Clayton had maintained an A22J as a personal plane. The long-range interceptor was a superb achievement in aircraft design. It could cruise transcontinental distances effortlessly at twelve hundred miles an hour, and Clayton had logged over seven hundred hours in the sleek little machine hangared at Andrews.

"Sir, I think you're making a mistake," Lieutenant Commander Daniel Soltani said emphatically. "It will be touch and go even for the A22 by the time we get it rolled out and do the preflight."

"Danny, it is crucial for me to get to Denver and I can do it. Let's move out and get the ground crews cracking. I'll go change into a flight suit."

"But, sir . . . !"

Admiral Clayton did not see his pilot's helpless shrug as he walked away. Muddled by fatigue and nearly consumed by the secret he was carrying, he had made his decision not out of cool logic but out of a simple yet overpowering human need to talk about the hideous truth of Project M10.

A feverish burst of preparation quickly brought Clayton's stainless-steel-and-titanium jet to the end of the long concrete ribbon of Runway 31 at Andrews. The low rumble of its twin-jet engines changed to a deafening roar as the takeoff clearance crackled into his helmet earphones from the tower. It was 4:50 P.M. in Washington as the A22J thundered down the runway and the brute strength of the two huge General Electric engines catapulted it into the air. Forty-five seconds later, at an altitude of 66,000 feet, Clayton set his electronic course computer and autopilot, then checked the three small electronic screens of the DIAS, the Digital Integrated Avionics System, which gave him status reports on all critical components in the plane. Everything was in good order.

Dazzling white against the blue-black sky of the edge of space, the sun bathed the cockpit in hot streaks of light. Clayton adjusted his sun-visor screen as the plane hurtled westward twelve miles above the earth. The slightly acrid sensation of tank oxygen reminded him to check his life-support reserves. Everything okay. Shifting his shoulders back and forth in his warm flight suit, he stared dumbly at the electronic screens and panels that lined his cockpit. Sleep began to drag heavily at his eyelids and he dozed. Awakening with a start, he settled deeper into the padded ejection seat. His eyes fluttered closed, open, then closed again. Finally, as his plane was crossing the eastern edge of Indiana, Admiral Clayton slept—a deep, dark, quiet sleep.

Approaching air space under control of the Omaha, Nebraska, Air Traffic Center, Clayton's A22 began a slow roll to the right and shuddered slightly. Clayton did not awaken. On the DIAS indicator panel, a small red light began flashing. Ninety seconds later, a second indicator light came on. The roll had increased to ten degrees and the plane's course had altered so that it was now vectored toward the northwest corner of Wyoming.

In the crowded avionics compartment of the A22, a single electronic chip of the fifteen hundred such devices in the plane's exquisitely tiny course computer continued to overheat and cascade its overload to other chips nearby. Redundant safety circuits in the plane were dutifully responding. More warning indicators sprang into life and finally a buzzer sounded in the cockpit. Still Admiral Clayton slept, his unconscious brain réliving a time long ago when he and Todd had spent a lazy Sunday afternoon flying a scale model of an old crop-dusting biplane whose engine noise was like a flight of angry bees. Covered by the artful magic of the dream, the cockpit alarm buzzed on fruitlessly, unperceived and unnoticed.

Clayton's jet was cutting through the cloudless skies over the North Platte River when a dozen electrical channels in stressed and overheated computer chips fused into vapor in a tattoo of microscopic explosions. The attitude of the A22J responded immediately. Its nose shook once, then dropped off the horizon as the craft sagged downward in a steepening arc.

Somewhere far off, there was a strange and persistent noise. Admiral Clayton pulled himself up through the darkness toward consciousness. What was that noise?

Instantly he jolted to full alert! The noise was the aircraft's emergency klaxon. Alarms were flashing on every video screen in the cockpit. The autopilot system, in spite of its carefully designed backup circuits and redundant modes of control, had failed catastrophically and the A22 was in a crazy rolling dive at full power. The altimeter was spinning down through six thousand feet. Clayton switched to manual control and pulled up hard. Suffocating G forces crushed down against his chest, driving him deep into his seat. The plane thundered on. His right hand strained toward the ejection seat lever, then hesitated. Years of flying high-performance aircraft told him he was too low and moving too fast. Looming slabs of the snow-drowned Grand Tetons filled his canopy from horizon to horizon. His knuckles white on the controls, Clayton's eyes bulged wide in terror. His dream! It was his dream, and it was too late! The sharp ice-covered blade of rock whistled forward through the bright sky to meet him as he screamed, and screamed, and screamed.

9

Tuesday, October 23

> a211 AP
> BULLETIN WASHINGTON D.C.
> THE DEPARTMENT OF DEFENSE ANNOUNCED THIS
> MORNING THAT ADMIRAL RANDOLPH G. CLAYTON, RE-
> CENTLY APPOINTED CHAIRMAN OF THE JOINT CHIEFS
> OF STAFF, WAS KILLED YESTERDAY EVENING. THE
> CRASH OF HIS A22J AIRCRAFT OCCURRED IN THE GRAND
> TETON MOUNTAINS APPROXIMATELY 20 MILES SOUTH
> OF MORAN, WYOMING. THE CAUSE OF THE ACCIDENT IS
> NOT KNOWN AT THIS TIME. AN INVESTIGATION TEAM IS
> NOW AT THE SITE.
> 0940 A ED 10-23
> MEMO TO NEWS DESKS: OBIT TO FOLLOW.

The sobs were coming more slowly. She could pull the cold air deeper into her lungs and her small shoulders stopped shaking under the wrinkled plastic of her rain cape. From someplace far away, the minister's voice droned on. She gazed at her shoes, watching the driving rain run in crazy little lines across the shining black patent leather and down into the brown grass. Finally, the last salute began. The guns.

Her fragile control shattered like glass with the first shot and her eyes flooded with tears. The emptiness surrounded and engulfed her, drowning the sounds. What can she do now? What can she possibly do now? No more trips to prepare for; no appointments to make. No crises. No victories. The little things were gone—the kidding, the stern but loving orders for sandwiches and coffee, the warm comradeship when the others had left the office. She had been cut in half and part of her was being buried this day in Arlington.

She gathered the translucent raincoat a little closer against the cold.

How could fourteen years have gone so quickly? It was

just yesterday. He was young and she was younger, quietly
in love with his little-boy grin and unruly red hair and all
the strength that lay beneath his gentleness.

And what about his appointments? His calendar was
filled into the middle of next month. Do you just telephone and say: "I'm sorry, sir, the admiral will not be
able to see you today. The admiral is dead." And the
nights? The suddenly endless empty nights. What will she
think about before she sleeps now that she can no longer
think of him?

The slow, sad tattoo of the rifle fire, the last farewell
to Admiral Randolph G. Clayton, was ending. A final
lonely shot echoed across the white stones of Arlington
and was gone.

Kathy Myrdal raised her bowed head and tiny needles
of rain jabbed against her cheeks. Higher up the gentle
hill and a few feet to her left, she could see the dark
figure of Mildred Clayton, her face covered by a veil.
The admiral's widow stood stiff, and silhouetted against
the sullen sky. Silently nodding, Mrs. Clayton acknowledged the parade of people stopping briefly, one after
another to hold her hands in theirs before moving on toward a long line of waiting automobiles with purple-and-
white funeral crosses on their wet windshields. In moments,
only the two women remained, left to stare at the black
earth and the cold dying grass. "Mrs. Clayton, I'm so
sorry," Kathy murmured after a long time. "I loved him
very much and I think you knew that. If there is anything
I can do to help you, I'll try to do it. I think you know that,
too."

Mildred Clayton lifted her veil. Her normally flaccid
skin was somehow clear and tight. To Kathy's surprise,
her eyes were steady. No great sighs of grief had etched
them. "Kathy," she said with soft bitterness, "thank you,
but you needn't worry about me. I lost him long ago, long
before that airplane crashed, so I'll get by fine. Believe
me." Lowering her veil again, Mrs. Clayton turned away
and, without a backward look, walked briskly across the
brown lawn, silver-mirrored by the rain. She disappeared
into a long black limousine in which the gray-haired figure
of her brother, John Schotty, sat waiting. Finally, Kathy
herself trudged toward a last remaining car. The funeral
was over.

* * *

Rain continued to fall in Washington during the rest of Friday and into Saturday morning, changed briefly to wet snow, and was changing back to rain when John Schotty lifted the brass door-knocker at his sister's home. He touched his knuckles gently to her chin as he greeted her. "Sorry, I'm late, kiddo. I had a few things to take care of at the paper. It took a bit longer than I thought." He stamped his wet shoes hard on the rough brick floor of the entrance hall. "Okay, let's go to it," he said without ceremony, while he hung his topcoat over the edge of a closet door to dry. "You'll feel better when it's over."

Mildred smiled at him wanly, her eyes still brighter and clearer than they had been in years. "Have some coffee with me first. I know we've got to do it and we will, I promise. It's just that it will bring back so many memories, things I've let slide away. I was almost hoping you weren't going to come today."

"I understand, but now's as good a time as any. Once it's over, it's over. We'll have coffee later. Let's start through them now; then it will be done with." Schotty was speaking of Admiral Clayton's personal papers. It was time to close the record of a man's life.

Mildred sighed with resignation. "All right. Come to the den. Anything important is in his desk."

Mrs. Clayton and her brother walked through the deserted living room and on into the small oak-paneled den where the admiral had so often worked. Opening the center drawer of Clayton's desk, she felt around toward the back, where the extra key to the locked side drawer was hidden. She fumbled briefly with the small iron key and the lock snapped softly. Inside, four red-brown folders, each tied with cord and fat with papers, were piled on top of other loose documents and an old cardboard box. The box was, Schotty knew, something very special and private to his sister. Her fingers caressed it, lingering lightly on the tape that held its well-worn edges. Slipping off the cover, she began to toy idly with the pile of disarrayed snapshots and letters it contained. Schotty pulled a chair up to the deak. "Any special place you want me to start?" he asked in an intentionally businesslike tone.

"No, just see what's here. I guess these folders are the most important. John, I don't think you'll need me for a while—at least till you have gone through things once—so I'll leave you alone, okay?"

Schotty squeezed his sister's hand and nodded with understanding. Taking up the box of photos and letters, Mrs. Clayton gave him a weak smile and headed for the living room to relive bittersweet old memories, leaving John Schotty in the den to deal with the realities of her present and future.

The admiral had been a well-organized and fastidious man. Those characteristics were evident in the precise way in which the important papers had been arranged. Each of the folders from the desk contained material on a different subject: the Clayton will in the thinnest one, family financial data in the second, property and deeds in the third, precisely arranged in chronological order, and finally the fourth folder, bulging with insurance policies and related correspondence.

In an hour Schotty had paged through all the material. His survey of the crucial items apparently complete, he stretched his cramped arms and shoulders, then rubbed the back of his neck until the stiffness eased. Refolding Clayton's three active insurance policies, Schotty reinserted them in their transparent window envelopes, stacked them carefully on each other at the edge of the desk, and reached for another sheaf of papers, lying on top of an old job offer from a large aerospace company. Schotty scanned the title of the stapled document: "A Synopsis of Project M10." From simple curiosity, he opened the cover and began to read. Outside, the icy rain that had been pelting Georgetown all morning continued to beat against the leaded glass windows of the den.

By the time he had finished the third page of the Clayton report, Schotty's hands were perspiring. A tingling had started in his scalp and his eyes were racing hungrily from one paragraph to the next. Thirty minutes later Schotty closed the last page of the document and, in a voice hoarse with excitement, shouted to his sister: "Millie, come here a minute, will you? Come in here *now,* please."

"Do you know what this is and where it came from?" Schotty asked, shoving the M10 report toward her. "It's dated the day he left for Denver. . . ."

After listlessly flipping through a few pages, Admiral Clayton's widow shook her head and shrugged. "John, I have no idea. I know Randy was very upset when he left. He did spend some time in here. Maybe he put it in the drawer just before. . . ." She paused to regain her composure. "He spend the last few days working all hours at the Pentagon. But," she added, "he's done that before in emergencies, so I didn't think too much of it. He might have been working on this. What's it all about, anyway?"

Schotty studied his sister's face carefully. Her open and innocent expression made it obvious that she knew nothing of the incredible pageant of deceit and death which her husband had chronicled in the papers on the desk before her.

"Look," Schotty whispered as though they were surrounded by hidden microphones. "If what Randy has said in this report is really true, it could mean . . . well, it could mean anything. It could mean a nuclear war; it could mean the end of the world." He drummed his fingers on the report. "I don't know what to do with this," he said, his voice louder and more agitated. "If this material is legitimate, then, in a sense, I have an obligation to publish it. But God knows what would happen to all of us if I do. . . ."

Fear began to squeeze at Mildred Clayton's stomach. She had never seen her older brother so concerned. What was supposed to be a quiet Sunday spent going over Randy's papers had become strangely ominous. "I don't understand any of it," she cried, stepping back with uncontrolled revulsion. "and I don't want to. I'm not even going to read it. Do whatever you want. I don't care. If it was what Randy was working on, then I hate it. I want it out of my house! It killed him, didn't it, John?" She was retreating toward the door. "This is what killed him, isn't it?"

Schotty did not respond. Instead he followed her, put his arm around her shoulder, and hugged her reassuringly. "Let's go make some coffee," he said.

"Okay," she replied, beginning to relax again. Together they walked toward the kitchen, leaving Clayton's M10 report behind them on the desk—waiting.

10

By Monday morning, Schotty had read and reread "A Synopsis of Project M10" a dozen times. Although there were large gaps, the report had the clear ring of truth. The deliberate omissions and the many complex acronyms and project designators with which the report was filled, Schotty realized, might be mysterious to him but would be entirely understandable to the reader for whom the report was intended. An electrifying hunch had grown toward certainty in the columnist: the unnamed addressee of the M10 report was the President of the United States himself.

Tired and anxious after an almost sleepless night, he arrived at his cluttered office in the Washington Globe Building about 10:30 A.M. and immediately waved his investigative assistant, Willis Tauber, into a quick conference. The two men, drawn together by their common interest in athletics—Schotty as an amateur, Tauber as a second string but always aspiring pro-football running back until a ruptured Achilles tendon ended his career—had been good friends as well as associates almost from the day the still-limping Tauber was hired. The bull-like ex-pro had been a journalism major at college and had nothing else to fall back on after his injury. Schotty had decided to hire him as much out of sympathy as out of conviction about his abilities and over the years had been pleasantly surprised at Tauber's tenacity and resourcefulness.

Tauber's wide, heavily muscled frame dropped obediently into a chair beside Schotty's paper-littered desk as Schotty, speaking very softly, began to relate the events surrounding his possession of the M10 document. "I think Admiral Clayton wrote it for the President," Schotty concluded after a few minutes, and shoved the document toward his immensely curious assistant.

It was almost noon when Tauber's stubby index finger swept slowly over the final lines of the last page. "Christ!" he said, with a long, low whistle, settling his thick body down on the end of his spine. "It's the biggest story in history!"

"Well, I'm not so sure," Schotty replied cautiously. "You can see all the parts that don't make sense unless you have the background. And there isn't one word about who has been running the project . . . assuming it is actually happening. That really bothers me. Is it the government or some privately organized team? We've got to be sure of ourselves. Besides, if we do publish this damn thing, we could blow the top right off the whole world. What will the Russians do when they find out about it? I think it scared the hell out of Clayton and that alone is enough to scare the hell out of me."

"Listen, John, forgive the lecture, but we're *reporters*. The public has a right to know what the United States has been doing. You can't sit on a story like this. Corny as it sounds, you have an obligation to the people and to your profession. If the report isn't true, publishing it will smoke that out. If it is true, then the world should know about it, and the sooner the better."

"Maybe you're right," said Schotty, squinting through a cloud of cigarette smoke at a badly tilted photo on his wall showing him as a young correspondent in Korea surrounded by a dozen battle-weary soldiers. "But maybe you're not. Before we decide anything, you and I are going to confirm every bit of it. We're going to know ourselves whether it's factual and who's been managing the project before we decide how we'll handle it. . . ."

Tauber held up a hand to interrupt his boss. "Do you think it could be Donley himself?"

"I don't know," Schotty answered. "I thought of that, of course. But then wouldn't Randy have been in on it? After all, he was *Chairman* of the JCS. Why would he be caught so completely by surprise as he obviously was, judging from the things he wrote? And if it wasn't to see Donley, then why the hell was Clayton charging out to Denver?

Tauber considered Schotty's logic a moment. "I wonder if the President has even seen a copy of this yet. They certainly didn't recover anything from the crash if Clayton was carrying it out there with him. I hear that hole in the ground was forty feet across—" Schotty grimaced and Tauber stopped abruptly. "Oh, Christ, John I'm sorry! I forgot he was your brother-in-law. You made so little of it all these years that I don't think of him as family."

"It's okay; forget it. Let's get on with what we're going

to do. I think it's at least fifty-fifty that Donley hasn't seen anything yet. We know there were only two copies, according to the cover page, and this is number two. You're right. Number one was probably burned and buried in the Tetons."

"And," Tauber said, "that means the President doesn't know what Clayton was going to tell him—"

"Or had partial knowledge, maybe from phone calls," Schotty suggested.

"Or was running M10 himself," Tauber said with quiet emphasis as he leaned closer to Schotty. "John, you realize as well as I do what we have here. It could end up making us a lot of money, on top of everything else."

Schotty laughed. "The thought of a few dollars had crossed my mind. But, Will, I'm not going to let us dash off in all directions even if we could end up with a Pulitzer or two and a Watergate best seller. This one is too dangerous. We're going to go a step at a time."

Like a man about to dive from a high rock into waters of uncertain depth, Schotty paused. When he started to speak again, there was new conviction in his voice. "Now, here's what I want you to do. Make up a list of every goddamned source you can think of who could possibly give you any background on a project of this kind. Hit them hard and fast. I'll do the same thing. You work the DOD and I'll see what I can do about going in as high as possible at the White House. But let's get one thing straight, Will. We don't publish anything until we confirm that Project M10 actually exists and we know who's behind it. And let's not drop a hint about what we're really after unless we absolutely have to, even at the highest levels. Okay?"

"Okay," Tauber responded, with obvious exasperation. "Let's spend some time on it, but one way or another, I think we ought to cash in quickly and I think it also ought to get out before the election. There are only a few days left and if this administration has been pulling something like this, think what that would mean to the voters." Tauber catapulted his weight lifter's body out of the chair, shaking his head. "Let's not check too long, John. This has got too much going for it and I've been hungry for a long time."

Schotty grunted. "We'll worry about what to do with it once we know more. Now get going." He lowered his head to his hands and stared morosely into an ashtray filed with stale cigarette butts as Tauber left the room muttering to himself. The meeting was over and two people now knew the secret of M10.

11

By Thursday, November 1, John Schotty and Willis Tauber had spent almost four days and nights digging into their story, with little to show for their efforts.

Schotty had tried every trick his years as a reporter had taught him, but his best sources of information were completely absorbed by the accelerating tempo of election activities. Those people he could get to knew nothing; those he would have liked to reach most were completely unavailable.

In desperation, pushed by his desire to act responsibly and by Tauber's incessant pressure to publish before the election, now only five days away, Schotty decided to step into an arena where he knew he would be neither competent nor comfortable. Since his political and administrative sources seemed useless, he would try to authenticate the feasibility of M10 on purely technical grounds. Were known carcinogenic chemicals actually suitable for the type of random, prolonged, and secret attack the Clayton report described? Schotty rubbed his grizzled chin and lit another cigarette. Whom could he contact? He didn't know anyone in the scientific community. Perhaps a medical school was as good a place as any to start.

After a series of telephone calls, Schotty jotted an entry in his pocket calendar. The Head of the Department of Physiology at Johns Hopkins was willing to meet with him early on Friday morning.

"Come in, Mr. Schotty, come in." Dr. Winston Kecht's crisp British accent beckoned Schotty into an office lined with bound volumes of medical journals and neatly shelved box files. Kecht, a picture-book British professor in a tweedy herringbone jacket with the obligatory leather patches at the elbows, had spent nearly two decades at Johns Hopkins and was widely recognized as an outstanding teacher and researcher in internal medicine. "You know, Mr. Schotty, I'm delighted to meet you in person. I've always enjoyed your *Globe* column. I think it's one of the most perceptive I follow. But I can't imagine what you would want with me. I don't know anything about politics."

"I'm a little out of my element myself," Schotty said, smiling. "I've got a few technical questions about a story we're working on, but first let me give you a little background. . . ." Warily and without referring specifically to M10, Schotty set about constructing a series of hypothetical situations, each of which depended on whether it would be possible to develop materials that could be deliberately introduced into the environment to cause various chronic human diseases. Kecht listened intently. At the end of Schotty's monologue, the professor stared silently for a moment at a bookcase filled to the ceiling with thirty years' issues of the medical journal *Lancet* bound in black and gold.

"You certainly pose some interesting possibilities, Mr. Schotty. I presume they are purely theoretical. By the way, would you take some tea or coffee?"

"I'll have coffee, thanks. Yes, they're theoretical right now, but I think some people are beginning to worry about their becoming real problems someday. That's the key to my story. Suppose someone decided to try to use the method, say, to murder a high official. Could he do it?"

"Murder by cancer!" Kecht exclaimed, carefully stirring his hot tea into the spoonful of milk in the bottom of his cup. "What an extraordinary idea."

"Well, it doesn't have to be cancer," Schotty emphasized. "It could be any natural disease—say, heart trouble or liver disease—almost anything that we have figured out how to induce as a result of medical research. That's my point. It seems to me that all our efforts in ecology and our understanding of what causes problems for people as a result of environmental contamination give us precisely the knowledge someone might need to use an environmental disease agent for murder with impunity. My problem is: Does the basic idea make any technical sense and should the police or the FBI be on guard against it?"

Kecht looked at Schotty searchingly, then turned again toward the wall of his office. "Yes, I suppose it would be possible. But I don't think it would be . . . no, I don't think it would be very practical. In the first place, you'd have to be a bloody patient murderer. You'd have to be willing to wait five . . . ten . . . fifteen, perhaps even twenty years to kill your victim. If you had to wait that long what's the point of committing the murder in the first place? On the other hand, it might be possible to develop some very active agents that could do it more quickly, but those agents would usually be detectable, more or less like poisons. We have some very good methods now—spectroscopy, chromatography, fluorescence techniques—"

"If the agents were still in the body of the victim at the time people became suspicious," Schotty interrupted.

"Well, I admit that's a point. But with so many other ways to commit murder, why go to all that trouble?" Kecht laughed lightly. "Besides, the human body has many defense mechanisms, some of which we only dimly understand. Now, as I think about the types of materials that might be used—I'm not really an expert in this, you understand; it would take someone more into biochemistry than I am—but as I think of some of the materials, most of them could be detected rather easily. They would have characteristic responses or properties. No, I don't think it would be anything very practical. Furthermore, you would have to be around the person targeted for the murder for a long time, all of those five or ten years, if you had to give him the kind of chronic dose you're talking about. If you give him one great blast, that won't work at all.

"And another point, Mr. Schotty: the body tends to *adapt*. We know that very well. Small doses delivered over a long time tend to develop a threshold effect, so that you might have to increase the levels to what I suspect would be very easily detectable amounts in order to accomplish the job. . . ." Kecht's voice trailed off. Schotty studied him, trying to judge how sure the man was of what he was saying.

"All right," said Schotty. "Let me give you a slightly different hypothetical situation. Assume you were aiming at some kind of a vendetta, where you wanted to get revenge on an entire family. Do you think it would be possible? Could you arrange to get some cancer-causing or heart-disease-causing agent into the environment of a whole family so that not some specific person but just *somebody* in that family finally came down with the disease years earlier than he might have otherwise? Do you think that's possible?"

Kecht's dark-brown eyes narrowed under his bushy but carefully barbered brows. "I suppose, I suppose, but it would take an absolutely insane mind to do such a thing. And it would take a great deal of knowledge as well. If you're going to do something like that, you wouldn't be patient enough to wait for the result, nor, for that matter, would you be satisfied with just killing at random. I should think you would want to do in specific people. . . .

"My, my, what a strange set of possibilities you do bring up, Mr. Schotty," Kecht continued, shaking his head vigorously. "I don't like them, but I can certainly see what you are saying. The very knowledge that we're so busily uncovering about how to improve our medical practice and our environment carries with it the possibilities you speak of. It's something I've not thought of, never really considered: that even these humanitarian areas of research have their peculiar two-edged swords. The nuclear physicists have had to worry about such difficult matters of morality ever since they developed the atomic bomb, but I shouldn't have thought that true of us until now—thanks to you.

"I presume I'll take comfort in the fact that the good that comes from all of our research far, far outweighs the bad, especially since the techniques you're propounding have never been used and I trust never will be. They haven't been used, Mr. Schotty, have they?"

Schotty rose from his leather chair and shook Kecht's hand firmly. "Thank you, sir. I do have some information that suggests somebody may be starting to work on the kind of thing we've been talking about, but it's so sketchy that I think all I'll do is turn the matter over to the FBI and let them worry about it from here. In the meantime, I hope you'll keep this inquiry of mine confidential. Thank you very much."

As the outer office door closed behind his departing visitor, a curious and vaguely disturbed Winston Kecht reached for his telephone and dialed a number in the Biochemistry Department. In his office minutes later, he was telling a senior professor in the Department of Biochemistry about John Schotty and his "hypothetical" questions. The biochemist concluded, along with Kecht, that there was some possibility Schotty's method of murder could be used without anyone ever finding out about it. But the biochemist waved his hand airily as he left. "Who would want to bother with it?"

Winston Kecht did not know it, but the biochemist, upon returning to his own office, immediately dialed a private number in Rockville, Maryland. "General Mallon," he said, "something has just happened that I think we ought to talk about. . . ."

12

"What do you mean, you're going to hold it up until after the election? That's ridiculous!" Willis Tauber's eyes were flashing with anger.

John Schotty gestured weakly at the small bull of a man glowering at him over the desk. "Willis, I've been agonizing over this for days. I think Clayton's M10 claims are very likely to be true. As a matter of fact, I'm scared to death they are. This is death to millions of people—millions. That Johns Hopkins guy was damned well scared, too. But that's precisely the point. We haven't got to the people in the government who really know. They are the ones who will have to take responsibility for what will happen after we publish. They deserve the chance to react—to give us their side. I've finally gotten to some people who are trying to get me an appointment with the President himself."

Schotty continued, his voice soft and reasoning. "I hope to be able to see him late this weekend. I'm going to show him the report and I'm going to ask him what he knows about it. Until then, we aren't going to do anything. The consequences could be too horrendous either way—whether it's true or even if it's not."

"You're losing your nerve!" exclaimed Tauber, shaking his head furiously. "I've been going practically twenty-four hours a day for most of the past week," he said through gritted teeth, his face beginning to turn a dark red. "It's the story of the century, and furthermore, we'll make a mint on it. And now you want to bury it or hand it over to the politicians? What kind of a newsman are you? The public has a right to know about this before they go into those election booths. Did somebody get to you, John? Are you trying to save the election for Donley?"

"Crap," Schotty growled. "I'm not trying to do anything except what's right. If the M10 story is legitimate, we could have a nuclear war on our hands in hours. The poor bastards who are going to have to live with what happens deserve a chance to confirm or refute the story before we go to press. As a matter of fact, depending upon what I find out—I hope from the President himself—we may sit on this thing forever. I'm not going to risk the whole fucking country for a story—not even one as big as this one!"

Tauber's face was now gray with fury. "I've thought about that, too. All that will happen is that we and the Soviets will set up a committee or something. Then there'll be U.N. debates and a lot of talk. You've gotten too comfortable and cozy with the power structure to be hungry anymore. You've lost your balls."

Schotty's fist pounded hard on the desk. "That's enough, Will!" he roared. "That—is—enough! The subject is closed." He picked up the M10 report and with slow deliberation, his eyes fixed all the while on the fuming Tauber, opened the drawer of his desk and slipped the papers inside. Once more, a lock clicked shut on "A Synopsis of Project M10."

Without another word, the furious Tauber stormed out of Schotty's office, almost shattering the glass door behind him. He stalked down the long corridor, his heels hitting the worn marble floor like the hoofs of an angry horse. At the elevator, he mashed the black Down button with his fist and paced in a tight, nervous circle while he waited.

An idea which had been whispering to him insistently for days now began to shout in his mind. His angry movements stopped abruptly. Unaware of the curious looks of passing clerks and secretaries, he leaned back motionless against the cold gray-and-white marble slabs that lined the Globe Building hallway. The elevator came and went once . . . twice . . . three times. Finally, Tauber pushed himself off the wall and walked calmly down the corridor and into his own office. When he emerged, he was carrying a thin Manila envelope.

Willis Tauber was pleased with himself in a way he had not been in years. The sense of time flying past him was at least temporarily gone. Even his approaching fortieth birthday—only days away—no longer filled him with dread. Since his injury, each successive anniversary of his birth had sent him into a deep introspective gloom. Every year around this time he would find himself compulsively reliving the meaningless preseason game and the three pointless operations which had left him hobbling the sidelines like a sad old has-been. Tauber smiled at the envelope in his hand. Here was the antidote, the promise of an end to his ruminations about failure, the escape from a newspaper career mired in permanent mediocrity—a career submerged in the towering reputation and success of the man for whom he worked. No more second string, no more waiting on the sidelines. Tauber picked up his pace as he moved down the Globe Building corridor. His moment had come. Willis Tauber was doing something at last to make himself feel like a man again. He was stealing the story of M10.

Tauber's fast walk turned into a sprint, his limp barely perceptible. He stuck a big hand into the elaborate 1920s ironwork of the elevator safety gate just as the rickety old cage was departing from his floor. With one great tug, he pulled the doors open again, surprising and annoying the two young women inside, who were in a great hurry to do their Friday-afternoon shopping now that the rain had stopped. They glared at him, but he ignored them. Seconds later, squinting against the bright light of a clearing sky, he headed up New Hampshire Avenue toward the Ink Spot Pub, a favorite hangout for most of his years in Washington. The streets and sidewalks were already beginning to show spots of dry concrete when Tauber turned into the darkness of the bar, perched himself on a padded stool in his customary corner, and ordered a soda-backed straight double bourbon from Sammie, the chatty but efficient little Filipino bartender.

Four doubles and a couple of hours later, Tauber had had time for a lot more thinking, and all the details of his strategy were in place. Young and vigorous again, thanks largely to the alcohol, and convinced that what he was about to do was right, both for his country and for himself, he lurched off the bar stool and walked unsteadily toward the pay telephone near the glowing rear Exit sign of the Ink Spot. John Schotty's familiar "Schotty—go ahead" greeted him after only two rings.

"John, this is Will. I . . . ah . . . called to apologize,"

Tauber said, struggling to sound casual. "There was no
cause for me to lose my temper like that. You have every
right to decide how we should handle things. After all, it's
your story."

"It's *our* story," Schotty replied, "and I'm delighted you
called. I was down after you left. We haven't ever gone at
each other like that before and I didn't like the way it felt.
Let's forget it happened. Now, how about coming over for
a drink? I'll even pop for steaks down at Blackie's if you
haven't eaten."

"Tell you what, John. I'll take a rain check. I've had
time to do a little thinking since I left you, and I think I
need a couple of days off. Maybe that's why I'm so edgy.
Since you're going to hold up on the story till after the election anyhow, would you mind if I went to Florida for a
while and did some fishing? I'd be back right after the election and then we'd have a better chance of getting to the
right people. We'll only be spinning our wheels in the meantime."

Schotty paused before responding to Tauber's proposal.
He'd not planned to drop M10 so completely. But then
again, he could carry on himself: the highest-level contacts
were those he alone could make. "Okay, why don't you do
that. It'll probably do you a world of good."

"Fine. I'll see you Wednesday and I'll stay in touch just
in case," Tauber said evenly. "Have a good weekend. . . ."

Willis Tauber was a passenger on the last Eastern Airlines shuttle flight of the evening from National Airport to
La Guardia. He carried a small suitcase containing a few
shirts and other personal articles. The case also contained
a photocopy of the Clayton report on Project M10.

13

At 8:35 A.M., Saturday, November 3, John Schotty received
another telephone call. It came almost exactly twelve hours
after his conversation with Will Tauber, but this time he
was awakened from a sound sleep by the honey-warm voice
of a woman. Dorie Wilcox, personal secretary to the President of the United States, sounded solicitous but firm.

"I am sorry to disturb you, sir, but the President has asked if you could be at the White House by 10:30 A.M. He would very much like to see you for a few minutes."

Struggling to keep astonishment from creeping into his voice—he had not expected that his request for a presidential audience would work its way up so quickly—Schotty cleared his throat. "Why, yes, I could make it by then."

"Fine," Mrs. Wilcox said pleasantly. "We will send a car by for you shortly before ten. And thank you, Mr. Schotty."

Hitching up his rumpled pajama trousers, the columnist dashed for the bathroom. As he scraped the gray stubble off his face, he told himself he really "owed one" this time. Talk about quick results! He had had no idea he could get to the President this fast, especially with the election only three days away. He grinned and the razor caught at the deep cleft in his chin. A large drop of blood formed instantly. "You dumb sonofabitch!" he said aloud as he pawed through is medicine chest, looking vainly for a styptic pencil to stop the bleeding.

After a fast bachelor breakfast of overdone scrambled eggs, toast, and black coffee, Schotty sat in his little kitchen, fussing with the bit of Kleenex on his chin while he chain-smoked cigarettes and struggled to contain his excitement. The White House car arrived ten minutes early.

As John Schotty walked through the open door of the Oval Office and into the presence of the President of the United States, he was dumbfounded to find himself the center of attention in a meeting that included not only the President, but also the Deputy Chairman of the Joint Chiefs of Staff and the Director of the Central Intelligence Agency, to whom he was briefly introduced, along with several other aides, who remained anonymous.

"I take it, sir," Schotty said, feeling uncertain of how he should handle himself in the presence of so many people, "that this meeting is the result of my request through Senator Davidson. I must admit I hadn't expected quite this—"

"I haven't talked to Senator Davidson in several weeks, Mr. Schotty," the President replied. "We asked you here at our initiative because we have become aware of certain inquiries you have been making. I assume you are pursuing a story for your column. Mr. Schotty, have you heard of a Project M10?" Donley asked pointedly, as he leaned forward over his ornately carved desk.

Schotty knew there was no sense in lying, even if he had been inclined to. The pressure he had put on his White House sources had been too obvious to go unnoticed. "Yes, Mr. President, I have," he said, still trying to conceal his surprise at the audience he was facing.

The tall, aristocratic man who had led the United States for the past four years tilted his chair back and seemed to relax. Then he fired his second question. "Are you familiar with a report on M10 written by your late brother-in-law?"

Schotty hesitated.

"I think I should tell you, Mr. Schotty," the President continued, "that we know from our computer records and other investigations that Admiral Clayton printed just two copies of his report. He was bringing the report to me when he crashed. Is it possible, then, that he was carrying only one copy with him and that you know the whereabouts of the other?"

The President waited for a reply, but Schotty said nothing. His mind was racing. If Donley was, in fact, aware of M10 all along and was the power behind it, then Schotty could be in a very dangerous position. If he admitted he had the Clayton report, what might the President do to protect the secrecy of the project?

Before the columnist could decide how to respond, Donley commenced speaking to him again, as if reading his mind. "I should perhaps also tell you, Mr. Schotty, that you should not feel any coercion here. Frankly, I am appalled—more than that, I am revolted—by what I have learned thus far about the intended objectives of the M10 operation. We have a special computer system that has allowed us to reconstruct much of what Admiral Clayton had discovered. On the assumption that the propositions he put forth are true—and I want to emphasize most strongly that we are not yet certain that is the case—I have only two reasons for asking you here to meet with me. First, I am hopeful that you have somehow obtained the full report and will let us see it. It is essential that we know whether our reconstruction of it is complete so we can proceed with our effort to find those behind the project and stop their further activities. Second, assuming you do have the report, I intend to ask you to keep it secret until we can take steps to minimize the . . . ah . . . reactions of other world powers. Those reactions, Mr. Schotty, could be very dangerous, to say the least, as you must have already surmised."

John Schotty met the President's steady gaze squarely. Something in the man's deep-set eyes reached out to him—openness, sincerity, concern—Schotty could not be sure, but it was there and Schotty responded to it. "I do have the report, Mr. President," he said simply as he opened his briefcase.

Sunday church services in St. John's Church, across and beyond Lafayette Square from the high wrought-iron fence surrounding the White House grounds, were just commencing as the man in the Oval Office began to page through the M10 document. By the time the minister had finished his sermon, each page had been compared with the President's own ACA computer print-out. Perhaps a dozen items in the original had been missed in the reconstruction, but these did not change the report materially.

Satisfied that he possessed all of Clayton's information about M10, the President smiled across the desk. "Mr. Schotty, you have done your country a great service. I now believe we have what we needed from you. I do have another question, however." Before Donley could continue, he was interrupted by the buzz of his intercom. "Yes, Dorie?" He stopped to listen. "Yes, I'll talk to him a moment. Put him on Line Two. . . . Hello, Jack, I hear you're having problems, eh? . . . Yes, I can imagine he is. . . . Listen to me. You tell him we desperately need those labor votes up there. If he can't move them himself, I'll just have to squeeze in a visit myself. Call me back. . . . Okay. Good luck!" The President hung up the phone and turned again to John Schotty.

"It's going to be a very close election, Mr. Schotty. That's off the record, of course, not that you don't know it. But enough of that. Let me get to my question: Have you made any other copies of the M10 material?"

"Yes, sir," the columnist answered honestly, "but only two. I have one hidden in a safe place, and my associate, Willis Tauber, also has a working copy, which he is guarding carefully."

"We would like to take possession of those copies," the President said. "If some unauthorized person were to—"

"They are safe with us, Mr. President, and I have already told you we will not publish anything for a reasonable time. I don't intend to precipitate an international confrontation without giving you a chance to avoid it. Surely my actions up to now should demonstrate that."

"They do, they most certainly do," said Donley. "It is simply a fact that DOD security for the documents is better than yours."

"May I ask how you can be certain of that until you know who is behind the project?" Schotty replied with a touch of annoyance.

"Touché, touché. All right, keep your copies, but please, please be careful with them," said the President, retreating hastily. "Incidentally, I want to be sure you know how much I appreciate your cooperation in this matter . . . how much I respect the statesmanlike way in which you have conducted yourself to this point." Donley rose from his chair and Schotty and the others in the room immediately understood. The President had a way of signaling that a meeting was over without ever quite saying so.

"You know," Donley said as he put an arm on the columnist's shoulder and escorted him across the polished oak floor toward the door of his office, "you could have really caused great trouble for the world if you'd published this material when you first got it. It might even have meant a nuclear war."

"I know that, sir. What bothers me is where this is all going to end. It's a horrible business, to say the least. I can't begin to imagine where it will lead. . . ."

The President stopped walking, his arm still on Schotty's shoulder. The sincerity Schotty had seen in his eyes was still there, but there was something more. It might have been fear. "I share your concern," Donley said quietly. "I'm not sure where it's all going to lead, either, but I know this: What we've decided to do here today is all that we can do. The problem is basically in our hands now, not yours. All your country can ask of you at this point is to keep absolutely silent for a time. I would also urge that you reach your assistant as soon as possible, and in some very, very private place, explain the situation to him. Tell me once again, are you certain of him? Are you sure he'll understand?"

"I'm absolutely sure of Tauber," Schotty nodded vigorously as the two men started walking again. "He's been with me for ten years and he's hard as nails—reliable beyond question. You need have no worries about us, Mr. President. We've had a long talk about the gravity of the situation. He understands it very well. Just remember, in the end we intend to be the ones who will publish the story. No deadlines, of course, but frankly, I would hope we could do it in, let us say, a week or two."

The President laughed lightly. "Ah, you're very much a newspaperman, Mr. Schotty. Yes, I assure you, and regardless of how the election comes out, when we have made the appropriate preparations and found the culprits, you will be the one who can tell the world about M10." Suddenly serious again, he added, "I'm not sure how I'll do it, but I promise you I will." The two men had reached the entrance of the Oval Office.

"Three last questions, Mr. President, if you don't mind," said Schotty quickly, as if he were conducting an impromptu interview. "In all candor, there is really little doubt that Admiral Clayton was right about M10, isn't that true? There is just too much evidence not to believe someone has been doing just what he said they've been doing, isn't that so, sir?"

"I'm afraid you're right, John," Donley replied sadly, using Schotty's given name for the first time.

"Well, then, sir, how do *you* feel about the people who did this . . . just as a human being. Those people have really been haunting me. How could they? I mean, I was wondering if you have any idea who . . ."

"M10, if it is confirmed, as I fear it will be, is an obscenity—perhaps no less than the worst obscenity in all of history. Those who did it must be totally mad. But that cannot become my first concern. I am a politician as well as a human being. Of course, I want the people behind M10 brought to justice—I am taking certain steps—but above all, my problem is the Soviets. I want my country to survive and I intend that it shall. There must not be a war over M10. Now, what was your other question?"

The stocky columnist turned to face the taller man more

directly. "With all due respect, sir, how do I know you, yourself, are not running M10?"

The President was completely surprised by the question, and his face fell, then he chuckled. "I'm afraid you don't," he said, "but it may help to remember that Admiral Clayton was prepared to trust me. Furthermore, John—if you'll allow me to call you that—I meant what I said a moment ago. M10 is despicable and disgusting. I have had nothing whatsoever to do with it."

Schotty nodded gravely and shook the President's hand. The flesh, he noticed, was cold, a sure signal of the enormous tension the Chief Executive must be feeling.

A smile from Dorie Wilcox sent Schotty through the outer door of the reception room and into the hallway. He took a deep breath, becoming suddenly aware that his own hands were clammy, too, then began to analyze what had just happened. The President had said it well. It was no longer Schotty's problem. In the depths of his soul, he was glad to escape. He shuddered. Those men in the Oval Office must now face M10 squarely, whatever the consequences, and he did not envy them. They, not he, were the ones who might have to look into the mouth of hell itself. Relief that was almost exhilaration spread through his chest.

Putting his lighter to the last cigarette of his first pack of the day, the columnist walked down the corridor toward the driveway where the White House car was waiting to take him home. The warm blue smoke felt good and he sucked it deep into his lungs. Yes, thank God all he had to do now with M10 was wait. Rubbing his chin thoughtfully, Schotty's fingers caught on something foreign. He smiled sheepishly. The bloodsoaked little bit of tissue had been stuck on his chin the entire time he was with the President! Red with embarrassment, he exploded with a huge laugh. He did not see the second car swing into traffic behind his own as they pulled out of the White House grounds and onto Pennsylvania Avenue.

In New York, just a few hundred miles to the north, another man who knew about M10 did not plan to wait, as John Schotty had promised the President he would. Waiting was something Willis Tauber planned never to do again. He had done enough of it for a lifetime. His private photocopy of the Clayton report was to be used as barter in a crude exchange: an exclusive on the story of the century in return for a large sum of money and a long-term national syndication contract for his own column. As far as Tauber was concerned, the bidding started at $250,000, and he knew exactly who the first bidder would be.

14

Newspapers such as the *Globe* were once the unchallenged providers of news and information to the world. But in the last few decades of the twentieth century, a new trend, which had started with radio coverage of the day's important events and had gathered enormous momentum with the advent of television, was threatening to become an electronic tidal wave that would sweep the old print media into history. In this new age of high-technology journalism, tough old newspapers like the *Globe* were struggling for their lives, while others of lesser strength and stature had already succumbed to the onslaught of an army of eager young reporters carrying pocket-sized TV cameras and tape recorders everywhere they went. So-called all-electronic news services, which fed detailed news programs and other special services into video terminals by wire, cable, and satellite, competed in a wild melee of information vending. The explosive growth of electronic communications systems had made great diversity possible. Dozens of new services collided head-on against the larger but more traditional television networks and newspaper syndicates. Some of the young all-electronic news organizations grew rapidly in spite of the competition and already served millions of private clients in the United States and abroad. Others were struggling hard just to stay alive. Among the marginal systems was one called VEI—Videowire Express Incorporated.

Videowire had been tiptoeing along the edge of bankruptcy ever since its establishment, and the president of Videowire, a former sportswriter for the *Globe* named Steven James Contos, had a spreading reputation for being willing to do almost anything, legal or extralegal, to strengthen his tottering company. In an effort to boost income, his reporters had torn and pried their way into the private lives of hundreds of people and had, in fact, uncovered perhaps half a dozen minor scandals. In the process, however, their overzealous search for news, their looseness with facts, and their occasional outright lies had hurt many innocent people. Repeatedly they had published unconfirmed rumors as major stories and then later transmitted meek, but almost invisible, retractions which left the damage mostly unrepaired.

In spite of its unbridled sensationalism and a well-founded rumor of a standing "kickback" deal to any news director who would buy its services, Videowire's client list had grown only slowly. The basic reason was to be found in the *Congressional Record* and in transcripts of hearings of the Federal Communications Commission. Several times in the past two and a half years, the practices of Videowire had come under congressional investigation as the lawmakers prepared to revise the statutes governing FCC operations. During the thrashing out of the new laws regarding government authority over the burgeoning crop of small news sources, John Schotty had been outspoken in his criticism of the tactics used by Contos and his associates. His criticisms, delivered from the witness table at the hearings and published in his carefully reasoned and carefully read column, "Schotty Says . . . ," had earned him the permanent animosity of Steve Contos. Contos would never admit to it, but close observers also knew that he was immensely envious of Schotty as well as bitter about being a target for Schotty's precise logic. The columnist's impeccable reputation and personal success contrasted painfully with the grubbing and clawing that had become the Contos trademark, and Contos was not inclined to forgive him for it, at least so long as Videowire remained just one of the crowd.

Past collisions between Contos and Schotty had not gone unnoticed by Willis Tauber. He had confronted Contos himself a number of times, although never with any ferocity, and had sensed the burning hunger and jealousy in the man. Given Videowire's "flexible" ethics and the general street knowledge about its fragile financial condition, it was easy for Tauber to settle on Videowire as a vehicle to achieve his own success, no questions asked.

At one stroke the story of M10 could move Videowire into the big leagues, provide sweet vengeance for Steve Contos, and make a former second-string football player rich and famous as the latest lead dog of the Washington press corps.

At a few minutes after 11:30 A.M. Saturday, Willis Tauber dialed the Videowire offices. As he had been every weekend for the past six weeks, Contos was at his desk struggling to prepare financial statements and cash-flow projections that would calm some very nervous men at First Capital Bank of New York.

"What do you want from me, Tauber?" Contos asked with honest surprise. "Is the great crusader about to howl for my blood again?"

"No, nothing like that. This is strictly between you and me and it's very special," Tauber answered. "Now, can I come over or can't I?"

To Contos, Willis Tauber had always been "that muscle-bound jock" who worked for Schotty at the *Globe*, but the sensitive entrepreneurial antennae that Contos depended upon to stay alive told him there was no harm in listening to what Tauber had to say. Something in Tauber's voice more than in his words suggested it would be well worth the time.

"Okay," Contos agreed. "I've got something to finish up, so why don't you come by about one-thirty."

"I hope you're prepared to spend the afternoon," announced Tauber as he lumbered into the Videowire offices.

"Good to see you, Willis. Sit down. Sure, I'm ready to spend as long as you like, provided you've got something worthwhile." Contos's dark, almost black, eyes flashed hungrily as he shifted a half-smoked, half-chewed cigar from one side of his mouth to the other, only to have the cold ashes drop off and land on his highly styled but very wrinkled white shirt. Contos brushed at them with an annoyed grunt. "Okay—what's going on, what have you got, and what's it got to do with me?"

As if to emphasize his confidence, Tauber did not bother to sit in the chair to which Contos had pointed. Instead he hoisted his wide body up onto the edge of the desk and directed a conspiratorial whisper at Contos's ear.

"I have got nothing less than the story of the century, and you can have it if we can make the right deal."

Contos looked at him dubiously. He'd heard stories about the story of the century before. "Oh, come on! What are you handing me? Are you setting me up for Schotty?"

"John Schotty has nothing to do with this. This is my story and my deal. Now, do you want to talk business or am I wasting my time?"

"Okay, okay—don't get yourself in an uproar," Contos said, wondering what the game really was. "What's the big scoop?"

"In good time, my friend. First let's talk about what I get if you go with it." In smoothly rehearsed phrases, Tauber named his price: a five-year contract for an electronically distributed newspaper column and a video-cable commentary slot, plus a flat quarter of a million dollars for the story.

"Man, you have got to be kidding!" Contos chuckled sarcastically. "I'm having a helluva time finding two dollars to tip a waiter, and you want me to give you a $250,000 guarantee? What's the matter with you? You know we're in trouble."

Tauber smiled indulgently at the impatient and annoyed man behind the desk. "I know you're in trouble and that is exactly why I picked Videowire Express to work with. That's what makes me so valuable to you. Once you start running with this story, VEI's going to have more subscribers than you know what to do with. That's why I'm worth at least a couple of hundred thousand dollars and more to you."

"Willis, I don't think you'd be worth that kind of money if you brought me the autobiography of Jesus Christ. You are off your nut!"

The smile on Tauber's face broadened; he was feeling absolutely sure of himself. "Well, I suggest you might want to reconsider that after you see what I've got. Incidentally, if we do make a deal, there is one other matter. I want you to put real promotional push behind my joining you. I want it spread all over the place. We may as well get people used to thinking of me as the country's new fountainhead of political news."

"You are out of your mind," said Contos, shaking his head. "I keep telling you that I haven't got a nickel. VEI is on edge of bankruptcy and you're giving me all this bull-shit about hundreds of thousands of dollars and big public-ity campaigns. Don't you hear what I'm saying?"

"Yes, I hear very well. But *you* don't seem to under-stand. Your savior has arrived, and I'm it, baby."

Contos breathed out an exasperated rush of air. "Oh, shit what the hell have you got? Let's look at it."

Tauber pushed a slightly worn Manila envelope across the desk to Contos, who was about to open it when Tauber dropped a hand gnarled by several enlarged knuckles onto the papers. "Let's be very clear with each other. My posi-tion is not negotiable. You have heard my minimum deal. That is what I get if you go with this, and nothing less."

Contos looked up at the rock-hard man seated imper-tinently on the edge of the desk. "I keep telling you you're out of your mind. Okay, sure, if we go with 'this,' what-ever it is, you've got the deal you've asked for. But it's got to be a cold day in hell when we take it on."

"Contos, listen to me. I'm trusting you now. I'll let you look through the first five or six pages, and that's all. Af-ter that, we draw up the contracts before you get a crack at the whole document. And let me make another little item clear to you: There is nowhere else that you can get this stuff, even if you tried and even knowing what you're going to learn in the first pages. It'll take you months to dig up the rest, if you ever do. By that time, I'll have an arrangement with someone else and you'll miss the whole ball game. Besides, if you try to screw me out of this, I will personally break you in half. So let's understand each other. You look at a little and then we deal, okay?"

"Yes, yes," snapped Contos impatiently. "I'll play your little game with you."

Lifting his hand away, Tauber tilted the envelope so the report inside slipped out onto the desk's walnut Formica top. The title of the document, "A Synopsis of Project M10," meant nothing to Contos. Opening the cover page, he settled back in his chair and began to read as Tauber heaved himself off his perch and strolled to a window to watch the New York pedestrians on Sixth Avenue far be-low. Tight smiles flickered around the former athlete's mouth as he waited for a reaction from the man behind him.

By the time the head of Videowire had turned the third page of the report, color was rising in his face and his jaw had begun to work nervously. Silently he continued reading. At page seven, he slammed his palms down on the desk with a loud whack.

"Are you putting me on, you sonofabitch?" he asked incredulously.

Tauber turned from the window to face him, grinning broadly. "No, baby, I'm not putting you on. It's all straight material. Now, do we deal, or don't we?"

"Wait a minute, wait a minute," Contos exclaimed. "How do you *know* this is not some crazy kind of joke?"

"Listen to me," Tauber replied with oily smoothness. "This document came directly from the Chairman of the Joint Chiefs of Staff himself—that guy who died in the plane crash. But you get nothing more from me until we have signed papers. After that, believe me, you can have it all. And I'll make another deal with you: we can put it right into the contract. If the story of M10 turns out to be a big nothing, the contract between us is canceled. How's that for being fair?"

Tauber's last words gave Contos what he had been looking for since page two. A fail-safe deal. He had also heard something else, which told him a good bit more about the man Willis Tauber than Tauber realized.

Without a moment of thought about a serious effort at verification, nor an instant's sober assessment of the political and military consequences that might follow running the M10 story, the president of VEI exploded with enthusiasm. This was news, the newsbeat that could make his company and make him. The demeaning struggle of the past five years could suddenly be worth all the blood and sweat and sleepless nights. Contos leaped from his desk to Tauber and practically pulled the heavier man off his feet with a handshake. "I apologize for doubting you, Willis. This is going to make us both millionaires!"

A happy leer spread across Tauber's face and a childish giggle erupted from his throat. "You're right, partner. You are absolutely right," he said.

Within a half hour, the two men had hammered out an agreement. It was not an elaborate document, only a few typewritten paragraphs, but it was enough to do the job, and their signatures were on the paper. A contract that could precipitate a global nuclear war between the Soviet Union and the United States had been executed.

"Now that we've got that settled," Contos said as he put his copy of their agreement into a file cabinet, "I want to ask you something. Where did you steal the report? Was it from Schotty himself or from his sister? You don't really think I didn't know Admiral Clayton was married to Mildred Schotty, for chrissake?"

Tauber blinked innocently. "Just how I got the material is not important. All you need to know is that Schotty won't be doing anything with it, if he has it, too, for at least a week and maybe longer."

"Mr. Tauber, I can see right now I'm going to have to watch you rather closely. You may be too much like me for my own good," the VEI president said with a cold smile.

"I'll be watching you too," Tauber muttered humorlessly as Contos began to devour the rest of the M10 report. If Contos actually heard Tauber's icy response, he did not react to it.

Later in the afternoon, Contos looked up from his non-stop study like a student who had just decided he could not possibly pass the next exam. Tauber, who had been working across the desk from him, sketching out his first series of columns, coyly entitled "Tauber Talks . . . ," paused expectantly.

"You know," Contos meditated, "we're going to have one hell of a time exploiting all this. There is just so much we ought to do. There's so damn much preparation we ought to make. I'm beginning to wonder whether we're not rushing it a bit, trying to get everything out before the election. It would shake the system something fierce, but I'm not so sure that's the smartest thing for us to do. It's just too big, and once we blow it, we blow it. We'll never get another chance like it." Contos talked on, not really addressing his words to Tauber but thinking aloud about how to maximize his profits. "Maybe we'd better slip the schedule a bit. Maybe we'd better get the boys out pushing for clients first. We could get people signed up on contracts that are cancelable if they don't like the story, but maybe we don't publish until we've got the whole crowd already with us."

"It's up to you," Tauber purred, his protestations to

John Schotty about early publication now conveniently forgotten. "I'm not worried about anybody else beating us to this story for at least a week or ten days. I'll tell you that."

"Seven to ten days . . ." said Contos, aware of Tauber's presence once again. "I told you before that I'm having trouble finding the money to tip a headwaiter, so we can't take too much time. Otherwise the banks are going to shut me down before we get the story on the street. But I guess we'd better take a few extra days," Contos mused. "I guess we'd better. . . ."

The prospect of having hitched his wagon to a star that was possibly nearer to financial death than he had previously allowed himself to think shook Willis Tauber momentarily. "How much time will the banks give you?" he asked.

"I'm not sure. A week or two, anyhow, Contos replied reassuringly. "Look, I've got to get my boys in on this. They're the ones who are going to have to make it go. I'll make a few phone calls."

For months, the entire VEI sales team of eleven men scattered around the U.S. and foreign countries had been struggling to survive on the pathetic one-hundred- or two-hundred-dollar commissions their occasional sales had produced. Many had been forced to take on extra or part-time jobs, but they were all long-time acquaintances of Contos's and most of them were willing to sell anything, from encyclopedias to panty hose, as long as it meant a buck.

In quick succession, Contos fired staccato sentences at the three of his four New York men whom he could reach. Two of the conversations were not altogether coherent. It was the cocktail hour in New York; one man had been drowning his sorrow in martinis, while another was following his usual Saturday formula of four hours of college football on the color TV in his house in Yonkers mixed with a quart of straight vodka on the rocks. All three men, grumbling and filled with doubt about the need for it, nevertheless obediently headed for the meeting Contos had scheduled for 7:00 P.M. at Videowire.

The luxuriously long Hauptmann Claro y Claro that Contos lit up after completing his phone calls had burned down to a soggy stump by the time the third and last salesman arrived at the VEI offices. As the man slouched through the outer door, Contos shot him a disgusted look and began a choppy, excited monologue addressed to listeners who were making it obvious by their manner that they were present only because he had demanded that they be there. About halfway through the Videowire chief's explanation of the basic structure of the M10 story and the promotional campaign he had formulated to go with it, Contos began to see the visible reactions in his audience. The man from Yonkers had shaken off the effects of his contest with vodka and was sitting rigidly upright in his chair; the martini drinker, unable to fully control his excitement, had got up and was pacing at the rear of the room; the third salesman, his eyes narrowed to thin slits, was hunched forward, attending carefully to each word.

"But for chrissake," Contos concluded ten minutes later, as he leaned against a desk, "be careful with what you say! I don't want the details of this story getting out prematurely. Work your sales pitch around the cancellation clause we'll put in. If the clients want their money back after we publish M10, we'll give them their money back. That's the guarantee—that's how they can't get hurt. But except in the most general terms, I don't want anybody knowing too much about M10 before we publish. No one even mentions the word 'cancer.' Is that understood?" Contos looked around the room.

If it had been possible to crawl inside the minds of each of the Videowire salesmen at that moment, one would have found few worries over the possible consequences of publishing M10. These were men who sold elaborately embellished stories of corporate sex scandals one day and overblown interviews with the disgruntled wives of philandering moving stars or with flying saucer nuts the next. They were intent on assessing exactly what M10 would be worth to them in cold cash. Nothing more.

"And remember this," Contos added as an afterthought. "You each have more details than I want the other fellows to know. You're the hot shots—the ones I'm looking to for the big buck. The other fellows . . . just tell them it's a big story and give them the same generalities I told you to give the clients. That'll be enough for them to work the small fry. . . .

"Guys, I can't stress this too much," Contos emphasized

"My friend Willis Tauber here doesn't seem to worry about getting scooped. But I do. All we need is for some sonofabitch to publish a cancer-war story as a rumor and that'll cream the thing for us. I want it to hit like a ton of bricks starting Thursday morning. Now get going!" The formal meeting at Videowire was over.

Clustered around Contos's desk, the salesmen pressed their boss for more details. Where did you get it? Who's behind it? Why not blast Donley with it before the election? What'll the Russians do? It's all really science fiction, right? "Hey, that's enough, guys!" Contos shouted with good-natured glee. "I'm giving you a package that can make you rich, but you're goddamn well not going to be able to blow it for me. All you need to know, you've already been told." He laughed happily. "Now get your butts into the other room and start selling. You've still got time to hit the U.S. and the Pacific if you use home phone numbers. We'll start on Europe tomorrow morning. Remember what I said: for every client you line up, assuming they stay with us for twenty-six weeks of service after M10, you get a thousand bucks. Remember that—a thousand bucks a client. Now move it."

It was about 8:30 P.M. when the salesmen filed out of Contos's office, to the accompaniment of wisecracks about where Videowire was going to get a thousand dollars to pay one bonus, let alone dozens. To them it was just another sales job, another story to sell—a beauty, in fact. Besides, in reality not one of them believed it was true.

15

About the time Saturday-night theater-goers in Manhattan were starting to fight each other for taxis home, the drum-beat of telephone calls from VEI had reached across the country and was leapfrogging the Pacific to Japan and Australia. For the first time in a year and a half, all the lines that Steven Contos had installed in the expansively optimistic early days of Videowire were in use. Salesmen's fingers danced over the touchtone dial pads and one potential customer after another was dragged from dinner or cocktails or pulled from the closing moments of a Saturday-afternoon tennis game. "Sign up and you'll get a guaranteed exclusive for your area in the very first package. It will be bigger than the atom bomb and Watergate put together. What do you mean, you don't trust us? This one is guaranteed, and if you don't want it, I'll sell it across the damned street to your competition! Yes, yes, you can cancel anytime."

Almost oblivious to the frenetic campaign in the next room, Willis Tauber had settled behind Contos's own desk and was well into the first segment of the series that would tell the entire world about M10. On the wall behind the desk, in a kind of opening ceremony, he had posted a piece of paper. It had pained Steve Contos to watch him do it. Masking tape slapped on a nicely painted off-white wall as if it were a locker-room door was hardly the image the Videowire president was trying to project. But Contos was feeling so good, he decided not to voice his objections. The paper displayed the following publication schedule from Tauber's typewriter:

Thrusday, November 8	Pre-publication promotion— early A.M.
	1st piece—11 A.M. EST, 5,000 words
Friday, November 9	No. 2—10,000 words; sidebar interviews
Saturday, November 10	No. 3—10,000 words plus charts and graphs, interviews; world reaction; guesses re whodunnit?
Sunday, November 11	No. 4—10,000 words plus graphics; congressional/DOD interviews as available; probable statements by Donley/ Soviets?
Monday, November 12	Complete Clayton Report Follow-ups U.S. and abroad; more whodunnit?
Tuesday, November 13	We celebrate.

16

Under the same early-winter weather system that had blanketed New York with black clouds and cold rain for an entire week, another group of men, three high officials of the United States government, were also completely absorbed with the subject M10. Unaware that Videowire was preparing to publish the story of M10 in less than a week's time, the Director of the CIA, the new Acting Chairman of the JCS, and the President's senior personal aide were wondering how they could help Frederick Donley keep the project secret.

"I think we'll have to give him all of what we've gotten tonight. It's so bad, he's just got to know what he's up against. We can't take this material much further without getting too many people involved. He said he didn't want to do that before the election, so this is about all we'll have until Wednesday or Thursday." The Director of the CIA stopped talking and paused to wipe his steel-rimmed bifocals. Although not a scientist, slight, balding Charles Frydon, at fifty-one and with nearly twenty years in the agency had developed an extensive technical background. He was also generally conceded to be the brightest mind in the entire administration and the essential scientific issues behind M10 were easily within his grasp.

At the other end of the table, General Mike Kallen, Deputy Chairman of the Joint Chiefs of Staff and now its acting chief, arched his back. "Let's go over that last part again," he said, stretching his arms wide. It had been a long session.

"Okay," sighed the CIA Director. "Here it is. Our ACA data, as well as information from the National Center for Health Statistics, show that the overall crude cancer death rate since 1933 was increasing annually by about one percent in the United States. That was until 1975. Then the rate appears to have jumped to something like 2.3 percent. One way—I repeat—one way we can explain that now is by assuming that the people behind M10 somehow grossly underestimated the feedback of their cancer-inducing

agents from the Soviet Union to the U.S. population."
Frydon paused to see if Kallen was following him. The
general nodded and Frydon resumed. "We haven't traced
all the possible routes of commerce that could be responsible. There are just too many—specialty foods, beverages,
drugs, even contaminated fabrics and furs. On the other
hand, we've gone over all the Clayton data. The calculations there seem right and yet the total population affected
seems to be much greater than it should be. Just look at
the charts."

Frydon held up a graph he had copied from a computer
display and pointed a red ballpoint pen at a line that moved
smoothly across the page, then abruptly turned upward.
"In 1975, for instance, there were 665,000 new cancer
cases diagnosed in the U.S. About 365,000 deaths, as you
can see. That year alone, the rate was five times higher than
the total U.S. military deaths in the Vietnam and Korean
war years combined. Our own HEW statistics say that the
direct and indirect cost of cancer for one particular year
in the 1970s, including the loss of earnings due to illness
and during the balance of normal life expectancy, was
around fifteen billion. Every cancer patient in the U.S. rep-
resents a direct-care cost of five thousand to maybe over
twenty thousand in 1975 dollars. One rather interesting
little question is how much of that cost could be the result
of the feedback of M10 materials into our own economy.
In any event, we figure, according to the M10 data, that
the impact of M10 on the Soviet Union in 1975 was at
least fifteen times greater than it was for us and the ratio
has been going up ever since. These excess cancer deaths
starting in '75 on our side shake me up a great deal. My
God, if they really are due to M10, we've got to find how
the active agents are coming back into the country and
stop them before even more damage is done."

"Charley," interrupted General Kallen, "this whole thing
is utterly unbelievable, but that's the part I don't know how
Donley can possible handle. In plain language, what you're
saying is that the idiots who are running M10 have been
murdering us right along with the Soviets. Clayton figured
eighty thousand deaths and you are pointing at data that
suggest over a million already, with more to come. If that
ever gets out . . . well, I can't imagine what will happen.
One thing is certain," Kallen said with a grim chuckle. "It

damned well better not get out before Tuesday, or Donley can forget about the next four years."

"No one's going to argue that," Frydon replied quietly, peering over his glasses at the Air Force officer.

"In fact, he might be better off that way," interjected another voice from across the table. The expression on Jim Willoughby's boyish face carried no suggestion that he was joking, because, at that moment at least, he was not. "Excuse me, Charley," the President's embarrassed personal assistant added. "I don't mean to get us off the track."

Charles Frydon could feel Willoughby's anguish. The thirty-eight-year-old summa cum laude from Indiana University had worked for Fred Donley for over fifteen years and was almost a second son to the President. He was thoroughly frightened about what M10 was likely to do to the man he both served and loved. "You can put all this another way," the CIA Director said, picking up the threads of his discussion. "Since 1933, the year the National Center for Health Statistics was established, our staff study shows that the standardized U.S. cancer death rates increased overall by about eleven percent up through 1975. How much of that eleven percent, we now have to wonder, was due to M10 getting started? We've agreed on the need to get later and more fine-grained data, but not at the risk of getting people too excited about why characters like us would be interested in it now. There might be too many questions, so we'll wait until after Tuesday. But then we really have to dig into this from a technical point of view as well as keep up the other investigations."

There were mute nods around the table as Frydon paused and drifted off into thoughts he did not voice. An invisible pressure to have the resourceful and controlled CIA man continue talking began to build in the other men in the room. They wanted the frightening silence filled with words. Talking seemed to shrink M10 to human proportions and, for a little while at least, make it appear to be a problem that could be solved. "Go on, go on," urged Kallen and Willoughby in unison.

"We have also agreed," Frydon said obligingly, "to inform the President that we have confirmed that detecting M10-style attacks is unlikely and that we are stuck for countermeasures in the event a similar operation were tried against us. We're really much more vulnerable than the

Soviets because our society is so open. There'd be a thousand ways to get M10 toxins into our streams of commerce —everything from meat inspectors to agents operating at grain elevators or factories. If they ever did try the M10 approach, think of the position we'd be in. In the first place, the toxicological testing of experimental animals or epidemiological observations in a large exposed human population both have their limitations. One can't detect an epidemic caused by the M10 carcinogens until the population is already affected. Furthermore, one needs some kind of clue—perhaps from the timing of the outbreaks or in the geographical clustering or *something*. But no clue we can think of is going to be quickly apparent to us.

"We've checked carefully with the National Cancer Institute. Any tests they do on laboratory animals are relatively insensitive and they have problems detecting the action of a cancer-causing agent where it acts individually, let alone in combination with the natural environment. Mostly they have to test with very high concentrations of the material. Certainly they have no very good techniques to reflect the role of changing patterns of an actual chronic environmental exposure such as M10 is using. They'll admit it right up front: the only times they've been able to get at such things in the past is when they could discover some kind of sharply differentiating factor in the general population's exposure. That was the secret of proving that cigarette smoking caused cancer. They could study those who smoked and those who didn't and look at the differences. But with these M10 agents—well, hell, *everybody eats!* So I conclude we are just helpless. The techniques for uncovering it simply do not exist."

"And it's obvious the Russians are not any better off then we are," General Kallen cut in. "They haven't got a chance of detecting M10, either. In a way, I suppose, that's a blessing and we must emphasize that point to the President. It gives us time to shut M10 off and, hopefully, get out of this with our skins whole." The Air Force officer frowned. What he had just said was as much a prayer as it was a prediction.

A silence again settled over the three men in the White House conference room. Each had thought of little else but M10 for over a week. During a frantic blur of nights and days, each had tried in his own way to deal with it and where it might lead and had been overwhelmed by the same sense of dread. Struggling to treat M10 as just another situation, just another job, each man knew it was different. Unlike any previous international crisis since the atomic age began, M10 was not merely a threat. In this instance, millions of people had *already* been killed and that single unalterable fact could mean the beginning of the end of everything.

Charles Frydon, his bald head glistening under the ceiling lights, took a deep breath and plowed on through the agenda to be discussed with the President. "Okay, now, we've checked on the TLVs for the carcinogens that M10 apparently is using. There just aren't any. Nobody knows the Threshold Limit Values—the concentrations humans can safely tolerate. Here are the print-outs from the National Center for Toxicological Research in Pine Bluff, Arkansas." He rolled open a large sheet covered with data. "If anyone would, the center would have the carcinogenicity data, but they don't have a thing. I've circled in red pencil the substances that are chemically closest to the M10 agents, but they are actually miles away and the numbers are worthless. I also asked the center whether they had any more relevant carcinogens in their large-scale 'megamouse' experiments. Those are the ones in which a huge mouse population is used to test the effects of chronic doses of a foreign substance. Unfortunately, at the moment they've got nothing going and they've got nothing planned. They really didn't think materials in the M10 class were very interesting compared to others—mostly industrial contaminants—that they are working on. Of course, I didn't tell them exactly what materials I was thinking of, but I gave them the general chemistry and they couldn't care less. They don't feel the area to be important simply because they don't realize the potencies M10 is able to achieve."

"Doesn't that mean it will take us months or years to get the data we need once we dare ask them to start testing?" Willoughby asked.

"That is exactly what it means," Frydon replied soberly. "Too bad—but it's true and there's nothing we can do about it. Leaving aside the biology, even the straight chemistry and physics are troublesome. We can get down to the detection levels and sensitivities that we would need to find the M10 agents—methods like laser fluorescence analysis will do it—but the hooker is we have to know what to look for and we have to know where to search. There are a thousand substances that might be synthesized that would have the potency necessary and most of them would be damn hard to find if you didn't know exactly what you were seeking. The question is: How do you know what to look for unless somebody tells you? I've already got a couple of our people working on that part of the problem and we'll certainly scale up the effort after Tuesday, but meantime, as Mike says, I think we can be certain that the Russians don't have a chance of detecting any of the M10 agents with the kind of environmental monitoring and quality testing we know they're doing. Hell, we couldn't do it ourselves!" Frydon stopped for another deep breath. He had been talking nonstop, running on nervous energy as much as air.

"Charley," General Kallen said, speaking very deliberately, "it seems to me we must remind the President that M10 materials are flowing into the Soviet Union not only directly but through Argentina, Yugoslavia, and Japan as well. There may be a dozen or more entry points, for all we know. M10 personnel have to be active in each of those places, and if so, they could be discovered at any time. That could blow the lid off, too."

Charles Frydon nodded and stared for a moment at Kallen. The general was gazing straight into space, his mind grappling with impossible probabilities. Frydon turned toward Jim Willoughby, who was chewing gently on the end of his pencil.

"We'll also have to tell him we haven't gotten any further on tracking down the crazies who started all this," Willoughby said. "It's going to be awhile unless we get a break of some kind, right?"

The CIA man did not respond directly. Instead he merely shrugged. "It's almost time to go," he said. "I'll sketch a few things on some viewgraphs and we'll be ready. I don't know exactly what we can expect him to do with all this. The man's more than got his hands full already with the election. I think it's going to be damn close myself."

The intruder, oscillating, bending, coiling tirelessly—a million million times each second—floats aimlessly in the infinite primordial fluid. At one end, an electric charge dances and whirls and sends its fingers of invisible force reaching outward across space. Numberless other molecules tumble in crazy frantic orbits around it . . . colliding . . . shivering . . . decaying . . . reacting.

From far off, the huge sinuous coil of the gene slowly approaches. As if transfixed by the same hypnotic fascination that holds the cobra for the mongoose, the gene drifts toward the intruder, drawn by its relentless electric field. A final fateful dance has begun. The gene has never approached so closely nor been so closely approached. There have been other encounters, a thousand near-collisions with other intruders, but always the gene had escaped as protective clusters of other molecules chanced to intervene. This time is destined to be different.

A chance thermal vibration passes through the warm ooze of the cell—the merest statistical fluctuation—a microscopic deviation from the norm. The intruder ricochets forward, its electric charge snapping like an angry whip. Slowly, inevitably—in timeless obedience to the old immutable laws—the shimmering double helix of the great gene bends forward, strangely contorted by the giant power of the intruder's electric field. The gene pulls closer. Suddenly, for an incomprehensible millionth of a millionth of a second, its delicate structure separates and rejoins . . . a spider's web struck by invisible lightning that both rends and repairs. The gene, intact but somehow changed, drifts on in the jelly of the cell. The primal dance is ended and the cancer has begun.

On a scale immensely grander, halfway in size from the molecules to the stars, Nikolai Lobachevsky, deputy director of the Volgograd power plant, is having his lunch. As is his habit, he asks his wife for yet another piece of that good bread—the kind she always makes with that wonderful but expensive American wheat.

Tuesday, November 6

> a1296 AP
> BULLETIN WASHINGTON D.C.
> PRESIDENT FREDERICK R. DONLEY CONCEDED DEFEAT
> TONIGHT AT 10:47 P.M. EST IN A DRAMATIC TELEVISED
> STATEMENT FROM THE WHITE HOUSE. HE DECLARED
> THAT HE FELT HE HAD RUN A GOOD STRONG CAMPAIGN
> BUT THAT—QUOTE—THE RAPID INFLATION AND LARGE
> BUDGET DEFICITS OF THE PAST TWO YEARS HAVE
> BLINDED VOTERS TO THE MANY SOUND ACCOMPLISH-
> MENTS OF MY ADMINISTRATION—CLOSE QUOTE.
> MARGIN OF VICTORY FOR PRESIDENT-ELECT C. BOYCE
> WILLIAMSON IS RELIABLY PROJECTED BY COMPUTER
> TO BE SLIGHTLY MORE THAN TWO PERCENT. WILLIAM-
> SON STATEMENT WILL FOLLOW IN 30 SECONDS.
> FULL TEXT OF DONLEY STATEMENT NOW ON B WIRE
> TELEPRINTERS.
> 1049 P ED 11-6

Drowned in the torrent of news about the election and its aftermath, a vague rumor which had begun over the weekend up in New York, and which had reached Washington Sunday night, continued to spread. On election day and throughout the orgy of second-guessing to which all Wednesday was devoted, it circulated around the city like a persistent wisp of smoke, moving mostly among newsmen and publishers and never getting space in the media. Something, it appeared, was going on at one of the electronic news services, a little outfit called Videowire Express Incorporated—something about a big international story that they were about to break. On the strength of it, they were pushing for clients in every direction, but no one seemed to know what the story was, and furthermore, the outfit had a sleazy reputation. Apparently there had been other times when it had made claims that fizzled into nothing. Probably it was merely the dying gasp of another desperate company about to go under and nothing worth losing sleep over.

"Willis, we are bombing out," a scowling Steve Contos said as the two men lounged in the VEI offices after a fruitless telephone conference with the head of the big German network Sudwestfunk. "I can't blame the boys for getting discouraged. People aren't buying our promises. I guess we're paying for our past sins. Everyone is afraid it's just another cheap-shot series." Contos reached for a sales tally sheet. "We've only got seventeen agreements signed, fourteen more tentatives, and maybe twice that who are serious but still on the fence. That's just not enough—maybe $300,000 in gross fees if they all stayed with us."

"But when the subscribers we've got start running the story, that ought to pull a lot of others in, don't you think?" Tauber asked, seeking desperately to protect the grand dreams he had been building over the past days.

"Well, maybe, but it's a hell of a way to run a railroad," Contos grumbled. "I admit I don't see any alternative but to start the releases on schedule. Christ, it's a gamble, though."

"Why not hold up until Friday?" Tauber suggested. "That will give us another twenty-four hours of selling time."

"No, all that would do is confirm the doubts. We'll have to charge ahead. But what we might do if it begins to look a little better after the first installment is hold up on the second one, or just do a rehash of Thursday for the second release. That would give the big systems time to buy in before the heavy material goes out. Meanwhile we'll continue to sell our tails off. I'll tell you this, Willis—you better start burning up the phone lines right along with the rest of us or that contract of ours may not be worth a dime."

Tauber eyed the glum VEI president, then silently hauled himself erect and lumbered toward the outer office and a telephone.

On Thursday morning, November 8, a sleepy-eyed young technician unlocked the heavy tempered-glass door of the Videowire offices and flipped a light switch. He walked over to the five-foot-high electronics rack which held the input equipment and video recorders that fed the Videowire word-and-picture-processing computer. Late Wednesday night Steve Contos had placed a prerecorded cassette in the little video player used to send short special announcements to VEI subscribers. Following the twice-repeated instructions he had got from Contos to initiate distribution of the content of the cassette precisely at 6:00 A.M., the technician whistled softly as he finished programming the computer to repeat the Contos announcement once every half hour. After checking to make sure the video cassette was properly threaded, the young man pressed a red Start button on the automatic sequence timer and the tape began to roll through the machine. It merely confirmed that distribution of the Videowire special series entitled "Project M10—Secret Government Project Revealed" would begin at 11:00 A.M. EST. The tape was only thirty seconds long, but the first tiny pebble of the avalanche that M10 was to become was moving.

The young man strolled over to a desk, shoved to one side the lists and sales notes that cluttered the top of it, opened a white paper bag, and took out a small Thermos of hot coffee and a cheese-filled "Danish" wrapped in wax paper. Through the floor-to-ceiling glass windows he could see that it was already snowing softly, although the morning weather report had predicted no snow until early afternoon and no significant accumulation. He yawned and sipped carefully at the steaming cup in his hand. By the time his lonely breakfast was finished, the Videowire announcement had traversed the globe and had been duly stored in the robot recording equipment of VEI subscribers across America and in six foreign countries. The total number of people the system served numbered approximately fifty thousand—about the population of a single smallish town like Hempstead, New York, or perhaps Severomorsk on the frozen Kola Peninsula north of Murmansk.

At his home in Stamford, Connecticut, Steve Contos was dressing, and on this morning for once he was not thinking about how he was going to make his next eight-hundred-dollar mortgage payment. This was a day for a businesslike look. Dark wool pin stripe, light-blue shirt, red-and-blue tie. No sense looking like a crapshooter even though that's what you're doing, he thought, nervously combing his glossy jet-black hair for the second time. He patted the pocket of his suit coat to make sure he had his cigar case and shouted an automatic good-bye to his still-sleeping wife, then dashed for the commuter station without stopping for his usual hamburger-and-eggs breakfast down the hill at the Woodfield Inn.

Contos was tired. Along with the rest of his sales team, he'd worked until almost 3:00 A.M., pressing for sales so hard that his hand still ached from squeezing the telephone handset. A few more subscribers had joined him—dubious, reluctant, and not enough. Staring at his image reflected in the train window, he practiced smiling confidently. Yes, it would all work out fine. Yes, he'd pick up clients in bunches after the first release hit. Maybe he could even raise his rates. Their contracts were all cancelable in just three months, so why wouldn't they go along? Contos stopped practicing his smiles. If the M10 series didn't go over big, he'd be out of business in less than a month. As his commuter train eased away from the empty platform at Greenwich, he looked up toward the glowering snow-filled sky and prayed.

Thursday, 11:00 A.M. Moving at the speed of light through the earth's gigantic nervous system of undersea cables and telephone lines, through the communications satellites hovering in the vacuum of space, and over the microwave relays that leaped the continents, the first lines of the Videowire story flashed across the world. Phototypesetters hummed into action, composing electronic newspaper copy at the baker's dozen of small newspapers that carried VEI releases. Another few dozen all-electronic video news distribution systems began preparations to channel the story to TV sets in private homes and offices. The secret of M10 was now flowing out into the open from Videowire's New York offices at the rate of five hundred words per second.

COPYRIGHT, VIDEOWIRE EXPRESS INCOPORATED.
NOTICE: NO PORTIONS OF THE FOLLOWING MATERIAL MAY BE REPRODUCED OR DISTRIBUTED BY ANY MECHANICAL, ELECTRONIC, OR OPTICAL MEANS WITHOUT THE EXPRESS WRITTEN PERMISSION OF VEI.
U.S. WAGING SECRET WAR ON RUSSIA! PART ONE OF AN EXCLUSIVE FIVE-PART SERIES BY WILLIS TAUBER. INDISPUTABLE EVIDENCE THAT THE UNITED STATES

IS USING LETHAL BIOMEDICAL AGENTS AGAINST THE
ENTIRE POPULATION OF THE U.S.S.R. HAS BEEN UN-
COVERED BY THIS REPORTER. . . .

Videowire's clients had expected a bombshell and a few
were actually prepared to believe the sales pitch they had
been given, but this was incredible! No one in his right
mind could run such a story from a source with VEI's
history. In the VEI offices, telephones were instantly
jammed by worried editors and video-service managers,
screaming for reassurances.

"Contos, I can't run your series unless you give me
names of sources I can check, and I mean right now!"

"Contos, do you have any idea what they can do to you
under the new FCC regulations if you can't back this
stuff up?"

"Contos, what the hell is this bullshit? Are you trying
to start a war?"

Perhaps the conversation with the ex-sheep rancher and
copper miner who controlled Austranews, an embryonic
cable-news system in Sydney, was most typical. Certainly
it was among the most gentlemanly.

"Mr. Contos, I'm afraid we'll want to hold up this
Willis Tauber material you're currently running until
we see the whole of it. I've done a bit of investigating
about VEI after our people bought your service and
frankly, I'm not at all sure we wish to be associated with
you."

"I assure you, Mr. Brightson, the M10 story is legitimate."

"Perhaps so. In which case I'm not certain it should
be told to the world just yet. In any event, sir, I should
like to consider our verbal contract with your salesman
as open to renegotiation or cancellation after we've received all of the installments, provided, of course, we do
not use the series."

"As you wish, Mr. Brightson. That seems entirely fair."

Contos hung up the phone, breaking the transpacific
connection. "The frightened little sonofabitch!" he said,
pounding his desk.

Later analysis of the events surrounding Videowire's
first release on M10 showed that only nine subscriber
systems were apparently willing to risk everything, in-

cluding the wrath of the FCC enforcing its new regulations on responsible use of telecommunications media. They picked up the copyrighted story and ran it "Subject to confirmation—may hold up."

In Washington, John Schotty was starting an early lunch in the dark-wood-and-white-linen surroundings of Chez Camette with Senator Tom Lynch of Texas. A colleague from United Press approached their table just as Schotty was taking a first sip of his Bloody Mary. "John, how are you? Say, when did your buddy Tauber decide to join that crummy Videowire outfit?"

Schotty nearly dropped his drink. "What? What are you talking about?"

"That cancer war baloney your partner is writing for Videowire Express in New York."

Now Schotty knew the meaning of those rumors he had picked up about a big story soon to be broken in New York. Now he also knew what Tauber had been doing on his so-called vacation in Florida and why he hadn't come home as scheduled.

Livid with rage, he stumbled toward a telephone and dialed Tauber's apartment, knowing there would be no answer, but having to do something. Moments later he was shouting over long distance at the Videowire receptionist in New York. The girl flinched at the stream of invective but remained calm and followed her instructions. Over and over again, she repeated her quiet answer, "Mr. Willis Tauber is not at Videowire and is not expected."

At the White House, Frederick Donley had slept late while his wife had gone downstairs to meet with the staff about preparations for vacating their quarters. Falling asleep had not been easy for the President, and for one of the few times in his long career, he had resorted to sleeping pills. His defeat and the end of the great ideas to which he had planned to give so much of himself had emptied his life. And on top of everything else, there was the unspeakable sickness of M10 which would inevitably have to be dealt with in the closing days of his term.

According to the official log of telephone calls received by the President for the day, Jim Willoughby dialed him only eighteen minutes after the VEI release on M10 was first distributed. The unrelenting buzz of his green bedside phone pulled the groggy Donley toward wakefulness as he felt around in the darkened room for the handset.

"Mr. President?"

"Yes."

"Mr. President, are you awake, sir?" Jim Willoughby's voice sounded both insistent and frightened. "Mr. President, I'm sorry to disturb you but I'm afraid we have a major problem."

Willoughby's last words tore through the soft gray veil of the sleeping pills.

"Details, Jim," Donley snapped. "I'm awake."

"The press monitors at State just sent a story over here via the video intercom that is running out of New York. They didn't know what it meant so they wanted to check with us. It's by some little news service that usually handles scandal and sex junk. Maybe you'll remember them from the FCC hearings a year or two ago. They call themselves Videowire Express."

"So what's the problem? Give me the bottom line."

"They're carrying a story about M10, sir."

"What!"

"I'm afraid so. It's billed as the first of a five-part series and—get this, Mr. President—it's by Willis Tauber, John Schotty's assistant, the man our FBI surveillance team has been looking all over the Florida Keys for."

Tension and anger sent a wave of nausea through the President's stomach. If the man Tauber had been within reach, Donley would have struck him with all the force he could have summoned. "Where is John Schotty in this?" he asked, with cold fury in his voice.

"I dunno. We've had a surveillance team on him ever since your meeting with him before the election. He's not left town. He hasn't done anything suspicious. Could be Tauber sold him out."

"All right, we'll get back to that later," Donley said grimly. "How bad is the story? How much detail?"

"It's bad, sir, but it could be worse. VEI doesn't have a large following anymore so it isn't getting much play yet. But if you read between the lines, it's obvious that Tauber's going to march right through the whole Clayton report. It's about five thousand words. Shall I put it through on Channel 80?"

"Okay," the President said, "and then meet me in the Crisis Center in fifteen minutes. Does Charley know yet?"

"Yes, sir. He's here with me now. We'll see you downstairs."

The President leaned his long body over to his nightstand, shoved aside the old Thomas Harris novel he had been trying to use the night before to help him fall asleep, and flipped a switch. One of six TV monitors that covered the far wall of his bedroom flashed brightly, then settled into a dull, expectant glow. A text began to scroll up from the lower edge of the screen and a stream of strange, wrong-looking words filled Frederick Donley's eyes: PROJECT M10 . . . RUSSIA . . . CANCER-INDUCING BIOMEDICAL AGENTS. . . . The terrible shock of final realization pounded against his senses. The secret was out.

Donley fell back against the soft, warm comfort of the pillows, his eyes closed, a quick pounding in his chest and at his temples. Opening his eyes again, he was almost surprised to find the White House bedroom still there and the madness of the television set still there also. In the silver half light of the room, the dancing white of the moving text was strangely out of place—too cheerful, too animated. The individual words seemed no more important than if they were conveying the latest stock reports, but to Donley they meant a crashing of worlds. The roaring in his ears increased abruptly and a mounting tide of vertigo swept through him. Struggling to regain his composure, he rose to one elbow and squinted in the direction of the flickering TV image. The text of the Tauber story had just ended and was starting over again. Without warning, the nausea leaped in a crescendo and shapes in the room began to weave crazily. A quick, sharp pain raced up the left side of his head, thudding furiously. Was it a heart attack? Control it, he thought fearfully. Fight it down. Relax. Breathe deeply. Nausea was storming over him like a great yellow-green wave. Weak and trembling, soaked with cold sweat, he bolted from the bed and raced for the bathroom. Hanging his head over the toilet, he fought back again, unwilling to give in. Then, finally—in huge, wrenching spasms—he vomited.

Although, to his distorted sense of time, it was much longer, Donley's writhing stomach began to calm in seconds and he eased himself weakly over to the sink, twisted on the cold-water tap, and splashed the icy liquid against his face, letting the coolness cascade down his neck and chest. That was better, much better. He stood erect and studied himself in the mirror, feeling suddenly old and feeble, trying to decide whether to leave the bathroom and dress to go downstairs. Not yet, not quite yet, he thought. No sense getting sick in front of the others at a time like this. He was shivering as he walked slowly back to the comfort of his bed, peeling off his wet and clammy pajama top on the way. Give yourself ten minutes more. It won't make any difference.

For Donley, the last two days had required Herculean self-control. His defeat, the first political loss he had ever suffered, had been shattering, although not entirely unexpected in view of the final preelection polls, which had shown an electorate divided almost exactly in half. Nevertheless, the broad, smooth highway of his life had ended abruptly at a chasm—a chasm of the unknown, the unplanned for, the unanticipated. He was not accustomed to losing and the shock of it had tested him almost to the breaking point. An hour before his concession speech and for the first time since he and Laura were young lovers, he had cried with her—put his arm around her, put his great leonine head down on her shoulder, and cried. The tears were no longer visible when he bravely congratulated Boyce Williamson on election night, but Laura could see that something very important was gone from behind his eyes, though they were dry and he was smiling.

In truth, it had only been in the past twenty-four hours that he had finally conquered his bitterness and self-pity —both strange emotions to him—and had begun to adjust to the idea of living and working through the weeks until Boyce Williamson was inaugurated. He had reestablished the strong self-image of the man he wanted to be. He had been a leader; it was necessary to him to remain one—even in defeat. Since he was twelve years old, almost from the exact day his grandfather died and left "the youngster" thirty million dollars' worth of Donley-Pioneer Oil stock, he had thought of himself always as pointing the way, directing, urging, achieving. Both his friends and his enemies would have used these same phrases, plus one more: "persuasively decisive," to describe him and what he did to and for those with whom he worked. He exuded an aura

—a certain dimension and way of thinking—that made it easy for people to follow him. Having recovered his equilibrium, he was not willing to stop being that kind of man now. In characteristic manner, he had started thinking about how best to organize the transition, how to smooth Williamson's way into power, and how to help his successor deal with the ugliness of M10 in a nonpartisan way.

It is true that he had briefly considered just relaxing and enjoying all the perquisites of his office, which he had been too busy to exploit before. But that was not his style and he knew it immediately. Nor did it make sense to launch a flurry of projects during the last moments of his term. Williamson would have his own ideas and there was no rational point in starting anything new. No, the logical role for him, the only one he could be comfortable in, was working constructively with the President-elect, a man he respected for his drive but whose consistency he doubted. Regardless of his formless concerns, his policy would be to cooperate fully with Williamson for the sake of his country. He had even convinced himself that he and Williamson, working carefully and cautiously, could develop some kind of accommodation with the Soviets if his worst fears about M10 proved true upon detailed and extended examination. And if that could be achieved—he was not clear exactly how—he could next turn to the problems of regrouping his party and go all out in another assault on the White House in four years' time.

Such, at least, had been Frederick Donley's plans until Jim Willoughby called him. Now those ideas for the forthcoming phase of his political life were grotesque absurdities and, instead, he was to be chained naked and unprepared to the festering sore called M10. It did not matter that he had known nothing about it, nor did it matter that whoever was behind it was not acting for the United States government. That the plot had also run undetected through the administrations of his predecessors was irrelevant. History is a harsh judge and what mattered was that M10, instead of being brought out in a carefully orchestrated fashion, with the problem and solutions announced together, was to burst upon an unprepared, dangerously overreacting world while he was at the head of his country. M10, regardless of its final disposition, was a curse from which he would never escape.

Donley rolled his body to one side, pushing away the slowly returning nausea. Fixing his eyes on a thin line of light at the edge of the dark shade on his bedroom window, he tried to anchor himself to the steady white streak as the darker corners of the room started to float amorphously. The nausea worsened. He recalled a trick he used as a child in Austin when he was sick to his stomach—a series of very deep breaths, each one let out as slowly as possible. That helped; the nausea retreated and he could think again. What could he do to head off the stampede, the headlong panic that M10 could trigger? How should he deal with the Russians? What would they do when they learned of M10? At that instant, and in the deepest part of him, he accepted the blunt truth for the first time: He and his country might be only minutes from disaster even as he lay there.

Shifting farther to one side in the warm bed and pressing a cheek down into the comfort of the pillow, he saw his travertine-and-rosewood night table with its two phones: the green for relatively ordinary matters, and the red, which rang only when the unthinkable might happen. During his forty-six months in the White House, the red phone had rung only for tests, never in an actual emergency. In many ways, before the twin disasters of M10 and his election defeat, Donley had been a fortunate President. His term in office had spanned one of those unusual times in world history in which there had been no significant shooting wars nor, except for recent sputterings in Burma, even a credible threat of one. Now, in an ultimate irony, his administration—"the great peace of the Donley era," as he had called it during his campaign—was likely to end in the explosion of a thousand hydrogen bombs.

What was the probability of any other result? he asked of himself. When the Russians learned what M10 was doing to them, their reaction was likely to be instantaneous, massive, and deadly. Donley understood the Russians very well, having studied their history carefully and dealt with them often during his term. Overwhelming strength and fury was their style of reaction. Although he had made great progress in other issues, his disarmament negotiations always had stumbled when he wanted the Soviets to scale down their very largest weapons systems—the basic tools of their rage. And if they did react, he mused, what would

I do? What would I *really* do? Could I give the orders that
would end the lives of millions or perhaps billions of
people? Reaching out his hand, he ran his fingers over
the smooth plastic of the red telephone and wondered.

When he was first elected President, leaving the relatively easy life he and Laura had enjoyed while he was
governor of Texas, a rich and happy life insulated from
most problems by thick pads of dollars generated by Texas
oil, he had thought frequently about the red phone. Why
not, he had once suggested with gallows humor to Jim
Willoughby, mount a death's head on the thing instead of
leaving it so innocent-looking? In the early months, during
the briefings and the procedural drills filled with megatons
and MIRVs and MARVs, the whole lexicon of atomic
death and destruction, he sometimes caught himself making comforting rationalizations. These were merely
projects and plans that had to be carried forward. As the
DOD people were always saying, the United States could
not become a second-rate power because political pressure,
whatever its lofty motives, could be too easily ignored
without military might behind it—but all the projects, all
the appropriations, all the statistics, were just that: projects, appropriations, statistics. They were never truly steps
on a path toward the red phone—never, until now. At
night, with Laura sleeping at his side, he would try to comprehend how it would feel to use the red phone in anger
or in ultimate despair. In those dark moments, as now,
the instrument was no longer merely a telephone but rather
a symbol, as the cross of Christianity and the Satanic head
of the devil are symbols—invested with the same awful
omnipotence and incomprehensibility. Could I use the
power? he asked himself again as he lay there on his bed.
Yes, I could, he answered.

19

On Sofiyskaya Quay, near the British Embassy in Moscow,
there is a roughly constructed poured-concrete building.
Built only a scant year after World War II ended, with the
poorest of materials and more manpower than machinery,

it is six stories high and from it one can see the ancient walls of the Kremlin across the river. On the third floor of the building is a room where shifts of intelligence clerks work twenty-four hours a day. Most of them have grown oblivious to the buzzing old fluorescent lights and the cold of the musty office. Monitoring and summarizing world news for relay to Premier Alexei Stepanovich Kirov and other important members of the Soviet hierarchy is their task and they do it with precision and pride.

One of the clerks on duty the night of November 8 was a heartsick twenty-two-year-old lieutenant who had just returned from a week's home leave in the Black Sea port of Odessa. The thin, blond young man was upset for several reasons. First, there were the arguments with his fiancée, who refused to set a specific date for their wedding. Second, his own mother had taken every opportunity his visit had afforded to express her disapproval of the girl, whose reputation for being a "little easy" was widely known all along the cobblestoned run of Sochi Street. Finally, now that he was back in Moscow, the dreary weather of the capital had made him wish desperately to be home again at the edge of the warm sea, even if it did mean more fighting with both his mother and his girl.

He was forlornly fingering the small oval frame of a photo of his sweetheart when a hand landed heavily on his shoulder, jarring him out of his reverie. The hand was attached to a uniformed arm, which, unfortunately for the lieutenant, was encircled with several rows of gold braid and belonged to the senior colonel in charge of the Press Intelligence Section. As the young man realized the moment he turned to face the humorless scowl of his superior officer, it was past the time for filing the midevening news summary. Burning with embarrassment, he shuffled the little portrait of his girl into a drawer and began to paw furiously through stacks of press reports. Using computer analysis methods that searched for Key Words in Context—much like the so-called KWIC system developed years earlier in the United States—the Soviets could easily find and isolate any stories in which topics listed in the computer instructions were mentioned. News items or features using terms such as "Cruise Missile," "ICBM," "Soviet Union," "Premier Kirov," or any of approximately 3,500 other "flags" were automatically stored by the

machine and also forwarded to the third floor on Sofiyskaya
Quay for further assessment. The Videowire release on
M10 was Number 27 in a group of forty-six items that had
accumulated since the early-evening report was filed at
5:00 P.M. Moscow time. When the young lieutenant began
to read it, he promptly forgot about the ugly weather, his
mother, and his fiancée.

As closely as can be ascertained, it was through the
Sofiyskaya Quay facility that knowledge of the existence
of M10 first reached the leaders of the Soviet Union.
Apparently, during the many years it was operational, no
inkling of the project had ever filtered into a single Russian
intelligence assessment prior to the initial VEI release.
Remarkably, however, the Russian press monitors forwarded their preliminary but formal comments about the
Videowire story headed with a date-time group which
read: 11082024M—eleventh month, eighth day, 2024
hours (hence 8:24 P.M.) Moscow time. The time difference
between Moscow and the U.S. East Coast is eight hours.
Only eighty-four minutes had, therefore, elapsed between
the time when Steve Contos anxiously entered a "Distribute" command into the computer at his office in New
York and the time when the Soviet intelligence apparatus
began to react. Later in the evening, this reaction culmi-
nated in a long encrypted message to the Soviet head of
state, carrying both the full text of the VEI story and
several pages of comments by the Chief of Intelligence,
General Vasily A. Levrov, regarding the nature and history
of the American entity Videowire Express Incorporated.

Ordinarily, a document considered to be of such importance would have been delivered to Premier Kirov by
Kremlin courier, but on this occasion, the Soviet leader was
not in the capital, having started a diplomatic visit to
Yugoslavia two days earlier. Alexei Kirov, like his peasant
grandfather, loved to hunt, and he, the Yugoslavian
president, and a party of nearly twenty high officials from
both countries had settled in at a comfortable state-run
hunting lodge overlooking one of the sixteen placidly
beautiful lakes of Plitvice in the heart of Croatia. The long
cable from the Intelligence Section in Moscow was decoded
in the temporary Soviet communications center in a timber-
walled first-floor room at the lodge, whose normal floor
space was reduced almost to half by great stacks of

firewood. It was handed to the sleepy Soviet Premier about 11:30 P.M. and did what the rain had already been threatening to do. It completely ruined his holiday plans.

Somewhat under 1800 miles to the north of Croatia and almost on the same line of latitude, the night was much clearer, but very cold—minus eighteen degrees Celsius and going down—as the director general of the Royal Nobel Institute of Cytobiology in Stockholm arrived at his home. He was a bit tired but otherwise content. The day had been a good one, he decided, as an elevator of teak and stainless steel vaulted him high above the city to a skyscraper apartment at Danviksklippan, which cost too much, but which overlooked the city from the south and gave him a view so breathtaking he was willing to pay dearly for it. To the cozy sounds of his wife's rustling about the kitchen preparing their evening meal, the director poured himself a small glass of dry sherry, relaxed into a sling chair, and flipped his TV remote control to video news service from Channel 39—the city's latest experiment in providing "a worldview," as the Swedish planners had put it. Signals from Kahnäs Tower, Stockholm's 426-foot-high television antenna, leaped into the room. Ten minutes later, when their smörgås was ready, the director's wife called to him. Instead of answering, he remained in the living room, his face furrowed with thought. It was almost thirty minutes before he was willing to leave the television set to join his thoroughly chagrined wife, and throughout the meal, for reasons which he would not tell her, he only toyed with his sandwich. Most of the time he gazed past her into space and said nothing.

20

Although he was on a secure line, Jim Willoughby, his tie off and his white shirt open at the collar, cupped his hand over the telephone with the reflex action people use when switching a conversation away from the distant party to someone nearby. "He's out on a picnic," he whispered. "They left about two hours ago and were going up toward the Wildwater Canyon. It will take our people about an hour and a half to get a message to him. They've got a detail with him, but their portable radio gear won't work because of the hills. Is that too long or should I order in a helicopter from someplace to go and get him?"

"No, no need for that. It'll cause too big a stir," President Donley replied. "We'll use the time to boil down our options and he can still be here by this evening sometime, so I can brief him. Tell them to send a car and also tell them to keep the whole operation quiet. Have them call us here via the car radiotelephone as soon as they get to a place where it will work."

The "them" to whom Willoughby proceeded to relay the President's orders were those members of C. Boyce Williamson's new Secret Service detail who remained behind when the President-elect left the Executive Suite at Huntley Lodge, Big Sky, Montana, in a small, snow-tired motorcade and headed for a winter picnic in a beautiful and unspoiled backwoods area known mostly to the local people in and around Bozeman. The senior senator from California, who two days earlier had defeated Frederick Donley for the office of President of the United States by only 581,000 votes, had started a ten-day rest and wanted no more of crowds and speeches for a while. Drawn as much by the early-season isolation to be found near the top of the Andesite Mountain ski runs as by the deep virgin powder snow that a series of heavy November storms had provided, Boyce Williamson had spent all of Wednesday afternoon hurling his wiry five-foot-ten-inch body down the slopes with more daring than the quiet and well-tailored young men of the Secret Service, who had joined him an hour after Donley's concession speech, would have liked. On Thursday, the soon-to-be forty-third President was paying for his sins of excess with two aching legs, a blister above his right ankle from an ill-fitting ski boot, and a host of minor sore spots. He was very happy to settle for the milder sport of a picnic in the gorgeous little canyon outside Bozeman, preceded by a search (from the comfort of his limousine) for the distant black spots that meant elk or bear feeding in the endless fields of white snow.

The orgy of activity of the previous day had been a kind of celebration for Williamson, a slashing, roaring victory dance of almost out-of-control skiing. Today, he promised himself, rubbing his legs, would see a quieter observance of his triumph. Nevertheless, he could still hardly contain his joy nor could he yet truly assimilate the idea that he had won. He had won! When the Secret Service first threw a full-scale protective cloak around him and his family, his intellect had agreed with the TV commentators—yes, he had won the election—but emotionally he had retained and guarded his childlike doubts and fears. *The candy is too good. There is too much and it is too wonderful. Someone will take it away from you.*

Those who were to start the process of turning Boyce Williamson's sweet victory into a nightmare of terror skidded around a sharp turn and into view along the Wildwater Canyon Road just as he was snatching his third piping-hot baking powder biscuit from the black iron campfire oven. The doors of the auto in which they came bore a white legend in small block print: U.S. GOVERNMENT —OFFICIAL BUSINESS. As the car ground to a stop on the gravel and mud of the road above the densely wooded picnic site, a man leaped out. He crashed noisily through the brittle black branches of the dormant undergrowth toward the President-elect's party. "Mr. Williamson, sir," he said, panting clouds of vapor into the cold, bright air, "I have an urgent request from the President. . . ."

Twenty minutes of driving back over the rugged canyon road were required before the radiotelephone unit in the car carrying Williamson to Big Sky could penetrate the craggy, snow-covered rocks and forests that crowded tightly around the frozen stream along which the road was built. The connection was still marginal whenever the twists and turns of the laboring car shadowed the radio system with huge blocks of stone, but in spite of the fading, Williamson clearly understood the President's carefully chosen words and sensed the urgency in his voice.

"We'll have an Air Force jet pick you up at Bozeman. It should arrive before you do," the President concluded, ending a terse monologue that told Williamson little beyond the fact that it was crucially important for him to get to Washington as soon and as quietly as possible.

"Okay," Williamson agreed, wondering exactly how serious the problem was. "I'll leave Annie and Mary Ann at the lodge for now. It will allay any rumors. After we talk, though, I may want to send for them, depending on what this is all about."

"Understood, Boyce. I'll see you this evening," the President replied, and Williamson's receiver crackled with the empty sounds of a terminated connection, leaving him to ponder the meaning of "international problem . . ." "No immediate crisis, but one could develop quickly . . ." "I want you fully informed . . ." and the other vague but ominous generalities that Donley had been willing to give him over the phone. Was this the start of some kind of political grandstanding to show how cooperative the defeated administration was going to be? Did Donley think he could use his famous persuasiveness better in person at the White House than in long-distance dealings with his successor? And if so, about *what?* How serious could the situation be?

Watching the dark-green pine trees whip past his car window as the driver raced along the well-plowed highway 191 toward Big Sky, Williamson suddenly sensed something strange. It was there around him . . . something dense and shapeless . . . something newly growing . . . a feeling. Forcing himself to seek it out, he realized it was not a single element but an amalgam of several—a fresh awareness of the immensity of the power of the office he had won, a new perception of the crushing responsibilities he was now to face, and underlying both, a building foreboding which stayed with him through his packing, the hasty but purposely casual thank yous and good-byes at Big Sky, and the fast drive back to Bozeman airport. As he boarded the waiting Air Force jet and strapped himself into his place for the three-hour flight to Washington, the feeling was still there, like a passenger in the next seat.

21

Behind the calm façade maintained by the White House throughout Thursday and into Thursday evening, shielded from occasional inquiries about "that wild story" by statements like "No official comment yet, and there may never be any; I personally think it's obviously more of

Videowire's usual nonsense" from the White House press secretary, there had been feverish activity and a long series of extraordinary conferences, mostly in the Oval Office itself, each attended by very quiet, very serious men.

On his occasional leg-stretching walks through the colonnaded corridor of the West Wing, the President had watched the sky gradually darken toward night and the streetlights come to life along the distant avenues. The bleak depression that had engulfed him early in the day had only deepened as he sat through meeting after fruitless meeting in which the conclusions had always been the same. He was caught in a monstrous trap from which, in spite of all of the power of his office, there seemed to be no honorable escape: If he acted to suppress the next Videowire releases, he would instantly confirm the existence of M10. If he did nothing, he was laying the nation open to uncontrolled Soviet vengeance—a vengeance that could mean mutual nuclear suicide.

Significantly, in the waning hours of Thursday and on into the early morning of Friday, Moscow time, no mention of the Videowire story appeared on Soviet television or in Soviet newspapers. The American Embassy at 19/21 Tchaikovsky Street, acting under secret orders from the Director of Central Intelligence and the CFI, the Joint Committee on Foreign Intelligence, was, of course, constantly monitoring all Soviet newspapers and broadcasts. Via facsimile machines operating through satellite channels, it had obediently relayed copies of anything remotely relevant to U.S.-Soviet relations directly to the White House and to the hulking marble-lined CIA headquarters building hidden behind a wooded hill just outside Washington. But there was nothing of more than routine interest in the constant stream of reports from Tchaikovsky Street. To President Donley and his associates, the silence in the Soviet press and on Soviet electronic media was deafening. Despite a Videowire release that had reached at least ten thousand people, to the Russian man in the street, and perhaps to most of the Russian government, M10 simply did not exist—at least not yet.

Repeatedly in the many meetings they shared on Thursday, President Donley had turned to Charles Frydon with the same question: "Are you sure there's nothing? Are you sure there's nothing anywhere?" And repeatedly the imperturbable Frydon had looked back over his glasses at the President and slowly shaken his bald head in the negative. During one break in the day's nonstop strategy sessions, while Mike Kallen briefed the other service chiefs and Jim Willoughby went off to check the latest surveillance summaries on Willis Tauber and Steve Contos, the President asked his question again. He got the same answer.

"Mr. President, according to every CFI report I have, the Soviets are apparently either ignoring the situation, which I doubt, or quashing the whole thing so completely that not one word is getting out. They are scared to death of it, too. There's no other reasonable interpretation."

The President sat up abruptly and nodded vigorously. "Dammit, that does become more and more convincing as the answer. We've been saying it is a logical Soviet response all day long. Perhaps it's about time we'd better believe it." Full of nervous energy, Donley pressed his palms tightly together. "If you were the Russians, what would you want—a nuclear war? Unthinkable. What you would want is for M10 just to go away or, at a minimum, you'd want a low profile on it until you knew all of the story and could arrange to control the reactions of your population. I agree with you. *That's* why we're seeing nothing in their press. They are trying, at least for now, to hush it up to avoid absolute pandemonium. It seems to me their first concern has got to be that. If their people begin to believe they've been under biomedical attack all these years, they could tear the whole country apart and Kirov couldn't stop them. The whole Soviet power structure could topple before they even got around to deciding how to retaliate against us."

"That very well seems to be the situation," Frydon concurred, "and if so, we are under even more pressure to stop the story now, before the second VEI installment digs us in deeper."

"On what grounds, Charley? We've been around and around on that, too. If we trample all over the First Amendment to shut Tauber and Contos up, everyone will be howling to know why and we will focus the whole country on M10 instead of just the few who normally read the trash Videowire spews out. We'll prove that this time, for once, they do have a real story."

"And that will mean the whole thing breaks open all the sooner and certainly before Kirov can prepare his population so they don't go berserk and force his hand," Frydon added, arguing against himself, as he often did before coming to a final conclusion. "But what if we use that idea we were discussing earlier—announce that the Clayton report was merely a *theoretical* study, not anything that was ever implemented, and also stop the further Videowire installments on national security grounds? That might get both us and the Soviet leaders another forty-eight hours or so." Frydon shrugged. "I'll admit it's a long shot, but the other alternatives are worse."

The President was about to respond when the door to the Oval Office opened. Willoughby and Kallen were returning from their errands.

"Well, they're still selling the hell out of it at Videowire," said Willoughby, flopping onto one of the two green-and-white-striped sofas near the fireplace opposite the President's big desk. "But it's just possible we'll be luckier than we deserve to be. Our on-site reports and phone surveillance all indicate people still aren't convinced their M10 material is legitimate. The clients are dragging their feet."

"That won't last," Frydon observed.

"I know," agreed Willoughby grimly. "However, the phone taps support our thought that Tauber and Contos are protecting the real guts of the story. It doesn't sound like they've even told their salesmen much beyond what is in the first installment—generalities and possibilities mostly, with not much hard data."

"And that won't last, either," Charley Frydon said, echoing his previous comment.

"Where are our two good friends now?" the President interjected.

"At dinner at Chez Pierre, with the head of the American bureau for Associated News Service of England."

"Ugh! Where's John Schotty?"

"Still at his sister's house, sir. I think he's calmed down, but perhaps not enough. He could still take off for New York at any time to strangle Tauber."

"He gave me his solemn promise he wouldn't do anything without clearing with us first," said Donley. "I trust that man. He's played it straight so far.

"Besides, he knows Charley's got two of his buddies from the FBI practically right outside his sister's door," Kallen observed with a cynical little chuckle.

"Be that as it may, I trust him," said the President, checking his wristwatch. "Boyce Williamson ought to be landing in a few minutes and I want to have a well-defined set of actions to discuss with him. I intend to make the decisions—I hope he'll go along with what I decide—but in any case, he'll be fully informed. Mike, what did the JCS have to say about current Soviet military posture?"

"All quiet, sir. Absolutely routine." Years of training made the four-star Air Force general stiffen slightly as he answered his Commander in Chief. "We recommend keeping our forces at routine, too, of course."

"And the JCS consensus on a hot-line contact with Kirov?" the President asked.

"We haven't got a consensus on that one, I'm afraid. It's an even split. Two suggest doing it right away. Two want to wait and see. I think they're hoping you'll come up with a way to handle it so well that everything will just fade away."

"All right, we'll come back to the hot-line issue," the President said. "Let's review the bidding on Videowire itself. First, we could ignore them—perhaps call the whole story a hoax. Second, we could acknowledge M10 as a theoretical study only. Third, we could shut them off officially for national security reasons. Fourth, we could detain them and try to plant a suitable cover story about their absence. Any other possibilities?" Donley paused and checked the faces of his three companions—Willoughby, slouched on the end of his spine on the sofa; Kallen, in a Queen Anne chair beside a huge world globe near the doors to the rain-drenched Rose Garden; and Charles Frydon, leaning almost casually against the mantel of the fireplace. A heavy silence saturated the room. The time for a crucial decision was almost at hand.

"I think," Frydon said, wiping the lenses of his glasses with his handkerchief again, "it's got to be number one or number two. You are right: shutting Videowire down for *any* reason will cause a sensation and everyone from the networks and the *New York Times* to the *Podunk Press* will be all over us in minutes; whereas now—as we must keep reminding ourselves—M10 is in the same junk-news category as that Los Angeles sex-ring story VEI ran last week."

"And what happens when they hit the streets with the whole Clayton report?" asked Willoughby rhetorically. "There are so many solid details in it, their credibility will take a big jump."

"True," Frydon acknowledged, "but our objective is not total and permanent containment; we know that's hopeless. Our objective is to prevent a panic here and a damned holocaust in Moscow. We've got to have time to develop an accommodation—some kind of acceptable way out for Kirov. We're only going to get a few days at best. The question is which way to do it."

"In that context, I think Charley's right," said the President. "It's got to be handled with a light touch, for a time anyhow. After that, all bets may be off, depending on Kirov."

"I'm sorry, I think you fellas are dead wrong," General Kallen declared, shaking his head. "We ought to take a good close look at the covert-action option with some sort of diversionary story. That could also give us some time, and more importantly, it would put off the release of the details from the Clayton report."

Donley was unconvinced. "But what makes you think it would work, Mike?"

"Say we detain Contos, Tauber, and their key staff in some secure place for a few days. And suppose we put our own people into the Videowire offices and announce that a new negotiation with some unnamed company which is interested in buying out VEI makes it prudent to hold up 'our' M10 releases for a while."

"Damned clever, damned clever, but you really mean their whole staff?" queried Willoughby. "Kidnap them all?"

"Hell, yes. Why not? We're dealing with dynamite here. If the Soviets go wild, you know what could happen as well as I do."

"Their families—what about their families? We're talking about more than a dozen people," the President observed, as he touched his fingertips to his temples. "I really don't think, quite aside from the ethical issues, that it—" Donley's intercom buzzed and he shifted gears. "Yes, Dorie?"

"Mr. President, two messages: Mr. Williamson has landed at National and the car picked him up in a cargo area about one minute ago. Everything went well. No one at the airport saw who it was. Also, Secretary of State Silverton received your message and is leaving Mexico City in one hour. He should be here by about two A.M."

"What about Bill Howetz? Has he made a decision about coming back?"

"Sir, the SecDef is still in an Autosevocon teleconference with his staff at DOD. I understand he'll make a firm determination shortly, but he's leaning toward staying in Germany for now. He could get from the Eighth Division HQ at Bad Kreuznach to Moscow very quickly if it became necessary for him to serve as an envoy, as you suggested. Meantime, he would use the automatic secure voice net to keep in touch with the Pentagon."

"Okay, break in on that teleconference. Tell Bill I think he's right to stay put. It will also look more like business as usual. When Williamson arrives, send him right in, of course, and make whatever arrangements he wants regarding his sleeping quarters. I'd recommend against Blair House, though. He might be seen too easily." Donley released the switch on his intercom and swung his long legs up onto the corner of his desk. "All right, I think I know what I want. I'm inclined to go with the 'theoretical study' angle, but not the rest. I don't like closing down Videowire and I certainly don't want to start kidnapping scores of people, at least not before I talk to Kirov and take his temperature. That's something I intend to do right after we brief Williamson. He should be here in a few minutes."

"Once you open the subject of M10 with Kirov, things could get out of hand very quickly," General Kallen said softly.

"I know," replied Donley, "but it will have to be done sooner or later and I think I want the initiative. It may help convince him M10 was not the doing of the U.S. government."

"What we really have to do is find the idiots who *are* behind it," Kallen growled. "It's hard for me to understand why we can't pin that down after a week of trying."

"They are very clever people, as you well know, Mike. And they're obviously insiders, high up," Frydon said. "Maybe very high up," he added with emphasis.

"Like who dammit?" Kallen snapped, thinking more

about what the Donley confrontation with Kirov might precipitate than about what he was saying.

The CIA Director felt the steel-spring tension in Kallen's tone. "I'm sure we'll get them, but perhaps not for some days," he said soothingly. "Remember, we went easy before last Tuesday. We've just added a fourth FBI/CIA task force to the job—any more people and we'd be risking a major leak. We'll get them. The ACA codes are giving us fantastic help."

"Are you sure we dare not put more people on it?" the President asked. "If I could tell the Soviets how it happened—who is doing it—I'd be in a much better position. After the initial shock is controlled, Kirov will need information to stop the toxins from coming in just as much as he'll need a proposal on compensation for the damage already done."

Frydon nodded. "I understand and I'll check again, but I think we're at maximum safe levels already. We're using nearly a hundred agents—almost every one of our Sigma Six or equivalent clearances."

"Okay, Charley," replied Donley as his intercom buzzer sounded and the paneled door to the Oval Office swung open noiselessly. C. Boyce Williamson, the next President of the United States, walked into the room.

To Frydon, Willoughby, and Kallen, the next hour was exceptionally interesting. It was not because of what was discussed, because they had already heard the facts of Project M10 scores of times in dozens of meetings. What made those sixty minutes so fascinating was the behavior of Boyce Williamson, who, after the usual greetings and amenities, fastened his icy blue eyes on Fred Donley and, for the entire time, never wavered or seemed to blink while the President spread the incredible panorama of the M10 problem before him. If, however, Williamson intended to conceal his emotional reactions to the briefing, then it must be said that he failed. His face was, in fact, a wide-open window to his feelings and it alternated rapidly between ashen gray and dull rose as Donley recounted the details of the long-continued cancer-induction attack on the U.S.S.R.

Finally, after the President summarized intelligence estimates of probable Soviet reactions, explained the

possibility of a raging runaway revolt which could over-
throw Kirov and the few other leaders in that tormented
country who might remain rational, and stressed how such
an eventuality could lead to vengeance strikes on the U.S.
by out-of-control Russian nuclear forces, Williamson seemed to be glowing like candle wax ready to melt beneath
the flame.

It was easy to understand his reaction. Thanks in part
to the leadership of the very man seated before him, now
quietly talking of war, most of his own career in Washington had been concerned with the important but not deadly
issues of peacetime: inflation, unemployment, social in-
justice. He had no way to know that the horror of millions
of artificially induced cancer deaths and the possible ultimate catastrophe of nuclear war would meet him at the
end of his first walk through the hallways of "his" White
House.

No one who knew him would have described Clarence
Boyce Williamson as a simple man. Unlike President
Frederick Donley, who had met him only casually before
the campaign, he was not the beneficiary of family money
but had accumulated a modest personal fortune as the
founder and owner of the San Calientas Vineyards in the
lush Napa Valley wine country of California. As his
financial strength grew—thanks to enthusiastic fans of his
better-than-excellent Chablis and one fortunate encounter
with the leading French wines in a blind tasting held in
Europe which, to the astonishment of Paris and the delight
of Sacramento, the San Calientas won—Williamson's
ambitions grew also.

It seemed almost preordained that Williamson enter
politics. His name was well known in California, he had
many powerful friends, and he had something else politicians liked: flexibility. If any one word might come close
to catching the essence of Williamson, it might be
"mercurial." But no one word could really convey the
nature of the man. He was also self-assured and honest
in his fashion. What kept him from being potentially great
was the fact that he could switch from one set of firmly
held convictions to another with such extraordinary quickness as to appear inconsistent. During his successful run
for the presidency, this was the facet of his personality
that his advisers worked hardest to keep from the public.

And fortunately for Williamson, they did it. In reality, he *was* consistent—consistently in need of shielding his easily bruised ego. Williamson did not enjoy situations in which he did not know more, understand more, initiate more, than anyone else. Not enjoy them? He hated them. They caused him to doubt himself. Rather than endure the pain of that, he would willingly shift his ground or invent improbabilities to reestablish himself. At such times he was given to screening his motives with sharp-tongued sarcasm that bordered on bullying. Strangely, he seldom, if ever, saw his flexibility as weakness or indecisiveness. He did not dare to. It would have hurt too much.

President Frederick Donley finished his lengthy, fact-filled discourse on M10 and looked toward the President-elect, who seemed unwilling or unable to speak. His eyes, although still fastened on Donley, were staring beyond him blankly. The puzzled President looked away in embarrassment, his own eyes coming to rest on the neutral ground of his wristwatch. It was a little after midnight. The public life of Project M10 had entered its second day.

Still the men in the Oval Office waited for a reaction from Williamson—a question, a comment. None came. The stillness became awkward. Suddenly, the shaken President-elect stood up and walked wordlessly out of the room through the tall double doors that led into the darkened colonnade along the West Wing.

It was a full ten minutes before Boyce Williamson returned to the Oval Office and when he reappeared his shoes and short brown hair were soaked from the night rain, but his skin color was nearly normal. "Gentlemen," he said, facing Donley's associates as he dabbed at his forehead. "I would like to speak with the President privately, please, for a short time. *Now*. please."

"Are you involved?" Williamson flung the question at Donley through gritted teeth the instant they were alone.

"No, I am not," the President replied evenly but emphatically. "I told you all I know and how I came to know it."

The two men gazed at each other—measuring, wondering.

"I intend to contact Premier Kirov," said Donley, breaking the mood.

"When?"

"In an hour or so. It will be morning in Moscow."

Williamson thought for a moment. "I want to wait, Fred." It was the first time Williamson had ever addressed the President by his given name and it was a symbol of equality and possibly of the beginning of trust or of a struggle for control. Donley caught the first meaning, hoped for the second, and calculated the likelihood of the third.

"Why wait? Kirov will need our help badly if the analyses and scenarios we've developed are correct."

"I know that, but I need time to think. I want to join you on the hot line and I have to decide where I want to go with whatever happens. It's a fair request—I'll be living with this mess after January, you know. Put yourself in my place and you'll agree."

"I am in your place, Boyce." Donley laughed gently. "Okay, we'll call tomorrow. Meantime, perhaps we'd both better get some sleep."

"I'm not planning to sleep tonight," said Williamson, shaking his head. "I want to read through these documents much more carefully and I've got a couple of ideas. I want to talk personally to John Schotty and Mildred Clayton."

"Are you serious?"

"Yes."

"To check us out, right?"

"Yes, in part."

"Boyce, you've got to remember something. Things are different for you now. You are, or soon will be, the President of the United States. You can't go dashing about interviewing people about this. The press would do handsprings. That's why I've been so circumspect myself."

"I realize that. I'll do it very quietly, and from what you've told me about Schotty, he's safe enough."

"But his sister is a drunk! Futhermore, she knows nothing."

"I'll be careful. Besides, Tauber and Contos are more of a chancy proposition."

"You don't intend to contact them, too? My God, that could be absolutely disastrous. Boyce, I don't want you to do that."

"I'm sorry. I think as President-elect—with that mandate—I might convince them to hold up publication where you could not. Regardless of how I feel about what you've said, to the press you are certainly suspect. M10 happened in your administration."

"Dammit," said Donley, a hint of the peculiar nausea that had assaulted him earlier in the day beginning to return. "I told you M10 was going long before I took office. You can see that for yourself in the Clayton material as well as ours."

"All right, I believe you. But I also believe I'll be able to reason with Tauber and Contos."

"You'll be reasoning with a thief and a scandalmonger."

"Perhaps, but I've got to try. They are, after all, Americans, too. They can't want to precipitate a nuclear war."

"Boyce, don't do it."

"Can you give me a couple of good, well-informed people as aides?" said Williamson, deliberately ignoring Donley's plea.

The President did not answer immediately. The situation was unprecedented. What meaningful force could a President exert on a President-elect? Confronted with the final boundaries of his power, Frederick Donley sagged back into his chair and sighed. "Yes," he replied as the rain fell against the blackness of the bulletproof West Wing windows and glittered brightly in the warm light of the desk lamp.

22

The ringing of the telephone did not awaken John Schotty. Even at 2:00 A.M., two hours after leaving his sister's home, the adrenaline level in his blood remained far too high for sleeping, and he was having considerable trouble convincing himself to stay in bed rather than leap into his car and race to New York to confront Will Tauber. He had no difficulty being dressed and ready at the curb in front of his apartment building a half hour later when the long black limousine drove up, its rear windows covered by opaque shades. Schotty stooped low to enter the back door as it swung open and found himself sitting next to a man about whom he had written often and sometimes critically over the years.

"Good morning, Mr. Schotty. Thank you for accommodating my request." Boyce Williamson flashed a courteous smile and the limousine glided out into the deserted street, followed closely by a second car, carrying four Secret Service agents.

It was over two hours and several slow round trips up and down the George Washington Parkway before the conversation between the columnist and the President-elect turned away from the history of M10 as Schotty knew it and to the matter of a meeting between Williamson and Mrs. Randolph Clayton.

"She has a severe problem with alcoholism, you know," warned Schotty.

"I understand," said Williamson, "but I'd still like to talk to her about things Admiral Clayton might have said and how he behaved in those last few days."

Schotty hesitated, squinting at his watch with eyes beginning to burn from lack of sleep. "If I call her now it will be a real shock. After all, it's four-thirty in the morning."

"These are not ordinary times, Mr. Schotty. Call her, please, and tell her you'll be in front of her house in, say, forty-five minutes. Do not mention me, of course. Tell her it is very important but nothing for her to worry about. Here is the phone."

The President-elect passed the handset of the car telephone across to Schotty, who filled his chest with a deep breath and gave the mobile operator his sister's telephone number. Following what seemed to be an interminable wait, Schotty began speaking earnestly into the mouthpiece with the exaggerated loudness and clarity of someone trying to communicate to a foreigner. He paused for an aside. "She's drunk, I think."

"How drunk?" asked Williamson anxiously.

"I've seen her worse."

"Okay, then tell her to be ready," Williamson ordered. "The sight of me might sober her up," he added lightly as the limousine and its Secret Service escort negotiated quick U-turns across the empty parkway and headed back toward the capital. Half a mile down the road, the little caravan passed a single outbound car moving at high speed and carrying three men. When the lone car reached the turn-around the limousine had used, it, too, reversed its direction, then slowed to match the pace of the government vehicles.

Mildred Clayton stared in wide-eyed astonishment at the man seated on the limousine jump seat in front of her. Meeting the President-elect face to face had, just as he had facetiously predicted, acted much like an ice-cold shower. She was thoroughly awake and alert; the cobwebs of Scotch were gone. Unfortunately for Williamson, twenty minutes of questioning her added little to what he already knew about M10.

"I know," she said again, "he was hard at work on it *or something* before he died. I know he was desperate to get to Denver—I assume to see President Donley. I don't even know that for sure, Mr. Williamson, honestly I don't." Mildred Clayton was repeating herself and running her fingers nervously through her streaky gray hair. Williamson changed the subject slightly.

"Did he ever suggest he was worried about a major scandal or a problem involving the President?"

"No, sir."

"Not in any way? Not even a hint?"

"No, sir. As I said, all I know is—"

"Okay, Mrs. Clayton. You've been very nice to put up with these strange goings-on at this hour and I appreciate it. As we've discussed, I have your word you'll tell no one of our little visit?"

"Of course not. I promised you that."

"By the way, did any reporters try to reach you yesterday after the Videowire story was published?"

"No. No one did."

"What will you tell them if they do?"

"That I don't know what they're talking about."

"Excellent, Mrs. Clayton, excellent. We'll let you and your very patient brother here get home for some sleep now."

The narrow streets of Georgetown had not yet begun to lighten from the faint glow in the eastern sky as Randolph Clayton's widow stepped from the big black automobile and walked toward the door of her home. Once inside, she stripped off her clothes and immediately slipped into the disheveled bed she had left earlier. She lay back, waiting for sleep. It would not come. Finally she groped for the TV remote control. After a fruitless search of empty channels for something to watch, she cut off the frustrating stare of the TV and, in disgust, turned her little bedside clock-radio to an all-night station. The sugar-sweet music and the chatter of the public-service messages didn't help, either. Unwilling to spend the rest of the night tossing around sleeplessly, she threw off the covers with a snort of exasperation and walked naked down the cold stairs to the living room. When she returned to her bed, it was with a bottle of Scotch whose seal had not yet been broken.

While Mildred Clayton was drinking herself to sleep, Boyce Williamson was getting a late surveillance report from Charley Frydon. The CIA Director had been up all night, but behind the bifocal lenses of his glasses, his eyes were very bright and alert, as usual.

"Tauber has just ordered breakfast in his hotel room," said Frydon matter-of-factly. "He's agreed to meet Contos at Videowire at 6:30 A.M .so they can decide what to do. Their last phone conversation was not a happy one. Tauber is blaming the salesmen and the VEI reputation for the relative lack of success they've had with new clients. Contos told Tauber nobody forced him to choose Videowire. They're now debating whether to put more or less detail into the Friday release. More facts would give them less to sell but make it easier. Fewer facts will give them more time but be less convincing to people that they really have a big story."

Williamson nodded. "Can you arrange to pick them up at Videowire and fly them down here to talk to me for an hour or so?"

The question did not take Frydon by surprise. "Of course we can, but I don't recommend it. What do you do if they decide not to cooperate?"

"Yes, that is a legitimate concern," Williamson agreed. "I've admitted that to Donley, as he's probably told you. But you people seem to want to just sit back and do nothing. You've been in this dilemma for over twenty-four hours and all I've heard suggested is a rather weak lie about a 'theoretical' study. I believe in action, not passivity."

"Sometimes," Frydon replied, "it takes more strength and wisdom to do nothing for a time. We need to lay the groundwork with Kirov. That is the first priority."

"We can handle *both* Kirov and the situation here if we do it right. Incidentally, Mr. Frydon, I really don't need the philosophical lecture, and speaking of priorities, I wish you'd put a little priority on finding the perpetrators of this outrage." Williamson looked hard at the self-assured, professorial Frydon. He did not like the man, but he did not understand quite why.

The CIA Director flushed but responded softly. "As far as I am concerned, sir, finding the culprits *is* getting plenty of attention. The wheels are in motion."

"Very well, Frydon, let's quit sparring with each other. I want to speak to Tauber and Contos *this morning* and as early as possible. Then I intend to cooperate with Donley on a hot-line contact with Kirov. Now will you get Tauber and Contos down here from New York?"

"I'll check with the President again," answered Frydon stiffly.

"You do that," growled Williamson.

Frederick Donley was already awake and the telephone in the darkened presidential suite on the top floor of the White House rang only once. He listened for a time, then nodded his head. "Okay, do it. I told him I'd go along with his wishes, at least up to a point. . . . Yes, I know. I told him the same thing. He's trying to help, but I think he's utterly naïve to think Tauber and Contos can be trusted. Then again, he doesn't really trust us, either. I'll be down in about thirty minutes. By the way, can you or Jim make sure Carl Silverton gets a wake-up call? He's only had about three hours of sleep since he got in, and at his age, he might not hear that old alarm clock he insists on carrying." Donley hung up, hoping his whispered conversation hadn't awakened his wife, but as he gazed trancelike for a moment at the shadowy outline of the red phone next to the green one he had just used, Laura Ann Donley stirred in the warmth beside him.

"Why don't you call them back and tell them to leave you alone for a while? You've been up so much already tonight," the President's wife murmured sleepily.

"I'm okay," Donley replied, brushing his lips gently against her silky hair.

"Is it getting worse or better?" she asked in a more fully awake tone, while she busily patted and smoothed the blanket over the two of them as she had done almost every night since they first married.

"That's getting down to essentials," Donley said, chuckling quietly. "I think it's too soon to tell, except that our Mr. Williamson is going to be hard to handle if it comes to a crisis."

"But he's not this country's President; *you* are."

"Only by accident of timing, honey. This could all be his problem, and it will be in just a few weeks, anyhow. Maybe I should give him his head."

Laura sat bolt upright in their bed. "Fred, I know you better than you know yourself. You are going to handle this mess your way, the way you think is right, until the day they inaugurate him. Now admit it."

Donley smiled in the darkness. "I admit it, but it won't be because I want to cling to the job. Boyce is a good, bright man, but he's inexperienced and he's very sure—maybe too sure—of himself. I think he's likely to be a little unsteady in a stormy sea. I've heard he changes positions awfully fast. Furthermore, he doesn't know Kirov or the Pentagon, and he hasn't had four years to find out that sitting in the White House doesn't make you a god. Ha! You remember how I felt in those first days? I thought I could do *anything*!"

"Well, you've done plenty."

"As the old saying goes: If I'm so smart, how come they didn't reelect me?"

"That's how the old saying goes, eh?"

"Around the Donley White House it is."

"Damn! It's good to see you laugh at it a little," Laura said softly as she encircled him in her arms. "I love you, Mr. President. In fact, if I weren't so worried about your not getting enough sleep, I might even try something downright sexy."

During the thirty-five years of their marriage, Laura Ann Donley had never wanted another man. The day she met young Frederick Donley, newly elected state representative, she had decided she would capture him even if it meant abandoning her ambition of being a concert pianist

in the great halls of London, Paris, Vienna—dreams her
teachers at Juilliard and the tutors that had followed had
all assured her were within reach—and she was true to her
decision. She had tilted her blond twenty-two-year-old
head to one side and had whispered to her astonished
mother, "He's the one I think I'll marry." After that she
traveled with him, slept with him, cooked for him, and
loved him. Eighteen months later she married him.

Her hair was no longer blond; it was gray, and she no
longer wore it long and loose but tied it back. Otherwise
the three and a half decades had not changed her much.
She was still a tall, beautiful woman with finely modeled
cheekbones and electric eyes. And she was still in love as
some people—mostly Southern men—say only a Texas
girl can be. Nuzzling down beside the body of her husband,
she listened to his breathing. Something was not quite
right. "Fred, are you okay?" she asked with sudden worry
in her voice.

"Yes, I'm fine," Donley answered. "I'm just debating
that last offer you made me. It's the best thing that's happened all week."

Laura giggled with relief. Nothing was wrong after all.
"I was only kidding, sir. We both know you need some
rest. Now go to sleep."

"I guess you're right," sighed the President, turning on
one side and reaching for his wife's hand. "I guess you're
right." The creeping nausea that had started with the phone
call and grown almost to the point where it threatened to
force him to race for the bathroom had eased. There was
now at least a chance that he might sleep.

23

Looking disgustedly at his expensive but annoyingly un-
reliable wristwatch, Steve Contos was uncertain about
exactly why he was where he was. It was so damned early
in the morning, he hadn't taken time for breakfast, and his
stomach hurt. I'll end up with an ulcer before this is over,
he thought, and decided to send his secretary for some food
as soon as she got in. Across from him, Will Tauber's mas-

sive shoulders seemed even bigger than usual as the unshaven ex-football player leaned silently on the desk, his head propped up by his knobby hands.

"By the way, Willis, without a shave you look like an ugly gorilla," said Contos. "Clients like neat people."

"Don't bug me with that shit," the sleepy Tauber grumbled. "I'll go downstairs to the barbershop when it opens. I need a haircut, anyhow. Now what the hell are we going to do?"

"Frankly, I don't know. I thought for sure that our pre-selling and the first installment would do it. On top of everything else, I've got to call my banker this afternoon and give him a report on new sales. I told him Wednesday that this story was going to solve all our problems, but I figure we need advance fees from at least thirty-six clients more than we've got to cover my loan."

"And if we don't get 'em?"

"Bankruptcy, and you damned well know it, my friend. Bankruptcy."

"Goddammit, Contos." Tauber's words snapped with irritation and lack of sleep. "You should have told me you were that close to the line."

"Now wait just a fucking minute! What the hell do you think I said to you when you first walked into this office?"

Willis Tauber was about to snarl his response to Contos's question when someone tapped hard on the glass doors of the VEI suite.

"Who the hell could that be at this hour?" asked Contos, and he headed toward the outer office. "The sales types are all either on the road or still in bed."

Left alone, Will Tauber walked to the floor-to-ceiling windows that overlooked Sixth Avenue. From the height of the thirty-sixth floor, the occasional taxis and buses of the early morning looked like the tiny Matchbox models he'd played with in his childhood. He swallowed hard. If he had it all to live over, he'd do it so differently. Christ, here he was, forty years old, it was almost all over, and what was he? Even his big gamble with M10 was going to end up just another washout. Tauber watched a young black boy with a stack of early editions bounce out of a red news truck far below. Sonofabitch! How great it would feel to be that young again. The boy leaped back into the truck. It sped off and Tauber's thoughts turned darker.

How would it feel to step back a few paces, hunker down, and charge that plate-glass window the way he used to hit the opposing line on a big play? The sweet contact and then ripping free—sailing for daylight. Tauber shook his head violently. Don't get suicidal, you idiot, he muttered to himself, then marched into the outer office to find out what had happened to Steve Contos.

"Will, glad you came out! Come over here, please," an exceptionally animated Contos called from the far doorway. "These gentlemen are from the FBI," he said, gesturing toward two well-tailored young men in their thirties, "and they'd like us to take a couple of hours off for a quick trip to Washington!"

While Tauber was recovering from his astonishment and shaking hands, Contos excused himself. "I've got to get a few cigars for this fancy trip," he said. When he returned from his office, his jacket's breast pocket was bulging with them.

The flight via government jet to the Anacostia Naval Air Station, immediately across the Anacostia River from the Capitol, took a little less than fifty minutes, thanks, in part, to quietly expedited traffic clearances at both ends of the journey.

As he and Contos were descending the aluminum steps from the plane to the tarmac of the taxiway, Tauber spotted a black limousine waiting nearby, its rear compartment shielded with curtains. "Look," he whispered, "that's a goddamned White House car. I've seen it before. You were right. It's the big man himself we are going to see!"

"If it is Donley who sent for us, it's the biggest break of our lives," hissed Contos excitedly, as they walked quickly through the morning drizzle toward the car. "Talk about confirmation of a story. Incidentally, you jerk," he added gleefully, "I'll bet you wish you'd shaved now."

The door of the limousine opened and the two men piled inside, expecting to be whisked to the White House. Instead, speechless with surprise, they found themselves suddenly alone with the President-elect of the United States.

The White House chauffeur's time sheet for that Friday in November shows that he left Anacostia at about 8:15 A.M., drove out and around in Prince Georges County for approximately one hour, and returned to Anacostia at about 9:30. His notes obviously do not record the fact that Boyce Williamson had a seemingly friendly discussion with the head of VEI and the "discoverer" of Project M10. Nor do they indicate that the President-elect got nothing that could reasonably be termed new information. Nevertheless, Williamson had said good-bye to his guests with a genuine feeling of accomplishment. Steven Contos had agreed, much to the surprise of his startled partner, to consider holding up publication of the third, fourth, and fifth installments of the M10 story for a few days. Regarding the second installment, Contos had argued, and Williamson had accepted his position, that it was too late to stop without arousing many questions. Instead a very co-operative Contos had proposed that Installment Two be watered down considerably, but transmitted on schedule. Thus, as far as Williamson was concerned, at the very worst he had gained a full day and possibly much more. And in case Contos and Tauber thought about breaking their promise, Williamson had made a mental note to see to it that a careful surveillance was maintained on their communications system, which could, he was sure, be cut off the national network at a moment's notice.

Of course, these facts and feelings were not the only important elements of the situation that could not be expected to be found in the simple time sheet of a White House limousine chauffeur. For example, because he did not know it, he did not record that the same nondescript tan car with a dented left front fender that had followed him up and down the George Washington Parkway much earlier in the morning had also followed him, at a respectful distance, during his trip around Maryland and back to Anacostia.

"What the hell is going on? Didn't we resign from the league with Williamson?" asked a bewildered Will Tauber the moment he and Contos separated from their FBI escort at the busy entrance to the New York building housing the Videowire offices. Half a dozen times during the return flight, Tauber, burning with tension and curiosity, had tried to whisper his questions at his partner. But Contos stubbornly refused to do anything except shake his head silently and gaze out the oval plastic window at the heavy winter undercast fifteen thousand feet below. Now Tauber meant to get his answers. "All right, dammit, we're alone, so answer me! How do we move the story now? How do we cash in on this? We wait as you promised, and everyone in Washington will be all over it."

"Okay, okay, hang on to your jock," said Contos, smiling like a self-satisfied hyena. "I'll give you the picture, but *not* in our offices. From now on, we assume we're being bugged. Everyplace we normally go and everything we normally do is being watched. Let's take a walk. I feel like going to church."

"To church?" Tauber exclaimed.

"Who's going to bug a church?" asked Contos with an innocent grin.

Pulling his puzzled companion with him, the Videowire president marched jauntily up Sixth Avenue, weaving through the midmorning sidewalk crowds like a broken-field runner. Turning crosstown, he guided Tauber up the aged and stained steps of St. Clement's Catholic Church; a small painted sign to the left of the entrance announced MASS 7 A.M. WEEKDAYS, 9 A.M. AND 12 NOON SUNDAYS. The church was empty except for the sound of someone practicing Bach on the great gold and walnut pipe organ. Peering up toward the loft, Contos tried to see who was playing. "He's good, whoever he is. I hope he keeps it up." He motioned Tauber into the fourth pew and giggled. "This is perfect! Even a remote mike couldn't work in here."

"Okay, Contos," grumbled the thoroughly impatient Tauber over the music. "Will you quit stalling and tell me what is going on?"

"What is going on, Willis, my friend, is this. We have got it made. We have what we needed. We can prove to everyone that our M10 story is factual and we are going to sell a million bucks' worth of subscribers today!"

"How can you possibly believe that?" asked Tauber. "We're worse off than we were before. You agreed with Williamson that we'd—"

"Sure I did. I agreed to gut the second installment. So what? All that does is give us the extra time we were thinking of taking anyhow."

"But that was to make more sales. If you're not going to publish the last three installments, what have we got to sell and how do we convince anyone to buy now when we couldn't before?" asked Tauber, as confused as ever.

"We publish on schedule, my friend."

"But you promised Williamson—"

"Sure I did. I wanted to hear him out," Contos agreed gleefully. "But I certainly don't intend to participate in the suppression of important news and I doubt that a President-elect would like to admit he proposed such an immoral action," he continued with look of exaggerated piety. "Furthermore, if we wait too long, someone else with good connections will have time to get into the story. Hell, they might even get the Clayton report itself. That's not a gamble I'm prepared to take."

"Contos, you crazy bastard! You're talking about double-crossing the next President of the United States."

"I'm talking about avoiding bankruptcy, making a ton of money for us both, and making you into the biggest political columnist of this decade. That's what I'm talking about."

Tauber stopped to consider the list of goodies he had just heard. How he wanted them! But still he was doubtful and more than a little frightened about going up against the raw power of the U.S. government. Ironically, as the racing themes of the Bach Passacaglia and Fugue in C minor cascaded over him, he gave no thought to the enormity of the international confrontation that was already building around Project M10. "So suppose we do publish on schedule," he whispered directly into Contos's ear, so as to be heard over the organ. "We still haven't got any better credibility than we had yesterday. We're still up against a hard sell."

Contos shook his head and smiled again. "Not at all. We now have President-elect Williamson's personal confirmation of the story."

"But who'd believe us? We've got no proof that we even know the man, let alone discussed M10 with him."

"Willis, would you like a cigar?"

"Oh, come on, you know I don't smoke—and anyhow, this is a church."

"Take a cigar," said Contos insistently, holding open his jacket so the left inside pocket and its row of cigars could be seen.

"Dammit, I don't want a cigar!"

"Look *behind* the cigars, Willis."

Tauber peered into the dark area near Contos's left armpit. It was difficult to see in the church, lit only by a few high chandeliers and several rows of votive candles. He could make out an extra bulge behind the long cigars. "What is it?" he asked.

"It's a tape recorder."

"What?"

"It's my Memo-Corder. I've used it dozens of times on hot stories. I've got every word Williamson said on this thing."

"Jesus Christ!" Tauber whistled. "You are a—you are a son of a bitch. That's why you went into your office for more cigars before we left and that's why you kept fussing with unlit cigars in that limousine."

"Sure, I was checking to be sure that the damned thing was still running," explained Contos to the awed Tauber. "Listen a moment. . . ." The Videowire president glanced around to make certain they were still alone, pressed a black plastic button on the top of the tiny recorder, and smiled malevolently at his stupefied partner as Boyce Williamson's voice, slightly distorted but quite recognizable, emerged from under the cloth of his jacket.

"Now, here's what we do," Contos continued confidently, his demonstration over. "First we edit the second installment down, as we promised. We get to the sales staff and explain the whole situation, *not* on the phone but in safe places like this. For the rest of the day they hit all the biggest cliffhangers among their potential clients. They work *from public phones* or by direct visits only. They reiterate the guaranteed money-back deal *and* they promise them a listen to this tape tomorrow. I'll have a dozen copies or so by then. As a matter of fact, I just had another idea. At the right time, we might think about calling a news conference for our beloved press colleagues and let them have an earful, too. That could only whet everybody's appetite for the rest of our stuff. Furthermore, we'll give any reluctant clients a look at the first couple of pages of the Clayton document itself, just like you did with me when you first brought it in. If that program doesn't close deals and get cash on the line by tomorrow, then nothing will."

Willis Tauber looked at the face of his partner, silhouetted against the candle flames and the rich reds and blues of the stained-glass windows of the church. Time stopped for him. It is all on the line right now, he told himself. It is this chance or none for the rest of your life. "Let's go," he said with finality.

The last notes of the Bach dwindled into silence as the two men walked quickly up the aisle past row after row of empty wooden pews and out into the daylight of the busy street. A husky college student wearing a dirty gray Columbia University sweatshirt, who had been sitting on the church steps, slipped a textbook into his scuffed plastic briefcase and nodded to a businessman standing on the corner. In response, the businessman fell in step behind the departing Contos and Tauber, staying within fifty feet of them all the way into the Videowire building. They never noticed him. Across the street, two other men paralleled the same route. Contos and Tabuer did not notice them, either.

24

The President toyed glumly with the remains of the scrambled eggs and toast on his desk. The dark whole-wheat bread was beginning to dry out and curl at the edges in spite of the margarine that had soaked into it. Seated on the green-and-white sofas near the fireplace in the Oval Office, two worried men, former Senator Carl Silverton, now the Secretary of State, and General Mike Kallen, fingered half-empty cups of cold coffee. Silverton, at sixty-nine, and until Donley asked him to serve one stint as Secretary of State before retiring—head of the Senate Committee on Foreign Relations, was one of the most respected of the Senate "elders" and also one of Washington's more colorful characters, thanks to his flowing white mane and his biting upper New England twang. Jim Willoughby, the youngest man in the room by far, was slumped in his characteristic pose in a leather lounge chair with tie pulled down and collar open. For the moment, he was dozing. Charles Frydon, standing at a window catching a November sun that had finally routed the clouds of the past few days, was reading from a pad of legal-size yellow paper as Boyce Williamson absent-mindedly scanned the titles of books in the President's bookcase.

"I'll read it through once more," said Frydon. " 'The following action items have been agreed upon as of 1:00 P.M., Friday, November 9: *One:* As a precaution, Trident Groups A and B and other Nuclear SSBN Submarines will be ordered to Alert Level Four via the SeaComm communications system. Responsibility: Acting Chairman, JCS.

" '*Two:* All other forces will go to Level Five status— one step above routine. Responsibility: Acting Chairman, JCS.' "

General Kallen rubbed his finger over his clipped black mustache and nodded his agreement.

Frydon continued. "We now get into the civilian sector. . . . '*Three:* National Institutes of Health will issue news release knocking down Videowire story and DOD Public Affairs will state that Pentagon once studied idea but found it impractical. Responsibility: Willoughby.' "

"Jim, do you know whether Brondoff's in town?" the President asked. "We might need his help." Albert Brondoff was the director of the National Institutes of Health and a long-time friend of the President's, as well as a credible spokesman on scientific matters.

"I'm not sure, Mr. President," his aide replied as he straightened himself in his seat.

"I think he is," Frydon contributed as he looked up from the action list. "I'll check after we finish here. . . ."

"I want to again register my doubt on Item Three," declared Boyce Williamson before Frydon could move on through the list. "In my opinion, and I'll say it again, it might goad Videowire into releasing material I feel they will otherwise be willing to delay. I intend to call Contos in the morning. He'll give me a few days, I'm sure."

"We've got to provide some answers before then, Boyce," said the President. "We're getting more inquiries already and 'No comment' just won't hack it. We've agreed to keep a low profile on the rebuttal: no DOD news conference or anything; just a routine distribution like M10 was merely another example of misinterpretation or bad communication. I definitely feel we've got to do that much, otherwise we're too naked when and if something more pops open."

Williamson hesitated, grimacing with distaste, then finally shrugged.

"Go ahead, Charley," said the President with a wave of his hand.

" '*Four*,' " Frydon read aloud. " 'Tauber, Contos, and other Videowire personnel will remain under surveillance but no effort to block Installment Two will be made. Responsibility: FBI.

" '*Five:* All available intelligence data on possible Soviet reactions to M10 will continue to be evaluated with hourly reports from CFI. Responsibility: Joint Committee on Foreign Intelligence (CFI).' "

Frydon paused for comments. There were none.

" '*Six*,' " he continued. " 'Attempts to find credible scenarios that do not lead to full disclosure of M10 will continue. Deadline midnight Friday, Washington time, and 8:00 A.M., Saturday, Moscow time. Responsibility: CIA Director and Secretary of State.

" '*Seven:* Assuming failure on Item Six, above, the following steps will be taken at midnight tonight, *assuming no overt response from the Soviets*: (*a*) The President and President-elect will contact Premier Kirov via video hot line, confirm M10, emphasize it was not an official U.S. project, and urge restraint and secrecy while we investigate further.' "

"Now, there's the one I'm worried about," said Donley. "My instincts are screaming at me to get in touch with Kirov *now*." He looked at his watch. "It's a little after 7:00 P.M. over there. Our embassy people say he's definitely in the Kremlin. It's time to face the music, I think. He's no doubt well aware of the VEI story and is moving to check it out. If we call him and open it up ourselves, it gives us greater believability. The critical point is that he understands it is not anything the U.S. government initiated or condoned. I agreed last night to wait so Boyce here could have more time to brief himself and try what I consider still to be a dangerous game with Videowire. Now we're saying wait again. I want that reconsidered. Why must we wait?"

"There are at least two arguments for waiting," Boyce Williamson replied, "both very strong. First, as your own people have admitted, we can't be sure how Kirov will react. The longer our military can continue contingency preparations before facing that reaction, the better. Second, we can plan for the reactions of Congress and our own population. I don't have a good feeling for what's been done so far. I must tell you I'm not impressed. You should be much further along."

Now it was Donley's turn to grimace. The points Williamson ticked off were telling ones—especially the matter of triggering events that could lead to panicky reactions by the U.S. public, for which no preparations had been made. Earlier in the discussion, Frydon and Silverton had emphasized another factor: In the peaceful atmosphere of the past four years, the old Civil Defense Agency and the Office of Emergency Preparedness had been allowed to wither into mere boxes on the federal organization chart. Time could indeed be very important. "Okay, Charley, keep going," said the President, reluctantly accepting the time-table.

" 'Seven (b),' " Frydon announced, picking up where he had left off. " 'After the Kirov discussion, the Secretary of State will brief the ambassadors from the People's Republic of China, Britain, France, Germany, Japan, and Iran. He will urge secrecy and restraint.' "

Charles Frydon's voice turned to a breathy whisper and he flipped his glasses up on his forehead. "That's it, gentlemen."

The President sighed. "Pretty thin, I'm afraid, pretty thin. All these damned meetings and it comes down to very little—very little indeed. Are we getting anything at all from the Soviet side, Charley?"

"I checked ten minutes ago. Still nothing, sir."

"God, I hope that holds," said Donley, looking down at his desk as if studying its polished surface. Carefully he pressed his finger against a tiny speck of dust and lifted it away. "I certainly hope it holds," he repeated distantly.

"By the way, sir," said Jim Willoughby after a few seconds. "I have a couple of messages. The Vice President's yacht has returned to Bimini. Should we consider telling him to come back to D.C.?"

"No," answered Donley, raising his head again. "Let him stay on his vacation schedule. Bringing Carl and Boyce here was chancy enough. I don't want any suspicions

aroused." Although everyone in the Oval Office knew he
was too much of a gentleman to say it aloud, they all were
quite aware that the true reason Donley did not recall the
Vice President was because the man was a lightweight,
added to the ticket four years before only for geographic
and class "balance," who had spent his term in office being
more of a giddy dilettante than the administration's number
two personality. At the recent convention, much to Donley's relief, the Vice President had not even attempted to
capture a renomination. Instead he had left the field wide
open to the young governor from Illinois, with whom
Donley would have been delighted to work . . . if only
they had won the election.

"My second message is from Mrs. Donley," Willoughby
resumed a little sheepishly. "She called from her luncheon
meeting and asked that you be reminded that you promised
to take a nap when you had a chance. Frankly, I think she's
rather concerned about you."

The President smiled at the young man. "Between Laura
and you, I've got lots of people worrying about my getting
enough sleep, haven't I?"

"Well, we all know you didn't get much last night, sir."

"Neither did anyone else here. What do you say, fellows?
Maybe we really should break for a few hours," Donley
suggested, uncoiling his long body and stretching. "Even
our friend Boyce, here, seems to be sagging a little. What do
you think?" The Chief Executive scanned the faces around
him, sensing acquiescence but wanting confirmation.

"Danged good idea," piped up Carl Silverton. "These
old bones are getting very creaky and I've got a feeling it
could be a long night, especially after we tangle with our
good and dear colleague Mr. Kirov."

"What time do you want to reconvene?" said Williamson, giving his tacit approval to the recess as he massaged
the day-old stubble of brownish whiskers on his face.

"Let's say at T minus nine," suggested Frydon.

"What the hell does that mean?" asked the instantly
annoyed President-elect.

"He means nine hours before we contact Kirov," said
Donley calmly. "That sounds okay to me. I'll see you all
here at 3:00 P.M. Jim, Mike, Charley—get those action
items under way, then let's all get some rest."

25

Within minutes after the meeting in the Oval Office adjourned and just as Frederick Donley was closing the blackout shades of his bedroom against the brilliant afternoon sun, the huge one-hundred-mile-square antenna of the Navy's SeaComm communications system began rumbling out its coded instructions to the great Trident submarines that lurked a thousand feet down in every ocean of the Northern Hemisphere. Each of the huge Tridents carried twenty-four launch tubes, and each of the launch tubes housed a missile capable of raining a nuclear hell of multiple warheads over thousands of square miles. Nor were the Tridents the only instruments of death alerted by the President's command. Forty-one operational SSBN nuclear submarines, each with sixteen launch tubes, responded as well. Hydrogen bombs with a total explosive force equivalent to thousands of millions of tons of TNT were being prepared for use.

Created by the uniform and synchronized chanting of dozens of electrical generators connected to a thousand points on the gigantic gridwork of the SeaComm antenna which sprawled across miles of America's heartland, the radio signals of the SeaComm were modern man's version of the war drum. Once a hundred drums beat out a primal rhythm to speak the message of tribal warfare; now great power plants drove electrical signals from finely tuned metal wires upward through the atmosphere and beyond.

The radio waves sailed along the curve of the earth for ten thousand miles and more, then struggled stubbornly downward again, carrying their message—"Make Ready" —into the dark waters below. The slowly varying waves, backed by the prodigious power of the generating plants, could penetrate the murky depths of the sea despite its heavy shielding of salt. But only with the greatest effort could they reach the depths at which the submarines waited. When the signals finally reached the receiving sensors of the submarines, swaying back and forth in the deep currents of the ocean like the antennae of gigantic insects, their power was almost spent and the most sensitive equipment engineers could devise was required to detect the few simple on-off pulses of the SeaComm message—a trivial digital code repeated over and over to ensure that no errors occurred.

The message SeaComm carried to the submarines on that afternoon in November was couched in obscure operational jargon, but its real meaning was starkly simple: "Prepare for Armageddon." In response, one after another of the enormous whalelike vessels of the American fleet filled first with a frenzy of activity and then with a tense, even frightened, silence, broken only by occasional staccato commands from the bridge. America's sea-based nuclear deterrent force was at Alert Level Four—two steps above routine, four steps from hot war. The avalanche of M10 was gaining momentum.

President Donley fell wearily into bed and pulled the sheet and blanket over his shoulder, then reached up and snapped out the light on the bedstand. A warm blackness enveloped him. For the moment, unable to fall asleep in spite of his weariness, he lay still with his gaze again fixed on the dull outline of the red telephone. How had the others felt? he wondered—Carter, Nixon, Johnson, Kennedy, and all the others. They, too, had stared at that red phone. With each successive presidential term, with every passing year, the power which it could unleash had grown until it had swelled beyond the comprehension of any living mind. Donley's thoughts drifted back in time. Long ago, during the first year of his term, he had been given Department of Defense briefings on nuclear weapons effects. Briefings, dozens of briefings. They were whirlwinds of data and statistics and he had not taken them very seriously, nor could he remember now exactly what he had been told. He knew only one thing with certainty: No human brain could contain an understanding of the devastation that would follow if he picked up the red telephone.

In the darkness, a couple of ironic phrases from one of those early briefings came floating into his consciousness and he grinned sardonically to himself. What was that fellow saying all the time? Yes, that silly phrase "a nominal large nuclear war." Donley grunted aloud. How could a large nuclear war be *nominal?* Yet that was the phrase—

"a nominal large nuclear war." How had the man defined it, again? Ten thousand megatons of explosive force released in the Northern Hemisphere? With loving detail, the speaker had described some of the less obvious effects of such an assault and it had occurred to Donley that the man was trying to be comforting by describing subtleties so he did not force either himself or the President to face up to the millions of casualties and the unimaginable destruction that would immediately follow a nominal large nuclear war.

The briefer, Donley now recalled quite clearly, had been a typically crisp colonel from ACDA, the Arms Control and Disarmament Agency. He was summarizing a National Academy of Sciences study on the long-term worldwide effects of multiple nuclear weapons detonations. The paper-bound two-hundred-page volume had been given to Donley, but it was very technical and Donley never had got around to reading it. He had, however, requested a briefing and a couple of the points obviously had stuck in his subconscious for nearly four years. That neat ten-thousand-megaton war with half the weapons exploding at ground level would excavate roughly twice the volume of material blasted loose by Krakatoa in 1883—twenty-five billion cubic meters of rock and soil. The eruption of Krakatoa was the most powerful terrestrial event ever recorded by man and the dust reddened the skies for decades. But even Krakatoa would be dwarfed by a nominal large nuclear war. Such are the "subtle" effects of a thousand hydrogen bombs.

The ACDA colonel had waved off the dust problem, but had expressed a more fashionable concern about the ozone issue. Back in the seventies, as Donley himself could remember well, everyone from competent scientists to dismal quacks had opinions about ozone depletion caused by certain classes of aerosol spray can propellants. Bold black headlines foretold the disasters that might follow reduction of the ozone layer by a few percent. With the typical perversity of the American press, the National Academy report on the effect of high-yield nuclear explosions on the ozone layer issued at just about the same time never got much attention. Now, by some quirk of memory, the story it told was starkly clear in Donley's overstimulated mind.

A substance called nitric oxide is normally responsible for fifty to seventy percent of the destruction of ozone in the earth's upper atmosphere. The National Academy had estimated that about five thousand tons of nitric oxide would be produced for each megaton of nuclear explosive power. What, then, would ten thousand megatons do to the ozone? The answer was that it would deplete the ozone level by an astronomical thirty to seventy percent.

The man from the Arms Control and Disarmament Agency had admitted that he wasn't sure of the consequences of such an enormous drop. He had speculated that the weakened layer would surely keep in less of the earth's heat than normal, causing a drop in air temperature, perhaps enough of a drop to produce serious damage to agriculture for decades or even centuries to come. Probably more important, the weakened layer would also let in more solar ultraviolet light. Since life on earth had evolved for eons within the protective ozone shield and was presently precisely adapted to the amount of solar ultraviolet which gets through, the change in the layer might mean nothing less than extinction to many species.

Almost every living thing on earth had defense mechanisms for use against the normal low level of ultraviolet that penetrates the ozone. External shielding, such as feathers, fur, or the waxes on fruits, had been tirelessly perfected by nature. Internal shielding, such as the melanin pigment in human skin or the flavonoids in plant tissue, had also been exquisitely tuned to the normal ozone levels. Avoidance strategies had been built into the instincts of everything from plankton, which migrate to greater depths in the ocean in the daytime, to the desert iguanas, who carefully seek the shade during high noon. Furthermore, elaborate natural repair mechanisms to cope with sunburn damage had evolved in almost every exposed organism. How well would they work in a world suddenly overwhelmed with ultraviolet light? No one knew.

But what, Donley had asked impatiently, were the best available estimates of the *overall* consequences of nearly destroying the ozone instantaneously in a nuclear war? The Arms Control and Disarmament man had held up his hands in a gesture of hopeless uncertainty. The major increase in solar ultraviolet that would follow such a war would likely overwhelm the defenses of some, and perhaps many, terrestrial life forms. Both direct and indirect damage would then occur among the bacteria, insects, plants, and other links of the ecosystem upon which humanity depends. This disruption in the aftermath of the major war might be just another "subtle" effect or it might match the gigantic scale of destruction of the nuclear war itself. No one, the colonel from ACDA had repeated meekly, really knew.

Donley had shuddered at that answer and now, years later, with the theoretical discussion of that long-past day on the verge of becoming reality, he shuddered again. Alone in the darkness of his bedroom, and as a gesture to his own soul, he reached out to the red phone and shoved it farther from his bedside, then turned his body to face the other way. He could no longer see it, but he knew it was there behind him, just a few feet away, ready for him.

The small amber light on the machine flashes on. Just above it is a single word in neat white letters: SILA—the Russian word for "power."

The child looks at the light and turns her thin, pale face toward the young radiologist. Fear is in her thirteen-year-old eyes.

"This won't hurt, Maria Ludmilovna. I promise it won't," he says as tenderly as he can. "Now lie flat on your back, please. Everything will be fine, but you must lie very still. These will help you." He presses the small towel-wrapped sandbags into place. Then he moves the four sponge-covered chrome-steel clamps into position and tightens them carefully against the translucent skin of her skull. The girl's eyes grow wider, and like a small trapped bird, she begins to quiver.

The radiologist looks helplessly over at the girl's mother and father, standing outside the thick green viewing window.

"Maria," he whispers, "I think it will be best if we give you something. It will be easier if you are asleep. We will get better results. Remember, Maria, this is not an operation; it is only a test—a diagnosis. It will help us find out about what is wrong." He picks up a small package from a tray next to the girl and strips off the plastic. Inside is a hypodermic syringe.

In a few seconds, the child's rigid body sags under the loose and faded gray cotton of the hospital gown. She no longer trembles and her frightened eyes cease their searching. As the radiologist slowly withdraws his hand from hers, she does not fight to hold it. Her eyes flutter and close. With a relieved breath, the man straightens his back and pushes the canvas table carrying the girl's inert body along the track, sliding it into the center of the detector array. He turns his head and sights through the eyepiece of the alignment optics. After one small adjustment, he locks the wheels of the table firmly into place.

Above the girl's small body an archway of five hundred detectors is waiting. Each detector is a small and shining crystal, a cubic centimeter of almost inconceivable perfection. In some distant laboratory, the crystals had once been painstakingly pulled and solidified from a white-hot glowing pool of molten chemicals and now they are in place, positioned with exquisite precision and waiting to deliver a decision.

The radiologist returns to the control unit and flips another switch. Under the canvas stretched taut by the child's weight, a hundred miniature x-ray tubes warm with life. They, too, are ready.

The man steps behind the lead-lined partition in the small space next to the observation window and smiles quickly over his sholder at the man and woman pressed close against the glass, then nods to the technician waiting before the color television set. The technician swings a camera into position in front of the screen and pushes a square green button under a plate engraved with the words PRIOBRETJENNYE DANNYE—"Acquired Data."

Instantly a hundred pencil-like beams of radiation streak through the body of the child. With infinite delicacy they search and probe and finger their way among her entrails. The beams, so fleeting and subtle that they cannot damage even the most fragile living structures, emerge from the girl's body, and whisper their secret messages to the waiting detectors. Five hundred radiation levels keyed to different combinations of source and detector positions funnel through a maze of cables and into the small computer next to the technician's left shoulder. For twenty-five one-thousandths of a second the computer calculates, correlates, and then commands. Again the pencil beams shoot through the girl's flesh.

With never-ending patience and perfection, the machine repeats the sequence over and over again: expose, detect, calculate; expose, detect, calculate—until, on the face of the TV screen, shapes and outlines begin to appear. The girl's brain and bones and lungs, her heart and stomach and intestines, every detail is being meticulously painted into view.

The young radiologist leans closer to the glass of the picture tube and narrows his eyes to suppress distracting flashes in the still-forming image. He whispers a request to the technician and the gaudy colors on the screen grow even brighter and more garish as adjustments are made. Several small round pinkish areas emerge from the orange-red that is, in effect, a slice of the child's liver. Both the technician and the radiologist see them at the same instant. Pointing to one with a pencil, the technician looks up with a question in his face. The young doctor's shoulders sag and his head drops. Yes, take a photograph of the screen for the record. But the doctor already knows. He glances back toward the two faces straining at him anxiously through the observation window. He cannot bring himself to meet their eyes just yet, so he directs his gaze toward his logbook and writes a few words of Russian: Case 76087—Computerized whole-body x-ray tomography of liver and surrounding tissue shows probable metastasis.

The verdict has been rendered and the verdict is death.

26

Watching his chief operator ready the Videowire computer for transmission of Friday's installment of the M10 story was essentially a sexual experience for Steven Contos. Caressing the blue and white paint of the metal boxes which housed the operating circuits of the machine, he felt as if he were on the verge of taking a willing and voluptuous woman who had promised to do anything he wished, even those wildly exotic acts of love with which he had often entertained himself in his imagination while perfunctorily going through the motions of intercourse with his thoroughly bored and quite disinterested wife. To say that he was excited is to understate badly. He was ecstatic. His mood did not come from the content of the second installment—he and Tauber had carefully edited it back to the point where it revealed little new material—but from the list of subscribers to whom it was being sent. There were twelve extra names. True, none of the big and cautious systems had yet signed, but twelve additions in the few brief hours since the new sales pitch began was intoxicating stuff, out of which Contos could make marvelous dreams.

The VEI president fingered the sensuous electronic warmth of the machine under his hands and smiled, knowing that it was, at that moment, pumping the Tauber by-lined story out to the lacelike combination of satellites, microwave links, wires, cables, and glass fibers that comprised the global distribution system through which Videowire reached its customers. The system, an outgrowth of the direct-dial telephone network of the 1970s, could deliver news, entertainment, words of rage or love or politics, anything that one person might wish to communicate to another, to any spot on the planet in an instant. During the few years since it began full operation, physical distance had been practically destroyed. Man's world had been made profoundly smaller. Most of the time delays that physical separation had made an inherent part of the large social interactions of mankind for hundreds of centuries had been annihilated. What vanished along with the delays was the stabilizing and moderating influence of time on the flow of events. In an earlier era, the disaster of M10 might have spread more slowly. But it was not an earlier era, and word of the project was not destined to move like a glacier but like an avalanche, fated to sweep a world before it.

While apparently being faithful to the Contos agreement with Williamson, the second portion of the Videowire series, moving to clients under the headline BIOMEDICAL ATTACK BY U.S. ON SOVIET RUSSIA!, nevertheless discussed the dramatic ten-year rise in cancer of the stomach and intestinal tract—diseases which were epidemic almost everywhere but by which the Soviet Union had been particularly hard hit. In cold statistical terms, the story also recounted the terrifying acceleration of liver cancer that had begun in the late seventies and pointed out how deaths from natural disease could easily mask additional deaths induced by U.S. biomedical agents delivered by

Project M10. The text hinted at how the agents were introduced into the Russian food chain and environment: Starting in the early 1970s, U.S. trade with the Soviets had expanded each year until currently Russia was America's single largest customer for food and for many other articles of commerce. The article concluded by stating that incontrovertible evidence had been uncovered showing that this expanded level of trade could provide the vehicle for a U.S. attack on the Russian population. In the next installment (schedule to be announced), Videowire promised to reveal much more detail.

A careful reading of the edited piece shows how skillfully Contos, a true professional at the scandal-sheet style, which twists ideas into facts and juggles tricky phrasing loaded with double meanings, had done his job. To a client or potential client who received a hard-hitting sales pitch from one of the Videowire salesmen, the words assumed enormous significance. To a general readership, however, the story of M10 had been given the coloration of a typical VEI exaggeration. Most importantly, the watered-down content of Installment Two provided false encouragement to Boyce Williamson. It even cheered Frederick Donley measurably, because it made his proposed "theoretical study" cover look enticingly more feasible as a means of buying a little more time.

Following the first VEI story, there had been a few sporadic inquires from Capitol Hill to the White House. A couple of curious congressmen, hesitant about even admitting they read that brand of news, had called Thursday afternoon and were easily mollified by generalities and vague remarks regarding overly imaginative reporters. Understandably, it was hard to find anyone in Congress who really wanted to be distracted from the process of assessing the consequences of the two-day-old election surprises. A new President was coming. That was important. Why get all excited about an unconfirmed bit of puffery being promoted by a cheap little news service?

With the second installment of M10 on the streets, the tempo of inquiries accelerated slightly. In the White House Press Office, still strewn with the remnants of election night, telephones were ringing more insistently and the two young assistant press officers who had been left to man the post-election battlements while their seniors

launched a scramble for new jobs, handled the queries
the best way they could: "No comment." "Yeah, we heard
about it yesterday and it's still baloney." "We may have
something later."

At the time of the second release, the White House
press secretary himself was being interviewed for a key
position in a top Washington PR firm. To him, M10 was
an absurdity. If there had been anything to it, wouldn't
he have been thoroughly briefed by Willoughby? The fact
that he had not been available to Willoughby for a briefing
because he had not told his office where to reach him, for
the obvious reason of wanting to keep his job-hunting
activities to himself, never occurred to him. He was almost
angry when one of his potential employers interrupted a
tantalizing sketch of what his new job might be to ask
about the truth of the "cancer war" stories he'd been
hearing around town.

The second Videowire story, anemic though it might
have been, was getting very serious attention in the
meticulously organized household of Lieutenant General
Robert Travis Mallon.

As usual, weather permitting, General Mallon was
walking his grounds after lunch, picking up twigs and
debris near the flagstone sidewalks and around the elms
and maples. But "Trav" Mallon was not thinking about
his gardening today. He had made a decision. It was time
to act. Intellectually, he had known this moment might
come someday, although emotionally he had never really
expected it, and certainly not so soon. Since Thursday,
when the first material on M10 was released, telephone
calls from people who seemed uneasy about using their
full names had been coming almost hourly. Each conversation was clipped and fragmented—the style of talk
between two people who were afraid someone else was
listening.

General Mallon strolled to the front door of his house
and opened it, ready to go inside. A surge of melancholy
brought him to the edge of tears, and he turned to stand
on the threshold, looking out at the late-fall landscape
and the golden afternoon sunshine. God, how he loved
those trees and that lawn, now touched with winter brown.
But there is a time to call an end. Today was the day

this great and productive phase of his life must be left behind. Mallon's eyes swept over the row of rosebushes to his left. Just last week he and Alice had been at work mulching them and preparing them for winter. She had chatted like a happy chipmunk about plans for more plantings next spring. He knew now that they would not be around to see their roses bloom again.

General Mallon retreated into the house and closed the door softly behind him. Picking up the hall telephone, he dialed the information operator. "Can you give me the number for Pan American Airlines, please? . . . . Thank you." After a short conversation with a bouncy female voice at Pam Am reservations, he put down the telephone and mounted the stairs to the second floor. His wife was busy making the bed.

"Alice," he said quietly, "I guess it's time, dear. I told you it might happen someday, and it has. We're on a Pam Am flight to Costa Rica at 1800 hours."

Alice Mallon stood erect, her hand still clutching the big pink-cased pillow she was about to put on the bed. She looked at her husband, eyes steady. Without saying a word, she placed the pillow carefully and flipped the flowered bedspread over it, then walked to the closet to get her first suitcase down. Trav Mallon smiled a small, tight smile and nodded. "We've got a few hours before plane time. I'll get a few boxes from the basement."

As Mallon was descending the stairs—there was a worn spot in the carpet on the third tread, which he'd always meant to fix—the telephone in his den rang again. The call was like the others. "Yes," he said softly, "we miscalculated. It's those associative codes they're using now-a days. We didn't anticipate them. We must presume they've got everything pretty well opened up. Yes, I know. . . . Yes, I assume the other side has access. Even if the U.S. folks have not given anything to them, some of their own people are probably in high enough positions to get it directly. Alice and I are making the assumption that they'll have identifications very quickly now and they'll be taking some overt action. If the other people have those same identifications . . . well, it might get dangerous. . . . What? . . Yes, we're leaving this afternoon. I would recommend that you do the same. The evacuation plan still looks okay and we can all get in touch after matters settle down. I'm sorry this is necessary, but we knew it might come someday, didn't we? . . . Quite so. . . . You've done a fine job and I'm proud of you and everyone else on the team. . . . Good-bye."

Mallon's hand trembled slightly as he placed the phone in its cradle and his clear brown eyes clouded with tears, but he squared his shoulders and continued toward the basement storeroom, where cardboard packing boxes were piled neatly in the corner.

"I say he's kept his word to this point and there's no reason to think he'll do otherwise tomorrow. This release says nothing that isn't common knowledge about either world cancer rates or international trade." Boyce Williamson was very certain of his feelings. The deal he'd made with Contos was going to hold up.

"Tie it to the first release, however, and what else they know and it says plenty," observed Charley Frydon. "We can't trust them."

"If you'll bother to notice, they even say the schedule of next releases is *to be announced*," Williamson replied, thrusting a copy of VEI's Installment Two toward the CIA Director.

"I know what they say, but—"

"All right, gentlemen," interrupted President Donley, "let's keep it calm. I want to hear logical arguments, not just a debating match."

The discussion, interspersed with reviews of intelligence reports from abroad and involving the President's "crisis group" of Williamson, Frydon, Kallen, and Silverton, had been washing back and forth across his grandly carved oak desk for nearly three hours. Most of the action items from the earlier meeting had been carried out or were in process. The point under debate was Item Three—the issuance of a low-key DOD press memo stating that the use of cancer-inducing agents as a weapon of war had once been studied theoretically but had been found impractical. The memo was to further state that the Videowire story was believed to have originated from a misinterpretation of fragmentary information about the old DOD study.

Williamson returned to a line of reasoning he'd used earlier. "Look, I expect to confirm my agreement with Contos in the morning. Now, why not hold off until then?

We'll already have talked to Kirov, too. That way, we won't push Videowire into defending itself."

"I'm afraid we're getting too much pressure to hold off with the usual 'No comment' treatment," replied Donley as he swung around to face Jim Willoughby. "Call the DOD Public Affairs people again, Jim. Ask them what kinds of inquiries they're getting."

"I did that a few minutes ago when I went out, sir," answered Willoughby. "They're getting at least a dozen calls an hour now and they're still answering with 'No comment.' One worrisome signal is that AP's Pentagon beat man and that hotshot new guy from the *New York Times* have both begun nosing around."

"I think we need that covering release," mused Donley aloud. "It will give us something to anchor to for, I'd guess, twenty-four hours or so."

"I agree, Mr. President," said Mike Kallen from across the room. "I'm thinking we will need that time and more to try to get our population-control plans cranked up—just in case. Are you sure, sir, you don't want to start that process now?"

Donley shook his head gloomily, "Not yet. It would bring in far too many people; we could never contain it." He looked away from Kallen and faced his Secretary of State. "Carl?"

"I dunno. They didn't teach us this kind of stuff when I went to school," said Silverton. "I guess I've got a feeling rumbling around in me that you should go ahead and do it. 'Course, at my age, it could be gas, too."

Donley's grin faded quickly as he pivoted toward the President-elect. "Boyce, I've decided I'm going to issue the cover story. We'll ask the DOD Public Affairs Office to release it after 10:00 P.M. so it will miss the big evening TV news shows and look very unimportant. But it will give the press staff something to defend themselves with."

The President-elect shrugged. "It's your decision," he said, thinking about adding: "at least for now."

27

Friday, November 9

a 989 AP
BULLETIN WASHINGTON D.C.
A PENTAGON SPOKESMAN QUOTED IN A PRESS RELEASE
THIS EVENING DECLARED THAT RECENT CLAIMS BY THE
NEW YORK-BASED VIDEO NEWS SERVICE—VIDEOWIRE
EXPRESS INCORPORATED—REGARDING AMERICAN USE
OF CANCER-INDUCING AGENTS AS A MEANS OF COVERTLY
ATTACKING THE SOVIET UNION ARE SPURIOUS AND
BASED ENTIRELY ON A CLASSIFIED THEORETICAL STUDY
OF SUCH METHODS PERFORMED ALMOST A DECADE AGO.
THE SPOKESMAN EMPHASIZED THAT THE SECRET STUDY
CLEARLY SHOWED THE TECHNIQUES TO BE IMPRACTICAL
AND THE UNITED STATES HAS NEVER TAKEN THE
METHOD SERIOUSLY NOR DOES IT INTEND TO PURSUE
RESEARCH INTO SUCH PROCEDURES IN THE FUTURE.
1036 P ED 11-9

When the Associated Press coverage of the Pentagon release on M10 hit the softly humming laser-driven teleprinter outside John Schotty's office at the *Globe*, he had just run out of cigarettes; otherwise he might not have seen it for hours. As it was, just as the story appeared, he happened to be passing the printer on his way to the chrome vending machine next to the elevator. He ripped the text off the long roll of paper and returned to his office without his smokes. "Those poor bastards!" he murmured, visualizing the agonizing discussions that must have been going on at the White House.

Since his remarkable ride all over the District of Columbia with Boyce Williamson early that morning, the columnist had spent the day vacillating between wanting to stay out of the way, leaving responsibility for M10 in official hands, and wanting to climb into the middle of the melee, starting, of course, with a trip to New York to find Tauber. His rapidly alternating moods had averaged neatly to zero, with the result that he'd done essentially nothing except prowl around his office asking himself whether he was, as Tauber had once suggested, getting too old.

Schotty reread the large block print of the AP story. What ought he to do? He knew the Pentagon release was an outright lie. He knew why they were lying. Was it his duty to tell the truth or was it a higher duty to keep quiet? If he kept quiet, what would it buy? Surely Tauber and Contos were hellbent on telling everything they knew about M10. Why didn't Donley just shut them up?

Schotty reached for a cigarette. The crumpled pack on the desk was just as empty as it had been before he'd been distracted by the teleprinter. Tossing the offending wad of paper into the wastebasket with a snappy overhand delivery, he growled obscenities at himself and decided it was getting late—after 11:00 P.M. and time to go home. A comradely "G'night, Johnny" from the night man on the city desk, whom he'd known for twenty-one years, followed him down the empty corridor of the Globe Building. When the wheezing elevator landed him at the ground floor, he realized that he'd been so wrought up while waiting for it that he still hadn't bought his cigarettes. "Jackass!" he said aloud, pushing the Up button again.

"Mr. Schotty?" a voice asked from behind him.

"Yes?" said the columnist, turning expectantly. He did not see who had spoken his name. Strong hands, the sharp jabbing pain of a heavy hypodermic needle entering his left upper arm through his topcoat, and a sliding, spinning fall into darkness prevented it. From far off, just as the blackness drowned his world, he did hear something: sounds—strange sounds. Someone was whispering orders, but the words did not sound right. It was because they were Russian.

In the neighborhood of the Globe Building, hard by the strip joints and the sleazy movie houses, it is not unusual for men to be seen late on a Friday night staggering home after an evening of cheap booze and cheaper women, who promise far more than they deliver. For that reason, the four men who piled unsteadily through a back alley and into a tan car with a dented left front fender and mud-smeared license plates were not noticed by anyone who might have been curious enough to provide useful information later. As a result, the single team of two FBI men parked outside the Globe Building and assigned to maintain loose surveillance on John Schotty had absolutely nothing to go on when they finally got curious and checked the columnist's long-empty office. By that time Schotty himself had been revived and strapped firmly into a chair in a concrete-walled room in the second basement of the Soviet Embassy.

"How do you feel, sir?" The man was about six feet tall, around thirty-five years old, with mousy hair combed straight away from a thin, high forehead that rose above an unusually sharp nose which twisted slightly to the right. He spoke with only the trace of an Eastern European accent. "How do you feel, Mr. Schotty?" he repeated.

The columnist pulled his throbbing head off his chest, the weakening aftereffects of the drug still not completely dissipated. "I'm all right," he croaked hoarsely, the light shining at his eyes. "What the hell are you doing? Who are you?"

"For our purposes tonight, my name can be Sergei. You may consider me a member of the auxiliary staff of the Soviet Embassy in Washington."

"Untie me, you idiot," growled Schotty, pulling at his bonds as his mind cleared.

"Of course, but first I need some information." Sergei's expression grew hard for an instant, then softened. "Mr. Schotty, I have been asked to obtain your files on a 'Project M10,' and most particularly, any official documents on the subject. We have reason to believe you have such papers in your possession."

"I don't know what you're talking about."

"Please, sir," the Russian almost pleaded. "We are on a very urgent schedule. Give me what I need and we can relax and go on to more pleasant matters."

"Let me go and you might get out of this with your hide whole," snapped Schotty, with more confidence than he actually felt.

Sergei bent down next to Schotty's left ear so he could whisper. "I urge you not to be difficult. You are a newspaperman, an intellectual. You are of a different world and you do not understand your position. You are—as you Americans say—beyond your depth. Now tell me where we may obtain your papers on Project M10. I repeat, sir, we are on a quick schedule."

John Schotty did not know whether he was an especially brave man. He did know his heart was already pounding fiercely in his chest, not only from fear, but from anger.

"I demand that you release me here and now!" he shouted furiously. "You must be crazy to kidnap me. The police and the FBI will be all over you! And I don't know what 'papers' you're talking about."

"Sir, we *know* of your involvement," Sergei replied icily. "We know of your discussions with Mr. C. Boyce Williamson this morning. We were right behind you. Now spare yourself and us. Give me the M10 documents."

"That meeting was pure politics," bluffed the columnist.

The Russian straightened up with a frustrated sign. "Very well," he said softly, motioning his two companions out of the shadows and into a quick conference. After a minute or two, the men left the room, leaving Sergei and Schotty alone.

Peering into the gloom beyond the blinding glare of the two-hundred-watt bulb in front of him, Schotty could just make out his tormentor's outline. He was leaning against the wall—waiting. When the other two Russians returned, one carried a small tray on which were several bottles, an alcohol lamp, and an eyedropper. Sergei put the tray on the floor behind Schotty's chair and gestured to his partners. Without warning, the men closed in, crowding tightly around Schotty, screening the light. His head was caught, cruelly twisted back and to one side, then held rigid.

"Listen to me, American," Sergei hissed at the side of his face. "Now we will do this my way."

Schotty tried to respond, but the callused hands clamping his head turned his reply into a meaningless grunt.

"You are a man of words, Mr. Schotty," said the Russian, "many words. I have read your column often. So I shall use words to tell you how we shall proceed. I shall gradually take your words away from you. Can you see this, sir?" Sergei held the eyedropper so Schotty could view it. It was filled with a water-clear solution. "This dropper contains a simple material—concentrated sodium hydroxide: You may know it as caustic soda or lye. You have probably used it yourself to open a sink drain. What you may or may not also know, my foolhardy American, is that lye dissolves human tissue very efficiently. I shall now put four or five drops of this solution into your left ear." The

Russian was close and whispering. Schotty could feel his breath on his cheek. "I shall count carefully. Four or five drops will be just sufficient to eat away your eardrum and all of the structure of your inner ear—perhaps it will not penetrate to your brain. You will, however, be irrevocably deaf in one ear. No words will ever come to you again from your left side. Do you understand, sir?" Schotty's legs were beginning to tremble uncontrollably. Panic clawed at him. He tried to speak. The hands would not let him. "If you still do not give us the information we want," Sergei continued, still whispering, "I shall next put the drops in your right ear. Then you will be totally deaf—forever unable to hear any words at all, Mr. Schotty. Yours will be a life spent in total silence. If there are still no answers, there is much more I can do. I shall place ten drops in your right eye. I think, by then, you will tell me. Feeling caustic soda digest away a living eyeball must be most unpleasant: Not painful—just unpleasant. I ask you to consider that well, sir." The Russian caught the lower lid of Schotty's right eye between his thumb and forefinger and pulled it away. He blew gently at the exposed tissue. Schotty moaned. The man returned to his whispering. "But if you still refuse me, I shall then put ten drops in your left eye also, and you will be deaf and blind for the rest of your life. I have never had a man require it, Mr. Schotty; however, there is another step after your eyes. I will burn away your vocal cords. Think carefully, sir. You will be deaf, dumb, and blind forever. *Forever*. At that point, I promise you, you will write me a note telling me everything and asking that we do you the kindness of shooting you."

Schotty's body quivered like a piece of spring steel struck with a hammer, his back arched wildly, his eyes rolled white with terror. He was howling and sobbing, but only a guttural chugging escaped through the fingers holding his teeth tightly together.

Sergei smiled at the frantic columnist. "Ah, you wish to say something, but I cannot be sure what it will be. I warned you that I was pressed for time. We shall make sure that you take us seriously when you do speak." He held the eyedropper directly over Schotty's ear canal, its tip nestled in the short gray hairs around the opening. One, two, then three more glistening drops fell from the end of the glass tube. A strange sensation of warmth laced into the side of Schotty's trembling head and he screamed hugely. Urine poured out of his bladder, staining his trousers with a great dark splotch. A rending sob bubbled from his lips. He was crying. He could hear himself only in one ear.

After a time the shriveled old man who had been John Schotty stopped shaking and the men holding his head eased their grips. His tormentor smiled and leaned close.

"Yes, Mr. Schotty?"

Schotty raised his eyes, sweat-soaked gray hair matted against his forehead. "The M10 report . . . in a suitcase . . . in the storeroom of my apartment."

"Thank you, sir. We have your key ring. Does it include the requisite keys?"

Schotty nodded weakly.

"Which ones, sir?"

"Small brass one . . . opens storage cage. Chrome one . . . marked with a piece of tape . . . opens basement door."

The Russian tossed the keys to the younger of the two men who had been restraining Schotty's head, leaving him free except for the straps on his hands and feet. "We shall wait here until my colleagues return with the papers," the Russian said quietly.

To get from the Soviet Embassy to the apartment building where John Schotty made his home, in the middle of the night when the streets are practically deserted, takes only seven or eight minutes. The two Russian agents reappeared in the embassy's second basement in less than half an hour. One of them was carrying a stapled sheaf of papers—the Clayton report on Project M10.

"Very good," said Sergei after glancing through the document, his narrow face beaming with satisfaction. "Very good indeed. Now, Mr. Schotty, we will put you back together again. You have a long trip to make."

"What do you mean? Please, please, let me go!" Schotty begged. "I gave you what you wanted."

"You are going to Moscow, sir, for further questioning. We have a plane waiting. That is why I was in such an unfortunate hurry." Sergei motioned to his silent companions. "Hold his head," he commanded.

Schotty tried to scream but could not. The rough vise

of the hands was on his jaw again. There was no strength left to summon as he tried vainly to twist his head free.

"Be calm, sir, be calm," purred the Russian as warmth cascaded into the columnist's ear again. "For a man of your importance, I used only a melted wax. The real caustic would have come much later. A little more washing with warm water and your hearing will be as fine as ever."

An hour later, John Schotty was en route to Moscow via a specially scheduled Soviet jet freighter that had landed at National Airport late Friday afternoon carrying "supplies" for the Russian Embassy.

"They've brought up the hot line for the T-minus-thirty-minute checkout. Everything is in good shape at both ends." Jim Willoughby was reporting in after a visit to the White House Communications and Crisis Center, constructed by Donley's predecessor and located in a deep subbasement under the main portion of the building.

"Okay," acknowledged the President, looking at his watch. It was twenty-five minutes to midnight.

"Will we both be visible to Kirov at the same time?" Boyce Williamson asked, his voice deeper and a little louder than usual.

"It can be set up that way," answered Willoughby. "Mr. President . . . ?"

"Yes, arrange for both of us to be on camera," said Donley, "However, Boyce, as we've discussed, I want it clear that you are an *observer* in these proceedings. Only I speak officially for the United States.

"Yes," said Williamson, "but I reiterate, so you also understand, I must reserve the option of commenting if I think it will be a problem for me to live with what you say."

"Look, you know what I'm going to tell him," said Donley with some annoyance. "We've practically scripted it."

"I'd suggest you work out that kind of thing off-camera," Willoughby suggested quickly. "We can interrupt the picture and voice transmissions at any time for private conversations."

Both Donley and Williamson nodded. It was like watching two very edgy prize fighters getting ready.

"Maybe you'd best go downstairs, gentlemen. General Kallen and Mr. Silverton are already in the Crisis Center."

The President stood up and straightened to full height so he towered over the smaller Williamson. He adjusted his carefully knotted blue-and-red-striped tie. "Where's Charley Frydon?"

"Getting a last-minute CFI briefing and checking with the surveilance teams," replied Willoughby. "He said he'd be in the Center by five of."

"Okay, then let's go," announced Donley, and the three men headed for a locked elevator that would take them 120 feet under the streets of Washington to the nerve center of the Executive branch of American government.

At exactly midnight, Friday, November 9, a series of computer-controlled relays in Moscow and Washington swung to their closed positions. Television transmitters and cameras in the two capitals waited, ready to feed their signals to communications satellites hovering high overhead. Automatic electronic translators stood by to convert English to Russian and Russian to English almost instantly.

In the White House Communications and Crisis Center, the atmosphere was thick with controlled tension. Two Department of State linguists, whose assignment was to monitor the automatic translation system for errors of meaning or syntax, hunched forward and adjusted their headsets and microphones. On the TV screen positioned in front of President Donley and President-elect Williamson, the Great Seal of the United States, which served as a final test pattern for the American end of the hotline system, wavered momentarily and was replaced by the red and gold of the Russian hammer and sickle. The connection was made.

Donley and Williamson, now visible in Moscow, waited expectantly for Premier Alexei Kirov's image to appear before them. It did not. They waited. Nothing. Donley shot an inquiring look at Willoughby, who then whispered a question to the chief systems engineer. A Signal Corps colonel raised his hands in a gesture of impotence. Knowing he could be seen in Moscow, the President looked straight into the lens of the TV camera picking up his image.

"Please connect us with Premier Kirov," he said.

The hammer and sickle remained on the silent screen.

"Please connect us with Premier Kirov," he said again, more firmly.

The bright-red field of the Soviet flag dissolved to black and was replaced by a Russian face. It was not Kirov's. The dark, square-jawed man, whom Donley did not recognize, began speaking rapidly and the soft hum of the waiting autotranslators cut over immediately to a stream of electronically synthesized English.

"I am instructed to inform you that Premier Kirov is not available. It is recommended that you call tomorrow."

Donley's blood pressure shot up fifty points. "This discussion has been scheduled for hours," he said, telling himself to remain cool. "Why is the Premier not available as promised?"

"I am instructed to suggest you call tomorrow," the man answered blandly.

"What time do you suggest?" snapped Donley.

"It does not matter," the Russian replied, as his face faded off the screen.

After more than a hour of rehashing, the consternation in the White House had subsided into grim worry. In his office, surrounded as usual by his advisers and Boyce Williamson, Frederick Donley stared over the rim of a cup of stale coffee. As he listened to General Kallen make a worried statement about the need to consider civil defense preparations, he idly raised the cup to his lips, his eyes trapped by a circle of light on the highly polished top of his desk. The spot of light from his reading lamp suddenly began to wave and dance across the old wood. Transfixed, Donley let the cold coffee wash over his tongue. The taste was bitter and he grimaced, but his eyes did not leave the circle of light. It was as if he were being drawn into it, his mind pulled from his body and into the solid surface of the desk—into the spot of light. Suddenly alarmed, Donley shook his head to stop the dangerous drifting. His hand instinctively returned the cup to its saucer, his eyes still unwillingly fastened to the shimmering, weaving glow.

And now Frederick Donley was no longer in the Oval Office of the White House. Time and space dissolved into the undulating pool of whiteness, and he and Laura were high above the beautiful water-filled fjords of Norway. It was their first trip abroad together and from the hilltop they could look down and see their cruise ship far below. The sunlight glinted off the deep blue waters of the fjord and into his dazzled eyes. He turned away from the pain, closing off the scintillating fire of the sun. Donley clamped his eyelids shut and the images disappeared instantly. Once again he was in the Oval Office, facing the torture rack of M10, a growing spiral of nausea starting in the pit of his stomach and reaching upward. That goddamn cold coffee, he chided himself. I should know better by now.

"Say that again, will you, Mike?" he said aloud, as his left eye began to twitch slightly.

"I was saying, sir," obliged Kallen with only a hint of curiosity, "that it might be prudent to alert the Civil Defense Regional Offices. If they have to disseminate crisis procedures to their field personnel and to the general population, they'll need all the warning time we can give them."

Donley shook his head with frowning distaste. "That will bring in hundreds of outside people. We'd have panic in the streets by morning."

"I think you're all reacting like a bunch of scared kids," said Boyce Williamson airily. "Kirov is not about to start a nuclear war over a news story."

"M10 is a great deal more than just a news story," Donley observed, "and you know it."

"But Kirov doesn't know it," answered Williamson.

Charley Frydon sat up in his chair. "There is no doubt Kirov knows M10 is not just a story. They have an intelligence machinery. They have computers. They have brains. They *know*. You can bet on it."

Williamson glared briefly at the CIA Director. Right or wrong, competent or incompetent, he just did not like the man and he did not like being treated as if he were a naïve boy scout. "I still feel you're blowing this all out of proportion. We can contain it and quietly negotiate—"

"Speaking of containment," interrupted Frydon, his transparent blue eyes peering at the President-elect over the steel rims of his glasses, "what have you heard from Messrs. Contos and Tauber? Are they going to hold up further releases?"

"I was saving that," said Williamson, smiling triumphantly. "I got a call from Mr. Contos a couple of hours ago. He has agreed to a delay of several days. I am to call him Sunday. He may even be willing to bury the whole story for weeks in return for guarantees of exclusive material later."

"Then why are all his sales people running around like madmen?" Frydon shot back, with the tone of an attorney beginning a cross-examination.

"What do you mean?" asked Williamson warily.

Frydon flipped his glasses up on his bald pate. "I mean just what I said. All during this afternoon and evening, the VEI salesmen have been playing very funny games. They've been making calls from public phone booths, never from Videowire. They've worked very hard to confuse any surveillance. They meet people in strange places like the New York zoo or in subway stations. . . ."

"What's going on, Charley?" Obvious tension was in President Donley's voice.

"I think they're pulling something," answered Frydon. "I think they've got no intention of slowing up on this story. They're out to make a quick killing financially. We've established that Contos is under very heavy pressure from his backers. It's as simple as that."

"Frydon, I think you're paranoid," said Williamson. "What have they been saying in these wonderfully peculiar meetings of yours?"

"We don't know. I'm afraid we haven't been able to stay close enough."

Williamson snorted. "In other words, these meetings could be quite ordinary, for all you know. Isn't it reasonable to assume they still plan to publish the story *someday* and they want to line up their customers?"

" 'Ordinary' meetings don't happen in churches," said Frydon.

"Churches?" exclaimed Donley.

"Yes, sir. Tauber and Contos and their people have taken a liking to St. Clement's Catholic Church. They've gotten together there twice—the last session was just an hour or so ago. They've also visited St. James' Episcopal. They sit in the pews—different areas each time—and whisper. We can't even get close."

"What about parabolic microphones?" suggested General Kallen.

"What do we do, ask the priest or pastor to lock the

doors of the place while we install the equipment?" responded the CIA Director. "Besides, they use several churches, as I've said, and an empty church is so reverberant it would probably take heavy computer processing and a long time to pull out the words."

"I don't like the way any of this sounds," declared Donley. "What do you think, Boyce?"

"I don't have an opinion yet," Williamson hedged. "It could be much made of nothing."

"We're losing sight of our main problem, aren't we?" suggested General Kallen. "I'm much more worried about what's happening in Moscow and what we ought to be doing about it. Why didn't Kirov talk to us?"

"It's all of a piece, Mike, it's all of a piece," said Donley. "Dammit, I certainly don't want to start the civil defense business yet. I really don't."

The Acting Chairman of the Joint Chiefs was preparing to reply when a bell rang. It was the "black circuit" telephone on the heavy oak credenza near the President's desk, used to obtain direct access to the U.S. intelligence community from the White House. Donley waved Frydon over to answer it.

"This is Frydon," said the CIA Director, and waited. The caller finished his message in less than thirty seconds. With the look of a vaguely preoccupied owl, Frydon replaced the phone and turned toward Donley and Williamson. "John Schotty has disappeared," he said softly.

At Scandia, the fashionable Los Angeles restaurant, late diners were leaning back in luxurious leather-covered chairs, enjoying coffee and a final cognac before calling it a night. The fancy establishments along America's East Coast had already closed their doors and counted their receipts, leaving their clients to go elsewhere to finish the evening's seduction, argument, deal, or philosophical discussion on the state of man. Whether any of the billions upon billions of words spoken that Friday night in the places where America plays on its weekends dealt seriously with the subject of M10 is impossible to say. It is probable that a few people did discuss the subject, but it is also probable that even the most perceptive of them did not comprehend what the remainder of the weekend was to bring. Nor would they have believed it if they had been told.

On the top floor of the White House, in his private quarters, protected by inches-thick bulletproof glass so subtly installed in every window that only its aquamarine tint gave it away, the one man who knew better than any other what might be coming was undressing for bed.

Laura Donley eyed her husband with loving concern. "Fred, I don't like the way you look."

"I'm okay. I'm just tired—and tense, of course. This is an ugly business. Too many people are climbing aboard. . . . Something is going to leak badly somewhere and I'm terrified of what could happen. People could lose their heads."

"What are you going to do about Kirov?"

"The ambassador's checking. The CIA's checking. Everybody's checking. Meantime, I'm going to sit tight for a few hours. As long as everything in the Soviet military remains in routine status, I guess we're okay. I've moved our Tridents up to Level Three—just in case."

"Just in case . . . ?" repeated Laura fearfully as she watched Donley's back, now clad in the silky wine-colored pajamas she had given him for his sixty-second birthday, disappear into the bathroom. She smiled briefly to herself at the absurdity. Even on the world's last night, men would still have to brush their teeth.

"Fred, where is all this going to end?" Laura whispered a few minutes later as her husband slipped into bed beside her. "I've never seen you looking or acting quite like this before. You're on the verge of exhaustion. I know it. I feel it. And I keep thinking about Billie and the kids, too. You know if anything happens, his ship—"

"Yes, honey, I know," Donley interrupted. "I've been thinking about Billie, too. As far as I'm concerned, though, don't worry, I'm fine. I really mean it. Now let's discuss something else. I think it's very important that you go on with business as usual tomorrow. It's a good day for it. You've got all those women's club presidents coming to lunch. We'll arrange some headlines for you and everybody will realize that things can't be very serious if the President's wife is busy having a Saturday luncheon right out in the open. I also want you to make a special point of those national arts awards you're giving tomorrow morning. Talk up the politics of music and painting or something like that. Express sorry over what Williamson might do to financial support for the arts. It will divert attention from M10, and if any damn reporter asks you about it, just laugh it off. Say you know nothing about it. You've been too busy with matters of more importance to you than reading that kind of thing."

"I can do that"—Laura nodded with conviction—"but afterwards I was thinking that maybe I should go to Norfolk on some pretext or other to be with Mary and the grandchildren. With Billie away, they'd have no one except Mary, and I don't know how good she'd be in a crisis. I'd go do it in a minute except I don't want to leave you here, either. You look so tired, and there's a twitch in your eye that worries me."

The President sighed. Planning at such a personal level for a possible disaster was somehow more frightening than anything he'd been through during the day. "Laura," he whispered, "I don't know. I don't think it'll come to it, but I thought maybe we'd send for Mary and the grandchildren and you could take them all with you to the Alternate Command Center."

"You mean inside the Mountain?" Laura exclaimed aloud.

"Yes, I mean inside the Mountain."

"My God, then you really do think it could be that bad? Oh, my God, Fred, I love you! I don't want to leave you. I don't want to be anywhere if you're not there."

"We'll see, honey, we'll see. I think everything's going to be all right. I really do. I was just thinking about it, that's all."

For a long time, Laura Donley lay still and silent by her husband's side. Her eyes, like his, were open and searching in the velvet black of the bedroom. Sleep did not come for either of them. Finally, at nearly 3:00 A.M., Laura turned toward her husband.

"Fred, are you still awake?"

"Yes."

"Fred, I love you so. I was just thinking. This might be our last night together . . . like this." Laura paused. She ran her tongue over her lips and could taste the salt of tears. "Honey, could you . . . could you hold me? Could we . . . make love tonight? Please . . ."

The President shifted on his side and reached toward his wife's familiar body. "Laura . . ." he said very quietly as he buried his face in the softness of her. "I can't. I just can't now."

28

0700 EST SATURDAY NOVEMBER 10

FLASH ANNOUNCEMENT TO ALL VIDEOWIRE EXPRESS INCORPORATED CLIENTS. VIDEOWIRE PRESIDENT STEVEN J. CONTOS DISCLOSED THIS MORNING THAT HE AND VEI COLUMNIST WILLIS TAUBER WILL HOLD A SPECIAL NEWS CONFERENCE IN THE COMPANY'S NEW YORK OFFICES AT 3:00 P.M. TODAY. CONTOS STATED THAT NEW AND EXTRAORDINARY EVIDENCE REGARDING U.S. CANCER WAR PROJECT M10 WILL BE REVEALED. BECAUSE OF ITS SIGNIFICANCE, THE NEW MATERIAL, SAID TO INVOLVE TOP GOVERNMENT OFFICIALS, WILL BE MADE AVAILABLE TO ALL LEGITIMATE NEWS AGENCIES AS WELL AS TO VEI SUBSCRIBERS. HOWEVER, ONLY CLIENTS WILL RECEIVE SUBSEQUENT INSTALLMENTS OF DETAILED TAUBER SERIES ON PROJECT INCLUDING ACTUAL SECRET GOVERNMENT REPORT ON M10 BY ADMIRAL RANDOLPH CLAYTON, LATE CHAIRMAN OF THE JOINT CHIEFS OF STAFF, TO BE RELEASED MONDAY. END.
ADMINISTRATIVE ANNOUNCEMENT TO ALL VIDEOWIRE EXPRESS INCORPORATED CLIENTS. INSTALLMENT THREE OF TAUBER SERIES ON M10 FOLLOWS IMMEDIATELY. TRANSMISSION WILL COMMENCE IN FIFTEEN SECONDS. SYSTEMS WITHOUT AUTOMATIC GRAPHICS TERMINALS SHOULD SET CONTROLS TO CONTRAST 2.8, RESOLUTION 6, FOR PROPER RECEIPT OF PICTORIAL MATERIAL. END.

Installment Three of Willis Tauber's stolen story of M10 rolled out across the world to a list of subscribers which included thirty-eight new clients, two of whom were major sources for South America and Africa.

No longer hiding his strategy, Contos let Tauber unload

great chunks of information about the purported first phases of M10 in the Saturday-morning release. Among Tauber's claims was that the basis for Phase One of the actual attack was the massive export of food products from the U.S. to the U.S.S.R. that developed after the mid 1970s. Cancer research had, by then, uncovered a probable causal relationship between the nitrite treatment used to redden and preserve meats such as ham, sausage, corned beef, and bacon, and the incidence of cancer in the human digestive tract. The mechanism seemed to involve the natural formation of substances called nitrosamines during the process of digestion itself.

Nitrosamines had long been known to be very powerful cancer-producing agents, but the fact that the body could synthesize them, using nitrites and similar chemicals in foods, came as a rude shock. During the period from 1974 onward, intensive research into the mechanisms and effects of nitrosamine formation in humans was carried out in the U.S. and elsewhere. At first the problem was treated cautiously by the scientific establishment. Admonishments from the National Academy of Sciences and other scientific bodies to use nitrites with discretion were accompanied by comments regarding the dangers of food spoilage if nitrites were not used. Except for a few neurotics and food faddists, the public barely took note of the nitrosamine problem. But the research continued.

It was finally shown that the chemical structure of the nitrosamines was peculiarly suited to blocking cellular defenses against certain viruses, including the four or five cancer-related types that by then had been clearly identified. Happily, it was also shown that many foods contained natural agents antithetical to nitrosamine formation and that adding vitamin C to nitrite-treated foods inhibited the formation of most of the troublesome substances. There was, however, one dangerous exception.

A particular nitrosamine, known as NARX and found almost accidentally by workers at the Kaiser Wilhelm Institut für Biochemie in Munich, was revealed to be an incredibly powerful and very stable carcinogen. Fortunately, it did not seem that nature tended to synthesize this material in the human digestive tract. Thus NARX was relegated to dusty medical archives amid millions of other bits of miscellaneous information.

But to the people behind Project M10, NARX provided a crucial opportunity, and they apparently seized upon it immediately. It could be easily made, and it was effective in submicroscopic amounts. Its structure was very close to that of natural substances, so discovery of its presence would be extremely difficult with the best of analytical techniques, let alone those routinely used to check food-stuffs. Furthermore, NARX could be got into the food chain in a dozen different ways.

One way, for example, involved salting U.S. facilities used for the processing or storage of large quantities of grain or meats prior to export to the U.S.S.R. New Orleans, through which forty percent of U.S. grain exports passed, was an ideal base of operation for M10 personnel, who might include, according to Tauber, various government grain inspectors. Another technique seemed to have involved adding NARX to the liquid nitrogen used to freeze foods prior to shipment. There were only a few suppliers of liquid nitrogen to the food industry. The key to the scheme was always that there was only a long-term and quite random relationship between additions of NARX to exported food and actual deaths in the target population. In short, there was simply *nothing* to cause alarm. Over the years, people—more and more people—just died.

Tauber then became philosophical. He declared M10 and the techniques upon which it depended were clearly the inevitable and logical next step in the chronology of warfare and weaponry. Nuclear weapons made overt attack too dangerous. Shielded by détente and mutual deterrence, the dogs of war, therefore, turned quiet but no less deadly. They began to kill under the cover of natural human disease and misery. Closing with speculations on who in the U.S. government had been behind the project, Tauber hinted at a final bombshell: M10 effects had fed back into the American environment and caused many U.S. casualties.

"Well, now we know, don't we?" said Fred Donley, still dressed in his pajamas and a white terry-cloth bathrobe.

"Yes, sir, now we know," agreed Jim Willoughby, who had brought the news of the VEI perfidy to the President.

"Where's Williamson?"

"He's getting dressed. He feels pretty bad."

"What does he think they're planning at their three o'clock party?"

"I don't think he has any idea. If they are planning to talk about his visit with them, he's sure they have no proof—"

"Dammit," said Donley, rubbing his left eye. "He's been around long enough to know they don't need proof. All they need is attention and now they look like they're getting it. Have we got any word on Kirov and a hot-line schedule?"

"No; nothing yet, sir."

"How about on John Schotty?"

"Nothing there, either, I'm afraid."

"Okay," said Donley wearily. "I'll be down in a few minutes. Round up Carl and Charley and Mike."

Willoughby nodded and padded across the thick Oriental rug of the presidential bedroom toward the door, just as Laura Donley, looking beautiful, but concerned and tired, entered from her dressing room.

"Hello, Jim." She smiled bravely.

"Hi! Good morning."

"Stay a moment," the President's wife invited, seating herself in a beloved Louis XV chair. "I want to talk to you. What do you think of our friend here? I don't like the way he looks and I need your help. Let's gang up on him and make him set up a time today for Doc Phillips to check him out."

The President grinned, but shook his head. "Not today, kids. I'm perfectly well—just tense. I'll see Phillips in a few days, when this situation has cooled off."

"Fred . . ."

"Not today, Laura," said Donley firmly.

Willoughby started a strategic retreat toward the door.

"I'll see you downstairs, Jim," declared the President, as he put his hand gently on his wife's shoulder.

"Oh, I've got one more thing to ask you," recalled Willoughby as he stopped, his hand on the heavy brass doorknob. "The Public Information staff is getting more pressure. Any new instruction?"

Donley stood silent, moving his hand lightly back and forth across the crisp white linen covering Laura's shoulders. "No; no new instructions. M10 was a theoretical study done some years ago."

* * *

The Washington offices of the CNS television network were about a ten-minute walk from the White House. In the marvelously jumbled, very casual atmosphere of the second-floor news room, where several dozen gray metal desks were crowded into a space originally designed for half that number, a twenty-seven-year-old investigative reporter named Hugh Callaway was reading a copy of Videowire's early-morning announcements. In his left hand he held a copy of Tauber's third installment, which a girlfriend and former colleague, now working for Bethesda Cable Service, had supplied him with. His eyes shifted quickly over the words. He reached for the file of background material he had been accumulating since Thursday. As he paged through the folder, an idea hit him and he dashed to a row of well-worn reference books stacked on a nearby black file cabinet. Seconds later, he was excitedly pawing through the Washington, D.C., telephone directory. His index finger swept down page 194 and stopped at a name: "Clayton, Adm. Randolph G. 3104 Old G'Twn Rd. G'Twn. 766-2487." He dialed the number.

"Hello? Mrs. Clayton?"

"Yes?"

"Mrs. Clayton, my name is Hugh Callaway. I wonder if I could talk to you about a rumor that's going around about—"

"What . . . you want?"

Callaway hesitated. Something was not quite right. It dawned on him that Mrs. Clayton sounded a little too sleepy. She was having trouble forming her words.

"Mrs. Clayton?" he repeated, listening to the sounds of her watery breathing.

"Who's this? What d'ya want?" mumbled Mildred Clayton.

My God, the reporter told himself. It's Saturday morning and she's drunk as a skunk! He hung up.

The young man spent the next thirty minutes alternating between frenzied searches through files and reference books, and times when he assumed the absolute immobility of a cat on the stalk. When, at last, he charged two at a time down the stairs of the CNS Building, his overcoat was flying behind him and he had a wide smile on his face. A little later, the smile had been replaced by a serious and very solicitous expression. He shifted the paper bag he was carrying to his left hand and pressed the doorbell at 3104 Old Georgetown Road.

"Hello, Mrs. Clayton," he said when the door swung open hesitantly. "My name is Hugh Callaway. I was your son's buddy and I just thought I'd come by to see you, ma'am. I'm on leave from the Marines and I heard about the admiral's tragedy while I was stationed in Japan. . . ."

Even when drunk or badly hung over, Mildred Clayton tried her best not to be stupid. This time she asked all the right questions—or almost all of them. She asked where "Captain" Callaway had met her son. What experiences had they shared? Where had they been stationed together? She got all the right answers. If she had asked to see the "Captain" 's government ID card, she might have caught on, but she didn't think of it and she didn't ask. Partly out of conviction, partly out of the depths of her own loneliness, she finally took the bait. "You know," she said, her eyes swimming with tears, "it was really nice of you to stop by . . . really very nice of you."

"My pleasure, Mrs. Clayton. It's the least I could do. Shall we drink to them both? I brought a little something for a toast."

Half a bottle later, after the stories of the time her son got his tricycle, the time he hit his head in the living room, the time he broke his wrist in high school, and five or six more, Callaway figured Mrs. Clayton might be about ready. "This M10 cancer war scare is pretty awful, isn't it, ma'am?" he said casually.

"Certainly is," she agreed, reaching for the Scotch. "Certainly is. . . ."

"What do you think of it, ma'am?"

"It's awful. . . . I don't want to talk about it."

"But do you think it's true?"

Mrs. Clayton shook her head vigorously. "Don't want to discuss it. Promised I wouldn't."

Callaway's heart started pounding. Fighting to keep his voice steady, he poured himself a drink. "Promises are important," he said.

"Very important . . . very important," agreed Mrs. Clayton. "Mr. Williamson can count on me."

It wasn't much of a slip and it was all Callaway got, even through the rest of the bottle. But it was enough.

29

The skin of the man's abdomen is very pale. The tissue under the skin is soft and watery with age. Sparse strands of curled hair lie matted and flattened against the white skin, which rises and falls slowly as the man breathes. Images of the old man's body undulate in grotesquely distorted reflections on the polished chrome of three funnel-like cones which lightly contact his stomach. The cones are positioned like the legs of an inverted three-legged stool. From the small tips, which almost touch the wrinkled skin of the abdomen, they each splay upward and outward until they are almost a foot in diameter. The old man's bony knees are upraised under the sheet and the force of the stirrups holding his heels presses them high against the cold metal of the cones.

Inside each of the brightly polished funnels, buried deep in thick insulation, is a coil of metallic alloy—a precisely contrived combination of exotic elements: niobium, zirconium, samarium, and tantalum. The coil, built on a base of the purest silver, is motionless and seems perfectly inert, but it is not. Immense electrical currents roar through its every twist and turn. So powerful is the current that were the coil at normal temperature, its entire structure would vaporize instantly in a dazzling white flash. But the current has been tamed. The coil has met the challenge with ease by becoming like an idea—effective but impalpable. The coil's secret is in the dancing fluid that constantly caresses every minute portion of its surface: liquid helium, the coldest substance known to man, an ephemeral material which can exist only at temperatures of 452 degrees Fahrenheit below zero or colder—a material so dependent on cold that to survive it must always remain within a few degrees of what scientists call absolute zero, the ultimate minimum of temperature, which nature herself cannot surpass even at the furthest edges and the dying endings of the universe.

By opening the deep electronic structure of the coil's alloy, by arranging the electrons of the metal to create a new and frozen order out of chaos, the cold has removed all resistance to the flow of electricity through the coil. The coil has been rendered superconductive. The smallest electrical current, once started, will flow in it forever, unceasingly, to the end of time. It asks only one condition to perform this seeming miracle: final, inestimable cold.

But current flows that can last into eternity are not the reason these coils with their cold jackets of liquid helium hang suspended over the anesthesized body of the old man on the stirrup table. The same cold that brings order out of chaos, the same total lack of resistance to electrical current which can stretch the lifetime of a small pulse of energy toward infinity, also allows a relatively small coil to shape and handle huge amperages. As long as the coil offers no resistance, the greatest currents that man can generate cannot destroy it. Can one destroy the air by striking at it?

Thus the huge currents flow harmlessly in each of the three coils above the man. And the currents in their turn create great magnetic fields—almost one hundred thousand times as strong as nature has placed at the surface of the earth.

The immense magnetic fields from the coils are like invisible forceps. Painlessly they can penetrate through the bone and tissue of the human body and fasten with tight fingers on any magnetic object inside the living flesh.

Surgeons, in masks and gowns and paper-thin latex rubber gloves, are clustered close around the table surrounding the old man's body as it rests, like a sacrificial offering, beneath the chrome funnels. Farther away, in positions at the glazed white outer wall of the operating theater, nearly a dozen technicians wait, eyes intent on arrays of dials, gauges, and screens.

"We are ready, Academician Shevchenko."

The head of the surgical team, a small woman in her late forties who is dwarfed by the apparatus she commands, nods her acknowledgment, then turns momentarily in the direction of the anesthesiologist. Her eyes, the only part of her face visible above her mask, ask a silent question.

"Yes, Dr. Shevchenko, the patient is sedated and ready," comes the quick reply.

"Very good, then. We shall insert."

To Academician Antonina Feodorovna Shevchenko, full member of the Russian Academy of Sciences at age thirty and winner the past year of the Pushkin Medal for innovations in surgical techniques, these preparations are like the countdown before a space launching. They are familiar but fascinating. She has been through them nearly three hundred times before, and still the same exhilaration fills her. In a few seconds she will literally be piloting a tiny television camera and a laser torch the size of a matchhead through the intestine of the unconscious patient on the table before her.

Dr. Shevchenko picks up the wandlike instrument she has given ten years of her life to develop. It is light and flexible, covered with a sterilizable sheath of black plastic. The sheath connects, in turn, to a long cable, which leads away toward racks of equipment spread everywhere around the room. At the end of the plastic tube the tiny zoom lens assembly of an exquisitely small TV camera peeks out. The lens is a little over one eighth of an inch in diameter, but it is a masterpiece of the optical designer's art. Along with the microminiature gastrointestinal camera unit itself, it was built in the United States—one of several medical breakthroughs shared between the two countries in recent years. Around the eye of the camera is an annulus in which three microscopic high-intensity lights are mounted. Immediately behind the tip of the wand is a stainless-steel ring penetrated radially by a dozen holes, each a light port the diameter of a single human hair. A solid-state laser is positioned inside the ring. Upon command, it will send a fiercely intense, perfectly focused needle of light outward through any one of the dozen ports. Tissue in the path of the emerging light beam will be steadily eaten away and vaporized into nothing but wisps of carbon dioxide and steam. Not even the smallest particle of char will remain as the beam chews through the flesh and bone toward which it is directed. Capillaries across which the beam may pass are instantly cauterized and sealed before a single drop of blood can escape.

Shevchenko leans forward. She inserts the black tube into the patient's anus. Carefully she slides it forward along the large bowel, then stops. The bloodless, incision-less surgery has begun and they are at the first turn.

"Have the magnets take over now, please," she says. "We'll use the usual image-intensifier guide markers."

Instantly the end of the tube is caught in the unseen grip of three magnetic force fields from the metal cones.

Guided by live television images from inside the patient's living bowel and checked by x-ray images and computer calculations, the fields from the three coils pull the camera and laser scalpel assembly through the dark passages of the old man's body. Slowly responding to the delicately modulated but powerful fields, the tip of the Shevchenko wand, as it has come to be called all over the world, moves steadily through the convolutions of bowel. Like a line of barges snaking up a river, the device is urged on by the tug of the magnetic fields, first ascending the large bowel and then threading its way almost twenty feet into the moist maze of the small intestine.

"We are at reference point one," announces one of the technicians from a chair in front of an x-ray display.

"Yes, I confirm that from the television picture. Please verify orientation for me," Dr. Shevchenko replies.

"It is correct."

"All right, we will now begin excising the tumors. But I want the patient's vital function alarm monitor set as close as feasible. This is a very weak man."

"Yes, Doctor," answers some anonymous voice. Dr. Shevchenko does not hear the response. She is already intent on the task of controlling the tiny laser now preparing to attack the first tumor. Shevchenko turns a pair of controller wheels. Inside the old man's intestine, the head of the wand turns also, its movement locked and controlled by the invisible forces which emanate from the three great pools of magnetic energy above the patient's abdomen. Shevchenko presses a trigger mounted on the controlled held by her right hand. Inside the intestine, a tiny thread of light of incredible intensity leaps forward. It smokes and sears its way into one of the bloated growths that is strangling the man's digestive tract. Shevchenko pauses.

A nurse dabs at the perspiration on the surgeon's forehead. There is no sound in the room except the raspy breathing of the old man and the low hum of the massive racks of electronics. Shevchenko returns to her work. Again she squeezes on the trigger. Again the threadlike flame of light leaps forward.

The operation continues for twenty minutes. Shevchenko is oblivious to time. She does not notice the movements of her colleagues in the surgical theater. She is aware only of the tumors, her enemies.

"I think we have that one," she sighs finally. "Let's move on up."

The wand renews its journey through the frail body on the table. A foot farther and it is at the second tumor. Shevchenko adjusts the magnetic fields to swing the laser ports to the left position. She is about to switch on the full power of the system when the silence in the room is shattered by an alarm buzzer.

"His ECG monitor has triggered, Doctor. He's going into fibrillation!"

Antonina Shevchenko's body jerks back from the table. "All right, all right! Kolganov, take over! Get your cardiac people in here! Pull him out of it!"

Thirty minutes later, the old man's body, his legs released from the absurd humiliation of the stirrup table, is wheeled through the sterile airlock and out into the hallway beyond.

Dr. Shevchenko, her surgical mask pulled down from her ruddy and normally animated face, leans against the cool tile of the corridor wall. There is a sadness in her eyes.

"Tonia, you tried your best. He was too old—even for your techniques. It couldn't be helped," Nikolai Kolganov says, trying to comfort his colleague and friend.

"Oh, Nikolai, he was such a giant, such a mind. We will never see his kind again. Never."

Kolganov puts his arm around the woman surgeon's shoulder and hugs her gently. "I know," he murmurs, "I know. Come with me now. You haven't eaten all day. That fat senior cook—you know her, the one with the huge front—told me this morning that she had some leftover beef from that Argentine shipment the hospital council arranged. She promised to make me piroshki."

A week later at Moscow University, six hundred kilometers from the Leningrad hospital in which Antonina Shevchenko had fought to save his life, a few students of Professor V. A. Gorichev gradually drifted into a lecture hall for the start of a new semester.

"Is this Advanced Astrophysics?"

"Yes."

"But where is everybody? When Gorichev teaches a course, it's usually crowded."

"Gorichev died last week. Hadn't you heard?"

"No!" The young student felt a wave of disappointment sweep over him: he'd been looking forward to this course all through the year. There was nobody like Gorichev. Listening to that man was like having your mind zipped open and the physics poured in. Last year, sitting in the front row, he'd watched the beads of perspiration on Gorichev's face as the old man worked, and worked hard, to put science in their viscera as well as in their heads. He'd sat there and marveled: here was one of the great men of history, trying to pass his insights—his genius—on to the next wave. All of it became clear, so sharp, so true. It was as if you'd climbed a single solitary mountain and could survey the plains in all directions. But now Gorichev was gone; probably one of the deepest minds in all human history, and he was gone.

"What was the matter with him?"

"Don't know for sure: Cancer of some kind: They tried a very advanced operation at Leningrad, but it didn't succeed. Mukhin is taking over his courses."

"Mukhin! But he's no damned good at all."

"I know it—that's why the place is empty. I'm staying with it because my adviser said I'd better or I'll lose a whole year in the course sequence. But I'm not about to learn anything, that's certain!"

"Well, I don't have to take it, so I guess I'll just see you around."

The young student walked out, suddenly aware of the catch in his throat. He realized then how much he'd loved that old man.

30

Carl Silverton eased his creaky body onto the sofa in the Oval Office. "Ambassador Riley claims he's finally gotten a hint out of Kirov's staff. The Premier may condescend to talk to us this afternoon sometime. Riley says the Kremlin folks he's working through seem to be pretty edgy. Something's afoot, no doubt of that."

"Something indeed," responded Donley, fingering his left eyelid in a habit that had grown obvious through the day. He exhaled slowly through tightened teeth and pulled his lanky frame fully upright. "Well, I don't see any alternative. We're just going to have to hang in there and wait for Kirov. Meantime, Contos and Tauber are going to have a picnic at our expense. We certainly can't admit to anybody that M10 is real at this point. We'll just have to stick to our story. Even so, this whole thing is going to be beyond our control very quickly. The best we can hope for is a statesmanlike response from Premier Kirov. Damn him. Why doesn't he answer our calls! He's got to give us time to handle this thing. Everything that we know so far makes me feel that we have got the Russian strategy figured out. They want to close this off and handle it quietly. And we've got to avoid turning our own people into a mob, which is exactly what will happen if they get to thinking about Russian retaliation. Convince them that the Videowire story is true and they'll figure that the Soviets will be jumping down our throats. That will be the ball game. Kirov's got to understand that we both have the same problem. We both have to control our people. Am I right? Have we got any other alternatives?"

There was silence around the table. Carl Silverton, normally a man who might be expected to come up with some tart New England witticism, quietly rolled his white-maned head back and forth as if he could not believe what was happening. Charley Frydon, looking thinner and more worn than usual, held his hands to his lips, his eyes closed in thought. Mike Kallen was sitting bolt upright in his chair, his shoulders very square and his deeply lined face stern and impassive. Only an alternate loosening and pursing of his lips revealed the tension he was feeling.

"Haven't we gotten anything that suggests a Soviet military response?" inquired Boyce Williamson in an uncharacteristically subdued voice. Since the disaster of the morning and the crushing of his expectations regarding Videowire, he had said almost nothing. His main energies were going into worrying about what Contos and Tauber might say at their 3:00 P.M. news conference, now two hours away.

Both Frydon and Kallen shook their heads negatively. "Just as it's been—routine," said Kallen.

"That fact strongly supports our feeling about what Kirov is doing," said Frydon. "It's the one bright spot in this entire situation. He's hoping to let it ooze out instead of hitting all at once. There is nothing on Soviet TV or in their newspapers. But to change the subject slightly, I think you all might be interested to know what the last courier handed me. We seem to be converging toward a specific possibility on the people who started all this."

"For heaven's sake, who?" Donley asked, his pulse accelerating.

"It's what our people have been calling the Fort Deterling 'alumni group.' We've had investigators working with the DOD budget people and the ACA codes. The further they go, the more it's beginning to look like it's Fort Deterling high-level people. Perhaps including the commandant. The incredible thing is the M10 team appears to be spread all over the system, in finance, research, operations—everywhere. We really haven't got a good handle on it all yet."

"Well, keep going on it," the President said earnestly. "Those people have to be brought to justice. Charley, don't let them sneak away on us. Do you understand? Use everybody you need. My God, leaving aside what they have done to the Soviets, whenever I think about the fact that they've been willing to induce cancer in *our own population*, it makes me literally sick to my stomach. It will be decades before this thing has run its course and all the casualties are known." Donley paused as a new thought occurred to him. "I'll tell you this: I only hope the long-term effects do become a problem we can worry about someday. I hope we're all around to testify at the investigations. Right now, I'm not sure there are going to be any investigations, because there may not be any of us left to investigate!"

Carl Silverton, having got up to stand behind the sofa, stopped shaking first one aging leg and then the other to restore circulation, and settled back down into his seat. "Seems to me," he said cautiously, "we'd better set up those briefings with our allies. I was going to do it yesterday, right after we had planned to talk to Moscow. If I call them now, and tell them that you are getting in touch with Kirov about M10, but that we frankly aren't sure when it is going to happen, I think that would be the fair thing to do, don't you, Mr. President?"

"Yes, I suppose so, Carl. The way the world press is picking up on the story, everybody may be facing a stampede by tomorrow or Monday. We'd better give them at least the broad outlines of what we're doing. Go ahead, set up your briefings," the President concluded gloomily.

Within himself Donley felt a growing sense of alarm. It was one thing to sit in his own private world and talk with a few trusted associates about M10 and its consequences; it was quite another to watch the process of diffusion and dissemination begin. The actions he was now approving were irreversible. Most of the governments of the world would soon realize that M10 was not going to go away. It was a matter all humanity would have to deal with, in whatever way it could.

General Kallen also seemed to sense the fact that they had crossed an invisible line. "Mr. President, in view of the other actions you are taking, I think it would be appropriate if the Joint Chiefs meet this afternoon a little earlier than we had scheduled. I intend to propose, sir, that we take all our strategic forces at least to Level Four or maybe to Level Three, depending upon what the other commanders think. I would guess that we will want to move the Trident squadrons to Level Two this afternoon. After all, we don't really know how your conversation with Kirov is going to go."

"Mike, do you really think that's necessary?" the President asked painfully. "Never mind, don't answer that. Of course, it's necessary. Go ahead. Go ahead and do it. I'll also want a full briefing on civil defense planning in one hour. Arrange it, please. . . ." The President's voice trailed off into introspective silence. He rubbed hard at the left side of his face and put his forehead down into his hands for a moment. An instant later he looked up again, facing Frydon. "Charley, have you got anything solid on John Schotty? We really do have enough coming out of the woodwork at the moment."

"Nothing, Mr. President," Frydon replied, "other than what I reported to you before. The apartment is empty. He is just gone. We've searched the whole place twice. There's nothing there. No one has seen or heard anything of him since last night, when we lost him at the Globe Building."

"Do you still feel it's the Russians?" asked the President.

"Maybe; in fact, probably, sir. We're continuing our checking, but I think it's a good bet."

The President's brow knotted into deep furrows, blood vessels on the left side of his face pulsating annoyingly.

"There are a couple of other things I think you'd better know," continued the CIA Director. "We've been monitoring the situation around the country and there are some worrisome signs. First of all, it appears that a number of New York and Washington people are beginning to travel. It's been exceptionally busy at all the airports, and there's a great deal of talk about M10. We've been monitoring foreign bookings and quite a few whole families are to be taking off for other countries. Too many people are flying to smaller towns for one reason or another. I think, frankly, they're anticipating real trouble. There's a fairly heavy buildup of automobile traffic for this time on Saturday, most of it outgoing. We've had our people spot-checking the big city food stores and we're beginning to see a tendency toward buying up groceries and supplies. If that gets to be a big thing, we might get into a hoarding problem and even some shortages. You ought to know that, sir."

Donley's stomach tightened further. "Well, I'm hardly surprised. We knew we couldn't keep things on a close-hold basis, given how hard we're pressing to locate the M10 personnel. Considering the details in the third VEI release, there must be a hundred damned reporters on the scent by now."

"I'm getting a hell of a lot of calls from congressmen and the media," Jim Willoughby contributed ruefully. "We're giving them the 'theoretical study' line. They are buying it fairly well so far."

"I'd give that about four more hours," observed Donley. "Which brings us back to the Videowire news conference. Since we don't know what they've got, I find the decision on blocking it one way or another a difficult one. Have you got any ideas, Boyce?"

Williamson, who had been following the discussion with a worried scowl on his ski-tanned face, chuckled bitterly. "My ideas so far have been pretty lousy, Fred. It's nice of you to ask for more. Well, clearly, shutting down Videowire is a major escalation. Unless we did it very cleverly, it would amount to instant confirmation, as we've been saying all along. I think we've got to tough it out. If they come up with something about me at three o'clock, I'll merely deny it."

"You're not even supposed to be in town," noted Frydon quietly.

Williamson blushed. It was a detail he himself would have thought of in a moment, but the CIA man was right again, damn him. "True enough," conceded the President-elect, thinking fast. "I would just issue a statement through my press staff. They're still out at Bozeman, and I'd say I was up in the mountains but I'd be down in the morning. That would give me plenty of time to get back there for a personal appearance."

"Might work," agreed Frydon, who was about to say something more when the black circuit telephone buzzed. Frydon was next to it and he picked it up immediately. "Kirov is ready to talk!" he said after three seconds of listening.

The President vaulted from his chair like a man who had received a galvanic shock. "All right! Boyce, let's get downstairs to the Crisis Center. Carl, get your translators down here. Jim! Call down, tell them to check out all the equipment. I don't want any technical problems." In long, loping strides, Donley moved rapidly toward the door, Williamson right with him, his legs pumping to match the taller man's pace. "Now remember our agreement, Boyce. This is going to be hard enough, without making it a three-cornered debate. Right?"

"Yes," answered Williamson breathlessly as they raced

for the waiting elevator. "I will just listen, provided you tell him what you told me you're going to."

"That's the way I'm going to handle it. I'll inform him about M10, explain that it's not an official project. I'm pretty sure from the strategy they've been following that he'll go along with giving us time to get to the bottom of the whole thing and discuss ways to recoup."

Williamson was dubious. "I warn you, Fred, if I were he, I wouldn't stop there. But if you think that's the way he's going to react, you know him better than I do. I hope you're right."

The key entry in the records of Crisis Center communications for Saturday, November 10, discloses that the hot-line connection between Washington and Moscow was first established with video imagery at precisely 1322 hours, or 1:22 P.M. EST and 9:22 P.M. Moscow time. The technicians had done their job well and the audio and visual fidelity were perfect.

"Mr. Premier, how are you?" said Donley to the image on the monitor.

"I am well, Mr. President: What is it you wish?" The face spoke in a flat, emotionless monotone, but the eyes under the heavy, dark brows were burning, the wide, heavy-jowled jaw set with determination.

"Mr. Premier, President-elect Williamson is also here with me, as you can see. He is an observer only. I speak for the United States." Kirov looked at Williamson and nodded. He had dealt with Donley before, but Williamson was an unknown quantity. Realizing what was coming and that the speed with which events were moving would make Donley the key to their course, he decided the President-elect was not important. His eyes turned back to Donley. It was a decision both Americans sensed immediately. Donley continued his introductory remarks. "We wish to discuss an unofficial project we have recently uncovered—"

"I assume you mean M10, Mr. President?"

"Yes, we—"

"Mr. President, perhaps I can save us valuable time. I am in possession of the complete M10 report. Mr. John Schotty also was kind enough to provide additional details to us. He arrived here just a short time ago and will, I think, be visiting us for a time. I wished to talk to him at length, which was, in part, the cause of my being unavailable when you first called."

Donley's eyes flickered at the mention of John Schotty, but he proceeded without hesitation. "Mr. Premier, you must understand—the government of the United States had no knowledge of M10. We do not condone it. We are doing all we can to find out who was behind it."

"My dear Mr. President, let us not waste words. Even if I were to believe you—believe that a two-hundred-million-dollar project could exist without your knowledge —what am I to tell my people? Am I just to say forget it? Do I say never mind that your fathers or brothers or daughters are dead or dying; the Americans really didn't mean it? We *know* what has happened. Our statisticians have confirmed the report of your Admiral Randolph Clayton." The face on the monitor seemed to turn darker and redder under the straight black hair combed stiffly back. "Mr. President, do you know that *my wife* died of cancer of the liver last year?"

"Yes, Mr. Premier, I know. . . ."

"Mr. President, I will say the obvious: We are at the edge of the cliff."

Donley nodded. "I am fully aware of that."

There was a long pause as the two men stared at each other. Though they were half a world apart and separated even further by history and by background, they were very close as they faced this moment together. At last the Premier spoke:

"Mr. President, what is the current status of your nuclear attack force? Do not lie to me."

"We are at Level Three."

"Mr. President, we monitor your global transmissions to your Tridents. We cannot be sure, but we think you have them standing by for a preemptive strike."

"We plan no first action of *any kind*. You must believe me. I have given the alert only as a precaution."

The audio signal between Moscow and Washington wavered slightly as Boyce Williamson cut in with a whisper to Donley, his voice quivering with tension. "Does he understand our alert system? Make sure he knows there are still many controls!"

"Boyce, he understands. We've exchanged these protocols for years, just in case of something like this."

"President Donley." The voice of Kirov boomed through the autotranslators. "I do not quite follow what Mr Williamson is saying, but I will tell you both this: I have had forty-eight hours with this nightmare and and I see only a very few possibilities. First, there is war, and I must tell you the odds are great for that no matter what we do. Who could blame my people for demanding revenge? And how could even nuclear attack match the unspeakable thing you have done?"

"Mr. Premier—"

"Let me finish, Mr. President! As I have said, we have had only a day or two to face this horror you Americans have visited on the world. But we believe, some of us, that there may be a way out."

"What, in God's name?"

"Not in God's name, Mr. President, but in the name of the Russian people. There must be reparations. There must be—there will be *justice*."

"Reparations. What manner of reparations?"

"First, you must pay for and provide the care for those you have affected. Your own report estimates twelve million at the present, with five more probably to come.

"Second, we must have material compensation. I have given much thought to that matter, Mr. President," Kirov said slowly. He paused, his eyes like black diamonds in his wide, ruddy face. "I want Alaska!"

The hot line went dead with a dumfounded silence.

Donley recovered himself. "Alaska?" he asked incredulously, "Alaska? Mr. Premier, you can't be serious! It is impossible! I could never convince the American people. It would destroy us."

"So it might," Kirov responded coldly, "But it is the only feasible possibility that has suggested itself. Your wonderful capitalist system, with all its initiatives and freedom, has brought this upon us. It should pay the piper. But money means nothing. It is just paper. Gold means nothing. The West could merely abandon it as a trading commodity. *I want Alaska*. There are relatively few Americans there. It could be evacuated readily. In a sense, Alaska should properly belong to the Soviet Union. It was only an accident of history that it was sold out from under our people without their consent. It is appropriate; in a way it is a justice long overdue. Even so, I am not confident that we can save the situation. And there are other conditions, Mr. President."

"Yes, go on," said Donley, now determined to be rational and detached, whatever Kirov said.

Boyce Williamson began fidgeting in his seat. "Donley," he whispered again, "what the hell are you doing? This whole discussion is insane—it's insane!"

"Pardon me, Mr. Premier. I'll be back on the line in a moment," the President said, as he gestured to a technician to cut the connection temporarily.

"Listen, Boyce! We have to hear what he has to say. There is time to argue later, is that clear? *Is that clear?*"

"Yes, it's very clear," replied the President-elect, glaring at Donley. "You are headed down a road to disaster."

"Would you prefer a nuclear war this afternoon?"

Williamson did not answer.

"Very well, then," said Donley. "I will proceed with Kirov. But let's have no more spontaneous assessments or decision-making—even by you. We will listen, think, and respond later."

"Now, Mr. Premier," said Donley, repositioning himself before the video camera with apparent calm: "What other points did you wish to make?"

"First of all, Mr. President, I am not sure that I will be able to contain the situation here as these revelations about M10 continue to gain credibility. The Soviet people, fortunately, are not yet aware of what has occurred; nor are most of my associates. That is a very important factor. I cannot overstress it. But in spite of the control I can exercise over our press and television . . . well, you can see what will happen. It will gradually spread across our borders. I do not know what will then happen. There is grave danger of outright rebellion and I need time to neutralize certain dangerous trends. You must stop any further stories about M10. Do you understand me? *There must be no more announcements.*"

"I understand completely," replied Donley. "I have serious problems there. I face severe legal limitations and if I act too precipitously against Videowire Express, the American population itself could panic."

"We have considered your limitations, and that is your burden," said Kirov. "You must now pay for your precious free press and I trust the price will not be too high for both of us. Find a way, Mr. President. I may perhaps also have the means to assist you . . . but let me continue on other matters. We shall return to that later."

Kirov shifted his body, square-cut and blocky, to one side. The steady eye of the hot-line camera in Moscow followed him. He slipped a hand into the jacket of his dark-gray double-breasted suit and leaned forward as if trying to get closer to the men he was addressing. "I now wish to discuss the disposition of the perpetrators of this heinous—this unspeakable—attack. It is to be understood between us—and I am quite aware of the dimensions of your current search for their identities—that regardless of who they are, regardless of what positions they occupy, they are to be delivered to us. *We* are the ones who will punish them. Not your American courts and laws. Our courts, our laws, our justice, Mr. President. Is that clear?" Kirov was almost at the camera lens. His distorted face filled the color TV screen before Donley and Williamson like a great swollen balloon.

"I understand the feelings you have expressed," responded Donley, cringing inwardly at what would happen if the personnel of Project M10 were delivered to Soviet hands.

"Do you agree it is our right to deal with these people?" The Soviet leader was pressing.

"I understand your feelings," repeated Donley. "We will work something out."

"Work something out? Work something out!" screamed Kirov. "We have been murdered by the millions and you say you will work something out?"

"Alexei, listen to me!" Donley shouted at the raging face on the monitor. It was like trying to make yourself heard by a hurricane. "Listen to me, Alexei," he said again, more quietly. "You and I have worked together for four years. You know I cannot act on my own. You know our system. I must have time to arrange such things. My power is not absolute."

Kirov's image pulled back, jaw muscles corded and taut, then his expression suddenly relaxed. The towering fury drained away and he was a statesman again. "Very well," he said huskily, "let us proceed. Mr. President, in one area your power *is* absolute, and I expect you to use it. You must order a stand-down of your military forces. That you can do immediately. Surely your satellites and other monitors have told you we are not readying an attack . . yet." Kirov looked down at a single small sheet of paper in front of him. "Furthermore, I also demand that you arrange for Soviet technicians to witness a prompt disarmament of your land-based ICBM inventory. I will announce this in due time to the Soviet people as further evidence of American conciliation and reparation. I want a reduction to twenty-five percent of current levels. With your Tridents, you will still be able to hold our cities hostage against everything, even a first strike by us, which your intelligence satellite system would detect in any event. As I see it, this will ensure that the United States will never attack us even if there is a rebellion as a consequence of the reparations formula. You will not be able to completely preempt us, as some of your hawkish generals might be already suggesting.

"Frederick, I know some of these terms are harsh—very harsh. I realize they will give you great difficulties. I am sorry I grew angry a moment ago. It has not been the pattern between us. Who knows? We could turn this calamity into an opportunity for the true peace we both have sought. But most importantly and immediately, these terms give us a chance—just a chance, mind you—of convincing my people not to seek the revenge they will surely want if—no—*when* they find out what the United States has been doing."

To Donley, each word Kirov said was a physical thing, a ponderous object weighted with lead. "I simply cannot react now," he said gently to the TV camera in front of him. "You must give me time. . . . I must have some time."

"I understand, Mr. President. This may sound strange under the circumstances, but I trust you. Both the documents I have and Mr. Schotty's testimony make it likely that you have had nothing to do with this abomination. I intend to proceed on that assumption. But I am not sure how much time there is. There are some here who feel time has run out. I am not sure I can control them. I *think* we will be able to hold matters together only for a day or two. You must have your forces stand down from the alert and start the disarmament *now* to help me. I must have at least that to keep serious things from happening in the next few hours. You need not announce it; just do it. The rest can come later, but you must do that soon—I can have my technical experts ready immediately—and *you must return your forces to routine status.* Now . . . *now.*"

Boyce Williamson, trembling with indignation, looked hard at the man beside him. How could Donley just sit there as that Russian fired orders at him as if he were an Army corporal? Was he that intimidated? Was he really planning to consider *unilateral disarmament?* Could he imagine giving up Alaska to the Soviet Union?

Donley ignored his agitated companion. "Mr. Premier, I will order our military back to Level Five as soon as I confirm the status of your own forces. I shall call you again on the rest of your proposals within twenty-four hours."

Kirov's brooding peasant face hardened into granite with the intensity of his next words. "Remember, somehow you must suppress M10. Otherwise I fear I shall lose all influence on the situation. As it is, it will take a miracle to prevent the Russian people from rising like a tidal wave. Only if I can prepare them, only if I can control matters, do we have a chance. I will use force where I have to. I will give you help where I can. As we have talked, I have decided to take certain actions to assist you. You will not approve of them, my dear and moral colleague, but accept them nevertheless."

"What do you mean? Explain what you mean," demanded Donley.

"You will understand in due time, Mr. President. Just remember that there are many lunatics in your country who would have wished this M10 Project to go on without ever being discovered or discussed."

"I still don't understand," said Donley.

"Do not worry about what I have just said, Frederick," replied Kirov. "Think, instead, about the reparations. Perhaps they will make the Soviet people stop and think. We must *give* them something—do you understand me? We *must.* Good afternoon, Mr. President."

"I shall call you before 9:00 P.M. Moscow time tomorrow," said Donley, wondering what Kirov was planning to do to "assist" him. "Good night, Mr. Premier," he said with a nod, as Boyce Williamson sat stiffly at his side.

"Well, I must tell you I am amazed, Mr. President," Carl Silverton declared, shaking his head in wonderment as he shuffled up immediately after the hot-line connection was broken. "He sounds so rational. The man has obviously been looking at the same ugly possibilities as we have, and in spite of the fact that he's come up with an incredible proposition, he's certainly not losing his head."

"Ridiculous is the word for it," said Kallen as he joined the cluster of people gathering around the now blank monitor of the hot line. "The whole thing is preposterous. Alaska? . . . It's beyond belief."

"I'm not so sure," mused Charles Frydon from the edge of the group. "You know, what would we do in their position? What would we really do if we thought the Russians had killed twelve million of our people over the last few years? I think he's genuinely trying to find a way out, short of nuclear war, and I don't think he's got very many options."

"Even if we give them what he asks for—not that I say we possibly could," said Silverton, "I wonder if we can trust him. And if we do trust him, I wonder if he can hold things together at his end. My people have had a feeling for some time that Kirov's position has been slipping. I think Efremenko and Amosov had been undermining his power base, and if we're not careful, this is going to be the final straw. It won't do us very much good to be dealing with somebody who doesn't have any power to follow through on a deal."

With a wave of his hand, the President stopped the discussions swirling around him. "Look," he said decisively, "it seems to me we have got to at least start the process of defusing the situation. It may not work, but short of going for an all-out preemptive strike, I don't see any other possibilities. We don't have to go all the way down the road Kirov is asking us to take. We go one step at a time. And we watch the Russians closely. If Kirov can handle things, we'll at least buy some time to deal with the question of civil reaction and the reparations. There is no doubt in my mind we're going to have to come up with some kind of compensation formula. I'll admit Alaska sounds unreal, to say the least. Perhaps we can develop a new economic assistance program with them, but that's all to take weeks, or even months. And the thing he and we both need now, more than anything else, is time."

"But, Mr. President, you don't mean you're really

thinking of inviting them into our ICBM silos, are you?" asked an incredulous General Kallen.

"Mike, we can certainly get them traveling *toward* those ICBM silos. It will give Kirov something to bargain with. We've got to put ourselves in this position. If he's as tottery as Carl and the State Department people seem to think, well, then it behooves us to strengthen his hand. Doesn't that make sense?"

"Goddamned little of this makes sense!" shouted Boyce Williamson, bringing the discussion to a sudden stop. He was, if he had been honest with himself, even more angered at being essentially ignored in the hot-line exchange than than by its contents.

"I keep asking for your suggestions," Donley said very quietly. The effect on Williamson was instantaneous.

"Well, I'll say one thing," Williamson continued at a more normal level. "I've come to agree with Kirov that we'd better shut down Contos and Tauber. The rest of it is another matter. It is asinine."

"Okay, let's go a step at a time," Donley proposed. Knowing Williamson was being guided as much by his concern about covering his misjudgment of Contos as by anything else, he nevertheless knew it should be done. "We've got less than an hour before the Videowire press conference. I agree, let's cut them off. Now, what's the best way?"

"I suggest we play it as straight as possible," answered Charley Frydon, his head shining under the ceiling lights of the Crisis Center. "We'll have the FBI take Contos and Tauber into custody along with the rest of their staff and we'll shut down their transmissions on the grounds that they are causing harmful international tensions."

"It's going to bring every reporter in the world down on us," said the President. "Jim, you'll have to alert the press staff."

"We'll get at least a few hours out of it. We can also build some blank walls and blind alleys to slow things up," argued the CIA Director.

"Like?" asked Donley.

"Well, we haven't used Brondoff and the National Institutes of Health yet. And maybe we could develop and leak a *fake* Clayton report, which keeps things on a theoretical basis only."

Williamson grunted with indignation. "Frydon, you are born for this kind of thing, aren't you? There is no level to which you do not easily stoop."

The quietly furious CIA Director focused his myopic blue eyes on the next President of the United States. "Sir, if I did not do all in my power to avoid the panic and death that may be occurring outside our doors in the next twenty-four hours—if I did not do all I could to avoid a nuclear war—then, *and only then*, would I be ashamed of myself. And you, Mr. Williamson—under what circumstances would *you* be ashamed of yourself?"

"That's quite enough," interrupted Donley. "Charley, proceed with the Videowire shutdown. We'll think about the rest. Mike, I want to join you in a teleconference with the rest of the Joint Chiefs and the SecDef in five minutes. Then we'll discuss alerting Civil Defense. I'll certainly want to start preparations Soviet intelligence will be able to detect on Kirov's ICBM demand. But I do not propose to leave this country naked. I intend to maintain our current submarine alert levels until we are sure Kirov is in firm control. I doubt if they could read a SeaComm reaffirmation message."

"They certainly can't," agreed Kallen.

"All right then," said Donley briskly. "Unless you, Boyce, have something you want to add, let's move out."

Williamson shook his head in disgust, then looked toward the chart-covered wall of the Crisis Center, where a digital clock labeled the flow of events with the numbers men call time. It was 2:16 P.M., Saturday, and the juggernaut of M10 was rumbling steadily toward its victims.

31

Steve Contos beamed. With sybaritic pleasure he pictured the days ahead. A black Mercedes? Maybe even a Rolls some time off. Perhaps Vegas. No, Monte Carlo! And why shouldn't he indulge himself a little? He had a right to. Other millionaires did, and Contos was a millionaire, or at least well on his way to being one. Fifty-five new subscribers, not even counting the Metrotext Italia offer. Fifty-five signed-on-the-dotted-line subscribers. And begging. They were begging. All afternoon the calls had been coming as the M10 story gained momentum. They were believers now, the doubting bastards. After the news conference and the Williamson tape, they'd be frantic, climbing the walls.

The Videowire president smiled. Through the open door of his office he could see Willis Tauber putting a little last-minute polish into a biography of Randolph Clayton which would run with the final release. Tauber was absent-mindedly doing arm curls with a metal side chair in his left hand while he scribbled on his typed manuscript with his right. The musclebound ape was a pretty good writer, at that, thought Contos. Not smart, not really shrewd, but not bad as a craftsman. He'd be useful when it came to writing the books and covering the TV talk shows after the dust settled.

"Willis!" hollered Contos. "Come in a minute, will you?"

Tauber's shoulders were almost as wide as the door opening. He took his usual seat on the edge of the desk. "Have you decided?" he asked, like a kid who was hoping to go to a Saturday-afternoon movie.

"Yeah," replied Contos. "I think we ought to do it."

"So do I." Tauber nodded.

"We'll refund to the three or four others in the Metrotext service area and give 'em the deal," Contos said, pulling on his cigar. God, how he loved wheeling and dealing! he told himself. He was made for it.

"The deal" was an exclusive arrangement with Metrotext Italia, the huge electronic news subsidiary of a Rome-based magazine empire which served "people-oriented news," meaning gossip and scandal whenever possible, to nearly fifty-five million readers across southern Europe and the Middle East. "The deal"—which had been proposed a couple of hours earlier in a culminating twenty-minute phone call to a Manhattan phone booth from a majestic villa set behind the old stone walls of Via Appia Antica— was backed by a $500,000 telegraphic bank draft, now behaving like a lighted 500-watt bulb in the pocket of Steven Contos's black-and-white-checked jacket. "The deal" had only one catch. It was predicated upon immediate transmission of *all* Videowire installments and supplementary materials. The Italian company would not break the story early. It would observe all publication embargoes. But it would be free to resell the story rights in its own territory; hence the need for receiving the material ahead of time. Send the goods and cash the check. For a solid, nonrefundable half-million dollars, who could argue?

"Okay, so let's load the disks," Tauber said, breaking Contos's reverie. Pulling two gleaming disks out of a locked file, Contos headed for the outer office and the VEI computer. As his partner watched, he stacked them into an electronic memory unit about the size of a shoe box and capable of storing the equivalent of twenty thousand sets of encyclopedias. A green "Ready" light came on as the disks started to rotate. Contos moved to the computer control console and typed in a request for the proper routing and address code for Metrotext Italia. The video telex number appeared on the screen: ITALIA-MT—678-7874. Contos pushed a keyboard button labeled "Add. Entr."—Address Enter. Electronic pulses representing the routing instructions to Italy obediently flashed into their correct slots in the Videowire transmission circuits.

On the now rapidly whirling disks in the memory unit, Installments Four and Five of the M10 story were ready for flight. Once launched by a "Distribute" command, they would move through the global network of communications satellites and fiber-optical data connections that spiderwebbed the planet to the exact address Contos had commanded. At maximum speed, the great information highway that led away from New York could transport a full page of print a distance of twenty-five thousand miles in less than two millionths of a second. Maximum-speed international service was expensive and unnecessary. For the low-cost class of service leased by Videowire, it would take a relaxed thirty minutes, from the time Videowire's computer was told to Distribute, to send all the content of the two memory disks to Rome.

"We've got forty-five minutes or so before the news conference," said Contos, glancing at the IBM clock on the wall above the entrance. His eyes wandered down to the figure of a woman seated at the Videowire reception desk, her back toward him. It lingered there. "I think we deserve a drink on an occasion like this, don't you, Willis?"

"Barbara!" he called, without waiting for an answer. "How about joining us for a little celebration?"

The girl picked her head up out of the movie magazine she was reading and smiled. She stood up, smoothing her very tight slacks over a bottom that was, as Contos described it, built for both speed and endurance. Barbara was not bright, but she was blond and marvelously decorative. Contos had kept her around, even when he could hardly afford it, for the sake of appearances and in the hope that he might someday get a chance to slowly peel that bottom bare of the little bikini panties he could tell she always wore. During the two years she had worked for him, he'd tried and failed four or five times—there were always younger men interfering. As he watched her undulate toward him, he knew he'd succeed next time. Money is a great aphrodisiac.

"The usual?" said Barbara pleasantly, passing the two men on her way to a file cabinet where Contos stashed bottles and glasses.

"Sure," replied the VEI president. "You'll accept Wild Turkey straight, won't you, Willis?"

Tauber grinned and nodded.

"What are we drinking to?" asked the girl innocently, as her violet eyes seemed to be saying a host of other things to Contos.

"We've made a deal on that story."

"Oh, great!" Barbara read only movie and TV magazines. She didn't know anything about M10, although it had surrounded her for days. "What story is that?"

"Never mind," said Contos, laughing. He took a long slug of the 101-proof whiskey, and as it burned down his throat, he jammed a finger against a button on his keyboard. It was green and larger than the others and the word engraved on it was "Distribute." "Pour me another," he said to the girl, running his tongue across his lips.

Not quite ten minutes later, Contos had finished his third drink and Tauber was beginning to worry about his ability to handle the questions from the reporters who were due to begin arriving momentarily. "Let's knock off the booze awhile, Steve," he suggested. "I want to be sharp for these guys."

"Yeah, yeah. Where's the tape recorder for the Williamson thing?"

"You locked it in your desk."

"Right. Let's get it checked out," said Contos as he clapped a hand on Tauber's heavily muscled shoulder and shoved him playfully toward his inner office. He closed the door behind them, leaving Barbara alone at her desk with a four-page photo spread entitled "Divorce: Los Angeles Style."

The receptionist did not hear the outer door of the Videowire office suite open. Most probably she was too engrossed in the pictures of the pretty people and her own special dreams of joining them. When she did become aware that someone was standing in front of her desk and looked up, it was already much too late. She stared in speechless terror at the black hole of the muzzle of the gun, paralyzed with fear. Her breath caught in her throat and her mind simply stopped. She did not even feel the quick sting of something on her upper arm, and in the space of three or four heartbeats, she slipped noiselessly into unconsciousness.

The three men, one carrying a heavy attaché case, walked quickly past the Videowire computer, still spewing out the content of its two whirling memory disks, to the closed door of the inner office. One man, thin, with a narrow face and a remarkable nose that twisted slightly to the right, put his ear against the door and listened briefly. He signaled to his two companions and opened the door.

"Hi, guys, you're a few minutes early," said a smiling Steve Contos before he saw the guns.

"What the fuck is this?" roared Will Tauber, whose reactions were a shade faster.

"You will kindly raise your hands, sirs," said the man with the twisted nose. The way he said it, his slight but peculiar accent, perhaps, made discussion superfluous. Tauber raised his hands and a transfixed Contos followed his example.

"Thank you," said the man. "Now turn your backs, please."

Contos and Tauber turned, Tauber sensing out of the corner of his eye that the man was walking up behind Contos. He caught the flash of something metallic or glassy in the man's hand as it punched forward against the Videowire president's thigh. Contos crumpled like a puppet whose strings had been cut. He's dead! thought Tauber. They're killing us! In desperate panic, he whirled like a trapped animal as the man approached him, swinging his great shoulders heavily into the lighter man's chest. With all his strength, he clawed at the arm holding the hypodermic needle, catching it, twisting it up and away. Tauber could hear tendons snapping. His chest thudding with fright, he pulled the injured man's recoiling, flexing body in front of him. The man, reacting with cobra quickness, jammed a leather heel into the top of Tauber's foot; searing pain shot up Tauber's leg. The man bent down sharply, ramming Tauber hard in the stomach with his free elbow. Tauber flinched. For an instant the agony froze him and he was unshielded. Almost nonchalantly, the two men who had been watching the struggle squeezed the triggers of their guns. Gray smoke spewed simultaneously from the heavy, silencer-equipped weapons and two eight-millimeter soft-nosed bullets ripped through Tauber's shirt and into his chest. One tore out his right lung. The second crushed through pulsating heart tissue and exploded from his back in a yawning volcanic eruption of bone and blood. Willis Tauber's eyes bulged wildly, he lurched forward a single step, and then what remained of him slumped toward the floor. Small sharp pieces of bone and glistening pinkish-gray jelly-droplets of nerve fiber driven from his spinal cord by the impact of the bullet, began a slow slide downward across the blood-spattered glass of the VEI windows.

The man with the thin face, holding his mangled arm, said something to his companions. One of the men stepped over to the still-unconscious form of Steven Contos. He placed his weapon behind Contos's right ear, pulled the fabric of the Videowire president's elegant black-and-white sports jacket up and around the muzzle to avoid the spray of blood, and pulled the trigger. There was only a soft, meaningless *thunk*. Like a hammer hitting a melon. It was not the way Steven Contos had expected to die.

Ashen-faced and trembling from the savage pain in his shoulder, the leader of the killers led the way back to the outer office. He gestured with a tilt of his head and the case his men brought was placed against the warm metal of the Videowire computer. Sixty seconds later, a great roar cut through the Saturday-afternoon traffic noises of Manhattan. Three large plate-glass windows in the office building housing Videowire Express Incorporated leaped from their frames and showered down thirty-six stories toward startled shoppers on the street below. Premier Alexei Kirov was helping make sure no further details about Project M10 were disseminated.

32

Over a chorus of horns, wildly screeching brakes and frantic shouting echoed along Sixth Avenue. Within seconds after the explosion demolished Videowire, the street, checkerboarded with the shadows of the afternoon sun, was clogged by a milling crowd of New Yorkers gawking curiously at two people lying on the sidewalk in widening pools of blood. One great daggerlike shard of bronzed glass had sliced deeply into the shoulder of a well-dressed elderly woman and another had cleanly amputated the foot of a young man dressed in the uniform of the BestEver Messenger Service. Someone was sobbing uncontrollably. Wailing sirens and running men seemed to be everywhere.

A voice rose above the babble. "I'm a doctor! I'm a doctor, let me through. Let me through!" The crowd, hypnotized by the blood, parted reluctantly and then clustered around as a man bent over the injured woman and began cutting away the cloth of her blood-soaked coat with a pocketknife. There was a jostling nearby and the doctor, a tall black man in a stylish blue suit and light-gray topcoat, looked up from his unconscious patient to find himself facing the impudently protruding lens of a portable TV camera. He returned to his work muttering, shaking his head, and watched by three network camera crews, all of whom had been on their way to the 3:00 P.M. Contos/Tauber press conference.

Two screaming fires engines, an ambulance, and three police cars, blue roof lights flashing to the accompaniment of frenzied whistles, appeared at the curb, displacing the stalled taxicabs and swirling masses of onlookers. Gasps rippled through the crowd as paramedics and firemen in heavy rubberized fire gear dashed into the building and then emerged with stretchers, carrying a pair of mangled male corpses under dark plastic sheets and a horribly disfigured but still breathing blond woman. And everywhere the TV cameras watched, sending their lurching, rolling images into thirty million American homes to viewers who had, until that moment, been dozing lethargically in front of the Saturday-afternoon movie or rooting hard for their favorite college football teams. Breathless young reporters dispatched on routine assignment to cover the press conference suddenly found themselves getting the chance of a lifetime on network television with interviews or stand-up commentaries. In breathless, panting, nonstop phrases, they told all they knew about Videowire, about M10, about the rumors that had been rippling between Washington and New York in the past days, and anything else they could think of. Some of the newsmen, especially those from the print media, who were on the scene but not on camera, were well-informed about M10 and had read VEI's first three releases. The TV reporters, however, had not been specially assigned to investigate M10 and did not know much more than they had casually overheard around their offices. Desperate to compete on the breaking story and to exploit the big chance fate had given them, they filled their air time with ad-libbed, half-considered speculations: Could the U.S. really be attacking Russia with carcinogens? Was the CIA behind the bombing? Had the government ordered VEI destroyed?

One bright, energetic TV commentator, a thirty-year-old graduate of Northwestern University's School of Journalism, who had arrived in New York only two weeks earlier, turned his eyes away from the camera lens and scanned the mesmerized crowd while he continued speaking into his chrome-plated microphone. Standing on a mass of crushed, pebble-sized glass fragments and almost without realizing what he was saying, he pursued the possible logic behind a government attack on Videowire: ". . . and if the perpetrators were really from the CIA, for example, it would suggest that the published claims of Videowire Express regarding the so-called M10 Project are, in fact, correct. That, in turn, could easily bring the threat of a nuclear war between Russia and the United

States at any time. . . ." His voice trailed off and he stopped talking. The young man gaped stupidly into the unblinking camera lens as the immensity of what he had just said penetrated his brain. Millions of people were watching. In undisguised dismay, he swallowed hard and searched for something more to come up with. Feeling like a fish just pulled from a stream, he opened and closed his mouth helplessly until the camera finally swung away to a group of well-dressed civilians flashing government credentials at two stolid policemen guarding the entrance of the building.

So outlandish, so incomprehensible in its implications, was the reporter's suggestion that war might be imminent that almost all his audience rationalized it away as cheap sensationalism or avoided thinking about it at all. Americans, for the most part, were determined to continue the ordinary business of their sunny November Saturday. The Apocalypse was not yet in their plans.

Frederick Donley, gratefully alone for the first time in hours, hunched forward on his elbows and stared at the polished oak surface in front of him. Where was it all going to end? Should he move more aggressively to protect the U.S. population from itself? Should he call in congressional leaders for a briefing? Should he alert the Civil Defense forces? The National Guard? Each and every one of those actions could trigger riots and terror. Donley picked up one of the paperweights from the collection clustered like toys on the corner of his desk. Idly he fondled the smooth, heavy glass. A jewel-like facet caught in the afternoon sun and glinted sharply. In an instant, he was again with Laura in Norway. The fjords and the ship and the sunlight were clear and the water a dark-blue mirror. A shiver ran down Donley's back and wispy lines of nausea threaded their way across his stomach. He shook his head vigorously and grunted aloud. He was back in the present again, his left eye twitching annoyingly. Ignore it, he told himself. This is no time to be sick.

Donley flipped on the intercom. "Dorie, could you call the attendant? Have him get these plates out of here. Just the sight of them is enough to make me queasy."

"Certainly, Mr. President, right away," the honey-smooth voice replied through the little speaker. "Mr. President, is there anything at all I can do for you?" Worry and concern were in the words.

"No, not a thing. I think we've got everything about as under control as it's going to get. You're doing your part just by standing by out there. On second thought, since I've got a breather for a minute, maybe you'd better get me General Josten at the Pentagon. He's still the head of Public Information over there, isn't he? I'd like his firsthand impressions."

"Yes, sir, Josten is still there. I'll get him right away. Meantime, Mr. President, Mrs. Donley called. She asked me to tell you that she wanted to stop by to see you as soon as the meeting was over. Is it all right for her to come in now? She's just upstairs."

"Okay. Tell her now's as good a time as any."

Laura Donley peeked around the door of the Oval Office. Dressed in a beautifully tailored gray suit with black velvet collar and a single strand of pearls encircling her throat, she looked like what she was—the perfect presidential wife.

"Hi! How's it going?" she said softly as she walked rapidly toward him.

"It's moving along. How was your luncheon?" he asked.

"It went okay. At the very least, we gave the society pages and the gossip columnists something to write about. I don't know how much good we did for M10. Half a dozen of those reporters pushed me on it very hard, but I think I did a pretty good job of making light of it. I even got off a couple of jokes! But Fred, I'm worried about you. You look strange. Are you *sure* you're feeling all right?"

"Laura, I'm okay. It's just the strain. I promise I'll see Doc Phillips next week. Now, don't worry about it, Laur, please don't."

"Fred, when this is over, let's go someplace. I'm tired of Camp David. You can't relax there. Why don't we talk to some of your friends? Somebody with a place off the beaten path. Let's really hide away for a few days. We could even have Billie, Mary, and the grandchildren come out with us. We really need it, Fred. You need it, in particular."

Donley nodded. "Yeah, you're right. Besides," he added with a grimace, "we won't be able to enjoy the perquisites of this office much longer, so we may as well take advantage of them. We'll get things settled down and then we'll—"

The loud buzz of the green scrambler telephone on the President's desk interrupted his planning. It was Charles Frydon, using a direct line from the basement Crisis Center. "What's up, Charley?" the President asked tensely.

"Mr. President, I'm afraid all bets are off."

"What do you mean?"

"Well, sir, according to a National Security Agency intercept, the fourth Videowire story started to go out on a private wire to Italy about fifteen minutes ago. The bastards must have moved up their schedule for foreign customers. We thought we had an hour or more. It was going out embargoed—but it was going. Then the damnedest thing happened. It looks as if Soviet agents blew up the Videowire communications computer."

"What?"

"That's right, sir, they blew it up."

"The computer?"

"Yes, sir."

"Okay, Charley, call the others. I'm coming right down." Donley slammed the telephone receiver into its cradle and looked up at Laura, who had been standing next to him, her hand gently rubbing the taut muscles of his neck. "I've got to go. I'll call you from downstairs when I know what's happening." Donley rose from his desk chair and walked, at first slowly and then long, quickening strides, toward the door.

Laura Ann Donley's steady gray-green eyes followed her husband's tall figure. "I'll be here, Fred . . . and I love you," she whispered after him.

The President stopped. He turned and came back across the room. "I love you too," he said, folding her close into his arms and kissing her gently. "I love you, too," he repeated.

Then he turned again and was gone.

33

The orange-red numbers of the big digital clock on the east wall were just snapping to 1510—3:10 P.M. EST—as Frederick Donley opened the door of the conference room. Frydon and a worried-looking Carl Silverton, who had been using the Crisis Center facilities to call abroad, met him just three steps into the room.

"Okay, give it to me," snapped the President.

"Williamson, Mike, and Jim are on their way," Frydon answered. "Three Soviet agents raided Videowire. They've killed Contos and Tauber. Beat our FBI task force there by only a few minutes. They blew up the VEI offices with a high-energy plastic explosive. Woman employee, probably a girl named Barbara Schmidt, critically injured. The medics doubt she'll make it. Flying glass got two pedestrians in the street. One died on the way to the hospital. A young kid lost a foot but he'll be all right. No other injuries except a few scratches."

"Good God," breathed Donley, "Is that how Kirov thinks he can help me?"

"It's all over the TV networks. People are beginning to run scared," the Director of Central Intelligence added.

"Kirov's completely misread the press reaction he'll get," observed Silverton. "This will exacerbate everything enormously."

"Of course it will." Donley frowned in agreement. "We've got to find a way to contain both the press reaction and the damned public panic. And we've got to do it quickly—very quickly. Dammit, what could Kirov be thinking of? It's stupid—absolutely stupid!"

"He may try to set us up with a cover story, sir," suggested Frydon. "You remember what he said on the hot line? Something about lunatic groups in the United States. Perhaps he's got more of the plan than we give him credit for."

"Let's check the videotape, Charley," said Donley urgently, as Boyce Williamson and Jim Willoughby joined the tight cluster of men around him. Donley tilted his head in greeting. "Carl, brief them, while Frydon and I review the Kirov contact. I've got big decisions to make in the next five minutes."

With Carl Silverton's calm nasal voice in the background, the President and Frydon skipped rapidly through a large-screen video replay of the Kirov exchange. It did not yield any more than the Director of Central Intelligence had remembered. A well-timed call from the FBI New York agent in charge to his director, who promptly patched Frydon in on the conversation, was much more fruitful.

"The *New York Times* just got a phone call," reported Frydon to his colleagues as he hung up. "It was from a group calling themselves Americans for European Liberty. They claim they did the Videowire bombing. They say Videowire was Communist-controlled and was trying to put over the M10 story. M10, they said, was just a hoax to create sympathy for the U.S.S.R. as a victim of American aggression, and it never really happened. So they have now 'punished' Videowire. Apparently they're calling all the TV networks, too."

"It will never work," said the President glumly.

"I know," said Frydon quietly.

"But why not?" exclaimed Boyce Williamson, excitement illuminating his face. "Why, for that matter, couldn't all of this *really* be a hoax? How do we know M10 actually happened at all? It's based purely on Clayton's computer output. What a great way to stampede the United States into some quick concessions—like the ICBM inspections, for instance—simply to appease an excited Russian population. It could all be a fake. It really could!"

"Boyce, that is too fantastic to waste time discussing now," replied Donley with the shrug of a parent talking to a child. "M10 is genuine. There is no way anyone could have planted data throughout the ACA computer system. There is no way they could have forged the statistical information we've developed in the past days and weeks. M10 has done exactly what we think it has, and there is no sense whatever in hoping otherwise."

"I'm not so sure," grumbled Williamson.

"I am," said Donley firmly.

Frydon stepped into the silence that followed the President's declaration. "I think we'd better take a look at what the networks are feeding their stations. We still have to follow up your agreement with Kirov to minimize further information flow on M10, Mr. President. We should also have NSA show us the material that was sent to Italy before the explosion." Without waiting for comment, Frydon leaned over the edge of the long walnut conference table to an intercom microphone which connected him with the Technical Support Area and the masses of equipment undergirding for Crisis Center. Seconds later, four brightly colored television images appeared on the milky glass of the wall-sized rear projection screens. Two of the pictures showed Saturday-after-afternoon football games in progress: Southern California versus Notre Dame and Michigan battling Minnesota. Everything seemed normal. On the third channel, cartoon characters were cavorting happily, while a symphony orchestra was in full cry on the fourth. "That sure looks okay!" exclaimed Jim Willoughby, who had not said anything since coming into the room.

"We'll keep the sound off until something changes," said Frydon. "The Videowire transmission from the National Security Agency will be ready to roll in a couple of minutes. Meanwhile we can talk. . . ." Behind his thick bifocals, Frydon's eyes drifted back to the TV pictures and widened. "Wait a minute—look at those stands!" Instantly other eyes swung to follow his gaze. Although the big Notre Dame-USC game was just getting started, the huge stadium in which it was being played was heavily dotted with empty seats. Small, dark masses of fans were squeezing toward the exits.

"Turn up the sound on Channel 2," ordered Donley.

". . . six yards on that last play. Considerable numbers of people are still leaving. In one minute, we will return to our studios for further developments on the New York explosion and the rumors of an international confrontation between the U.S. and the U.S.S.R. Now it's third down for USC on their own forty-two . . ."

The President began rubbing at his left cheek. "It's beginning. It's going to turn into a stampede," he said. The room began to shift and waver before him. "We'll never hold things together with the 'theoretical study' cover story now. It's going to take something much more dramatic. I propose to watch these broadcasts for a few minutes and no more. From then on, we'll shift to intelligence summaries from Charley's people." Donley's left eyelid dropped. He covered it with his hand. "We'll have to spend our time building a plan for the next twenty-four hours. Charley, is the NSA material ready?"

"Yes, sir, it is."

"Okay, give me time to see this next news coverage on Videowire just to get the flavor of things firsthand, and then we'll look at it."

Little more than forty-five minutes had elapsed since the Videowire offices disappeared in a burst of yellow light and boiling gray smoke. It was already apparent that the explosion was acting like a gigantic alarm clock, whose sounding was awaking Americans not to escape a nightmare but to confront one whose dimensions would surpass their most terrifying imaginings.

The television screens in front of the President and the men around him shifted colors abruptly as one after another of the national networks cut away from their regular programming to their news rooms or to New York reporters still at the scene on Sixth Avenue. Channel 6, the CNS outlet in Washington, flashed the words SPECIAL BULLETIN in large white letters on a red background which dissolved to a set normally reserved for the 6:00 P.M. CNS evening news segment from Washington. Raymond Claridge, the CNS anchorman in the capital for twenty-two years, began speaking, his deep and carefully modulated voice sounding, as always, as though each word had been cut into stone and presented to him by a great unseen hand. "CNS News," he said ponderously, "has always been very mindful of its extraordinary obligation to the American viewing public. . . ."

"Oh-oh," muttered Jim Willoughby from his semiprone position in a chair near the screen. "Something's coming."

"For some hours," continued Claridge, "CNS News has been in possession of certain information which we have been attempting to confirm regarding the so-called Project M10, now being widely described as a long-term biomedical attack on the population of the Soviet Union by unknown factions in the United States. In view of recent developments, including the explosion at the New York offices of Videowire Express Incorporated, which, as you know, first broke the story, the CNS management feels duty-bound to report one of our Washington staff men-bers has personally interviewed Mrs. Mildred Clayton, widow of Admiral Randolph G. Clayton, until recently Chairman of the Joint Chiefs of Staff, and the man who is claimed to be the original source of the M10 story. . . ."

'Oh, Christ!" groaned General Kallen, who had just entered the Crisis Center. Boyce Williamson closed his eyes, his lips pressed into a thin, tight line.

"Hugh Callaway of our staff," said the mellifluous voice from the screen, "informs me that no less a personage than the President-elect of the United States, Mr. C. Boyce Williamson, visited with Mrs. Clayton and asked her what she knew about Project M10. In his meeting with Mrs. Clayton, which CNS News believes may have oc-curred late Thursday or early Friday, the President-elect also asked that she remain absolutely silent on the matter and not talk to newsmen about it. At the moment, Mr. Callaway and other CNS personnel are attempting to meet with Mrs. Clayton again. However, she has barricaded herself in her Georgetown home and is refusing to see anyone. Meanwhile, CNS news has confirmed that President-elect Williamson, who was thought to be va-cationing in Montana, is in fact someplace in Washington at this moment—perhaps at the White House itself. The implications of these facts, partially unsubstantiated, as we again emphasize, are of course very grave indeed. CNS News will continue to follow all developments on Project M10 closely throughout the remainder of the afternoon. This is Raymond Claridge in Washington, returning you now to our regular programming. . . ."

". . . and he cuts to his right, picking up the first down at about the twelve-yard line. That's the Wolverines' twelfth first down and brings . . ."

"Turn it down," ordered Donley, struggling hard against the rising pressure in his head and the tingling numbness that was creeping down his left cheek from his temple. Boyce Williamson, looking smaller and older than he had moments ago, opened his mouth to say something, then changed his mind.

"Do you want to run the text Videowire sent to Italy?" asked Frydon gently as he studied his boss. He sensed that Donley was not well and was getting worse. He shot a meaningful glance around the room at Willoughby,

Kallen, and Silverton, all of whom had already reached
the same conclusion. Only Boyce Williamson, who did not
know Donley well, seemed not to notice.

"Okay, let's see it," sighed the President, ignoring the
symptoms that were ebbing and flowing across his body
and haunted more by the sight of the emptying stands at
the football games than by the explicit facts about M10
that were being broadcast.

Frydon pressed a button and the network TV programs
disappeared. In their place, the wall of the conference
room took on a soft greenish-white glow. The text of the
fourth Videowire release scrolled steadily upward across
the glass of the screen:

ITALIA-MT-6787878
NOV 10 VDW
PROJECT M10—INSTALLMENT FOUR
COPYRIGHT VIDEOWIRE EXPRESS INCORPORATED
BY WILLIS TAUBER
SPECIAL TRANSMISSION TO METROTEXT ITALIA

NOTE: STRICTLY EMBARGOED FOR RELEASE AFTER
7 A.M., EST NOVEMBER 11
REPEAT—STRICTLY EMBARGOED UNTIL 7 A.M. EST
NOVEMBER 11.

M10 INSTALLMENT FOUR TEXT FOLLOWS:

THE ACTIVE USE BY THE U.S. OF NARX AS A SECRET
BIOMEDICAL WARFARE AGENT DIRECTED AGAINST
THE POPULATION OF THE U.S.S.R. CONTINUED TO
EXPAND EACH YEAR AFTER NARX WAS INTRODUCED.
SPECIAL DELIVERY TECHNIQUES WERE DEVELOPED
AND PERFECTED TO CONCENTRATE THE EFFECTS
OF M10 PREFERENTIALLY IN THE UPPER STRATA
OF SOVIET SOCIETY—THOSE WHOSE LOSS WOULD
WEAKEN THE NATION MOST IN SUCCEEDING DECADES.
PRIMARY TARGETS WERE SUCCESSFUL STATESMEN,
TEACHERS, INDUSTRIAL LEADERS, SCIENTISTS,
ENGINEERS, PHYSICIANS, ARTISTS, AND ATHLETES—
ALL OF WHOM COULD AFFORD THE LUXURY ITEMS
OF COMMERCE IN WHICH THE NARX COMPOUNDS WERE
EASILY SECRETED.

* * *

MEANTIME, INTENSIVE RESEARCH ON THE EFFECTS
OF NITRITES AND NITROSAMINES CONTINUED
THROUGHOUT THE WORLD. THE SUSPICION THAT
MANY DIGESTIVE TRACT CANCERS WERE
ENVIRONMENTALLY INDUCED WAS FINALLY AMPLY
CONFIRMED. THIS GHASTLY TRUTH BECAME, AS IS
WELL KNOWN, GENERALLY ACCEPTED WITH THE
PUBLICATION OF THE FAMOUS "WORLD HEALTH
REPORT." ENVIRONMENTALISTS AND PUBLIC HEALTH
OFFICIALS IN MOST COUNTRIES THEN RAPIDLY
SUCCEEDED IN CAMPAIGNS TO ELIMINATE MANY
NITRITE-TREATED FOODS. THOSE FOODS WHICH WERE
STILL NITRITE-PROCESSED WERE ALSO REQUIRED TO
CONTAIN QUANTITIES OF VITAMIN C DERIVATIVES,
WHICH ACTED AS POWERFUL BLOCKING AGENTS
AGAINST THE CARCINOGENIC ACTION OF NITROSAMINES.

ALTHOUGH IT WAS, OF COURSE, NOT KNOWN
AT THE TIME, MANY OF THE NEW REQUIREMENTS
TRIGGERED BY THE U.N. WORLD HEALTH REPORT ALSO
GREATLY REDUCED THE STATISTICAL DEATH RATE THAT
COULD BE ACHIEVED BY THE M10 ATTACK ON THE
SOVIET UNION. THE DIRECTORS OF THE M10 PROJECT
WERE, HOWEVER, NOT CAUGHT BY SURPRISE, SINCE
THEY THEMSELVES INCLUDED SOME OF THE MOST
SOPHISTICATED RESEARCHERS IN THE RELEVANT FIELDS.
PROJECT M10 QUICKLY CONVERTED FROM NARX TO A
NEW AND EVEN MORE EFFECTIVE AGENT——AN
INCREDIBLY POWERFUL EXTRACT FROM A RADIATION-
INDUCED MUTATION OF THE MOLD ASPERGILLIS-FLAVUS.

THE NATURALLY OCCURRING FORM OF THIS MOLD
PRODUCES A POISON KNOWN AS AFLATOXIN. THE MOLD
GROWS ON SUCH CROPS AS CORN, WHEAT, PEANUTS,
AND RICE. AFLATOXIN ITSELF IS TERRIFYINGLY
ACTIVE. ONE HUNDRED PERCENT OF RATS FED VERY
SMALL QUANTITIES OF AFLATOXIN DEVELOP CANCER
OF THE LIVER WITHIN TWO YEARS.

IN THE HUMID TROPICS AND SUBTROPICS, THE MOLD
PROBABLY ACCOUNTS FOR THE FACT THAT THE HUMAN
LIVER CANCER RATE IS 500 TIMES HIGHER THAN IT IS IN

OTHER AREAS. IT ALSO WAS SHOWN TO BE THE SOURCE OF THE "TURKEY X" DIEASE THAT KILLED HUGE NUMBERS OF TURKEYS, CALVES, CHICKENS, AND DUCKLINGS IN ENGLAND IN THE 1960s.

AFLATOXINS COMPRISE A SERIES OF NATURAL COMPOUNDS. THE IDENTIFIED MEMBERS OF THE DEADLY CLUB INCLUDE AFLATOXIN B_1, B_2, B_2-ALPHA, G_1, G_2, AND G_2-ALPHA. TESTS IN THE MID 1970s SHOWED THAT B_2 CAUSES THE HIGHEST CANCER SUSCEPTIBILITY.

BUT AFLATOXIN B_2, WHICH CAN MEAN SLOW LINGERING DEATH AT CONCENTRATIONS OF LESS THAN 100 PARTS PER BILLION, IS LIKE A MOTHER'S MILK COMPARED TO THE RELATED AGENT DEVELOPED BY PROJECT M10.

GIVEN THE INNOCENT-SOUNDING DESIGNATION AFLACOID-12, THIS MATERIAL IS BORN OF A MOLD WHICH FIRST GREW AND FLOURISHED IN THE BLUISH HELL OF A RADIATION FIELD PRODUCED BY A MILLION CURIES OF THE WELL-KNOWN RADIOISOTOPE COBALT-60. UNDER THE SEARING STRESS OF THE RADIATION, IT WAS EVOLVE OR DIE, AND THE ALREADY DEADLY ASPERGILLIS FLAVUS EVOLVED TO AN INCREDIBLE NEW FORM. WHERE TOXINS FROM THE NATURALLY OCCURRING MOLD WERE DEADLY AT CONCENTRATIONS OF A FEW HUNDRED PARTS PER BILLION, THIS NEW FORM PRODUCED POISONOUS MOLECULES WHICH COULD KILL AT CHRONIC DOSE LEVELS OF A FEW PARTS PER TRILLION OR LESS. PROJECT M10 NOW HAD ITS ULTIMATE WEAPON—AFLACOID-12.

AFLACOID-12 IS VERY EASY TO PRODUCE. IT IS AS SIMPLE AS GROWING MOLD ON PEANUT SHELLS.

AFLACOID-12 IS IMPOSSIBLE TO DETECT. EVEN OUR BEST INSTRUMENTS FOR ROUTINE ECOLOGICAL MONITORING DEAL IN PARTS PER BILLION, NOT TRILLION.

AFLACOID-12 IS EASY TO DISTRIBUTE. JUST ADD A FEW OUNCES OF IT TO A WHOLE SHIPLOAD OF GRAIN

BOUND FOR RUSSIA. IT CAN BE DONE AS EASILY AS
HUMIDITY IS ADDED TO THE AIR IN A ROOM.

AND AFLACOID-12 KILLS. NOT IMMEDIATELY, NOT BY
TRACEABLE ACTION, BUT INEVITABLY, OVER A
PERIOD OF MONTHS OR YEARS. IT IS A WIDELY KNOWN
MEDICAL FACT THAT THE CANCER RATE IN THE SOVIET
UNION HAS MOVED UPWARD IN RECENT YEARS FOR NO
APPARENT REASON. LEADERS AND COMMON FOLK
ALIKE HAVE DIED BEFORE THEIR TIME. NOW WE
KNOW WHY. THESE EPIDEMIC EFFECTS WILL
UNQUESTIONABLY CONTINUE FOR YEARS, IF NOT
DECADES.

AFLACOID-12 IS . . . GHTRZI . . . UT . . . RHTOM . . .

The video screen faded to black.

The Crisis Center was silent. In it, the most powerful
men in America were filled with a sense of utter help-
lessness. They would have to watch as the details they
had just seen rocketed out of Italy to join with the story
of the Videowire attack to produce only one possible
result: M10 was now possessed of a life and a will of its
own. It had broken loose to tear and claw its way toward
an independent destiny and could no longer be caged or
tamed.

"We'd better warn Kirov," the President said, almost
inaudibly.

"Shall I try to set up the hot line?" asked Jim Willoughby.

Donley glanced at the clock. "No. It's after midnight
in Moscow and there's little more we can do other than
tell him the facts. I'm not prepared to take up his demands
yet, so I'd rather not have another face-to-face discussion
unless he asks for it. Send him an urgent cable and include
the Videowire text. His agents are surely keeping him
thoroughly informed on the New York situation, but they
may not have the material that actually got out before
the explosion. Jim, will you take a first cut at a draft?"

"Yes, sir. I'll have something in ten minutes."

"Mr. President," asked Charley Frydon, "don't you think
we ought to reconsider one of the matters we discussed
earlier—blacking out our overseas communications traffic

for a while? There must be an incredible outflow going on. The less of it Kirov has to contend with around his borders, the more time he'll have. . . ."

Donley paused to think. "Opinions?" he asked, swinging his eyes from colleague to colleague.

"Do it," said Kallen firmly.

"I agree." Silverton nodded.

"Boyce?" queried Donley.

The President-elect casually picked at a fingernail and shrugged slightly.

Donley again considered the impact of a blackout—a possibility he had been toying with for over twenty-four hours. In reality, a full-scale communications shut-down would only replace increasingly damaging facts from the U.S. press with excruciatingly painful speculations from foreign sources—a small gain, at best. "Okay, Charley. It won't buy much, but let's proceed." He sighed. "Beggers can't be choosers."

Charles Frydon immediately grabbed the intercom mike and reeled off instructions to an officer in the Technical Support Area.

The response was immediate and razor sharp. "Yes, sir. We have information on the whereabouts of the head of the Bell Telephone Long Lines Division and his counterparts at three other major communications carriers. We also think we can locate the top authorities in two more companies in the next few minutes. That should give us almost one hundred percent coverage."

"Very well, said Frydon. "Patch those you can reach through to one of the phones in here."

"Yes, sir. When we're ready, the white control light will flash, sir."

The President leaned back against the padding of his chair to wait. His brief rest was terminated by a whispered request from Boyce Williamson. "Fred, could I speak to you privately for a moment?"

"Yes of course," Donley replied, rising to follow Williamson to a far corner of the room, as the others watched curiously.

"I have a favor to ask," said Williamson very quietly.

"Certainly, Boyce. What is it?"

"Will you arrange a plane to pick up my wife and

daughter at Bozeman tonight? I'd like to bring them here to Washington."

Donley nodded knowingly at the shorter and younger man, an almost physical surge of empathy filling his breast. "That would be no problem," the President whispered, "but I think you ought to consider a couple of points. First and least important, bringing your family here could add somewhat to public reaction. Second and more important, Washington won't necessarily remain a—a safe place. We may all have to go to an alternate location some distance from here. Frankly, both places are likely to be prime targets for very heavy weapons. Even afterwards, the . . . ah . . . environment will be extremely difficult, if not impossible. Dammit! What I'm trying to say, Boyce, is that you should seriously consider leaving your family out West but move them to a place far from any missile sites or other possible targets. Actually, Big Sky isn't a bad spot. It's upwind of the Ellsworth and Warren ICBM bases and well south of Malmstrom. And there are no large cities nearby."

Williamson looked up at the President. His eyes reddened, then cleared. "Yes, I see your point. I guess I'll have to think about that."

"One more thing, Fred. You and I both know I'm at a tremendous disadvantage in this whole situation. None of my preelection briefings went anywhere near *this* far. I'd like you to stop asking me for suggestions so pointedly. It makes me appear stupid in front of the others. When I have something to contribute, I assure you you'll hear about it."

"I'm sorry," Donley replied with some astonishment. "I had no intention of putting you on the defensive. I really wanted to give you the floor on the key decisions."

"Just keep what I've said in mind," whispered Williamson.

"Boyce, you and I aren't in a contest."

"I know that," responded the President-elect, "I know that." But there was no conviction in his voice as he turned to rejoin the others in the Crisis Center, leaving Donley standing alone and staring at the floor.

"Mr. President, we're ready with the conference call, sir," announced the audio speakers around the room.

Donley looked up from the spotlessly waxed floor tiles and walked around the table to pick up a telephone on which a small light was pulsing on and off. "Hello? Hello? All right, yes. Gentlemen, this is the President. There is a problem and we need your assistance immediately. . . ."

The conversation between Donley and the operating heads of the major U.S. communications carriers did not last long. The intensity of the President's words quickly cut through one or two very tentative questions about censorship and left no doubt that an extraordinary national emergency was at hand. Almost as the telephone conference call ended, the complex, multilayered communications Tower of Babel which welds the United States into the global community of nations fell eerily silent. Suddenly, it was as if intercontinental television, radio, and telephone lines did not exist. Far out in space, dozens of U.S. communications satellites continued to pinwheel along their mathematically precise orbits. But no longer did they swallow a million-millionfold, to waiting receivers far below.

"All right, that part's done," Charles Frydon seemed to tick an item off an invisible check list.

"Yes, that part's done," agreed the President unhappily, shifting his attention to General Kallen. "Mike, what's the current JCS recommendation on our force status?"

"I was in touch while you were setting up the blackout, sir. No changes are proposed for now, pending any alteration in Soviet posture. We're monitoring things minute by minute. The civilian side here is what is worrying everyone, Mr. President. We feel an official Civil Defense Alert may be in order. Also a National Guard call-up. Both might prevent a disaster."

"Or cause one," observed Donley acidly. "I propose to issue stand-by alert orders to the Civil Defense regional offices only. Classify the messages Top Secret. I don't want a Guard call-up yet. It's much, much too visible. We've got to lay the groundwork for something like that. I am coming to think I should address the nation via television tonight. . . ."

"And say what?" asked an openly surprised Boyce Williamson.

"Perhaps the truth . . ." answered the President.

Amid quick sandwiches eaten to the accompaniment of a shower of situation reports from alerted federal agency personnel throughout the country and accumulating stacks of Central Intelligence press summaries, which were obviously building in a seemingly limitless crescendo, another in the long series of crucial debates over the handling of M10 took place under the White House. The discussion stopped repeatedly to allow Donley to instruct Dorie Wilcox in the handling of urgent calls to the Oval Office from frightened cabinet members, senators, and congressmen of special power and importance. Finally, the President had no choice. "Dorie, cut off all the civilian calls. Tell everyone I'll be in touch as soon as possible to explain everything. I'm going to use only the National Military Command System for communications in or out, until further notice. You just sit tight up there meanwhile. Also, tell Mrs. Donley I'm fine and I'll drop up to see her the minute I get some time."

The President hung up and returned to an ongoing exchange about further cover stories versus open admission of the facts of M10. He and his companions were struggling to guess how the American public and press, along with world and Soviet populations, might respond. The real decisions were, however, being made elsewhere.

On Pennsylvania Avenue, 120 feet above the White House Crisis Center, people were beginning to behave as people do in the face of a common danger. Strangers waiting anxiously for buses in the bright Saturday-evening twilight asked each other what the latest news was about M10. Many pedestrians, coats flying, faces agitated, were running toward their destinations.

City families, those who were easily frightened, those who were perhaps more perceptive or more prone to decide the course of their own lives, were seeking cover in the countryside or, if they could afford to, were heading for Canada, Mexico, and even more distant places. In Washington and elsewhere, occasional fights were breaking out at airplane ticket counters and boarding areas. Airport security forces were gradually being stretched beyond their capabilities.

The roads out of major American cities were becoming clogged with cars. It was almost like one long and exceptionally massive rush hour, but the cars, instead of being loaded with businessmen returning home after a routine day at the office, were filled with men fleeing with their wives and children.

While most of the police forces in metropolitan areas were still doing their jobs, numbers of police decided that they, too, should join their families in flight. Since traffic on the U.S. telephone network had already reached mammoth proportions, police officials and fire chiefs, like many others, found it nearly impossible to get their calls through and were unable to reach potential replacement personnel at their homes. Instead they heard nothing but stubbornly unresponsive busy signals or no dial tone at all. A long, steep slide toward anarchy was under way as the services and facilities of civilized America threatened to crumble before the irresistible force of Project M10.

Three blocks from the White House, in the huge new A & P supermarket near the intersection of Connecticut Avenue and K Street, forty-two-year-old Alice Bolling clawed at a shelf on which there were only a few cans left. Around her, other people were grabbing for similar fast-disappearing foodstuffs. Howard Bolling shoved a small, well-dressed woman aside at the crowded meat counter and stared down at the frosty white slats of the refrigeration unit. The meat counter was empty.

Outside on Connecticut Avenue, young Eddie Bolling stood guard over a station wagon already loaded with three large cardboard boxes full of food. Leaning against the car fender in the manner of a typical teen-ager, a transistor radio jammed against his car, he was not listening to rock music. For one of the few times in his life, Eddie was listening to news reports, while an almost continuous stream of cars snaked past him toward the suburbs.

In the basement of the glistening, newly built Du Pont Building, the Black Diamond Lounge and Restaurant, which should have been filling with early-evening patrons, was deserted. While a bartender busily polished a glass, he and the maître d', the only people in the seductively lit rooms, debated whether they, too, should leave the place and join their families. "It's all bullshit," declared the bartender. "Nothing is going to happen. People get crazy about every damned piece of crap the TV types put out to hype their ratings."

Several miles from the White House, a line had formed and was gradually lengthening at the cashier's office of the Washington Hilton Hotel. Families from out of town who had planned to spend the weekend in Washington seeing the sights of the capital were checking out early. One heavily perspiring man, an electronic-parts salesman from Atlanta, shifted his weight from one foot to the other. Finally, as if something had broken inside him, he deserted the line, leaving his bill unpaid, and half-running, half-walking, bolted through the revolving exit door, dragging his wife and ten-year-old son behind him.

In Alexandria, Virginia, just across the bridge from downtown Washington, Roger Adamson and his wife, Grace, had spent a pleasant although tiring afternoon helping their friends, the Flemings. The four of them had been painting the Flemings' cozy new apartment in a high-rise overlooking the Potomac River. It had been a happy day. The walls were finished, the latex paint was already dry, and the hanging of the drapes had begun. Then Bill Fleming found his little transistor radio among the cartons and boxes. From that moment, the mood of the day changed and the beer, the ribs barbecuing on the balcony, the discussion of how to season the potato salad, all were forgotten. "Roger, please hurry, let's get home!" cried Grace Adamson as she pulled her husband toward the door. The Flemings were not with them to say good-bye. Instead they were standing on the balcony, gaping in astonishment as never-ending streams of cars and trucks funneled along the roads below.

The Adamsons arrived at their own home to find their all-day babysitter, a student at the nearby high school, gone. Their four-year-old son was sitting crosslegged on the floor of the living room, watching a television program he did not understand. He giggled happily. His mother swept him up into her arms, stepped over a spilled glass of orange soda pop that had seeped into the white living room rug, and headed for the bedroom to pack.

To the southwest of the capital, an ancient Ford camper piled high with torn duffel bags and tent poles lumbered toward Washington along the Skyline Drive from Charlottesville. With increasing puzzlement, Ronald Goldfarb watched the traffic headed in the opposite direction. "I don't understand it, Irene. I've never seen outbound traffic like this before."

The Goldfarbs had spent five beautiful days in the mountains. They had really needed a vacation, and the old jalopy, Ronald figured, had one more good trip left in it. He was right. The vehicle had held up admirably, although one taillight was out and the radio didn't work anymore. Nevertheless, and in spite of his conviction that they ought to get closer to nature and become less dependent upon technology, Ronald Goldfarb had agreed that he was going to buy a new car sometime next week if he could arrange the financing.

By the time the Goldfarbs reached the vicinity of Sperryville, the outbound traffic was practically bumper-to-bumper. No longer able to contain himself, Goldfarb turned off the Skyline Drive and headed into the town. He pulled up to a gas station to fill his tank and to find the reason for all the movement. A wiry old station attendant, who had spent all his nearly eighty years in Sperryville, casually wiped his grease-blackened hands on his shirt. "Hell, man ain't you heard?" he said "Surely looks like we're about to go to war."

34

Under presidential directive, the communications system linking America to the outside world had been silenced, but the operation of internal TV, radio, and videowire services, as well as of newspapers, continued. Every editor in the country was screaming for information about the blackout and every reporter in Washington was storming the Public Affairs Offices of the government. Television commentators and radio broadcasters launched a deluge of inquiries about both the shutdown and the attack on Videowire. Under all the words, like a persistent drumbeat, was one blunt and terrible question: Are we preparing for war?

In Europe and Asia, puzzled technical specialists tested and retested their circuits, only to find there were no equipment problems. The realization that the entire United

States had been cut off the line came slowly. But then, like an intensifying storm, the implications of the U.S. action engulfed the minds of those responsible for communications in London, Berlin, Tokyo, Paris, Buenos Aires, New Delhi, and other centers of civilization.

Although the panic in the soul of America was building with every news broadcast, every electrifying rumor, it was still far from producing all-out chaos. Hundreds of thousands of Americans were beginning to run for their lives, but many millions were staying put, unable or unwilling to believe they should do otherwise. The nation was edging toward mass hysteria; nevertheless, the final paroxysm—the climactic spasm—was not yet in process.

As the malignancy of Project M10 spread and enlarged, so did the circle of people around the President. He was moving closer to a final decision on making a broadcast to the nation, and the White House Communications Center was crowded with men called from cocktails or dinner tables. The full National Security Council staff, as well as all the Joint Chiefs and their deputies, had joined operating heads of every essential department of the federal government. National Security Agency experts, Defense Communications Agency representatives, and dozens of other specialists supplemented the President's close advisers. A full emergency staff of engineers and technicians was operating the communications apparatus deep in the rock under the White House and the once empty tiers of chairs around the main table were filled with quiet, somber-faced men.

For the moment, there was very little conversation. The President and his advisers were transfixed, their attention riveted to the glass screen of the large video display. Television cameras in Continental Defense Command reconnaissance helicopters, dispatched at the Chief Executive's order, were filling the room with images of traffic jams and sidewalks covered with tiny moving spots which were people walking rapidly or running toward unknown destinations.

"All right, all right, I've seen enough," Donley announced, waving his hand toward a colonel standing at the doorway of the Technical Support Area. "Shut it off so we can talk." For an hour at least, he had known what he must do. Only the full weight and power of his office could conceivably break through the tightening ring of fear that was beginning to strangle the country. "I see no other alternative," he said, addressing himself first to Charles Frydon and then to Carl Silverton and the President-elect. "I think the broadcast is the only way we can stop it. Otherwise it will be irretrievable by midnight."

"Every word you say will be around the world and into Russia within hours, regardless of the blackout," said Carl Silverton. "But I agree, you've got no choice." He brushed absent-mindedly at a long strand of white hair.

Charley Frydon pushed his bifocals up on his forehead. "It's a trade-off. Kirov's been trying to protect his people and his position with actions like the Videowire attack. And you must protect our population if you can. Protect it from itself. It's a clear and obvious obligation. Personally, I think everyone will react better if they know the truth and know we are negotiating directly with the Soviets. The rumors carry more *immediate* danger than the realities."

"If Kirov can retain control on his side . . ." observed Mike Kallen.

"We're not picking up anything to the contrary," answered Frydon.

"But just how good are our intelligence sources?" Boyce Williamson wondered aloud.

"Frankly, in this situation—at the very high levels in the Soviet government which would be involved—not all that great. Nevertheless, I think we'd sense something," Frydon replied levelly. Williamson looked at him, momentarily telegraphing both distrust and dislike.

"I'm going ahead," declared Donley firmly, looking squarely at the President-elect before turning to Willoughby. "Jim, have the Public Affairs Office put out a statement that I will be making an important clarifying announcement regarding reports about Project M10. The key word is 'clarifying.' Stress it. That will convey the proper tone. Set me up with the network people for 7:30 P.M. That will give us time to make some notes and get prepared. I intend to make only a few very strong points: First, M10 has done some damage to Soviet society; second, it was not an act of the U.S. government; third, we and Kirov are sanely discussing appropriate reparations, which I will not name; fourth, we cut off foreign communications to prevent the flow of wild rumors; and fifth, the perpetrators are being identified and will be punished. I then will urge everyone to remain calm and return to normal activity. Finally, I will announce limited activation of some National Guard units to help maintain law and order. Are there any comments?"

The men around the President said nothing. There were few meaningful alternatives. So dangerous was the situation that dealing with it had become simple. There were only two options: one unthinkable; the other possibly unworkable.

The first choice was to prepare the nation for full-scale nuclear war. The second was to gamble that words rather than force would resolve the tension. Could any sane nation really prepare for nuclear war? Better to try to convince the American people that there was no immediate danger and that both governments would continue to behave rationally. Donley would have to *make* the *people* believe that M10 was not the percussion cap that could ignite a nuclear holocaust. If they did not come to believe him, the nation would tear itself to bloody shreds escaping bombs that might never fall.

"I'm going to need all the backup I can get," the President declared, swiveling around in his chair to face the filled tiers of staff chairs behind him. He looked directly at a stocky, bearded man in the second row. "I'll want you to follow up on the technical side with the press after I'm finished, Dr. Brondoff. Make sure people understand we are *not* dealing with something contagious. This is not biological warfare in the usual sense and that is important for people to understand. Also, you should indicate we are already preparing detection and monitoring methods for both exports and imports. Don't go deeper for now. Is all that clear?" The bearded director of the National Institutes of Health nodded nervously.

"All right," said the President, turning his chair back toward the conference table. "Has anybody got anything else he wants to say at this point?" Silence. "Very well. We've only got minutes to get ready, so let's stop here. I'll want the NSC and all staff people back after the broadcast. Thank you, gentlemen." Frederick Donley smiled. There was a new ingredient in his expression. He was donning his political personality—the same smile and engaging look that, with one exception, had brought him sweeping pluralities during a lifetime of political campaigns. The Donley smile—the Donley look—were about to be put to a supreme test. The President was preparing to ask the nation to be calm in the face of death itself.

As the meeting recessed, Donley called across the table to the President-elect. "Boyce, come with me, will you? While I get a little make-up on, I'd like to chat a minute."

Williamson nodded and walked with the President, making a point, despite the pain in his legs from his overdone Montana skiing, of matching the President's long steps stride for stride all the way down the hall to the door of the small dressing room located just off the Communications Center's TV studio. Donley leaned forward into a mirror flanked by rows of small, bright incandescent lights, gazing first at his own image and then at Williamson's. He laughed softly. "Damn, I look awful, don't I?" He picked a small sponge out of a cardboard container half filled with reddish pancake make-up. "Boyce, I was wondering whether you'd like to appear with me on this broadcast. It would, I think, help considerably to have us both there. I think it would reassure the people a great deal to know we are in touch and cooperating."

The President-elect narrowed his eyes to cut the bright gleam of the lights around Donley's face, now partially coated with a healthy-looking tan. Donley's fingers, he observed to himself, were trembling slightly as he held the sponge. "I've been considering that, Fred. Frankly, I think it is wiser for me to keep my options open."

"What you really mean is you want to stay clear of any responsibility for what happens," replied the President, a touch of annoyance showing under his words.

"Put it that way if you wish," said Williamson, as he retreated umcomfortably toward the door of the barren little room. "I do intend to issue a statement after your speech, saying I am looking into the whole situation—and that, for now, is *all* I intend to say."

Donley caught Williamson's eyes in the mirror, hoping to make contact with some deeper layer in the President-elect. He failed. The door closed solidly and he was left alone.

At exactly 7:30 P.M. EST, November 10, the image of the forty-second President of the United States appeared simultaneously on almost every television set in America. Arrangements had been made for delayed broadcast to Europe and Africa—it was now the early-morning hours on the continent. South America was receiving the program live. Asian viewers, separated in time from Washington by anywhere from ten to fifteen hours, also were seeing the broadcast as it happened. Over a billion and a half pairs of eyes focused on the gaunt, but nevertheless imposing, face of the American Chief Executive.

Never in his long career of politics and persuasion had Frederick Donley faced a more profound challenge. It was, he knew, the most important speech of his life and down in the core of himself he also knew, regardless of the outcome, that it might be his last. Almost from the beginning, the possible finality of his words seemed to resonate under each phrase he uttered. Simply and directly, he declared his unlimited trust in the good judgment and wisdom of the American people. He asked for courage and maturity, for faith and forbearance. And he told the truth. Project M10 *was* real. . . . Damage, great damage, had been done by persons operating outside the government. . . . He and Kirov were negotiating. . . . We are alert but optimistic. . . . The Soviet government behaving very responsibly . . . no immediate danger . . . a long process of recoupment will be necessary . . . planning already underway. . . .

Donley paused to fill his lungs. Millions of viewers realized they, too, had hardly been breathing. Emphasizing that the Videowire attack was not an action of the U.S. government and that his temporary communications shutdown was designed only to help stabilize conditions abroad, the President pledged that as soon as the situation had calmed a full investigation would be launched to find and deal with those behind the project.

The words were coming more rapidly, Donley's apparent confidence building with each sentence. Urging all Americans who had taken what he termed "panic steps" to reconsider, to return to the safety of their homes, he repeated himself more emphatically. *There is no cause whatsoever for alarm.*

The speech was turning into a masterpiece—a tour de force. By sheer strength of personality, the President was reversing the nation's inexorable descent into chaos. With every word, his politician's intuition told Donley he was gaining. Oblivious of the cameras and of the technicians behind him, he was lost in himself, speaking from his soul, expressing not the present of M10 as he knew it to be but the future of M10 as he hoped it would be. And by convincing himself, he was convincing the world.

Then, as he was beginning the closing sentence of his remarks—a final testimonial to the strength and good sense of the American people—the President's left eyelid began to flutter and droop. In that instant, in his own mind, fearful reality replaced hopeful dreams. Quickly covering his eye with a movement that made it appear as if he were merely rubbing his eyelid, Donley motioned the camera up to the Great Seal of the United States, hovering in gold-and-white splendor on the wall above him. And he was smiling confidently as he did so.

The broadcast from the White House was finished by five minutes to eight and across the country its effect was immediate and substantial. Crowds who had been glued to television monitors at the airports and in the railroad and bus stations sagged with relief. Facts had finally replaced rumors. The situation was bad. A terrible wrong had been done. But there would be no war. So overwhelming was the sense of relief that some people, preparing to return home again from the ticket lines, made joking remarks about M10 being a damned smart trick for which we'd probably have to pay mountainous hospital bills. Harried ticket-counter personnel continued to process large numbers of customers, but their pace was less frantic and more routine. They, along with their clients, were convinced that their President had told them the truth. There was no immediate danger of war.

It was, of course, easy to convince them. Donley's magnificent performance had been received by an audience desperately wanting to believe every word he said. What human being wished to cope with a nuclear disaster that might be just hours or even minutes away?

Frederick Donley, not yet knowing with certainty how well he had succeeded, left the television studio and entered the long, bright corridor that ran along the backbone of the White House underground facilities. Boyce Williamson was leaning against a wall opposite the studio door.

"It was very convincing," said Williamson. "I only hope it was also right."

"It was right, Boyce. If you saw things from where I sit, and you soon will, you would know how right it was. You would have done exactly the same thing."

Williamson shrugged dubiously. In spite of himself, the manner in which Fred Donley was carrying his burden made Williamson wonder whether he could have done as well. He dismissed the thought as quickly as it came. "I think I would have left more doubt about the validity of the M10 damage claims. You admitted guilt very quickly. If the Soviets have tricked you, you'll look like an idiot."

"Perhaps . . . perhaps not," Donley replied quietly. "What I did was designed to help Kirov as well as us. Control is the important issue now, not guilt." The President pressed his thin fingers to the left side of his face and rubbed vigorously. He pulled himself away from the wall and started walking down the corridor toward the conference room that had become the center of his universe. "People are waiting for us, Boyce. I guess we'd better go in. We've got a lot more to talk about and I'd like to hear what the national reaction is like."

Williamson moved quickly to catch up, again matching the President's long steps as they walked together toward the gray armored-steel door of the Crisis Center. Donley had promised to call Kirov in less than twenty hours and respond to the Russian demand for unthinkable reparations.

As the President entered the conference room, a swelling outburst of spontaneous applause greeted him. Every man there was clapping. Carl Silverton loped to his side like a beaming silver lion and shook his hand in passionate congratulations. "Fred, you did what you wanted to do, and you did it magnificently! I'm sure of it. It may be that you have saved this country with that speech."

"Let's hope so, old friend," Donley replied. "We'll know pretty soon."

National surveillance reports began to arrive within minutes. The thick stack of White House records for the period between 8:00 and 9:00 P.M. clearly showed a rising tone of optimism as data from one section of the country after another told the same story. Traffic was slackening off. Action and flight were being replaced by analysis and talk. Despite dubious predictions of Soviet revenge from several observers who had followed Donley onto television at the invitation of the networks, a paradoxical ease was settling over the nation.

Sure now that there was more time to cope with his problems, the President focused discussion on the crucial reparations and disarmament demands proposed by Kirov. These were not matters he had dared raise in his speech. Even the basic question of how to broach such subjects to key congressional leaders was supremely difficult. The pros and cons of a closed Sunday-morning debate in a possible joint session of Congress with direct presidential participation were being argued when an intercom announcement took Charles Frydon to a black circuit telephone. The news he brought upon his return to the table completely swept away any hopes kindled by the President's speech. Donley might have succeeded in slowing the avalanche of M10 in America, but half a world away, it was gathering unstoppable momentum.

"Mr. President, I'm sorry to interrupt, but I have some information you had better hear." There was a stir in the room. People leaned forward expectantly. "Mr. President, as you know, the National Foreign Assessment Center, our best NFAC people, have been monitoring Soviet actions since M10 started." Frydon peered at the wall clock. "It's about 5:20 in the morning, Moscow time. Sir, there are significant troop movements beginning in and around major Soviet installations. They are moving some fairly heavy equipment, too. The problem is we don't know whether these are steps to control the Soviet population, as we have been assuming would occur, or whether they are organizing for evacuation of their urban centers."

"Evacuation!" exclaimed the President, as his stomach turned into a clenched fist.

"Yes, sir. Evacuation is a key element of Soviet civil defense. They try to move everyone in the urban populations out to a collective or state-owned farm. They have stated openly that they can hold casualties in a nuclear war to perhaps five to eight percent that way. And they've actually practiced a large-scale evacuation of several Siberian population centers. It was about three years ago, but was never generally reported. The procedures start very much the way they are doing things at the moment. It's all right in the *Grazhdanskaya Oborona*, their civil defense manual. And as you know, Mr. President, they've been dispersing their industry and building up underground food and supply depots for years. Combine those facilities with the fairly good previous preparation of their people and one can guess they might be willing to commit to a full-scale prestrike posture."

"Charley, my God—you've got to give me more than guesswork on their intentions," the President cried, his anguish evident in his voice.

"I'm sorry, sir, I can't. We're moving heaven and earth to get more, but we haven't got it yet. Meantime, it's at least reassuring that they have not given any formal evacuation signals. Of course, they could do so at any moment."

At the far end of the long table, General Kallen, surrounded by the uniformed four-star officers of the Joint Chiefs, shook his head sadly and got to his feet. "Mr. President, regardless of how we interpret this NFAC information, it is my opinion that we should alert all our own Civil Defense personnel and activate Phase One crisis procedures immediately."

The President stared intently at the dark, handsome face of the man in Air Force blue. Saying nothing, he shifted his gaze from Kallen to one after another of the men around the table. The Secretary of State was nodding slowly in apparent affirmation of Kallen's suggestion.

Donley's face fell in disbelief. "Carl, you don't agree, do you?" he asked his long-time ally and confidant. "You don't really think we ought to get Civil Defense into this. If we do, whatever time we've just gained will be lost again. The Guard people and local authorities need at least twenty-four hours more to get set, and that probably isn't enough."

Silverton looked like a very tired old man who was about to confess to a murder. "Mr. President, if the Russians are implementing an evacuation plan already—"

The President slammed his fist on the conference table, his head throbbing and his rigid stomach twisting again with nausea. "Damn it! Frydon didn't say that. Frydon and the NFAC said that there are some troop movements, which could be perfectly consistent with what Kirov said he had to do—namely, control the Soviet reaction so that he doesn't have riots on his hands, too. Futhermore—and check me on this yourself, Carl—we've got to realize that Kirov is perhaps being threatened by some kind of a coup. There are several people in the Politburo, as we've said before, who are just sitting back waiting for an excuse, and this goddamn M10 business may be just what they've been after. It is perfectly understandable that Kirov would want to protect his position with his army if he has to." Donley paused to look around the room to see whom he had convinced. The faces were mute. Each man to whom he turned simply looked back at him blankly or dropped his eyes.

"Sir," said Frydon finally, "there are some positive signs. Aside from local preparations, there has been no general Soviet alert ordered. Futhermore, we've had the NFAC watching for the start of construction of what the Soviets call 'dug-out' shelters. They count heavily on them for fallout protection and they can be built in the rural countryside in less than forty-eight hours by the people themselves. They're all trained in high school to do it. The idea is that a crisis usually takes time to build up— at least a few days—and that gives everyone time to dig in. In fact, according to one NFAC scenario, this whole situation and the start of a Soviet military response to M10, if there were to be one, could be judged precisely by their progress with the shelters when they do start making them. That is vital for us to remember. Down in Tennessee we once tested some designs they published in *Voyennye Znaniya*—their *Journal of Military Knowledge*—and untrained people can build them in less than two days. They use trees and mud, even reeds...."

Mike Kallen drummed his fingers on the table. "Christ, if we wait until they are all out in the countryside and dug in, while most of our people are still like sitting ducks in unprotected cities . . . Mr. President, please—admit the time has come: activate the Civil Defense Phase One program." Kallen knew he was urging a precipitous action that carried into territory where his boss did not want to go. He was trying to face the facts from a purely military perspective. And the facts were grim. The U.S. population was far less trained and far less prepared to take defensive measures against nuclear attack than were the Soviets. Purposely, and with the best of intentions, one President after another had considered massive civil defense efforts and had rejected them, opting instead for easier roads, such as marking "Public Shelters" with the little yellow-and-black signs that became ubiquitous in the 1960s and then gradually disappeared in the 1970s. The reasons for the deterioration of the U.S. civil defense posture were several: First and most important, détente seemed to be working—a stream of SALT agreements and other treaties between America and Russia attested to that. Second, it was successfully argued by many that strong civil defense efforts could themselves lead to war since they might convince our leaders that the nation could not only survive an attack but even "win" an atomic exchange. Believing one can win is the first step to proving it.

A third and very basic factor in the calculations of civil defense was the very heavy dependence of the largely urban U.S. population on essential skills and facilities supplied from elsewhere. The rural character of the Russian population was starkly different. The farmers of the Ukraine were infinitely more self-sufficient than the city dwellers of Detroit, and in the ugly aftermath of a nuclear war, self-sufficiency would necessarily replace high technology. To compensate, even partially, for the pampered life style of Americans, a prodigiously expensive U.S. shelter program and a dispersal plus partial evacuation program would be required. Shelter spaces, enough for one hundred million urbanites, stocked with food, water, and medical supplies for at least two weeks, would have to be constructed. Preplanned, thoroughly practiced evacuations of perhaps fifty to seventy-five million persons to specifically outfitted sites in the countryside would have to be implemented. It was all just too much—too big, too frightening, too expensive, too dubious. And so the United States chose another approach.

U.S. citizens, in the *three or four days* before a crisis, were to be instructed in what actions they should take to survive *in place*. Evacuation was not to be considered. Television programs illustrating methods of improvising shelters in urban homes and office buildings were to be shown, along with instructions on how to monitor for radiation, how to care for post-attack casualties, and other grisly but necessary matters. A cram course in atomic disaster. Military and paramilitary personnel, including police, firemen, and the limited number of civil defense trainees in each locale, were to maintain order, make short-distance shifts in populations to heavier, more shielded buildings, and organize post-attack operations and services.

If order could be preserved and *if* there was time enough —two very doubtful assumptions—everyone who did not have a better option was to construct a so-called expedient shelter in their basement or wherever possible. Total casualties in a full-scale attack, according to Department of Defense estimates, could be reduced by tens of millions by such steps and the nation, which otherwise might *never* recover from the indescribable aftermath of the holocaust, might have a marginal chance of surviving, albeit to face a future in which the living would probably envy the dead.

As Mike Kallen urged the President to start civil defense preparations, he was thinking primarily of those tens of millions of lives that early preparations might save. The post-attack recovery simulations of his Department of Defense computers played very differently with them or without them. But balanced against the benefits of starting civil defense actions were the heavy costs of potentially stampeding the American people into a frenzy of headlong flight. Kallen, basing his decision on decades of battle experience, was choosing to ensure maximum survival. He had seen too many blazing fire fights lost because there were too few left to do too much with too little. He was gambling that soldiers, guardsmen, and police could maintain discipline and keep the lid on the panic. The President, however, was unwilling to take that gamble, as Donley's next words made obvious.

"Very well," said Donley, pulling himself fully erect in his chair. "I've listened to all the arguments very carefully. We've been over them many times since yesterday. Here's what we're going to do. We are not—I repeat: *not*—going to issue a general Defense Alert. The regional directors have been notified and are quietly getting their trained cadres into position. That is consistent with what I said in my speech. I'm not prepared to go further just yet. I want the Joint Chiefs to review all reaction options to various Russian moves, including the evacuation, if that's what it is, and I want them to be ready to brief me if any confirmation of an evacuation develops. I also want a full recon effort on shelter construction. Now, it may be that I will have to tell the American people to prepare for a possible attack soon. If so, I will do it. But I do not feel that will become necessary."

The President was rubbing his left eye almost constantly and there was an unhealthy waxlike look to his skin as he spoke. "I expect all of you to proceed with the actions we've planned during the last several days. I expect absolute calm and deliberate, careful implementation. I propose that we now adjourn for a few hours to await clarifying data. Charley, Jim—I want to be informed instantly if anything breaks. In the meantime, from all of the inputs we have, I see no reason not to assume that Kirov is keeping to the positions we have inferred he is taking. We will reassemble as a group at 5:00 A.M. sharp. We will review everything then and make a final decision on how to bring Congress into the reparations issue before I call Kirov."

Across the fine grained walnut of the table from Donley, Boyce Williamson's thoughts were swinging wildly. From joining Kallen in his demand for a full alert, they moved to the possibility of ending the ambiguities of the situation once and for all with a massive preemptive strike against the Russians. At least all the doubt would then be gone. He could not yet bring himself to think through the idea seriously, but it was there in a dark niche of his mind and it was growing. With a conscious effort, he deliberately switched away to other possibilities. Seize the initiative from Donley. Take a plane and jet to Moscow for direct talks with the Russian Premier? What if Kirov lost control while he, Williamson, was there? No good. A hot-line conference with Kirov now? Perhaps. But if the Soviets were preparing for an attack, Kirov would merely lie about the meaning of his preparations. He would claim they were exactly what Donley hoped they were—only population-control measures. Christ! Why hadn't he got any preelection briefings on civil defense? Fly back to Big Sky and the family—then afterward return to Washington? Afterward? No good. Might look like a coward. Stay put and *lead*. You're a better leader than Donley. Find a way to show them, dammit!

"One moment, please." Boyce Williamson's voice boomed out over the rustle of papers being gathered into briefcases. "I'd like to make a few comments before we adjourn. With the President's kind permission, of course."

Donley blinked once in mild surprise. "Certainly, Boyce, please do."

Williamson moved to a spot in front of the projection screens, where he could be better seen by those in the tiers of staff chairs behind the main table. The change was intended as a clear psychological signal of assumed authority. "Now, I do not know you people and you do not know me." Williamson paused for effect. "You do know I'm getting a new job soon." The practiced and deliberate attempt at light humor was rewarded by an obedient ripple of tense laughter. "You also know that this grave and threatening situation has developed very quickly. I want to say here and now that I feel the President and all of you have behaved remarkably well throughout." Pause for solicitous nod in Donley's direction. "However, I feel myself to be at a grave disadvantage. During the recently concluded presidential campaign, fortunately or unfortunately, military matters were not major issues. I have, of course, had the usual very general preelection briefings from the administration." Another nod toward Donley. "But I have not had the benefit of the thinking of my own group of military advisers—an important omission in my planning. . . ."

"Where's he headed?" Jim Willoughby whispered to Carl Silverton.

"Danged if I know," the Secretary of State replied.

"Now, this is hardly the time to add a lot of new players to this game. I therefore request, in spite of the need we all have for some rest, that we spend a few minutes here and now getting to know each other better." The President-elect walked to where Frederick Donley was seated and spoke directly to him. "Fred, I know you're very tired, as are these other gentlemen. . . ." His waving hand swept over Frydon, Silverton, and Willoughby. "There is no need for any of you to stay."

The President's face reddened. He and his closest advisers were being firmly invited out of their own meeting. Donley rose slowly to his feet, seeming thereby to make his successor suddenly small by comparison, smiling at the obviousness of the power play. "I think that's a fine idea," he said wryly. "I'm sure everyone will cooperate and I'm also certain we all understand your very difficult position as an unofficial participant in these proceedings. Gentlemen, you may consider this my personal request that you be frank and open with Mr. Williamson. As usual, I shall welcome any ideas or opinions which come out of your exchanges and, as usual, I know you will all discharge your duties and constitutional obligations *to the letter*. And now I, for one, am going to get some rest. As I said a moment ago, we shall reconvene at 5:00 A.M. sharp."

Standing in the elevator on their way to the upper levels of the White House, Donley, Frydon, Silverton, and Willoughby were studies in contrast. The President and the Director of Central Intelligence were passing knowing little grins at each other. Carl Silverton looked worried and Jim Willoughby was furious.

"How dare he do that to you, Mr. President?" Willoughby asked angrily. "That man is going to set up his own damned shadow cabinet! There's enough division of opinion in that room as it is. He'll find the dissidents or the ones with ambitions for new presidential appointments and pretty soon, instead of a military line of command, we'll have a debating society."

"I understand exactly what he's doing and why," said Donley soothingly, "but unless or until he tries to give orders rather than advice, I intend to be fully cooperative. As for the others, they will stand by their oaths of allegiance. I will not even consider any other possibility. Now, Jim, stop worrying and get some rest. It will be a very short night."

On the top floor of the White House, behind the bullet-proof windows, the President of the United States felt his way in the darkness. Still several careful steps from the bed, he could sense his wife's presence and hear her soft breathing. Her voice, husky with sleep and with concern, welcomed him.

"What time is it? How's it going?"

"It's about one o'clock in the morning. It's going . . . I'm not sure how. . . . It's just going, I guess."

Donley slipped under the covers and told himself to relax. For the first time in hours, he became aware of parts of his body other than his throbbing head and churning stomach. His legs were shaking with fatigue and the muscles of his neck and shoulders were taut as bow-strings. With a long, low sigh, he settled into the downy comfort of the pillows.

Laura turned toward him and worked one warm hand under his neck. She began to massage the tightness away. "Do you think everything will be all right?"

He sighed again. "I don't know. I think it's too early to tell. I'm not even sure how to tell. I do know I'm betting very heavily on Kirov. And Williamson is beginning to play a few games, too. Nothing serious—at least not yet."

Laura Donley's fingers moved upward on her husband's neck. "Fred . . . I've been thinking about what we discussed last night and decided it's not the right thing for me to do—to go to the Mountain with you if there's a transfer of operations. I want to go down to Norfolk to be with Mary and the children; that's where I should be. You'll have enough to worry about in the Mountain, without me around. Besides, I know you. I trust you. You're not going to let anything terrible happen to this country, so it's perfectly sensible for me to be with the kids for a time."

Fred Donley only half heard his wife's words and did not reply. His eyes, now accustomed to the dark, were staring unblinkingly at the red telephone on the bedstand. The red of it seemed to be coming from deep inside—like the dull red of the coals of a dying fire. Great glowing cracks were opening in the inert plastic. It blurred and shimmered and the yawning red crevices reached across space toward him, wrapping themselves around him, enveloping him, strangling the air away from him. Donley pressed his eyelids together to escape the nightmare vision. Suddenly, a cool, refreshing breeze caressed his weary body.

"Look down there, Laura. What magnificent country! It's absolutely perfection!" Fred Donley was standing on the topmost point of a steep hill overlooking the dark-blue water far below. Laura Ann was there with him and they were young and happy, turned inward on themselves. The trip had been glorious. Days exploring, nights on the cruise ship, all wonder, all flawless. Tomorrow they were to leave for Stockholm and the trip would end. But here and now, in this magic moment, the sunlight on the water was a mixture of melted gold and blue enamel and Fred Donley was filled with more joy and contentment than he had ever known before. The woman beside him had brought total fulfillment to a life already blessed with more than an ordinary share of happiness and opportunity. Standing there on the high hills above the fjords of Norway, Fred Donley knew how lucky he was. There was nothing he and Laura could not do. There were no limits to what they could achieve together. The whole world lay open—waiting for them.

A short, sharp pain raced through President Donley's left temple. In the dark bedroom, he fought to control the creeping nausea that always seemed to follow the spasms of pain in the left side of his head. He turned his body so that he could no longer see the red phone and pressed against the warmth of his wife.

"Laura, do you remember that time we were in Norway?"

"When, Fred?"

"That time we cruised the fjords."

"Why, yes . . . of course I remember."

"That was lovely, wasn't it?"

"Yes, it was very lovely. Why do you ask?"

"I don't know. I just happened to remember it, that's all. It was a beautiful trip. I love you, Laura."

"I know, my darling. I love you, too. Please try to sleep now. You're so tired. You've got to rest." Laura Donley's lips pressed against her husband's cheek. This was not the time to decide about the Mountain, she told herself. Finally, after a while, she pulled her arm from under his head. The President was asleep.

For almost an hour, Laura Donley lay next to her husband, listening to his slow, steady breathing. The man lying next to her—her man—was being destroyed before her eyes. First, the rending defeat of the presidential campaign. And then the terrible curse of M10. He was withering, shriveling into a tired, empty husk and she could do nothing about it except watch it happen. M10 was like some thick corrosive liquid. With each passing hour, in ways only she could see, it was eating away more and more of the towering personality with whom she had lived most of her adult life. It was so unfair. No flesh-and-blood man ought to be asked to contend with the impossibilities that faced Frederick Donley. Tears spilled from the corners of Laura's burning eyes and spread into the pillowcase. She let them flow until, in the silence, there were no more. Then, brushing her lips softly against the raspy stubble of beard that shaded her husband's face, she turned on her side and waited, hopefully, for sleep. It was almost 3:00 A.M.

35

Somewhere in the darkness of the presidential bedroom, there was an angry noise—a ringing. Frederick Donley struggled to react. He dragged himself toward wakefulness and squinted at the small lighted clock on the bedstand: 3:42 A.M. The green telephone, as it had so many times before, was shouting for his attention. He pushed himself up on one elbow and reached for the handset. "This is the President."

"Mr. President, I'm sorry to wake you, sir." The voice was strained. "There is a major news conference now going on in Stockholm. It looks bad. A group of European scientists and medical people are confirming both the scientific feasibility and the casualty levels from M10. They've been putting a big effort into their own computerized statistical analysis since the first VEI release. A Professor Lindstrom of the Nobel Cytobiology Institute seems to be orchestrating the show. . . . The worst part is that they're beaming the program all over Western Russia through the Eurosat system. . . ."

The voice on the phone chattered on, but the President had stopped listening. His thoughts were far away.

"Mr. President, shall I pass this material to the others?" The question snapped Donley back to the bedroom and the telephone in his hand.

"Yes, you'd better do that right away. Get to everyone—including Boyce Williamson. Brief them and tell them to meet me in the conference room at 4:30 . . . and thank you."

The President eased his legs slowly from the bed onto the chilly floor at the edge of the carpet. His feet searched a moment for his slippers, then he trudged wearily toward the bathroom. Emerging a few minutes later, he was shaved and smelling subtly of menthol, but not even slightly refreshed. The few hours of rest were worse than none at all and had left him feeling drugged and light-headed.

Laura Ann Donley was sitting up in bed, the bedside lamp aglow. "What's happening?" she asked.

"There's a news conference in Stockholm. It's going to give Kirov fits. Could make for very ugly reactions in Russia."

"Fred, do you think . . . there's going to be a war?"

"I don't know. I hope to God there isn't, but I just don't know. Look, I've got to go downstairs. Is there anything I can do for you?"

"Fred, I think I want to leave now. I want to go to Norfolk. I want to be with the children. You can stay in touch with me by phone. I'm sure, though, that's where I ought to be. You're going to be tied up in this thing completely from now on. Can you understand?" She looked at him steadily. It was a conversation without the need for words.

"Yes, of course I understand. Go be with the kids and I'll see you in a few days. Jim Willoughby can get you a helicopter. When do you want to leave?"

"I guess I can be ready in an hour or so."

"Okay, darling." The President's voice trembled, his eyes brimmed with tears. He leaned down and gently kissed her hands, then her lips. "Thank you, my love, for everything. . . ."

"Kiss me again," she murmured.

The conference room of the White House Communications Center was crowded, but in spite of the large number of people, it was hushed with that feeling peculiar to very early morning. Boyce Williamson, still a little rumpled with sleep, watched impassively as Frydon and Silverton took their seats. General Kallen was already in his place, as were the other members of the Joint Chiefs of Staff.

The President himself was standing near the doorway in private conversation with Jim Willoughby. The young man was listening carefully and nodding. Occasionally, the level of Donley's voice was loud enough for Williamson to hear. The subject of the conversation seemed to be Mrs. Donley, but Williamson could not make out more and stopped his casual eavesdropping to smile and nod to others entering the room. He scanned their faces and let himself dream. In a few weeks, they would all be under his control. When they knew his plans for the future, when they saw how he would act in situations like this, they'd know how great a President he could be. Williamson breathed in expansively.

In spite of lack of sleep and the tension in the room, he was enjoying himself. It was still so new and intoxicating to be there. Boyce Williamson could enjoy himself for one very dangerous reason, although he did not recognize it: He had convinced himself that even after a war, or more accurately, *especially* after a war, a President could make truly historic impact on the world. Put simply, in the depths of his subconscious, he was coming to see a war as an opportunity. The challenge of recovery would mean far more scope for momentous accomplishment than merely trying to put a few percentage points off unyielding inflation and unemployment rates, as Donley and his recent predecessors had been forced to do. A war would change the rules of historical judgment. The President-elect was not aware that he was thinking in such terms. He had the ability of many men to conveniently close himself off from his true motivations. Earlier in the morning, he had listened carefully to those in the conference room after Donley and the others had left. Without trying, he had filtered their words, leaving behind a residual feeling that nuclear war need not be so different from conventional war as to be avoided at all costs. Thanks to successful test ban treaties, he and a whole generation of his colleagues had never seen a nuclear explosion, and he only dimly recalled seeing photos of H-bomb clouds in his youth. Reduced to an eight-by-ten picture, even a megaton detonation does not look like much. More significantly, he was nearly convinced that a nuclear exchange could be controlled and limited. Conveniently, the focus of the discussion had been largely on the use of one or several weapons on selected targets— "surgical strikes," as one general had called them. The possibility that such actions would bring an answering cascade of weapons that would build to an uncontrollable holocaust was brought up, greeted with shrugs and silence, and pushed into the background in favor of more "tractable" aspects of nuclear war. Intellectually, Williamson recognized the yawning gaps in the discussion. Emotionally, he decided to ignore them, at least for the present. Meanwhile, his lack of detailed knowledge and his own deeply buried psychological needs combined to push Boyce Williamson toward a dangerously presumptuous answer to the ultimate question about nuclear force: Dare it be used?

Red-eyed staff personnel continued to file into the room and arrange themselves in the tiers of chairs as President Donley left Jim Willoughby and walked to the head of the table. In a voice hollow with fatigue, he listed the matters for consideration. As he did so, an electronic typewriter displayed the same items in glowing letters on the large television screen behind him:

1. IMPACT OF STOCKHOLM ANNOUNCEMENTS
2. SOVIET MILITARY STATUS
3. U.S. MILITARY STATUS
4. PROBABLE NATURE OF U.S.S.R. POPULATION REACTION
5. STATUS OF U.S. POPULATION
6. STATUS OF NATIONAL GUARD AND EMERGENCY PERSONNEL
7. TIMING AND CONTENT OF NEXT U.S. CONTACT WITH KIROV
8. CONGRESSIONAL BRIEFING: TIMING AND PROBABLE REACTIONS

Except for Stockholm, very little had changed since the group had adjourned four hours earlier. Some uncertain indications from reconnaissance satellites and from data flowing in from the National Foreign Assessment Center, doing its round-the-clock duty in the CIA building, suggested further shifting of trucks and heavy equipment throughout the Soviet Union, especially near Leningrad and in the north. There was still no indication of any major evacuation or other preparations. On the other hand, the news from Sweden was only minutes old and the huge Soviet population had not had time to assimilate it.

Half an hour later, Charles Frydon was ticking off a summary of where the discussion had brought them thus far. "Okay," he said, touching one finger after another. "We presume Kirov can handle the impact of Stockholm; there's nothing to the contrary yet. Soviet military status is routine; ours is Level Four except for the Tridents. Talk about M10 is circulating in Russian cities, but up to now, nothing too ugly in the way of losing their heads. We don't know how the Politburo and the Kremlin bigwigs are taking it; our people are jittery, some still heading for cover, but the National Guard presence seems to be damping things down. Hell, I think we're in remarkably good shape, all things considered. . . ."

"If—and it's a big *if*," said the President, "we're not deluding ourselves about Stockholm's lack of impact, then I've got two immediate problems: Kirov's reparations formula and how to bring Congress into a discussion on it. Shall we call the joint emergency session for 10:00 A.M. today? It's not much warning for the Hill, but we could notify those who happen to be in town and we could fly in some of the other key people. It would seem the right way to go instead of trying to talk to everyone individually, as we've been doing."

Carl Silverton was about to reply to Donley's suggestion when a flashing warning light and a loud voice on the Crisis Center intercom stopped him, mouth agape. "Priority black circuit call for Mr. Frydon, please!"

Frydon picked up the telephone. "Go ahead. . . ." Seconds later, he turned to face the President. "There may have been a coup in the Kremlin. They've apparently shot Kirov."

"Dear God!" said Donley, wide-eyed. "Is he dead?"

The Director of Central Intelligence did not answer. Instead he spoke rapidly into the phone, waited for what seemed to be an eternity, then turned again to his boss. "More data. Several officials definitely killed. Don't know who. There have been some small explosions, too."

"Well, that tears it," said Mike Kallen. "Mr. President, without Kirov's moderating influence . . . Remember what he said about others around him wanting to . . ."

"I know, Mike, I know. You don't . . . have to say it," replied Donley bleakly.

According to data in the National Security Agency compilation of Presidential Orders, the message activating all U.S. regular Army personnel and other internal security forces and the full complement of National Guard units was dispatched from Washington at a few minutes before six o'clock on the morning of November 11. The Phase One Civil Defense Alert followed immediately thereafter, as did a major advance in American strategic posture. All U.S. submarine squadrons were brought to Level Three—a state just two short steps away from receiving Level One ready-attack instructions. At Level One, transmission of a few additional coded symbols over the massive SeaComm low-frequency radio link could launch 710 Poseidon C-3 and Trident C-4 MIRV missiles from forty-four nuclear submarines. Over a span of 185 degrees of longitude, more than half the distance around the earth, from airfields within sight of the Blue Mosque at Istanbul westward to the gray coral of Johnston Island in the Pacific, klaxons sounded and jet bombers carrying megatons of death in Cruise Missiles in their bellies or under their wings roared skyward on Level Three Airborne Alert. Across the central third of the United States, from the Malmstrom Minuteman farms in Montana and the Titan silos of Davis-Monthan in Arizona to the ICBMs of Little Rock, Arkansas, and Whiteman, Missouri, nervous men hovered over their control consoles, reviewing check lists and manuals of command procedure.

Just as a faint rosy glow was lighting the cloudless skies along America's east coast, hundreds of thousands of people who ordinarily would still be asleep were awake and frightened. Prerecorded voice messages, activated by a Pentagon mobilization computer, had delivered telephoned orders to the homes of off-duty police, firemen, National Guardsmen, reservists, and regular Army units, catapulting them out of their beds. And in turn, their mothers, fathers, wives, and children had begun their own panicky torrent of warning calls to relatives and friends. Something awful must be happening! War must be coming after all! The burden on the national telephone system skyrocketed to unprecedented levels. In the space of a few minutes, millions upon millions of local and long-distance calls were dialed and the national communications lifeline staggered under the enormous input. The more often people tried to place calls, the more the circuits jammed, lights flashing, relays chattering helplessly. As the orange-white disk of the sun became visible in New York, the system started an irretrievable slide into almost complete collapse. Except for special circuits protected by telephone company computerized contingency programs, few calls were getting to their destination. Like a frightened animal, America was ready to fight or to run, and uncertain of which was wiser.

"It is essential that we talk to Moscow," snapped the President. "Now keep trying, dammit. Any misinterpretation of our actions at this point could be disastrous. If Kirov is no longer in power, I'll speak to *anyone*, but it must be now!"

For the fifth or sixth time the Communications Center technician pressed the green "Auto-Connect" button at the left of the video console. Everything should be ready. The equipment had been checked out repeatedly over the past thirty minutes. Nothing happened. A nervous senior engineer leaned past the technician and pressed the "Auto-Connect" button himself. Still nothing. Several minutes elapsed. Donley drummed his fingers on the console nervously. "Someone over there has got to know exactly what we are doing and why." The men around him stood in their places watching the blank screen which should have brought a living Soviet's presence into the room. Nothing. The perspiring engineer dashed for the main communications control facilities, next to the conference room. He and an overweight Army one-star general, the current commander of the Center's Technical Support Group, made another series of hurried radiotelephone calls to key parts of the complex worldwide communications system that lay behind the simple-looking television set in front of the President. Whatever was wrong with the system, it quickly became obvious, was definitely at the Russian end. Apparently no one in Kirov's office was willing to answer the call from America.

As Donley was turning toward his colleagues in helpless frustration, a momentary pattern of light flickered across the video terminal and was repeated in enormously magnified form on the large-screen display at the end of the room. The image of a grim-faced Russian flashed into view before the President and loomed up on the wall. It was not Kirov.

Startled by the sudden appearance of the unfamiliar face, President Donley licked his lips and swallowed once. "I wish to talk to Premier Kirov or whoever is currently in command."

"Premier Kirov is not available," the grim-looking man replied in bland but perfect English.

Donley switched off the autotranslation system to halt the annoying snapping sound it added at the end of each computer-translated word. "When will the Premier be available?" he asked coolly.

"The Premier is away for today and perhaps for tomorrow as well," came the noncommittal reply.

"Can he be reached?"

"No, he cannot be reached."

"This is an emergency. It is necessary that I reach the Premier."

The face glared at the President. "The Premier cannot be reached," it repeated firmly.

"I wish you to understand," the President said, with every bit of authority he could muster, "this is an emergency."

The man looked at the President with unyielding eyes. "We understand your emergency. We also have certain problems here. The Premier is away. You may call tomorrow."

"Then let me talk to his deputy," demanded Donley. "I must explain certain actions we have been forced to take."

"Comrade Mihalas is not here."

"I will speak to the most senior official available."

A quick babble of words pulled the Russian's eyes off to the left for a moment. He nodded to someone and then looked directly at Donley again. "Call tomorrow," he said firmly.

The picture before the President abruptly vanished into blackness and Donley was left staring at a lifeless piece of glass. Behind him forty or fifty people sat rigid and voiceless. Donley's eye twitched reflexively. Another dull but insistent pain grew out of the back of his head and climbed slowly up his neck into the left side of his face. Different from the previous torments he had been experiencing, it changed into a peculiar numbness which spread from his eye and radiated outward over the full left side of his face. His eyelid drooped almost to the point of closing. The blurred reflection of a fluorescent lamp caught in the glass of the TV screen and burned into his vision. Instantly he was whirling on a wave of vertigo to a far-distant time and place. The waters of the fjords are deep blue. It is lovely and warm. . . .

A loud cough behind the immobile President pulled him back toward the present. Don't let them know, he told himself, as he climbed out of the dark-green clouds swirling around him. Cautiously, he faced directly toward the hot-line terminal and away from the room so those around him could not see what he was doing. His cheek was completely without sensation. He pinched at it several times and a tingling sensation thrilled through his left temple and into his neck and shoulders. Feeling began to return. Almost as quickly as it came, the numbness left. Weaving slightly, Donley rose slowly from his chair before the hot-line console, waiting for the familiar surge of nausea that had always followed such episodes. He turned toward the others in the conference room. The faces he saw were empty. There was nothing to say.

36

A few hundred feet from the subterranean nerve center of the White House, half a dozen men were going through a routine they had conducted daily for years. The security guards who man the tiny white houses with the thick blue windows that dot the grounds of the presidential residence at strategically placed points were changing shifts. On this shift change, there were none of the usual raucous jokes or complaints about the lousy sweet rolls and coffee from the refreshment counter near the locker room. This time there was only fear.

The veteran ex-policemen and MPs of the White House security staff looked at each other knowingly as streams of National Guard trucks rumbled past them and turned down Pennsylvania Avenue. Outside the high iron fence which enclosed the manicured lawns and trees and hid the seismic intrusion detectors, the electric eyes, and the acoustic listening devices, sidewalks that should have been deserted on a Sunday morning were, instead, crowded with people cutting around each other, running, most of them carrying packages. The scene was familiar. It was a repeat of the events of the previous night before the President's speech, but there was a greater intensity, a deeper desperation, in the actions.

The off-duty guards rounded a corner. Through the large plate-glass windows of the new quarter-block-long Dart drugstore, they could see a mob scene inside. People were buying everything they could reach, from toiletries to frozen candies and canned cocktail nuts. As the guards passed the store, two men rushed up behind them to one of the windows and smashed it. They grabbed at the items on display and in an instant disappeared around the corner. Except for the silent guards who stopped momentarily to watch, the passing hordes of people seemed to take no notice. On the street, the low, throaty groan of National Guard trucks continued.

Almost four hundred miles to the northeast, National Guard trucks were also rumbling through the streets. Boston, this Sunday morning, was bitter cold, although the skies were very clear.

Father Philip Coogan of St. Brendan's Church was donning his vestments in the sacristy to the left of the altar. Through the doorway he could see his parishioners gathering in the pews. To his astonishment, the church was filled and people who had arrived too late for seats at the mass were crowding in against the back wall. Father Coogan smiled sadly. What a shame, he thought to himself, that it took an impending national disaster to fill a house of God.

In a hilly and beautifully wooded suburb outside Pittsburgh, Pennsylvania, the residents of the Forest View Retirement and Convalescent Home were filtering into the dining hall as they did every morning. Normally, they seldom spoke. Petty hates and jealousies, shyness and sickness, prevented it. Living together while waiting for death to come does not make people very sociable. But this morning, they were chattering nervously to each other about the news broadcasts they had been watching. One after another, in trembling voices, they told of their unsuccessful attempts to reach their children or grandchildren by telephone. They settled down expectantly; it was time for Sunday breakfast to be served. After almost fifteen minutes, they became aware that not one of the kitchen help had appeared to serve them. Eighty-three-year-old Steven McLaughlin, unable to fight off his hunger and his curiosity any longer, tottered through the swinging doors that led from the dining room to the cooking area. The usually bustling kitchen was deserted. On the counter, there were only empty pale-yellow plastic plates and unopened cans of orange juice. Mr. McLaughlin returned to the thirty-four elderly people waiting in the dining room. "No one is here," he announced in a trembling voice.

Upstairs, in her small second-floor bedroom at Forest View, surrounded by pictures of her sons, grandchildren, and great-grandchildren, and the well-fingered and worn mementos of a married life that had ended almost twenty years before with the death of her husband, Mrs. Mary Harrison was still in bed. For the past three years, ever since her stroke, she had been unable to get to her wheelchair or to the bathroom alone. Now, terribly uncomfortable and very frightened, she was crying softly to herself. She had been ringing for the attendant for over an hour and no one had come.

Barely over the horizon from the 184th Street Marina in Miami Beach, the forty-five-foot motor cruiser *Happy Daze* rolled gently with the slight swell. Mark Pasternak and his wife, Beth, together with their weekend guests, Maggie and Sam Siegel, had been up late and were just arising. They had spent last evening under the dark, star-filled sky talking about the President's speech and how the United Nations might be used to facilitate some sort of people-to-people program to assist cancer patients in the Soviet Union.

Mark Pasternak yawned, scratched his bald but very tanned head, and shouted down into the forward cabin. "Okay, everybody. Up on deck. The Bloody Marys are ready!"

"Mark, you better put some suntan oil on," a voice replied from below.

"Okay, honey, okay, I will—but listen, c'mon up here. It's a beautiful day. I think we ought to go for a little ride and try for some fish before breakfast. We'll have a few Bloody Marys and maybe a snack from the refrigerator. Then about noon we'll go on in and have brunch at the Doral or something. How does that sound?"

By the time Mark had finished proposing the agenda for the day, his wife and his two friends were on deck with him, admiring the pink-and-white clouds of the morning. "I think you got a good idea there," said Sam Siegel. "Let's go!"

Siegel, an agile man in spite of his sixty-three years,

hoisted his scrawny, well-browned body out of the cockpit of the boat and onto the spotless white foredeck. Expertly he coiled the white nylon line that held the sea anchor and then dropped lightly into the cockpit again. The twin diesel engines of the *Happy Daze* rumbled into life, soiling the clear air momentarily with sooty black smoke. The Pasternaks and the Siegels were off for a morning on the beautiful Atlantic. It did not occur to them to turn on a radio or their television set until they were almost twenty-five minutes farther from Miami. It also did not occur to them, perhaps because they did not want it to, that the crisis of M10 had not disappeared simply because of the confident words of their beloved President last evening. When, finally, for no particular reason, Mark Pasternak did flip on his elegant multiband shortwave portable, the message traffic he heard was hardly typical Sunday boatmen's talk. Instead the airwaves were filled with strange codes and crisp-sounding official commands.

"There must be some kind of emergency ashore," Mark Pasternak said, turning to Sam with a worried expression.

"Let's see whether we can get anything on the television out here," Siegel suggested.

Leaving their wives sunning themselves on the foredeck, the two men slipped down the narrow ladder that led into the beautifully appointed interior cabin. Siegel dialed in Channel 5 on the little color TV. The picture was badly broken and rolling, but the two men could make out the face of a newscaster. The audio was coming through clearly as the commentator repeated the latest bulletins about President Donley's call-up of the National Guard and Army. "Everyone should remain calm and stay tuned for a repeat of civil defense instructions, which will be broadcast on all channels every fifteen minutes."

"Beth, Maggie—come here quick!" the old friends screamed in unison. "Quick, quick!"

Five minutes later the *Happy Daze* was making for shore under maximum power. Mark Pasternak was at the controls, and Beth was standing next to him, compulsively twisting her hair between her fingers.

"Mark, what will we do about the children?" she asked fearfully. Mark Pasternak did not reply. Cold sweat had begun to pour from his ashen forehead and sharp, crushing pains were assaulting his chest. Two minutes later, Mark Pasternak was dead.

In New York, the residents of Manhattan were pouring across the bridges and out of the city in a wild orgy of flight. The previous evening had been bad and only by the narrowest of margins had a full-scale panic been averted. But now New York had gone completely berserk. Wild-eyed, screaming men, women, and children filled the streets, running over each other, pushing, shoving, doing anything to save themselves from onrushing disaster and death.

On elegant Sutton Place, only a few people and no cars were left. A well-dressed man in a gray, fur-collared top-coat stood alone in the middle of the road, vainly attempting to flag a taxi. Occasionally, one of the big yellow automobiles streaked by unheedingly. Some were already loaded with passengers. Others were driven by men desperately trying to get around the traffic on the through streets to their families and then out of town. Finally, almost insane with fear, the man spotted another taxi, roaring down the empty street toward him at fifty miles an hour, and stepped directly into its path, waving his wallet. An ear-piercing screech brought the car to a halt inches from the man's body, its horn blaring. The man vaulted up on the front bumper and leaned over the hood, shouting at the top of his lungs to the hysterical driver. "I'll give you a thousand dollars," he screamed, "a thousand dollars! Just take me with you and let's get out of town!" The cursing taxi driver shoved his car into reverse with a tearing, grinding lurch and stomped on the accelerator. The quick movement of the automobile flipped the man off the front bumper and down onto the street. With a second grinding roar, the machine charged forward again. The man shrieked as the oncoming auto-mobile tore away the ligaments and crushed the bones of his right ankle and then was gone in a cloud of exhaust fumes.

37

"Mr. President," a voice said, "it's getting very bad out there."

In the crowded subterranean Communications Center, President Frederick Donley was trying to decide on another attempt to contact the Russians via the video hot line. His attention was finally forced away from his inner thoughts as colorless but devastating numerical summaries of national situation reports were replaced by too vivid telephoto pictures of specific towns and street corners. What had been, in the hours before the President's calming speech of Saturday night, an orderly river of people pouring from their homes and out of the cities to what they hoped would be safety in the country was reappearing as a monster tidal wave. Beginning on the East Coast, to the accompaniment of feverishly strident news flashes and TV reports, it was sweeping westward, engulfing the Middle West, the mountain states, and, finally, California and the Far West, touching every home and every human being in America. *Could a nuclear war really start today? Why can't I get through on the phone? The TV is saying the Russians are getting ready for revenge! Who could blame them? What would we have done if we were they? Are we really on full war alert? My God, it's coming! It's coming!*

President Donley forced himself to forget the terrorized faces the helicopters had just shown him. "I intend to concentrate on operational issues," he reminded everyone around him. "We must deal with the high-level problems. We can't start diverting ourselves to save a neighborhood and lose a nation instead. "We'll have to depend on the local on-site personnel to deal with the population. We can't help them from here. Our primary obligation is the Soviets," he added emphatically. "Charley, have we gotten anything else on the coup? Did it oust Kirov or did it not?"

The Director of Central Intelligence looked up from a stack of intelligence summaries and took off his glasses.

Using a rumpled white handkerchief, he began to wipe the lenses with a repetitive circular motion.

"Sir, I still can't give you anything on Kirov. We plain don't know where he is."

"But do you detect anything in the way of *someone else* doing things that Kirov ought to be expected to do?" Donley pressed. "That might be indicative."

"I'm sorry, sir, our sources just aren't that close. I can't tell you." Frydon shook his head helplessly and carefully fitted his glasses back onto his ears.

"Well, at least this solves the problem of your giving Alaska away to Kirov for the moment!" Boyce Williamson observed dryly. It was such a contrast to Frydon's quiet report that the President jumped slightly in his chair.

"I'm glad you think it's such a game, Mr. Williamson," the President replied grimly.

"No, not at all. I don't think it's a game. I just can't fathom how you could be caught with such inadequate emergency plans for controlling the U.S. population and the property of this country. The way this is working out is an absolute disaster. You seem very willing to forget that right over our heads there's practically a riot going on. And the same thing is happening in every other city in this country." Williamson's voice was rising with his every word.

"Dammit, Boyce," the President exclaimed impatiently. "When you're in this office you'll learn something you obviously don't know yet, and that is you have to work through other people and you have to depend on other people. I have given the proper orders. The National Guard and the military personnel of this country know what to do, and I assume are doing it competently."

"Mr. President, may I interrupt, sir?" It was General Kallen. "My colleagues and I here"—he gestured toward the other uniformed men near him at the table—"have been discussing the possibility that the Soviet Union is preparing to launch a first strike." Kallen stopped to let his words sink in. "That could be the reason for the coup against Kirov, and our Defense Intelligence Agency data cannot rule it out. They would not have to reveal their plans with a general alert first if, for example, we have somehow underestimated just two items: their ability to track our submarines and their ability to hit our missile silos accurately. We already know they have grossly under-estimated our air-launched Cruise Missile systems. These three miscalculations combined together could lead them to try to preempt us with a full-scale attack. None of our data are definitive, but it is our recommendation, sir, it is our strong recommendation that it is your duty to remove the center of command, civilian as well as military, to the secure facilities in the Rock."

The President studied Mike Kallen's face. The wide-set eyes, accented with deeply cut lines shaped by thirty years of flying through bright skies, were steady. Mike Kallen was a military man facing a military situation.

Donley pondered briefly and sucked in a very deep breath. The nausea was gone, at least for the time being. "Well," he said to the group as a whole, "you've heard General Kallen and the JCS recommendation. Does anyone have any comment?"

A few people in the distant tiers of seats nodded their heads. Carl Silverton looked across the table at the President. "I think he's right, Fred. Nothing like that may be necessary, but I guess it is your duty to this country to act on the presumption that it might be. It costs us nothing and it could be terribly important."

"All right, get the helicopters ready," the President declared softly. "Boyce, I'm not sure you understand what we're discussing here."

"Oh, I understand," said Williamson with a hint of haughtiness. "I've heard about the Alternate Command Center. But may I ask this: What do you propose to do, Mr. President, about the chaos outside. Are you really simply going to let it go on and on?"

"What I would like to do, Boyce, if you'll cooperate, is to make a joint appeal for calm. It's about all we can do beyond the procedures that have already been imple-mented. We can make the broadcast from the ACC as well as from here. Say, in an hour or so. I would like to tell the country what we know at that time and I'd like you to appear with me. Meanwhile, if things abroad go badly, we may have some actions to take that will be very difficult. Implementing them will be easier—no, that's the wrong word—more efficient and certain from the ACC."

Williamson tilted his head toward the ceiling and leaned back in his chair. The uneasy feeling that had accompanied him on his ride to the Bozeman airport had returned. The full weight of the responsibilities of the office of the President was apparent in Donley's last words, and it was pressing hard against Williamson's subconscious attraction toward a heroic role in the aftermath of war. He was unsure of what to do. That unknown Russian who had answered for Kirov on the hot line had shaken his confidence. He concluded that there was no reason not to go along with the President's suggestion.

"All right, Fred. We'll make the broadcast together from the Rock, as your people call it. But I insist that we pay more attention to the American citizens who are tearing themselves to shreds while we sit here and talk. My God, man, there must be something more we can do."

"I don't know what it would be," Donley replied almost inaudibly. "We'll check with the Continental Command people and the National Guard as soon as we get to the ACC. And, Boyce, thank you for your cooperation."

Donley swung around to scan the rows of faces behind him. "Gentlemen, we are moving to the Alternate Command Center. Mike, how long before we can have helicopters here?"

"About ten minutes, sir. It'll take that long to get them over from Andrews. We've had them standing by."

The President got up from his chair. "All right. I want everyone here to be on the South Lawn at . . . 11:25. *Don't be late,*" he said firmly, straightening his back and producing a small grin, which faded immediately. "I've got some packing to do. I'll see you all outside shortly." The room emptied in seconds as people moved out into the corridor and hastily headed for offices to pick up vital papers and personal belongings.

The President walked rapidly from the elevator and into his deserted private quarters. A bleak emptiness, made all the more melancholy by the sharp light of the winter sky, greeted him. Laura, whose presence had always filled these rooms with warm serenity, was gone. By this time, Donley told himself sadly, she was far away—in a small and vulnerable house in Norfolk.

The President's personal houseman was also gone, dismissed by Mrs. Donley hours ago. Packing a small brown leather suitcase with the President's personal toilet articles, a bathrobe, and light-green pajamas was the final service the fine old gentleman had performed. The Alternate Command Center, he had known, was fully provisioned and equipped. But packing that little case was a comfort and he had done it lovingly. It made it seem as if the President was going on just another ordinary trip.

Frederick Donley smiled faintly at the sight of the suitcase on the bed and he picked it up, grateful for the gesture of love that it was. He walked to the two-drawered bedstand next to his bed and pulled open the lower drawer, seeking an old silver goblet carefully wrapped in a worn red velvet cloth. "It's for the two of us!" Laura Ann had announced with excitement when she first gave it to him. "I found it in a little antique store in London, on Kensington High Street, and I've saved it till now."

"It's beautiful," he had replied, not knowing what it was to come to mean to him.

"Well, it's ours and tonight we'll drink champagne from it and get a little dizzy and make love all night," she said with girlish enthusiasm. "After all, it's our wedding night!" she continued, her cheeks flushing.

Through the early years of their marriage, the goblet had become a ritual. It meant "This time is ours!" They had used it everywhere—filling its rounded satin-smooth bowl with young red Beaujolais on picnics in the French countryside or toasting his election victories with biting-cold champagne late at night when they were finally alone. During a thousand other half-forgotten warm and happy moments, it had always been with them, and Fred Donley wanted it with him now, safe from harm. At least something of theirs would remain untouched by what might happen. He searched among the welter of socks, handkerchiefs, and discarded wallets in the drawer. The goblet was gone. Laura had remembered it, too. Donley smiled again. It was with her in Norfolk. Well, that's all right, he said to himself, as he fought against the loneliness. Perhaps that's really the way it should be.

The President picked up his suitcase and was about to leave when his eye caught the red telephone on the bedstand. He chuckled at the irony. "Well," he said, addressing the phone aloud, "I guess I won't be using you after all. It's going to be your bastard brother in the Mountain who may have that pleasure." In a dozen steps he was at the elevator and on his way to the first floor and the Oval Office.

There are more direct routes to the Executive Office in the West Wing, but something urged Donley to walk through the main hall, with its two great eighteenth-century cut-glass chandeliers and its wine-red carpet. His long strides carried him into the white and gold of the East Room, scene of dozens of concerts and other cultural events during his presidency. Slowly and reluctantly, he strolled west and opened the doors of the magnificent State Dining Room, at the other end of the Main Hall. How many spectacular evenings he and Presidents before him had spent there! How many times had the course of history been changed with conversations over coffee in that chamber? Donley's eyes drank in the grandeur of the place. Might he be the last President ever to see its splendor? He shut the doors gently and walked down a narrow flight of seldom-used stairs to the ground floor.

His quickening steps brought him through the vaulted-arch hallway and into his favorite place, the White House library, with its high book-lined shelves and splendidly scaled octagonal table. He ran his fingers over its inlaid surface. Time was running out. None was left for further good-byes. In seconds, Donley was crossing the long colonnade of the West Wing, headed for the reception area of the Oval Office. There, as always, was Dorie Wilcox.

"My God, Dorie, I should have been keeping you informed. You must have been going crazy, waiting here with all this going on."

Dorie Wilcox looked up at the President with small, bright tears in the corners of her eyes. "Mr. President, I figured you might need me and I just didn't know where else to go."

"Dorie, I do need you. You're coming along with the rest of us," the President replied firmly.

"To where, Mr. President?"

"We're going into the Mountain, Dorie."

The woman's eyes widened and her hand flew up to cover her mouth. She recovered in an instant. "Is there anything you want me to take, Mr. President?"

"Just the three or four folders in the Current Papers safe. Everything else is already out there. Copies are always automatically transmitted to the archives files in the Alternate Command Center. We'll have everything we need, except from the last day or so."

The President watched his secretary look around her office, knowing that in her way she was doing exactly what he had just done. She was saying farewell. Dorie Wilcox pulled her purse from a drawer in her desk and squared her shoulders. "I'm ready, Mr. President," she said.

Together they walked through the French doors leading to the Rose Garden and out into the strong and gusty winds. Dark clouds were whipping past overhead as the weather began to turn threatening. The magnolia trees planted by John F. Kennedy, their branches silhouetted against the dreary sky, waved and twisted good-bye, and in the distance, across the lawn toward the south, they could see three helicopters waiting, blurred rotors slicing through the chill air. Above the White House grounds, another half-dozen aircraft circled slowly. Lines of men were being loaded into the machines sitting beyond Herbert Hoover's white oaks and Franklin Roosevelt's lindens. Two of the craft rose noisily over the trees and whirled off toward the southwest as the President and his secretary bent low under whistling blades and climbed two perforated aluminum steps into their own craft. An aide slammed the door hard and the noises diminished. Through a plastic window, Fred Donley watched the weight come off the thick black tires as the helicopter lifted into the air. The South Lawn, he noticed, was turning brown with the approach of winter. The helicopter gained altitude and the White House grew smaller. In the distance, long columns of dense smoke were rising into the air from widely separated parts of the city. The streets of Washington were alive with a jumble of people and cars. Blustery November winds buffeted the helicopter and tipped it to one side. The President grabbed for an armrest. He could feel himself getting sick to his stomach again.

38

In the Appalachian Mountains, some two hundred miles southwest of Washington, D.C., and not far from White

Sulphur Springs, Virginia, is a secret chamber deep in a granite mountain. It is called by several names—the Rock, the Mountain, or, more formally, the Alternate Command Center, the ACC—and it is there because of the mountain and because of the prevailing winds, which blow across the continent from west to east but tilt somewhat toward the north. Fallout patterns originating in the great industrial heartland of the country, from Detroit, Cleveland, and Chicago, would not generally be expected to cross its location. Nor would the bomb clouds that might tower over Washington and New York, which would blow out into the Atlantic, to rain lingering death elsewhere.

The Alternate Command Center is a lonely place and not one that tourists visit. All that can be seen of it on the surface are six windowless buildings of poured concrete which are pressed tightly against the base of the mountain and are separated from each other by many miles. They are entrances and designed so there is no way a nuclear war could destroy *all* six, or at least so it is hoped. Across each entrance is a huge two-foot-thick steel door painted with black and white diagonal bands. Each opens on a tunnel, and each tunnel follows a long serpentine path into the solid rock of the mountain. The tunnels have round roofs and the roughly finished, solid-gray granite forms their walls. They are illuminated by two lines of fluorescent lights placed end to end behind heavy screening. The lights follow the tunnels for as far as the eye can see.

The tunnels seem to meander, but they do not. Proceeding through carefully planned right-angle turns, they zigzag back and forth toward their destination in a manner designed to reduce the effects of any nearby nuclear explosions. The gigantic shocks of the explosions are weakened by the need to turn the corners and thus, it is assumed, would never reach the center of the mountain.

Deep in the mountain's heart, where the tunnels converge under a five-thousand-foot layer of stone, is a group of rooms—a small underground town—designed for one purpose: to survive and make war.

Hacked out of the unyielding granite at enormous cost, the rooms are packed with the necessities of life for the several hundred people who might have to live there for months without ever seeing the light of day. The hub of this underground city is a single large chamber, which is actually a room within a room. If even the billions of tons of granite above it are not sufficient protection, the inner room is its own shelter.

This steel-walled central room, the ultimate Command Center of the United States of America, is like a brain. The human brain swims in a fluid inside its protective skull of bone. Nature intends the fluid to absorb external shocks that might threaten the brain. The U.S. Alternate Command Center is protected by the same principle and floats on an immense array of heavy metal springs and giant hydraulic shock absorbers.

The central hall of the Alternate Command Center is just over a hundred feet long and a hundred feet wide and rises fifty feet to its curved ceiling. One entire wall contains projection screens of unbreakable glass, behind which are mounted audiovisual devices of every sort and description. Projection plotters that can draw the most complex trajectories and graphs in less than a second sit side by side with television systems that can bring scenes from any part of the world into view at the flick of a switch. These, together with computer-driven alphanumeric text-display visual intercoms backed by automatic foreign-language translators and other gear, make up the most intricate electronic command, control, and communications systems modern engineering has ever devised.

In front of the projection screens on the main floor of the room are row upon row and tier upon tier of action officer desks. A series of electronic channels connects each desk to the communications systems, computers, and command and control apparatus in three other rooms, which have been gouged out of the rock and arranged radially behind the main command center and at different distances from it.

The three rooms hold three complete and redundant sets of equipment, connected to the outside world through a network of buried cables and almost invisible radiation-resistant and blast-hardened radio antennas. The entire facility is intended, as the jargon goes, "to degrade gracefully." If a nuclear fireball were to blow away part of the system, the rest could still function almost perfectly. The commands could still be given. The missiles could still be launched.

Hovering above the main floor of the Alternate Command Center, on a balcony enclosed with shatterproof, soundproof glass, is a room called Control Central, designed for the President of the United States, key cabinet officers, and a small cadre of top advisers. From Control Central it is possible to survey the entire main floor and to direct questions and commands by voice or by visual display to anyone below. Some of the desks on the main floor beneath the balcony are for damage control officers and attack assessment personnel. Others wait for senior officers whose duty it will be to forward attack orders to America's strategic forces.

At the same level as the enclosed balcony, but behind it, are a kitchen, a dining room, and a series of little chambers that resemble the sleeping cells of monks in a medieval monastery. They are spartanly equipped, but it would be possible to live in them for a long time under very difficult circumstances. There are beds, simple washrooms, compact closets, and small audiovisual intercoms.

In the granite a thousand feet to the east of the bedrooms are huge water tanks and stores of diesel fuel for three complete and independent sets of electric generators. A hundred different air tunnels crisscross the mountain and a hundred eight-foot fans are positioned to force outside air into the heart of the mountain—but only after it has passed through filters capable of removing almost every trace of nuclear fallout or toxic gas.

Behind the projection screens on the far wall of the Command Center is a small hospital finished in light-green ceramic tile and equipped with the best trauma and radiation-injury control devices available.

All the years of effort and the billions upon billions of dollars that have been poured into this worn and rounded fold of the Appalachians have had one purpose —that a small group of people shall survive to unleash the wrath of the United States against any attacker in case of a last, unthinkable cataclysm. Into this forbidding place, like men exploring a newly discovered and potentially fearful cave, walked Frederick R. Donley, followed by his personal secretary and his administrative aide, the President-elect, the Secretary of State, the Director of Central Intelligence, and the Chairman of the Joint Chiefs of Staff. Almost immediately they were joined by a paunchy man with a straggly blond mustache—Dr. Emmon Reid, Director of Defense Research and the President's chief adviser on military technology. With Reid was a crew-cut Army lieutenant general, the officer in charge of all Defense Communications facilities.

On the wall of Control Central, a digital clock exactly like the one the President had checked so often in the Communications Center beneath the White House flipped to 1:08 P.M. Eastern Standard Time. The Chief Executive and his party peered silently through the long glass wall of their conference room as uniformed men and women, the staff of the ACC, filtered into the main hall below them. They watched as equipment operators, in deceptively random fashion, settled themselves into black swivel chairs before the numberless electronic consoles, flipped switches, and fitted earphones and microphones on their heads. The staff of the ACC had been through dozens of crisis rehearsals and they had always assumed rehearsals were all they would ever be. This time, they, and the people in Control Central above them, knew they were not rehearsing.

Standing to one side, Dorie Wilcox looked through the windows at the surrealistic scene and began to tremble uncontrollably. The President put an arm around her shoulder and touched his cheek to her hair. "Dorie, everything is going to be all right. Don't be frightened. You'll see."

A few feet away, gaping down at the same scene, was Boyce Williamson. Donley looked toward him and smiled faintly. "Say, I just realized no one's had anything to eat. I'm told they have excellent kitchen facilities here. What do you say, Boyce? Shall we give them a try?"

The President-elect smiled back, matching Donley's gesture. In spite of himself, he felt an inexplicable and almost welcome excitement. "Certainly. By all means let's have some lunch."

"What about that, Jim?" the President said, turning to Jim Willoughby. "Hot soup and a sandwich might warm up this place."

"I'll see to it right away, sir," the young man answered. Carl Silverton shouted after Willoughby as he was disappearing through the door: "If it's all the same to you, son, make mine clam chowder." A ripple of laughter started, then died. For a moment, just a moment, the terror that had brought them there seemed to recede.

"I think we'd better try out the communications and computer data facilities," advised Charles Frydon.

"Okay, let's," agreed Donley. "Look, I promised Boyce here that we'd check in with Continental Defense Command and with the National Guard to see how things are going. Let's do that first. By the way, David," he said, addressing the three-star Signal Corps officer who had come in with Dr. Reid, "where is the crisis phone? I don't see the red phone."

Lieutenant General David G. Witzenhal had been head of the Defense Communications Agency for three years, and he was known throughout the Army as a demanding and by-the-book officer. DCA was his last assignment before retirement. "There isn't one anymore, Mr. President," Witzenhal replied, "or, rather, since we re-equipped the ACC, it's all around you. See the headsets and rows of switches at each position—they can tie you or any of the rest of us into the red lines directly from the microphones, or we can plug in standard back-up phones at the seats if you'd prefer."

"The headsets will be fine," replied the President, with a grim nod. "I just assumed there'd *always* be a red phone somehow."

As more men and women filled the action desks in the large room below, Mike Kallen and General Witzenhal slipped on their headsets and spoke quietly into the intercom circuits connecting them to specific desks on the main floor. The large-screen television display across from Control Central brightened with a parade of letters and numbers.

Running through the highly condensed data available in the Alternate Command Center computer file took only a few minutes, but the message was painfully clear. Behind the charts and tables flowing from the computer was a self-inflicted tragedy that had spread across the entire United States. Los Angeles, San Francisco, and other West Coast cities were reacting violently, joining the Midwest and the East Coast in a growing orgy of looting, rioting, injury, and death. The situation everywhere had reached levels at or beyond the outer limits of control. Some local police still remained on duty, but they and the National Guard were being decimated by desertion. Stores throughout the country had been stripped like carcasses in the desert. The national telephone network, which had collapsed earlier under the overload of millions of frantic and almost simultaneous calls, remained in a state of complete paralysis. Highways throughout the country were nightmares of heaving, immobile steel.

As the computer read-out ended, telephoto TV pictures relayed from military helicopters circling over the urban centers of America began to march across the wall. Times Square in New York paraded into view. Personnel on the main floor of the Command Center gasped and whistled softly in disbelief, while above them, the President of the United States and his party stared speechlessly at the huge screen.

New York was being dismantled by hysterical mobs. In Chicago's Loop, in downtown Detroit, in Denver, almost everywhere the images carried them, the situation was the same. The civilization called America was on the verge of disappearing in a calamity of unfathomable immensity.

Before the President or any of his party could react, a buzzer sounded and a second screen, to one side of the television display, scintillated with dots of light. The computer-controlled teletype, connected by redundant and secure scrambler links to the enormous white marble-lined CIA building a few miles outside Washington, was readying its first official message since transfer of the national command authority to the ACC. On the first floor at the CIA building, the National Foreign Assessment Center had continued its incessant twenty-four-hour-a-day sessions and its latest evaluation report was being sent far ahead of the normal every-hour schedule. The report, which scrolled up across the screen for all to see, needed no interpretation:

NO INFORMATION ON STATUS OF PREMIER KIROV. NFAC CANNOT ASCERTAIN WHO IS OPERATING SOVIET GOVERNMENT. NFAC DATA INDICATE LARGE

GROUPS BEGAN FORMING IN RED SQUARE
APPROXIMATELY THIRTY MINUTES AGO. FRIENDLY
AGENTS IN CROWDS STATE KNOWLEDGE OF M10
COMMON. SOME VIOLENCE. CROWD DEMANDING
REVENGE.

The President faced the tight cluster of people around him. "All right, all right, everybody settle in. We're going to have a long day." Like guests uncertain how to behave, the President-elect and the Secretary of State hesitated. Seats along the length of the conference table, which ran parallel to the window overlooking the main hall and the display wall, had not been specifically assigned. Donley motioned them into place and he himself tugged at a chair at the center of the table. As he waved Dorie Wilcox toward a location closer to him, the message buzzer sounded again and the screen of the electronic teletype flashed brightly:

1:37 P.M. EST
NFAC REPORTS RIOT DEVELOPING IN LENINGRAD.
FIGHTING ALSO REPORTED BETWEEN RED ARMY
UNITS AND CIVILIAN SCIENTIFIC STAFF AND SOVIET
ICBM TEST AREA PERSONNEL NEAR NOVAYA ZEMLYA.
NO DATA RE KIROV.

At one end of the long conference table, Mike Kallen's finger quickly punched four buttons, putting him into instant contact with his colleagues of the Joint Chiefs on the main floor of the ACC. He stopped his urgent conversation only to wave General Witzenhal of DCA onto the same line. Soon both men were grunting and nodding in agreement. In a firm but stress-filled voice, Kallen addressed himself to the President, whose eyes were still glued to the glowing letters of the NFAC report. "We all feel, Mr. President, that this NFAC report is very significant. Novaya Zemlya is dangerous, sir. The Russians have not only test facilities there but operational ICBMs and heavy SS-24 launchers as well. Given the Kirov coup, there could be a rebellion under way in the local Red Army units—and if that's what is going on, then those weapons could be launched at us."

The President drew a deep breath through his gritted

teeth but said nothing. His eyes were closed, his body motionless. A full fifteen seconds ticked silently by. Then Donley stood to face the people at the table. "Before this goes any further, I think there is something I should say to you. It is something I want you all to know. . . . With every fiber of my being, I do not believe there will be a war. I cannot believe that the God who made us placed us on this earth to be burned away in some radioactive hell of our own creation. But I also realize that nowhere is it guaranteed that we Americans or our potential attackers are destined to survive. Mankind will survive. Regardless of what today brings, man will survive. He will suffer, but he will rebuild and he will survive. And centuries from now, those who follow us will judge this day—and us. I want you to know that I intend to operate on the facts as they become known to me. However, there are likely to be times in the next few hours of this crisis when the facts will not be enough. I want you all to understand . . . I want you to know that if such times come . . . I shall be guided by faith and by faith alone if need be . . . and I shall do my very best for us all."

As Frederick Donley stopped talking and settled back into his chair, the doors stood open on hundreds of ICBM silos crouching under the heartland of the United States. Every ground-based "Central Strategic System" in the American inventory—54 Titan II's, 450 Minuteman II's, and 558 Minuteman III's—was only a few procedural steps from action.

It seemed an inordinately long time before anyone in the glass-walled room spoke, and when the darkly introspective quiet was broken, it was by Boyce Williamson. "Fred, we all fully appreciate the magnitude of the decisions to be made . . . and I am sure we all are prepared to protect and defend our ideals. If a war comes, the American people—the infinitely resourceful American people—will deal with it as they have with every other crisis in our history."

The President looked at Boyce Williamson with the expression of a man who had been completely misunderstood. He was about to respond, when two young Air Force majors entered the room carrying trays of food. Donley's jaw took a firmer than usual set. "Let's eat," he said, with an undercurrent of disgust and dismay. And then the intercom message buzzer went off again:

NFAC REPORTS SMALL ARMS FIRE NEAR KREMLIN.

The trays of food accumulating in neat rows on the conference table were forgotten.

NFAC REPORTS 40 TO 50 TANKS APPROACHING RED SQUARE.

39

Half a world away from the Americans under the Virginia mountain, a roaring crowd was sweeping headlong through Gorki Street in Moscow. It joined with another mass of humanity rolling like water down Herzen Street and still others storming up the Serpukhov Highway from the south and stampeding into Kropotkin and into Yakimanka from Gorki Park. The ancient streets of Moscow were filled with people, tens of thousands of them, all intent upon reaching Red Square and their leaders.

On Rozhdestvensky Boulevard, the hordes overpowered the thin line of soldiers vainly attempting to hold them in check. From Novoslobodskaya, more thousands added their pounding feet and angry voices to the din. It was eight degrees above zero and the breathing of the panting mobs filled the dark night with clouds of white mist. Their furious, rage-filled faces flashed past the glow of the streetlights, one following another faster than the eye could count—a great human implosion with the Kremlin at its center.

Transistor radios tuned to direct-broadcast satellites of the Eurosat system were everywhere. These satellites, operated by the international communications consortia of Europe, were capable of reaching directly into almost every Soviet home and of being received by the simplest of transistor radios and television sets. Since their launchings, they had provided the Soviet people with an unprecedented access to information, and the Russian government had been reluctant to blatantly set up a jamming apparatus. Now the Western news programs the satellites routinely carried were firing a gigantic outburst of wrath and hatred as they whipped the crowds with details about M10 from Stockholm, Oslo, Paris, Rome, and London. The reports and commentaries all led inescapably to one conclusion: For years, the United States of America had been waging a secret biomedical war on the Soviet Union and had been directly responsible for the agony and death of millions of Russians. Husbands, wives, lovers, children, relatives, colleagues—all had been victims of the American plot. And now, according to stories of U.S. blackouts and armed forces alerts, the Americans seemed ready to attack not only with cancer but with nuclear bombs as well. The crowds screamed at the bitter-cold night. *Vengeance! Vengeance now! Revenge now!* Like storm-driven ocean waves, they dashed themselves futilely against the old walls of the Kremlin, shrieking, crying, shouting at the dark, voiceless windows above them.

A huge mass of men and women suddenly boiled away from the main body of rioters in Red Square. As if possessed of a single mind and heedless of the cold and the night and the soldiers now appearing in greater numbers in the square, they charged down Tchaikovsky Street toward the American Embassy. In moments, two thousand wild, stampeding people were into the embassy grounds and tearing at the building. The doors opened, torn from their hinges by brute strength. Three American Marine guards inside were pummeled and beaten senseless, then trampled into bloody pulps. Unsatiated, the crowd charged furiously through the rooms of the embassy, ripping, smashing, pulverizing everything they could touch. Screams and then billows of smoke filled the hallways. The raiders retreated into the grounds and onto the street, where they were joined by thousands of their comrades. Howling voices shrieked Russian curses as bright orange-red flames licked out of the embassy windows and curled up and into the night. *Vengeance! Vengeance now!* A small group of anonymous Americans—perhaps five or six—trapped in rooms on the upper floor of the building cried out for help, but the crowds below were heedless. As one desperate American, his clothes already ablaze, leaped from a window to smash himself on the pavement below, a roar of animal satisfaction erupted from ten thousand throats.

40

In the glass-walled room, the President of the United States and his companions were reading a new NFAC report:

> 1:51 P.M. EST
> NFAC REPORTS SOVIET RURAL COMMUNITIES NEAR
> MOSCOW APPARENTLY TAKING INITIAL STEPS TO
> RECEIVE URBAN EVACUEES. WINDOWS OF BUILDINGS
> ARE BEING WHITEWASHED AGAINST NUCLEAR THERMAL
> FLASH EFFECTS. LENINGRAD AND KIEV BELIEVED
> ALSO INSTITUTING PARTIAL EVACUATION.

Charles Frydon whistled as he pulled off the set of earphones feeding him additional details from the NFAC via audio.

"They're actually doing it!" he whispered to his colleagues.

"But is it local panic or is it being ordered from the Kremlin?" the President snapped.

"We're not sure," answered Frydon.

"Charley, if you've got any deep agents planted over there, now is certainly the time for you to blow their cover wide open if it will get us anything."

"Mr. President, NFAC cashed our last big chip in the Kirov coup. We had a deputy assistant minister of defense—"

Boyce Williamson's heavy voice broke in. "Fred, I think the time has come to discuss—"

Before Williamson could continue, the President pointedly stood and walked to the glass wall to stare silently at the projection screens across the main hall. There was no respite for him there:

> 1:56 P.M. EST
> NFAC REPORTS SEVERAL SOVIET MISSILE-CARRYING
> SUBMARINES LOST TO U.S. NAVY LARGE-AREA

ACOUSTIC-ARRAY TRACKING COMPUTERS. IT APPEARS
THEY ARE ENGAGED IN TYPICAL PRE-ATTACK
EVASIVE PROCEDURES. NO INFORMATION RE KIROV.

The President slammed his hands against the cold glass
of the windows. The sound was like a rifle shot. It echoed
and reechoed against the hard stone of the room.

"I have got to talk to them," Donley growled. "I have
got to talk to them. They must understand we are ready to
do anything reasonable . . . anything reasonable. . . ."
The President's voice trailed off as he swallowed hard and
dug two fingers into his left cheek. He walked back to his
seat.

Donley leaned forward and pressed a button on the
control panel mounted in the conference table. "Communications officer, I want the Moscow link fired up, and I
want it fired up now. Where is the hot-line terminal in this
room?"

Through a loudspeaker, the voice of a man on the floor
below replied. "Sir, if you'll push circuit M, you'll be on the
hot line. If you want privacy and don't wish to have the
audio or the video relayed into the main room, turn the
switch immediately above the lighted push button. As you'll
see, sir, there is a small monitor mounted in the table in
front of you. Just slide the cover back and it will be there."

"All right, all right," said the President impatiently. "Get
that link up. It's very important."

"Yes, sir."

On the floor below, Donley could see the colonel at the
communications desk working feverishly. Two other col-
onels joined him, donning headsets. Donley lowered his
head to his folded arms on the conference table. "I'm tired,"
he said.

"Mr. President, why don't you eat something? In fact,
everybody ought to eat something," a female voice said
gently.

The President raised his head and looked up at his
secretary. Her face was drawn and cheerless. The warm
Texas smile was gone. He had almost forgotten she was
there. "Thanks, Dorie." Donley laughed lightly. "Leave it
to a woman to worry about us."

"All right," the President said in a louder voice, as he
resisted the dizziness that was making the room spin away

from him. "We've got to keep up our physical strength. Why don't you all eat?"

Jim Willoughby walked to the end of the table and inspected a plastic tray with its lukewarm cup of soup and its cold roast beef and mashed potatoes. "I'll send for something fresh," he said.

The President grunted and snapped on the intercom to the communications officer. "What's your status, son?" he asked impatiently.

The agitated young colonel looked back over his shoulder toward the lighted conference room hanging over him. "Mr. President, sir, we are not getting any answer. It appears that the Moscow line is blocked—perhaps permanently."

Consternation filled the glass-walled room. Kallen and Witzenhal accelerated their running telephone discussions with the Joint Chiefs. At his chair, Charles Frydon was pleading in low, earnest tones with the NFAC action center in the CIA building, while next to him Carl Silverton silently studied the several rows of push buttons before him. Jim Willoughby, looking far older than his thirty-eight years, pulled idly at his carefully knotted red tie and stared straight into space.

Rapidly losing patience and on the verge of losing control, Boyce Williamson bounded out of his chair at the table and stood behind it, his fingers closed tightly on its back. As if he were at an exercise bar, he rose to his toes and then dropped to his heels again, repeating the motion over and over again. "Christ, it's obvious," he said, looking at his reflection in the glass wall. "It's obvious as hell. Fred, I was going to say this a few minutes ago. You've got to face facts. The bastards are going to attack us. I know it. I just know it."

Instead of replying, the President pressed the button for the communications officer's position. "What do you say, Colonel? Can you find out any more?"

The metallic, electronically amplified voice responded. "Not likely, sir. We have to depend on the Soviet technicians and they're completely off the air in Moscow, as far as we can tell."

With a shrug of disgust, Williamson left the table and moved close to the long window. A hundred men and women were sitting stiffly ready at their control consoles.

Another voice from a PA system cut through the heavy air of Control Central. "Mr. President, this is the Continental Command control desk. I have an urgent call for you from the Continental Command Center in the Pentagon. It is General Schroeder, sir."

Donley picked up the telephone at his position and pressed a flashing button engraved with a *C*. "Yes, General Schroeder, this is the President."

Schroeder's report was a desperate one. Police, fire department, and National Guard forces in New York, Washington, and several other cities were being overwhelmed. Casualties were mounting with each passing minute. Confirmed dead—over 9,000. Reported injured—160,000. Actual figures probably very much higher. Schroeder wanted presidential permission to use the force of available U.S. Army personnel and equipment against U.S. civilians if necessary. "Mr. President, without such vigorous intervention, we'll be taking a great many more casualties and tremendous property damage. I need your answer, sir. Do I have presidential permission to use nonlethal chemical agents and live ammunition, if necessary, against civilians?"

The knuckles of the President's hand went white against the telephone, but he could not answer. He was, instead, transfixed by the teletype screen, which was crackling with another report from the National Foreign Assessment Center.

2:02 P.M. EST
NFAC, AS CONFIRMED BY DEFENSE INTELLIGENCE
AGENCY AND NATO SURVEILLANCE SATELLITES,
REPORTS SOVIET INTERNAL FORCES BEING PLACED ON
FULL ALERT. REPEAT FULL ALERT. MAJOR LEVELS
OF ACTIVITY OBSERVABLE AT STANGUSTA LAUNCH
FACILITIES. ELEMENTS OF SOVIET ATLANTIC FLEET
APPARENTLY IN ANTIDETECTION ELECTRONIC EMISSION
CONTROL EMCON STATUS. NO RADIO SIGNALS BEING
RADIATED. SIGNIFICANT ACTION BY THESE ELEMENTS
MAY BE IMMINENT.

The color drained from the President's face. On his forehead, beads of perspiration glistened in the cold greenish-white glow of the small video screen before him, which repeated the same ominous message as the large display of the main hall. Donley, his eyes held fixed by the NFAC report, murmured to no one in particular: "Tell him to do what he must. Tell Schroeder to do what he must. But minimum force—minimum force, do you hear? Minimum force. Minimum force." The Chief Executive seemed unaware that he was still connected directly to the Continental Command Center.

Dorie Wilcox, who had been standing close to the President, hoping to find a way to help, moved forward and reached for the phone held tightly in the President's hand. Donley's face was blank. He released the phone.

"General Schroeder, is there anything else you need from the President at this time?" Dorie Wilcox paused, listened, and then hung up, wiping her reddening eyes with her wrist.

"Mr. President, sir. Mr. President . . ."

Frederick Donley hardly heard the voice. There was a fierce roaring in his ears which did not go away when he covered them. Reluctantly he turned to face the gold-braided uniformed man standing behind him. "Yes?" Then, with a flash of recognition, "Yes, Mike," he said quietly. "What do you think?"

"Sir, it's extremely serious. The Soviets are moving very rapidly. The fact that their nuclear-attack submarines are using antidetection procedures under these circumstances is unprecedented. They have always followed the SALT-IV peace-keeping protocols before. Now that our Large Area Acoustic Listening Arrays and our DIFAR hydrophones in the deep ocean have lost them, we are almost blind to their intentions. If we couple that with their alert, then I think, sir, together with the EMCON status of the Soviet surface fleet, we, sir"—Kallen hesitated—"we perhaps should go to Level Two."

The President's eyes drilled into Mike Kallen's face. "You really think it's coming, don't you?"

"I don't know, sir, but at Level Two we'll be ready to react if it does. All we'll have to send out are the Level Two designators and launch orders. . . ."

"What's your feeling, Charley?" asked Donley.

"Before I answer that, I'd like to emphasize that things aren't shaping up like preparation for an all-out attack by the Soviets, Mr. President. It's out of whack somehow.

They still haven't put out a full alert to their attack units—their strategic forces; only to their internal forces. Those strategic groups that are taking action seem to be spotty—almost as if some local commanders are deciding for themselves."

"Part of the Kirov coup?" suggested Silverton. "Maybe we're into a many-sided power struggle and what we're seeing only looks like it's aimed at us. . . ."

"No way, Carl," said Kallen. "Stangusta and Novaya Zemlya? Whitewashed windows? Their missile subs? What good do they all do in a coup d'état? We are seeing a part of the preparations for a war—*period*."

"But there's been no all-out strategic alert," insisted Frydon.

"You have no guarantee you'd be able to intercept it," growled Williamson. "Now, Frydon, goddamn you, why don't you admit that?"

"The odds are very high that we would, Mr. Williamson. Using ELINT—Electronic Intelligence Systems—we monitor a huge number of factors: radio message traffic, satellite recon data, sonar use. It adds up to a definitive pattern. . . ."

"But is it one hundred percent? Isn't it possible you could be tricked?"

"Yes, of course it's possible," replied Frydon softly.

Boyce Williamson drummed his fingers on the table with annoyance. "You know, Frydon, you amaze me. Why don't you admit to the President the Russians could be feeding us the impression that only a few elements of their military are out of control as a cover story for a full-scale attack? They could be playing you and your fancy surveillance systems like a con man plays a mark. And you and your boys over at the NFAC could be in the process of being sucked right in."

Charley Frydon's face remained expressionless. "That is an ingenious suggestion, Mr. Williamson. It is also possible, in principle. But if you knew more about how intelligence estimates are put together, you would know it would be quite unlikely."

"Impossible?" snapped Williamson.

"No, not impossible," replied Frydon again.

"What's your best advice, Charley?" asked the President wearily.

"If Kirov were still in power, or if we knew who was and how he thought, I'd be against going higher. As it is, perhaps Mike is right—we may be in danger of some unauthorized strikes by factions no longer under Kremlin control. . . ."

Frederick Donley swiveled around to gaze out through the glass at the momentarily blank screens across the vaulted granite of the main hall. The long fingers of his right hand ran back and forth over the rows of buttons before him. Finally, he pressed one of them and said two short sentences. "This is the President. Move everything to Level Two." In response, the light over the button began blinking immediately.

The President slumped down on the end of his spine, breathing deep, slow breaths. Then, as if he had just remembered something, he leaned forward again and pressed another button. "Colonel!" he said, in a voice that crackled with a mixture of authority and strain. "Try Moscow again, now—right now."

The President's Level Two command was like a giant switch. It initiated a complex sequence of events that, in seconds, reached around the earth, out into the blackness of space, down into ICBM silos buried beneath tons of protective concrete, and deep into the souls of tens of thousands of officers and men of the U.S. military establishment. The United States was now fully poised and ready to make nuclear war on the Soviet Union. A few top-secret Level One designator codes were all that stood between the world and Armageddon. It was 2:14 P.M. Eastern Standard Time in the Mountain.

In accordance with long-preestablished procedures, dozens of huge reinforced-concrete slabs began rumbling ponderously into place, blocking the six access tunnels of the ACC and the hundreds of air intakes that honeycombed the mountain. Normally, outside air was used in the underground complex, but at Level Two it was mandatory that the Alternate Command Center of the United States switch to internal supplies to avoid the effects of unanticipated chemical or biological agents which might be distributed prior to or during the early phases of a major attack.

The people in the glass-walled room watched as the tempo of action on the main floor accelerated under the

Level Two command. All the hypothetical planning, all the theoretical procedures were suddenly real. Trident Squadrons I, II, and III Priority A targets in guidance computers . . . Minuteman systems in launch-ready status Priority A targets . . . FB111 Wings A through G leaving Level Three checkpoints for Level One positions . . . B-52 units report seventy percent Level One operational readiness for Cruise Missiles . . . Polaris squadrons . . . Poseidon squadrons . . .

The President covered his eyes with his hands, his index fingers pressed hard against his temples. Billowing blue-green nausea and dull red pain were engulfing his stomach, chest, and head, threatening to overcome his fading defenses.

"Mr. President . . ." It was as though the voice were inside his mind. Through his misery Donley struggled to focus on its source. There it was, the small man in front of him. . . . Despite the nausea and the throbbing pain, he fought to understand what it was Boyce Williamson was saying.

"Mr. President, as I said, I—" Williamson repeated more firmly.

"Just a minute, just a minute," the President cried, abruptly bolting from his chair and moving hastily toward a small door, which shut with a click. The President had locked himself in the men's washroom.

Williamson's shoulders sagged with impatience as he returned to his chair to wait for Donley to emerge. "Do you think he's ill?" he asked the others sitting at the table.

No answer was needed. From the direction of the men's room came the gagging, retching sounds of a man vomiting. Perhaps two minutes later, a pale and perspiring Frederick Donley emerged to take his seat at the center of the conference table. Williamson moved instantly to confront him.

"Mr. President, what is the matter with you? I think it's only fair to this country that you tell us, straight out. Are you ill?"

The President met Williamson's searching eyes squarely. "No, Boyce, I am not ill. I am perfectly all right except for a little stomach upset."

Boyce Williamson shook his head dubiously from side to side. The President, no longer able to stand the smaller man's steady measurement, looked away toward the other people in the hushed room. In the faces of his colleagues he could see the doubt. They knew. They all knew. The world was at the edge of the nuclear abyss and something was seriously wrong with the President of the United States.

In his certain conviction that Donley was both mishandling the situation and on the verge of a complete breakdown, Boyce Williamson became an angry bulldog remorselessly pursuing a weakening adversary. "Donley, I know you're under enormous strain. We all appreciate your efforts," he said, in a tone of insolence that bordered on insult. "But you must listen. The Russians are going to attack at any moment. You have got to do it. You have got to order a preemptive strike now! It's your duty, dammit! Your duty! A strike now would reduce our damage to manageable proportions. If you wait, it will be ten times worse!"

The excitement-filled face of his successor blurred and darkened in Donley's vision. For a moment, he could not reply. When he did, his lips formed slowly around a single word. "No." The word was spoken as a soft snarl. "No!" he said again, louder and more certainly.

The President-elect stepped closer, leaning down so his face was inches from the President's. "Listen to me, Donley!" his deep voice bellowed. "We all know you're lying and that you are sick. We all know you're afraid. That's understandable, but goddammit, it is no excuse for cowardice!"

At the word "cowardice," the President leaped to his feet, sending his chair crashing to the floor. Vibrating with rage, he loomed over the unflinching Williamson. "Now *you* listen to me! You only *think* you know what nuclear war means. You've read about it in the goddamned newspapers. But actually live with the fact awhile. Live with two hundred million corpses and a world bombed back into the stone age. Live with the disease and the hopelessness of the survivors. Live with it as a reality, not merely some damned theory or convenient opinion you've picked up in the last twenty-four hours, and then, goddammit, *then* come back and tell me what to do. But not until then, do you hear me? Not until then!"

Williamson's eyes flickered as though he were a little

boy being disciplined. He looked away from the raging mask of the President's face to the other dumfounded human beings in the room. But the President was not finished. Seizing Williamson's jaw, Donley pulled it around and upward so their heads almost touched.

"Futhermore, Mr. Williamson, I'll tell you something else. It may be that Kirov is gone. It amy be that some crazy Russian idiot—a man who thinks like you—sends one or even a dozen ICBMs at us. It may be that a million of us die! But even then, I will not order an all-out attack, because if I did—a hundred million of us would die! I will trade one for one hundred if I have to. I will gamble. I will not respond except to a full-scale, all-out attack."

Boyce Williamson's hand closed tightly around the President's wrist and he pulled at the iron grip on his jaw. "Donley, you're crazy . . ." he said breathlessly.

"No," responded the President, releasing his hold. "I am not crazy. You do not know what I know about this office—about the things you live with in this office. I only wish to God you did—and I did not. I wish you could sit here eating out your soul about what you should have done—and didn't—or did do and shouldn't have. I wish you could sit here and remember all the briefings that said a nuclear threat would come slowly—not in two days! And how everything would be rational and centrally controlled on both sides so we could use reason and logic to decide how to react.

"I remember a briefing I got once—maybe three years ago. The man quoted an editorial from back around 1977. It was a very convincing editorial about avoiding nuclear war. Beautiful logic. Perfect arguments. For instance, it argued against civil defense as an unnecessary and ineffective countermeasure. And it was probably right, Williamson, it was probably right. But toward the end of the editorial, the writer said there was no defense anyway against a desperate or insane Soviet leadership. What he didn't think of was a sane leadership, like Kirov's, which might not be able to control a few madmen with a few weapons at a time like this. And that small omission, my dear Mr. Williamson, could cost this country a million dead in the next few hours!" Donley paused for breath, his chest rising and falling rapidly, like that of a man who had just run a marathon. He was so near Williamson that tiny droplets of moisture from his mouth were causing the President-elect's eyes to blink repeatedly. Donley's face was a flaming red as he growled his final words. "But if a million is all that we will lose, then I will not let it cost it us more. *I will not retaliate!*"

Boyce Williamson turned from the tall, panting man confronting him toward the others. "Well," he said, speaking almost as if the President were not there, "I'm sure you gentlemen agree with me. A million dead and we would do *nothing?* This man"—he gestured toward Donley—"is ill . . . or if he is not ill, then he is a traitor!"

Frederick Donley, eyes blazing, took one step back and his right hand swept upward. The sound of a slap exploded in the room, bringing gasps and a quick cry from Dorie Wilcox. Staggered and surprised, Williamson retreated, then lunged forward as he doubled up his fists, his cheek going from a bloodless white to scarlet from the force of the President's blow.

"Enough!" someone shouted in a huge, strangely hoarse voice. Carl Silverton rose to his feet. "Enough!" he roared again, as his shaking hands pounded the table in indignation and outrage. The sheer intensity of the outburst froze both Williamson and the President. Williamson's fists opened slowly as the Secretary of State leaned forward over the table, glaring at both men. "I am ashamed! *I am ashamed!*" the old man hissed. "This republic has chosen you two men—you two men—as its leaders. It has placed its greatest trust in you both. It has honored you above all others. And here you are—like alley cats! *I am ashamed.*" Silverton sat down again, his mouth quivering, his eyes on the verge of tears. The President's head lowered, color draining from his face. He walked stiffly from Boyce Williamson to his seat. At least for the moment, the confrontation was over.

From his chair, Donley addressed Williamson, who was still standing where he had been struck. "Boyce, I am sorry that happened, and I apologize to you. But henceforth, I wish you to understand that you are here as a guest and I must insist that you keep your opinions to yourself unless you are asked for them."

The President-elect nodded sullenly, without otherwise replying. He motioned to General Witzenhal and Emmon

Reid, who moved their chairs closer to his. Purposely ignoring what appeared to be Williamson's open disdain for his instructions, Frederick Donley directed his attention to the panel in front of him. He pressed the selector switch for the Moscow communications desk. "All right, Colonel, what is the status of the hot line?"

"Yes, sir. The line is still blocked at the Kremlin, sir."

Donley frowned in frustration. "Okay, continue working on it and . . ." He paused. The voice he had just heard had sounded strange, perhaps embarrassed. Suddenly, he understood why. His fight with the President-elect had taken place right in front of the glass wall overlooking the main floor of the ACC. Every person down there must have seen him strike Williamson.

Donley cleared his throat and with a quick "That's all, Colonel," closed off his conversation with the communications officer. He was about to say something to Charles Frydon when the video-teletype buzzer interrupted.

2:26 P.M. EST
NFAC AND STATE DEPARTMENT REPORTS INDICATE
U.S. EMBASSIES MOSCOW PARIS STOCKHOLM BEING
ATTACKED BY CIVILIAN MOBS.

A strangled cry of alarm sliced through the sudden stillness. Carl Silverton slowly dropped his white-maned head. His son was first assistant to the American Ambassador in Moscow.

"Carl . . . I'm sure he's all right," the President said softly, touching his friend's arm.

"Yes, Mr. President, I'm sure he is," the older man replied with a weak smile.

Before anyone could say more, a bell shattered the somber mood. The "Flash" alarm, reserved for messages of extreme importance, had never been used before and signified an *immediate* threat to national security.

2:27 P.M. EST
NFAC AND SAT-TRACK BELIEVE LAUNCHINGS OF
LARGE SOVIET PAYLOADS UNDER WAY.

Eyes widened in fear in the conference room. The bell sounded again.

* * *

SAT-TRACK CONFIRMS LAUNCHINGS.

Ten terrible seconds elapsed. No one spoke.

SAT-TRACK CONFIRMS TWO LAUNCHINGS FROM
AMUR RIVER MANNED PLANATARY SPACE
EXPEDITIONS CENTER.

The President's face contorted with agony, his eyes
squeezed into narrow slits.

"For the sake of God, Donley—they're using Amur
River launchers. Do something!" someone cried.

At 2:28 another message:

SAT-TRACK WILL HAVE TENTATIVE ORBITAL
PARAMETERS IN APPROXIMATELY 30 SECONDS.

"We will wait!" whispered the President.

2:28:30
SAT-TRACK CONFIRMS TWO VERY HEAVY SOVIET
PAYLOADS IN ORBIT. NO U.S. IMPACT, REPEAT
NO U.S. IMPACT POSSIBLE WITHOUT ADDITIONAL
PROPULSION BURNS. MINIMUM THEORETICAL TIMES
TO IMPACT IN U.S. IF SUCH BURNS ARE MADE
SHOWN ON FOLLOWING CHART.

A series of sinuous red lines on a white grid snapped
into view on the giant projection plotter next to the video
screens. From the orbital locations of the Soviet payloads, a minimum of twenty-two minutes would be required
for them to reach the United States. The President had a
few minutes to think, but *very* few.

A hurried conference took place in the granite mountain
as a quietly glowering but secretly exhilarated Boyce
Williamson and a terrified Dorie Wilcox looked up. Computer analyses of probable Soviet-American nuclear en-
gagement scenarios prepared and refined over dozens of
years by hundreds of experts using millions of bits of
information were called up on the video displays. In less
than two minutes of discussion, dominated primarily by
Emmon Reid and Charles Frydon, the technical possi-

bilities were narrowed to two of maximum probability. Either the Soviet launchings could be the new high-performance reconnaissance satellites or they could be carriers for gigaton nuclear weapons.

First guardedly discussed in the early 1960s, gigaton bombs—bombs equivalent in energy release to a thousand million tons of TNT—had not been seriously mentioned in the public media for almost two decades. Small wonder. The effects of such weapons were almost beyond imagining. The blast from a single one-*megaton* bomb would level all structures within a distance of five miles and ignite fires ten or more miles away. A gigaton bomb was *one thousand times larger*. Gigaton bombs, if detonated in deep ocean near a continent, could launch monstrous tidal waves—perhaps three hundred feet high—whose awesome power would completely destroy coastal cities and all life for miles inland. Even one such bomb detonated in space high above the atmosphere could direct such searing blasts of heat at the earth that an entire hemisphere might leap into flames in numberless simultaneous fires. Gigaton weapons, each equal to fifty thousand Hiroshima bombs, were the machines of doomsday.

Whether they had used it or not, the technology for creating gigaton bombs had been available to the Soviets since the 1960s. The barrier to their development had been their prodigious size and weight, but several recent critical design discoveries had made them, in principle, small enough and light enough to be lifted into orbit by the huge rockets of the Soviet Manned Planetary Exploration Program. Such launchers were not controlled under the many SALT arms limitation agreements that had been concluded between the U.S. and the U.S.S.R. by Donley and his predecessors. While lacking the quickness of response of the usual ICBMs, the interplanetary rockets had both lifting power and the guidance capabilities to make them enormously effective *first strike* weapons if a superpower wished to put them to such use. And the final ominous fact was that such gigaton weapons were tailor made to Soviet thinking. From Stalingrad to the Sino-Soviet encounters of the late 1970s, the Russians had always followed a military policy of overwhelming force rather than precision bombardment. The two heavy payloads now in orbit high above the earth could be

precisely what the Soviets would rely on for an attack.
Or they could be relatively benign but marvelously complex
observation satellites intended only to gird the globe with
all-seeing Russian eyes. Heads or tails, life or death.
Until more data became available, the President of the
United States, the one man who had to decide whether
and how to react, had no way of knowing what those
objects really were.

"I should also point out, Mr. President," said Reid,
concluding a summary of his views, "that U.S. site-harden-
ing programs have not incorporated gigaton effects in their
thinking. One such weapon, I'm afraid, could even obliter-
ate the ACC. . . ."

Donley acknowledged the brutal facts of Reid's analysis
with a nod and pressed the switch that put him on the main
loudspeaker system of the ACC. "Notify all force elements
of the Soviet launches—but tell them to *hold current
status*. No execution sequences are to be started." The
President's voice was strong, but his flesh was a sickly
gray. His left eyelid was drooping again and the entire
left side of his face seemed to be sagging. A small cascade
of spittle rolled unnoticed from the corner of his mouth.

Ignoring the grim men seated with him around the
conference table, Donley switched his microphone to the
communications officer controlling the direct Moscow link.
To one side he could hear a rising volume of animated
conversation, with Boyce Williamson's voice recognizable
above all the others.

In the world outside the Alternate Command Center,
the ordeal of the American cities went on unabated.
Looting and rioting were everywhere. Human beings, each
trying to get out of the way of the rolling juggernaut
of death, were being crushed and mangled by their sheer
numbers.

In the ICBM silos squatting in the great open prairies
of the plains, in the soaring aircraft of the Strategic Air
Command, men fought to stay calm and rational and
attend to their duties. Don't think about home, the wife,
the kids. Don't think at all.

In the U.S. Trident submarine squadrons hovering
silently beneath the dark ocean depths, crews had been near
the maximum alert for over forty-eight hours. Those aboard
the boats, always tense and edgy in their close quarters,

were being stretched to the breaking point by the unremitting pressure. Many of the men on board did not even have the comfort of a bed of their own to escape to. The usual lack of space in all submarines, even the great Tridents, meant the crew must rest briefly in "hot bunks," narrow beds which had to be surrendered every few hours to other weary men. The submariners, living in daily intimacy with H-bombs and ballistic missiles, sleeping and eating within a few paces of a churning, glowing, pulsating nuclear reactor, had perhaps more than any other members of the U.S. military establishment come to understand what nuclear war could mean. And there had been time, too much time, during their long alert to wait and to think. What the action orders that the President might be forced to give at any moment would mean to them, to their families, and to the whole world stalked their every moment.

In the empty galley of the Trident submarine *White Shark*, Commander John J. Wiley was nursing his third lonely glass of "bug juice," the sugary orange drink to which he had become addicted in his early days aboard the tiny old diesel-powered boat *Grenadier*. In those times, the stuff had been essential because the taste of the water from the drinking water tanks of the creaky diesel was so vile. On the *White Shark*, the water was fine, but Wiley could never bring himself to drink it. Since his boat was first alerted, John Wiley had been unable to sleep even while off duty. Fifty-five hours without closing his eyes had lined their lids with sandpaper. Crazy haunting images formed before him and evaporated as he slouched on the empty bench. For several hours, and without realizing it, Wiley had been occasionally hallucinating from lack of sleep. Now he was hearing strange muffled voices that were not really there. They kept telling him things, "Do it, Wiley, boy," they whispered. "Do it, man."

"But it's dangerous," argued Wiley.

"Do it," the voices said.

"Are you sure it's necessary?" asked Wiley.

"Do it," insisted the hollow chorus of voices.

"All right, I'll do it."

Commander John Wiley drained his glass of orange drink and headed forward along the stainless-steel passageway. He banged a shin on the high lip of a watertight bulkhead door and cursed. He hadn't caught a shin in almost four months. He was more careful going through the next three hatches. Finally, he was standing on the thick shield of the *White Shark's* power reactors. His personal domain. Since the submarine was moving at about thirty-five knots, the radiation levels in the compartment were moderately high, but not lethal. Men were allowed in the area if necessary, provided the integrity of the shield was maintained. "Hell of a time for an inspection," Wiley mumbled to himself, as he began to loosen the safety covers on the inspection holes penetrating the main shield. Pulling off one of the heavy covers completely, a forbidden procedure when the reactors were operating, Wiley was about to insert a long inspection borescope when the excessive-radiation warning horns let loose. "Goddamned noise. Somebody oughta shut it off." Wiley peered into the inspection port. A deadly stream of high-energy gamma rays and an intense neutron beam from the reactor's core passed unfelt through his eyes and brain. It took ten minutes for his fellow crewmen to disable the safety locks on the hatch leading to the reactor compartment, which had been activated by the breach of the main shield. By that time, Commander John Wiley had completed his inspection and had absorbed enough radiation to produce severe temporary radiation sickness and permanent cataracts.

In Control Central, President Donley pressed his left hand against his cheek and watched the colonel on the main floor of the ACC confirm for the hundredth time that all the equipment of the hot line was operational. The problem was simply that no one in the Kremlin was willing to press a small green button labeled with the Russian equivalent of the words "Auto-Connect."

"All right, Colonel, thank you again," said Donley forlornly. "Keep at it. I want you working that line continuously."

"Yes, Mr. President, we are doing that. . . . Mr. President, hang on a moment, please!"

Donley peered down through the window. The man at the communications console was desperately manipulating his controls. Lights were appearing on a new sequence of circuits. Someone in Moscow had pushed the green button! Without warning or ceremony, Donley found himself staring into an enormous video image of a square-jawed Russian face. He recognized it instantly—Field Marshal Vladimir Mikhalevich, Soviet Chief of Staff. Mikhalevich did not bother with a greeting. The autotranslator equipment in the ACC barked out his angry questions. "Donley, why are you pushing us into a war? Why are you at maximum alert? Why are you ready to attack us?"

Taken aback, Donley recovered quickly. "We are not about to attack you! We have been trying to reach you by every means possible. We are only responding to your actions. We are only maintaining order as best we can. Now *you* tell *me* something. What have you just launched from the Amur River?"

The face on the video screen before Donley turned away abruptly. The President could discern a shadowy group of figures clustered behind Mikhalevich and could hear bits of conversation, but the audio volume was below threshold and too fast for the automatic translation gear. Donley waved frantically toward Charles Frydon, who dashed to his side as Mikhalevich turned again to face the hot-line cameras.

"The Amur River launchings were not authorized," said Mikhalevich crisply. "You must understand that there are people here who would punish you most severely for your accursed M10 project. Even I myself . . ." Mikhalevich's voice dropped below the translator threshold and only a series of clicks could be heard, but the Russian's face was contorted with anger. Suddenly Mikhalevich waved his hand peremptorily and continued speaking, now loud enough for the machine.

"Futhermore, Mr. President, those are merely reconnaissance devices. You have nothing to fear from them. They are exclusively a defensive measure. They are as much to help us control the situation here as to defend us against the insanity you are perpetrating at this moment. We do not intend to attack you, Mr. President. But I will assure you of this: If you strike at us . . . we will destroy you." Mikhalevich's dark eyes glittered like black glass as he ground out his next words. "For all time, Mr. President . . . for all time. We will leave nothing behind . . . *nothing.*"

The image before Donley seemed to grow even larger.

Donley covered the side of his face with his hand and looked down and away to hide the spasm that was twisting his face. He tried to speak. "We are not . . ." His voice sounded strangely hollow and muffled. The pain in his head, searing a path down the left side of his neck, was too intense. He could not form his words. Finally, the agony receded. "We are not going to attack you, Mikhalevich! Who is in control of your government? We are prepared to deal as constructively as possible with the matter of M10. Why can I not talk to Kirov? We had the beginnings of a plan. This can all be handled if we remain reasonable and responsible. The United States does not want this to go any further. Is Premier Kirov still in power? I must know. . . . I must talk to him. . . ."

"The Premier is not available. . . ." Mikhalevich was about to say more when a storm of Russian words from the men standing in the background interrupted. Mikhalevich again turned away from his video console and gestured to his side. Another, much younger face appeared before Donley.

"Marshal Mikhalevich states that he is closing the video circuit. He shall reopen it very shortly. Please stand by," the young man said in fluent English.

The huge video screen on the wall of the ACC and the small repeater screen in front of the President dissolved into incoherent bursts of brightly colored spots as Donley lowered his head into his hands. "Well, gentlemen, what do you think?" he asked in a voice muffled by his arms. "Before you answer, give me just a second to rest, then we'll discuss it. . . ."

Although he could not see them, the men around President Donley were wearing that characteristic expression of pity and concern that dying patients come to expect of their visitors. Even Boyce Williamson was silent. It was less than sixty seconds later that the connection with Mikhalevich was reestablished.

"Mr. President, I am authorized to make several points:

"First, you must realize that the reaction of the Soviet people to M10 has required us to take certain actions. These actions are directed only at our internal control problems and are not to be misinterpreted by you.

"Second, Premier Kirov's proposals are still in effect and we demand a response.

"Third, we demand that you order your forces to stand down from their alert condition immediately.

"Fourth, I am given to understand that Premier Kirov himself will be in contact with you shortly.

"What is your reply, Mr. President?"

Donley studied the thick Russian face on the TV console. Mikhalevich gazed back at the President, his face cold and impassive, his eyes unblinking.

"We shall, of course, consider these matters and respond as quickly as possible," said Donley with surprising strength. "In the meantime, however, I insist on immediate discussions with the Premier himself. I propose to deal only with him. Is that clear? We therefore demand to know if Premier Kirov is alive and well. If he is not, then we shall deal with your present head of state, whoever he may be. Assuming it is not you yourself, I demand that you have him contact me forthwith and hold yourself available as well. You may call me at any time." Donley flicked a determined finger at a switch and the video screens in Control Central and in Moscow went black again. Looking a thousand years old, Frederick Donley walked unsteadily toward the men's room, oblivious to the anxious eyes that followed him.

41

It was a beautiful sunny fall Sunday in Chicago. A crisp but not too cold winter air had moved into northern Illinois, but no one in Chicago was thinking about the weather. A heavy pall of smoke from out-of-control fires hung over the downtown area of the city and under the smoke, along Michigan Avenue and Lake Shore Drive, on the Eisenhower Expressway and the Stevenson, people were dying, dying not because of nuclear bombs or radioactive fallout, but because they were murdering each other.

Halfway up the newly rebuilt Fullerton Avenue entrance ramp leading to the Kennedy Expressway, a tiny white Chevaire was stalled in the right-hand lane. The car was part of Mrs. Betty Knudsen's divorce settlement, and now she was sitting behind the wheel paralyzed with fear. In the cramped back seat, six-year-old Cary and four-year-old Jennifer were screaming, filled with raw terror by the deafening noise of a thousand auto and truck horns behind them, the wild noise on the expressway above them, and more than anything else, their own mother's soft, helpless sobbing.

Three men suddenly appeared at Mrs. Knudsen's half-open window. "Get this fucking thing out of the way!" one of them roared. Betty Knudsen could not answer. She sat staring straight ahead and trembling violently, her hands frozen helplessly to the steering wheel.

"Lady, what the shit is the matter with you?" The man was screaming. "Come on, you guys, let's push this damned thing out of here!"

The man reached through the window, turning the steering wheel. His companions leaned hard against the back of the little car as Cary's and Jennifer's cries grew louder. At first the car did not move, but then it slowly began to slide forward and to the right. Gathering speed, it bounced lightly up over the curb onto the sloping muddy-brown earth, still crisscrossed with the marks of heavy construction. The men stopped pushing and stood at the edge of the concrete. The car continued to roll, swinging around backward. Faster and faster down the steepening slope it moved, careening crazily into the deeply excavated, unlandscaped area remaining from the just completed roadwork. Spinning to the left, it slammed to a halt with a heavy thud against the track of a huge bulldozer. The smell of gasoline instantly saturated the air and a small bright flame licked its way around the edge of the car's fender. Seconds later, there was a loud explosion.

While most Chicagoans were clawing and smashing their way out of the city center toward the illusory safety of the countryside, Mr. Isaac Tandy, aged seventy-three, walked slowly toward his shop on a now almost empty block of North Michigan Avenue. His tiny store, Boul Mich Rare Coins and Stamps, Inc., had been in its present location for twenty-six years, but Mr. Tandy had owned the business for almost half a century. He had started his collections in his teens—first stamps, then coins, beginning with usual items, and later, the beautiful and precious rareties. His collections were his family, his children; almost surely they were why he had never married. While other men were finding wives, Mr. Tandy was already in love with four-dollar U.S. gold pieces from 1879 and six-rouble commemoratives of the victory over Napoleon.

With reluctant, arthritic fingers, Isaac Tandy unlocked and opened the door of his shop. It felt strange being there on Sunday afternoon, but this was a very strange Sunday. As if to underline his feelings, the sharp report of what sounded like dynamite rippled down the street. Tandy looked in the direction of the sound. Smoke billowing out of the shattered windows of the Lakeside National Bank in the next block. Tandy's old man's hands, now trembling like leaves in the wind, were almost unable to close around the doorknob. Sighing with relief, he finally got the front door shut and locked, then shuffled toward the small round wall safe behind the curtain in the back room. After two attempts, he worked the combination properly and the safe door swung open. Inside were dozens of little transparent envelopes, each holding a single metal coin of glistening gold or silver. As hastily as the pain and stiffness in his fingers would allow, Tandy transferred the little envelopes to a small black leather bag. In ten minutes, the safe was empty.

As he was preparing to leave the back room, there was a loud crash and the sound of breaking glass somewhere in the front of his shop. Isaac Tandy's heart began to pound heavily in his chest. He stepped forward into showroom of the Boul Mich Rare Coins and Stamps shop to find that the window of his front door had been smashed away. Two men, one holding a brick, were standing in the shop looking directly at him. Isaac Tandy closed his old, tired eyes and wrapped his arms protectively around the worn leather bag as if it were the wife he had never had.

On the outskirts of Chicago, in a small white frame house where the Greenley family lived, fear was seeping through every crack like the smell of distant fires. "Jimmy, everybody's going. We got to go now, too. We just got to!" James Greenley's sister had been forced to grow up long before other kids and had been taking care of her younger brother Jimmy, now twenty-two, for nearly a decade. Jimmy couldn't do much for himself at first, but later he'd become self-sufficient enough to hold down a job; not much of a job, but a job. And Jimmy liked it. He liked working with the animals—especially the dogs. It bothered him terribly that the men killed most of the dogs. But that's what happens to strays, they always told him. That's what animal pounds are for. Nevertheless, it still bothered Jimmy, and even on his days off he went over to the pound—it was only two blocks away—to play with the dogs in their tiny cages and to bring them scraps to eat.

"Who's gonna feed my dogs, Sissy? Who's gonna feed them, and give 'em water? There's gonna be no one over there!" Jimmy Greenley's big eyes were red and desperate. Then his expression suddenly changed. "I'll be right back, Sissy," he shouted, as his thin body, clad only in a shirt, faded blue jeans, and gym shoes, vanished out the front door. "You wait right here!"

"No, Jimmy, no! Come back, please. . . . Please come back. . . . We got to go right now," his sister pleaded to the empty room.

Jimmy Greenley raced down the deserted side street toward the corner where Elston Avenue met the big highway. To his left, he could see the rushing stream of eighty-mile-an-hour traffic on the highway and in the distance sirens were wailing. In all the years he'd lived around there he'd never seen so much traffic and trouble on the highway. But it was not his business. His business was the dogs.

Panting with the exertion of his two-block run, Jimmy knocked hard at the front door of the office of the county animal pound. No one answered. He took out the keys they had given him for emergencies. That had been a proud day when they trusted him with them, and he smiled to himself as he remembered. Carefully unlocking the door, he walked inside. "Hello," he shouted. "Hello?" The musky, unlit pound was deserted. There were only the dogs.

Jimmy knew exactly what he must do. He moved quickly from cage to cage, throwing open the latches. In minutes, the parking lot inside the wire fence was filled with a hundred and fifty running, snarling, yelping animals. Jimmy Greenley picked his way among his friends, talking to them, smiling at them. He pulled out his keys again to open the padlock on the parking lot gate, which led directly to the main highway. In an instant, the dogs were gone and Jimmy was grinning happily. His pals would be okay now.

The seething, howling pack of animals, wild with hunger and the excitement of release and the roar of the traffic, stampeded directly toward the highway. Steering wheels were wrenched instinctively and brake pedals jammed to the floor. But the speeds were too great. A dozen cars plowed into the yelping, snapping dogs, hurtling some high into the air, crushing others into bloody, shapeless pulps on the concrete. And then the cars themselves began to pile into each other in a deadly chorus of squealing tires and grinding metal. The highway traffic came to a dead halt, its noises replaced by moans of pain and the squeak of engines still stubbornly turning under smashed hoods. On the shoulder of the road, Jimmy Greenley was screaming hysterically.

42

"I don't think there is any reasonable doubt, Mr. President. They are lying." Charles Frydon, in a rare show of emotion, was pacing back and forth in front of the glass wall as he worked out the logic of his argument. "There is zero likelihood that the Amur River staff would have launched unauthorized recon satellites. No way. I think Mikhalevich simply slipped. He probably didn't even know about them until you told him. Remember how he turned to those people behind him? Those unauthorized launches must be weapons launches. They've got plenty of recon systems up and they already knew what we were doing. Those are probably gigaton bombs up there."

"Okay, Charley, I'll buy your argument for now," replied Donley as he massaged his cheek and neck. "What's your feeling about his statement that Kirov will be in touch shortly?"

"Obviously a lie, too," snapped Boyce Williamson, ignoring Donley's earlier orders to remain a silent observer. "Donley, if you were thinking straight, you wouldn't even have to ask. They know you trust Kirov. They know your past relationship with him. Do you think they'd admit he'd been deposed or killed? Of course not. They're using his name just to keep up your hopes while they get set to blow us off the goddamn earth! Now I demand a final statement about those gigaton weapons. What can they do? Is Reid right? Can they prevent us from hitting back?"

"I'll answer that, Mr. Williamson," said Mike Kallen, "but first I'd like to point out that if Mikhalevich didn't authorize the Amur River launchings and, therefore, didn't know about them, someone above him—even Kirov himself, if he's still alive—might have."

"But it makes no rational sense, Mike," protested Donley.

"It would to them," replied Kallen, "if, as we've said before, they know how to track our subs and if they could hit our silos with more accuracy than we think with their new guidance systems. The gigaton bombs take us out here at Control Central—that answers your question, Mr. Williamson—and their subs hit ours before we can get off our sea-launched missiles while their ICBMs destroy or pin down our Minutemen and Titans."

"So we still have the third element of the deterrence triad," said Donley. "We've still got the planes and Cruise Missiles. They are enough to inflict so much damage, neither Kirov nor any other leader would risk it."

"Unless they've grossly underestimated the Cruise Missiles," said Charles Frydon unhappily, "which, I must admit, the NFAC has felt is possible for some months. In theory, they could have misled themselves into thinking they could knock out all three elements of the triad."

"This is the first time Frydon and I have been together on something," commented Williamson. "Also, why couldn't they have found a defense against the Cruise Missiles that we don't appreciate? Maybe lasers or something?"

General Kallen shook his head. "Very unlikely."

"Impossible?" Williamson asked.

"No; as usual, not impossible. Nothing's impossible."

"Dammit, Boyce," said the President, his voice rising. "You keep using the same line: Is it impossible? No, it's not impossible. Q.E.D., it's probable. We can't deal here merely in the possible. We have to deal in the probable and we've only got minutes to do it."

"Very well, I'll give you some 'probables,' as you put it," said Williamson, his voice growing louder to match

Donley's. "One, Kirov's dead. Two, an all-out attack is coming. Three, unless you launch a preempting strike, we will be annihilated and democracy on this earth will disappear for a thousand years."

"No! No! No!" shouted Donley. "They are lying about those launchings, I'll grant you that. But they also don't want a war. They are lying, but I trust their judgment. We will wait. We will do nothing. I am sure Kirov will call me soon."

"You know they are lying and yet you trust them?" Boyce Williamson exploded. "That's an absurdity! You are mad. Mad and sick. Everyone in this room knows it—everyone. Furthermore, it's been ten hours since we got the report of the coup. If Kirov survived it, where the hell is he? You demanded he call you, and has he? No, of course not! Because he's dead! And I don't know exactly what these damned gigaton bombs can do, but I sure as hell gather they are more than even you bargained for. They are no little toys that will let you sacrifice 'only' a million or so Americans, are they? Are they, Mr. President? Admit it, damn you!" Williamson roared. "Your easy way out, your hundred-to-one trade-off, isn't in the cards, is it? It is all or nothing now, isn't it? Isn't it?"

The President tilted his great leonine head toward the ceiling, clasping his hands behind his neck. He apppeared relaxed and calm. The tactic worked. Williamson, perplexed by the blandness of Donley's attitude, waited a moment for a reply, but got none. He addressed his final statement to the President more quietly.

"Donley, I do not intend to let you destroy this country. You have all the authority you need under the old War Powers Resolution Congress passed in the Vietnam era. You are simply not capable of making rational decisions and I demand that you either preempt the Soviets before they hit us or step down in my favor *here and now*."

A small, bitter smile crossed the President's haggard face. "I have several things to tell you, Boyce," he replied softly. "First, I remind you again that you have no official status here. Second, I am entirely capable of carrying out my duties. I admit I'm tired and my stomach has been upset, but I reject your more dramatic characterizations of my condition. Third, I would observe that the Constitution of the United States makes no provision for a President-elect to assume his office early, a fact you might be willing to ignore, but I am not."

"Your sarcasm does not solve anything, Mr. President."

"I am not finished, Mr. Williamson. I have one more thing to say to you and it is this: Get the hell out of this room before I summon the guards!"

Boyce Williamson sprang up, his face twisted into a snarl, his hands closing into fists. "You sick, gutless bastard! You are beneath my contempt. Come on, gentlemen," he said, looking to his left. "Let's go down to the main floor—where the *Americans* are!" As Williamson stalked from the room, a gold-braided uniformed man and a civilian stood to follow him.

Carl Silverton, a silent spectator since his lecture to Donley and Williamson, leaped to his feet. "Witzenhal! Reid! What the hell are you doing? Where are you going?" he cried incredulously. "Who are you working for—the President or Boyce Williamson? Frederick Donley is the Commander in Chief of this nation. You work for him!" The men kept walking.

General David Witzenhal stopped as he reached the door of the conference room and turned back to face the President. "Mr. President, it is my belief—our belief—that we *are* working for the United States of America." Witzenhal looked toward General Kallen. "So long, Mike," he murmured.

"Davie, don't do it," said Kallen softly. "Treason is an awful word. Don't do it this way."

Witzenhal nodded. "Knowing you as I do, Mike, I don't think you yourself would call it that." He closed the door quietly but firmly behind him. An open revolt was under way among the President's most senior advisers and commanders.

43

The discussion that followed Williamson's departure did not last long. Now was not the time to be concerned about issues like treason. Such matters would have to wait for later. Nor did it seem constructive to try to arrest the men who had just left. On the main floor of the ACC there were too many officers whose loyalties, under the strain of the moment, might run more toward their direct and immediate commanders than to a President about to leave office. There was also no practical way to ensure that the alerted U.S. forces would remain under presidential control. The long-established standard operating procedures had to be trusted to hold up in the face of anything Williamson and his cohorts might do. Besides, Williamson himself had not really *done* anything. So far, all he had done was talk and follow a presidential order to leave the room.

"We will wait," sighed the President once more. He glanced over at the glowing numbers on the digital wall clock: 3:12 P.M., Sunday, November 11. "It's a little after eleven at night in Moscow," Donley observed under his breath. "Mike, I want a reaffirmation sent to all force elements regarding presidential authorization sequences and confirmation programs. I want it very clearly stated that there are to be no contingency responses to an attack. I will not institute any 'launch on warning' or 'launch on detonation' instructions. Firing will commence only upon a direct and confirmed order from me. See to it, will you?"

"Of course, Mr. President," the general replied, his hand trembling very slightly as he reached for a button and adjusted his microphone.

Overhead, in a pair of dull metallic spheres, each three meters in diameter, two billion tons of explosive force circled silently in the cold vastness of space.

"Let's get some coffee in here," said the President. "Dorie, you look like you could use something to do. Go find some for us, young lady, will you?" The President's secretary was acknowledging his request with a frightened nod, when her eyes widened in astonishment. For no apparent reason, General Kallen had got to his feet and was staring straight ahead like a thin young recruit at attention.

"Sir, as Acting Chairman of the Joint Chiefs of Staff, I wish to make a proposal. . . ." Kallen's voice was a flat uncharacteristic monotone. He had pulled up his tie and buttoned the blue tunic of his uniform. In spite of the heavy air conditioning in the room, tiny beads of perspiration glistened on his forehead. "It is a damage-limit-ing proposal from a military point of view and it is, in my opinion, our only viable option."

"What are you doing, Mike? Sit down, *please*," the President exclaimed, his voice filled with apprehension.

Kallen continued, still unwilling to look at the others in the room. "I wish to observe that we have four Cruise Missile Airborne Platforms on station over the Sea of Okhotsk and within two hundred miles of the Soviet Amur River launch and control facilities—"

"Mike, for heaven's sake, sit down: I can't even concentrate on what you're saying while you stand there like that!"

Kallen ignored the President's plea, his voice droning on. "These aircraft could deliver at least twenty Cruise Missile nuclear warheads to the Amur River facilities within approximately twenty-five minutes of receipt of firing orders. The Soviet payloads now in orbit could then be deprived of control if there are no other backup control facilities, as we believe there are not. . . ."

"Brilliant!" declared Charles Frydon. "He is right, Mr. President!"

The President's mind was racing. "You mean we could catch the Russian payloads on the wrong side of the globe and knock out their control before they could be sent reentry or detonation orders?"

"Exactly, Mr. President. They are in orbit, not on straight-in trajectories. That's what Mike means," Frydon shouted, while looking at the still standing Air Force general. "If they are not fully automated, and our data suggest they are not, they have to go through another maneuver to get to us. That could be the Achilles heel of their use of the space-flight launchers."

"But," said Donley slowly, "if we do that, we foreclose any choices Kirov has left. It would mean . . . a first strike . . . a full-scale war."

"Not necessarily, Mr. President," Frydon replied quickly. "It would be a classic surgical strike. We'd only take out Amur River. The Soviets need not respond—"

"No, that's wrong, Charley! Kirov would lose all control. It would be all over," the President replied, pressing his left eye and cheek.

"But, Mr. President, we still don't know about Kirov. And if those launchings were really unauthorized and not preparation for a first strike, they would understand why we did it."

"What if they bombed Houston or Huntsville?" asked Donley.

"We didn't launch any weapons and if those gigaton monsters get over the U.S.—and they program them to detonate—we've only got a few minutes to decide, Mr. President," argued Frydon, his eyes now blinking furiously over the metal frames of his glasses. "It could be a way out with an absolute minimum of casualties."

"How sure a way out, Charley, how sure?" the President asked quietly, his hand on the side of his face.

"Not very, Mr. President," Frydon admitted with a helpless sigh. "Not *very* sure."

"Then we will wait," said Donley firmly, looking again at the ramrod-straight figure of General Kallen, still at attention, eyes unblinking.

Kallen's shoulders sagged. He turned very slowly to face his superior. "Mr. President, I would appreciate it, sir, if you would relieve me of my command responsibilities."

"What? Mike, please . . ."

"*Relieve me, sir!*"

"Mike . . ."

"Relieve me, sir!"

"Mike, there is no need . . . I don't . . ."

General Kallen's hand snapped upward and he saluted his Commander in Chief. Taking two quick steps backward, he turned as if he were a guard on duty and, without another sound, walked out of the conference room deep in the granite mountain.

Charles Frydon began another compulsive cleaning of his glasses.

"We will wait," said the President softly, as he lowered his face into the dark comfort of his arms.

44

Under the bright-blue winter sky, like lemmings to the sea, Americans were pushing and shoving each other toward death. Convinced that nuclear war was only minutes

away—ignoring half-hearted broadcast appeals for calm
voiced by officials who themselves were transparently
terrified—they were destroying themselves by the tens of
thousands with automobiles, guns, and knives, not with
nuclear bombs.

The odor of fear rolled across the planet like a great
fog. But in London, Tokyo, Berlin, Rio, in all the great
centers of civilization, there was an unearthly calm. The
other inhabitants of the world knew that in this final confrontation they were not the primary targets. Nuclear war,
if it came, would not mean quick and searing death to
them. In its stead, they would face another and different
horror—the slow, creeping spread of radioactive fallout
from a thousand million megatons of raw energy. They
would live and die in the radiation aftermath of the nuclear
spasm. They would not and could not escape. And somehow they knew: There was no sense in running.

45

At the brutal sound of the "flash" bell, the President's
head snapped up from his folded arms as if he had been
struck a physical blow. Under him, on the main floor
of the ACC, a hundred pairs of eyes stared at the large
display screen.

3:27 P.M. EST
UNCONFIRMED REPORT RELAYED FROM AIR FORCE
RECON CONTROL CENTER TO NFAC STATES THAT
U.S. ORBITAL TRACKING AND RECONNAISSANCE
SATELLITES MAY BE UNDER ATTACK BY HIGH-POWER
GROUND-BASED LASERS. ONE OF THREE MAJOR
UNITS NOW NOT OPERATIONAL. ABILITY TO
MONITOR SOVIET ACTIONS SEVERELY IMPAIRED FOR
AREA SHOWN IN BLACK.

A multicolored map came up on the large plotter
screen. A great black oval covered much of the Soviet
land mass. It stretched from Moscow on the east past
Novosibirsk on the west and from the border of Afghan-

istan to the frozen tundra of Novaya Zemlya. The United States was almost blind to anything happening over millions of square miles of Russian territory.

"That is an overt act of war, Mr. President. If they've attacked Watchsat II, things may be irreversible," Charles Frydon murmured.

"I know, I know, I know," replied Donley sadly, as he walked across the room to stare silently at the people milling around on the main floor of the ACC. After a fast conference, Carl Silverton and Charles Frydon followed him to the window.

"There are several possibilities to consider, Mr. President." The Director of Central Intelligence had returned to being his calm and analytical self. "First, it may be that Watchsat II is merely malfunctioning. We don't have any on-board diagnosis yet. Second, the Soviets might have done it, but it could have been unauthorized. Another group pressing for war—just as with Amur River and just as you are being pressed to preempt."

"Third," added Silverton, "we may not be able to trust our field reports now unless NFAC confirms them. Williamson and the others may be distorting matters. We don't know exactly what they're doing. Even though they can't override your command authority, they may be crazy enough—or sure enough of what is going on—to push *you* into action. They could feed you false impressions up here. Then you yourself might be forced to launch an attack."

"Dear God!" Donley cried. "Do you realize what you are saying, Carl? You are telling me I am to sit here deaf, dumb, and blind, or—or even worse—*misled,* and decide whether to destroy half the world and a billion human beings!"

"I . . . do understand, Mr. President," the old man answered with a devastated shrug.

"Well, look, those bastards are right here in this building someplace. Let's find them and damned well find out what they're doing! And furthermore, there has got to be some way to verify whether that satellite was attacked. Charley, get on that console over there and do it!"

"I'll try . . . I'll try, Mr. President," said Frydon. "But the best sources would be out of DOD, not the intelligence community. Kallen and Witzenhal are the ones who know the proper people on the floor to check with. I really don't."

"Then find someone down there who does know and get him going on it now! And pull the JCS folks up here immediately to take Kallen's place."

Donley sagged into his chair again, his body settling as if crushed by some great unseen weight. His eyes were rolling with pain and shadowy red splotches were spreading slowly across his face. His fluttering hands again pressed hard against his pulsing temples.

Inside a thousand ICBM silos and aboard a hundred Navy ships and submarines, countless tiny jewel-like computers pulsated with electronic life. Locked to the rhythm of exquisitely accurate clocks and navigational sensors, the computers were attending to their deadly business of preprogrammed target correction. If asked, they would do their jobs with unquestioning faithfulness and guide an infinite measure of death toward chosen destinations half a world away. And they would do it within an accuracy of fifty meters.

"If we get confirmation on Watchsat II and if one more major overt act occurs . . ." The President emerged from his minute-long reverie, speaking to no one in particular. Frydon and Silverton nodded slowly. They knew what had been decided. What remained now was only to wait—and perhaps to die.

"Frederick," said Silverton in a wispy, almost inaudible voice. "You must do what you must do. May God be with you."

The digital clock flipped to 3:34 P.M. The men inside the granite mountain had nothing more to say. There was no conversation . . . no comradeship. Each of them was totally and utterly alone. Even the video consoles and the sprawling communications network provided no contact with the outside world. The system and the men who created it were waiting . . . waiting . . . waiting.

46

"They're ice flowers, my love."

"But you really shouldn't have picked them. They'll die so soon."

"Oh, come on. There are thousands—look around us!"

Fred Donley put an arm around his young wife's waist. "Let's get back to the ship. I'm hungry!"

Far below them, nestled in the snug little natural harbor, they could see the excursion boat. People were moving like small black specks on the green deck. The sun glinted brightly off the water and into Donley's eyes. Dazzled by the hypnotic splendor of the light, he drank in the beauty around him. The light began to hurt. He closed his eyes against it. It would not go away. The spots grew hotter and brighter, burning into his brain. The left side of his head was throbbing. His cheek and jaw were numb.

"Mr. President . . . Mr. President." Charles Frydon put his hand lightly on the President's shoulder. "We have gotten the 3:30 P.M. systems check. There is no change."

"Okay, okay," replied the President, his fingers moving like butterfly wings—a man at the end of his strength. "Any word on Watchsat II?"

"None, Mr. President. I got hold of a General Johnson downstairs—a one-star. He says we should have something in five or ten minutes."

"All right. We will *wait*."

The glowing red numbers of the clock changed to 3:35, then 3:36. The President's lower limbs began to quiver. He crossed his legs firmly to hide the shaking from the others. The numbness was increasing. It crawled out of its hiding in his jaw and cheek and oozed onward, pausing briefly at his eye and then climbing up across the top of his skull. Lingering there, it toyed with going farther, then faded. Donley shifted uneasily in his chair. The nausea and the vertigo were bound to follow.

ALL SOVIET CITIZENS STAND BY!
IMPORTANT ANNOUNCEMENT AT 11:45 P.M.

* * *

The words, printed in the Cyrillic alphabet, blazed into view on television screens across the Soviet Union and on the monitors in the ACC that captured the Soviet signals via electronic intelligence satellites.

"Do you think it could be . . . a declaration of war?" asked Carl Silverton, hesitatingly speaking the unspeakable. They had never used the formal phrase before. Never, not once during the entire crisis.

"I don't know," said the President hoarsely.

"If it is . . . can we afford to wait any longer?" The words squeezed out of Charles Frydon's throat—slowly—one at a time.

"Can we afford not to?" responded the President. "Charley," he pleaded, "do you really want me to push the button?"

"Mr. President . . . I . . . If it is a declaration of war, they will have already launched an all-out attack and given the final trajectory data to those payloads. We've got only minutes to order a response if we are going to make one." The President looked into the face of his long-time friend with eyes that were bottomless pools of agony.

"Yes . . . that is true, Charley . . . and I know it."

At precisely 11:45 P.M., Moscow time, a young and very nervous announcer stepped into view before the television cameras in the main broadcasting studios of the Soviet Television Ministry.

"People of the Soviet Union," he said, "you are now to be addressed by Premier Alexei Stepanovich Kirov." Two hundred and fifty million Russians waited to hear their fate.

Frederick Donley's heart was pounding wildly. Kirov was alive! "He's still in control!" the President shouted.

"But he didn't call you to negotiate!" cried Frydon frantically. "I think we've been trapped. He's going to attack!"

As Kirov looked toward the camera and began to speak, the video teletype connecting the ACC to the NFAC and Sat-Track facilities also exploded into action. The message alarm bell tore into the President's eardrums:

* * *

3:45 P.M.
NFAC AND SAT-TRACK REPORT RAPID CHANGE IN
ORBITAL CHARACTERISTICS OF POSSIBLE SOVIET
GIGATON BOMB PAYLOADS. NEW TRAJECTORIES
AND IMPACT POINTS, IF ANY, AVAILABLE IN 23
SECONDS.

Overwhelming nausea swept across Donley's abdomen.
His hands tightened on the arms of his chair and his
fingers clawed uncontrollably at the leather-covered padding. Tiny red droplets began to ooze out of the torn
flesh under his fingernails. "We will wait for the trajectory
data . . ." he whispered, while scalding-hot steel rods
began to push their way into the left side of his brain.

Over the drone of Kirov's guttural Russian, the ACC's
automatic translators began their mechanical monotone.
The President, blood roaring wildly in his ears, could
hear only fragments. . . .

"Many of you understandably want revenge. . . . Many
of you will die because of the M10 cancer project of the
United States. . . . And many of you have died in the
last few days and hours . . . at your own hands. . . ."

A geyser of flame shot up the left side of Donley's
head and ripped at his pulsing temple.

"I tell you now that I have done what is necessary and
what is right . . . no more and no less. I tell you now
that I forgive those who, in these last terrible hours,
yielded to their hearts and attacked my advisers and
even me. . . ."

The camera in Moscow drew back from its close-up.
Kirov was in a wheelchair, his right arm and leg heavily
bandaged. Weak from his wounds, he bent forward, his
haggard, almost bloodless, face approaching the lens.

"Time is of the essence now. I must address myself
both to you, my countrymen, and to the American government, and especially to the President of the United States,
Frederick R. Donley." Kirov paused and lowered his head,
too weak for the moment to continue. He raised his eyes
again. "There must be no war! Even as I speak I know
there are many in our military forces ready to strike
at the United States with our full might. I beg them—do
not do so. Millions of our comrades have died, but if we

attack . . . millions more of us will perish, along with the Americans. . . ."

"It could still be a trick!" Charles Frydon shouted at the President. "A ruse to buy the last critical seconds—" The "Flash" message bell cut off all other sound.

Trajectory plots were coming in from Sat-Track. On the wall-sized screen, two blue lines snaked across a map of the world. Each of the lines could end in a titanic outburst of energy, perhaps over both the ACC and America's East Coast—a thousand million tons of TNT tearing and screaming into flesh and bone and dreams. The lines inched downward, moving in unison. The Russian devices were maneuvering! The great computers of Sat-Track struggled to keep pace with the flow of possibilities, but had too little data. The half-blinded U. S. recon system could not see clearly enough. The blue lines began to broaden into meaningless statistical blurs covering almost a third of the globe. Death for half of mankind could lie hidden under those dancing dots on the screen.

On the main floor of the ACC, disciplined military officers began to leave their consoles. Lighted switches and buttons were blinking, video screens were flashing everywhere. Men and women stood together in tight knots, looking up at Kirov's image and the plots on the large screens. Voices, first by ones and twos, then by dozens, began shouting up at the glass window. The shouts rose to a deafening crescendo. A man ripped at his headset and flung it at the floor. Another, two stars on each shoulder, screamed into a microphone connected to the room above.

"Mr. President," Charles Frydon said, in a voice quaking with tension, "they are asking us what to do! They know one of those gigaton weapons could take us completely out even here! They want the Level One command!"

Carl Silverton moved on rubbery legs to join Frydon next to the President. His anguish-filled eyes signaled to Dorie Wilcox. She rose from her chair, sobbing. As the old man put one comforting arm around her, he placed the other on Frederick Donley's trembling shoulder.

The President stared unblinkingly at the flickering light of Kirov's image, his teeth grinding against the terrible nausea and the blue-white flames consuming the flesh of his face and head. Merciful shadows suddenly moved across his vision, cooling and soothing the torture. Laura Ann was there, laughing at the playful squirrels on the soft grass of the mountainside. The green-and-white fjord ship was there also, far below them, a toy on the beautiful blue of the sunlit sea.

"I must tell you, my beloved and brave comrades, certain facts and actions which I have taken. I cannot be sure that what I have done is right. Only the future will judge me." Kirov's ashen face engulfed the screen.

"Please, let's not go back yet, darling." Laura snuggled into his arms on the picnic blanket. "Have just one more sip of champagne. . . ." She held the silver goblet to his lips.

"Comrades, I ask you to return peacefully to your homes. There is good reason to do so. Now hear me well, you who seek for nuclear vengeance on America: There is no need. For I tell you now that you are already revenged. You are already revenged!"

"Fred, I love you. I'll never forget this day. Promise me you won't, either. Swear it on our goblet!" She laughed. "Swear you'll never forget."

"Our hands, I am sad to say, are stained from the same vast pool of blood and tears as the Americans'. Yes, it is true. It is true! We, too, have been using biomedical weapons. Our procedures have been different and our programs more recent. But for us it has been even simpler than for the Americans. Theirs is a society that allows for easy access to their industry, their farms, their cities, their ships, their trucks, their railroads. Yes, comrades, yes! We have had our own disease-induction program in operation against the United States for over four years! There will be no escape for them. They have but to look and they will see the statistics for themselves—in their hospitals and in their cemeteries. So I say again, citizens of the Soviet Union, *you are already revenged! There is no need for more.*"

Bathed in a hot light of the setting sun, Laura's face was close to his. He could smell her perfume. He kissed her warm and smiling mouth and put his right hand on the gleaming silver of the goblet. "I swear . . ." he said, as the mountain air turned numbing cold. "I swear I'll never forget." The sun grew dimmer, its orange disk fading . . . fading . . . fading. "I'll never forget . . . I'll never forget. . . . " And then the sun was gone and there was only the cold . . . and the endless dark.

"I ask you now, and again, all of you—return to your homes peacefully. I have reason to believe the Americans will not permit this madness to go further. As their tracking systems have, I am sure, confirmed, I have directed that the two ultraheavy nuclear weapons systems which we currently have in orbit be jettisoned in the mid-Atlantic. I assure those responsible for the launching of these weapons and all other unauthorized acts of the last several days that they will not suffer the slightest reprisal.

"I appeal also to the President of the United States to contact me directly and immediately so we may avoid any possible mistakes. . . ."

Inside the granite mountain, tears rolled down Carl Silverton's weathered old face. He kissed Dorie Wilcox gently on the cheek.

"Mr. President . . ." Silverton's voice was the only sound in the room. "Mr. President, you were right to wait . . . you were right." He patted Donley's shoulder gently. Wordlessly, the President slumped away toward the left, his head lolling awkwardly on the back of his chair. The President of the United States was dead.

At 4:05 P.M. EST, ten minutes after the Kirov broadcast, Boyce Williamson burst through the door of the ACC conference room. In the intervening minutes, a stream of uncoded messages had been dispatched to U.S. forces across the globe and a careful step-by-step stand-down was underway. Every possible channel of communications with the civilian population was being used to halt the panic with which America had been inflicting death upon herself.

Williamson's strong voice thundered across the room from the open door. "Donley! My congratulations! You were right in how you handled this." Before anyone could speak, Williamson was beside the President, now seemingly asleep in his chair.

"Boyce, wait! The President is dead."

Williamson's knees buckled as if he had been struck by a club. "My God! When?"

"During Kirov's speech," someone replied. "It probably was a brain hemorrhage."

"My God . . . my God! Did he *know* Kirov was not launching an attack?"

"We don't know exactly when . . ."

"But . . . I mean, was he going to give the strike order?"

"We don't know, Boyce."

The President-elect stood silently by the side of his dead predecessor. After a very long time, he spoke only a few simple words. "I want this understood. President Donley was in full command of this situation at all times and was not going to launch any attack. He died only after Kirov's intentions became fully apparent."

"Yes, Mr. Williamson," said Carl Silverton, with a strange, sad smile.

Epilogue

The congressional investigations of Project M10 started on January 6 and have continued for over two years. While the full extent of the M10 plot remains unclear to this day, it is certain that at least seventy military and civilian personnel originally involved in U.S. Army chemical and biological warfare research, primarily at Fort Deterling, Maryland, were involved. These personnel included not only scientists and engineers but contract administrators, fiscal-control officials, auditors, and others. When the U.S. biological warfare effort was shut down in the early 1970s, these people were dispersed throughout the DOD system. They remained in contact, however, and ultimately were organized by Lieutenant General Robert Travis Mallon (U.S. Army, Retired—current whereabouts unknown) into an "invisible" project team. The dispersed and varied nature of the group was crucial both to the execution of the project and to its successful cover-up until the discovery of M10 by a newly appointed Chairman of the Joint Chiefs of Staff, the late Admiral Randolph G. Clayton.

Bilateral and multinational negotiations are currently underway on treaties designed to limit or forestall further use of biomedical "sub-statistical" attacks by one nation or bloc upon another. The enormously varied nature of the possible techniques, the difficulty of detection, the inherently long delays before effects become evident, and the near impossibility of monitoring for compliance using currently known procedures, have precluded effective agreement as of this writing.

According to the latest projections by the National Institutes of Health and the Soviet Academy of Sciences, cancer rates in both the United States and the U.S.S.R. will continue to rise for another fifteen to twenty years, although both countries are believed to have suspended all disease-induction projects.